I0712185

EMERALD CITY

ASTRID COLE

Emerald City © copyright 2024 by Astrid Cole. All rights reserved. No part of this book may be reproduced in any form whatsoever, by photography or xerography or by any other means, by broadcast or transmission, by translation into any kind of language, nor by recording electronically or otherwise, without permission in writing from the author, except by a reviewer, who may quote brief passages in critical articles or reviews.

Hardback: 979-8-9881469-5-7; Paperback: 979-8-9881469-4-0;
eBook: 979-8-9881469-3-3

Editing by astridcolebooks
Cover design by Kira Rubenthaler and James T. Egan
Book Design by Mayfly Design

Library of Congress Catalog Number: 2023916707

AUTHOR'S NOTE

Emerald City is an adult novel that touches on mature themes that include but are not limited to sex, drugs, rape, suicide, explicit descriptions of gore, and intense child-bearing scenes. For a full list of warnings, please visit astridcolebooks.com.

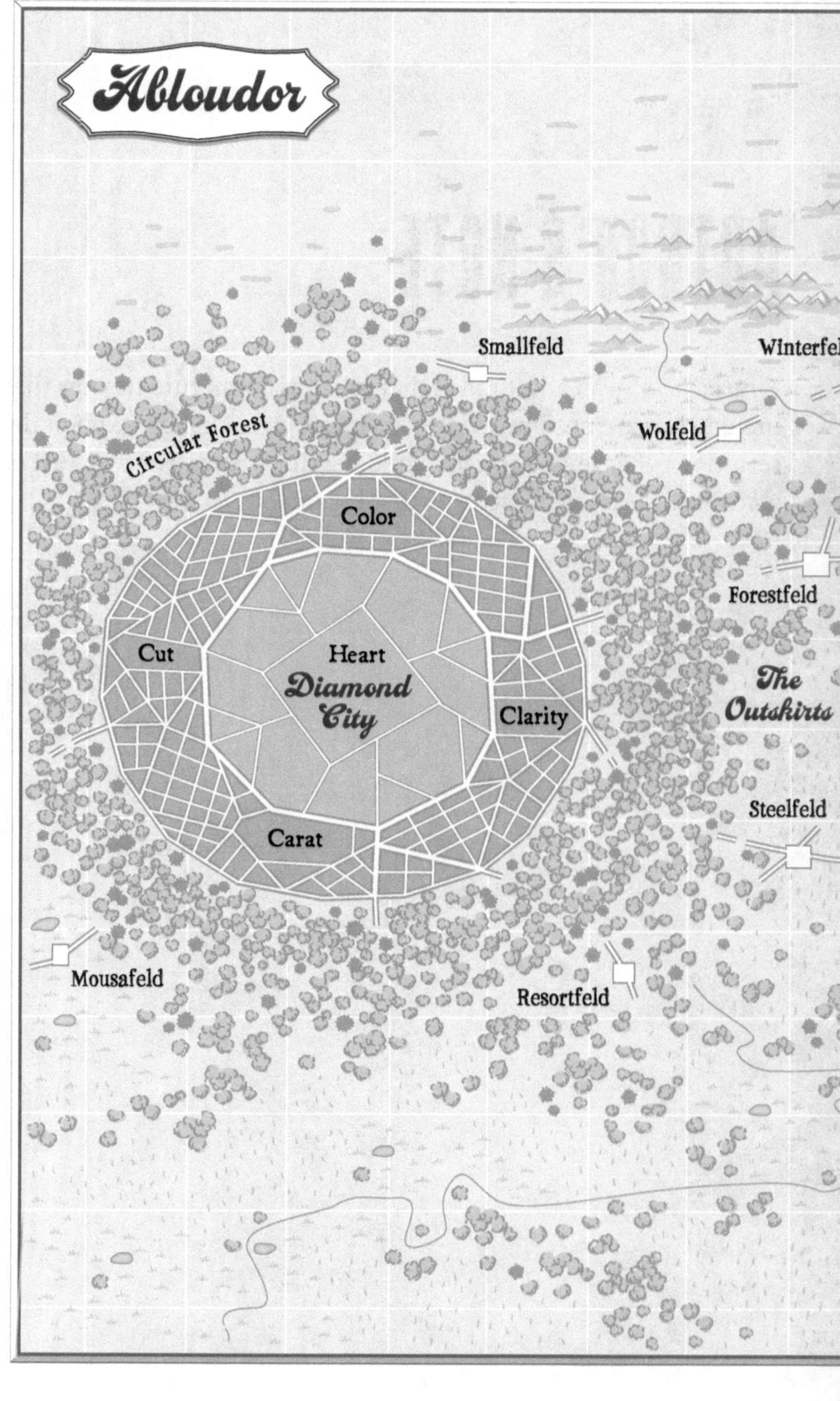

Abloudor
Smallfeld
Winterfel
Circular Forest
Wolfeld
Color
Forestfeld
Cut
Heart
Diamond
City
The
Outskirts
Clarity
Steelfeld
Carat
Mousafeld
Resortfeld

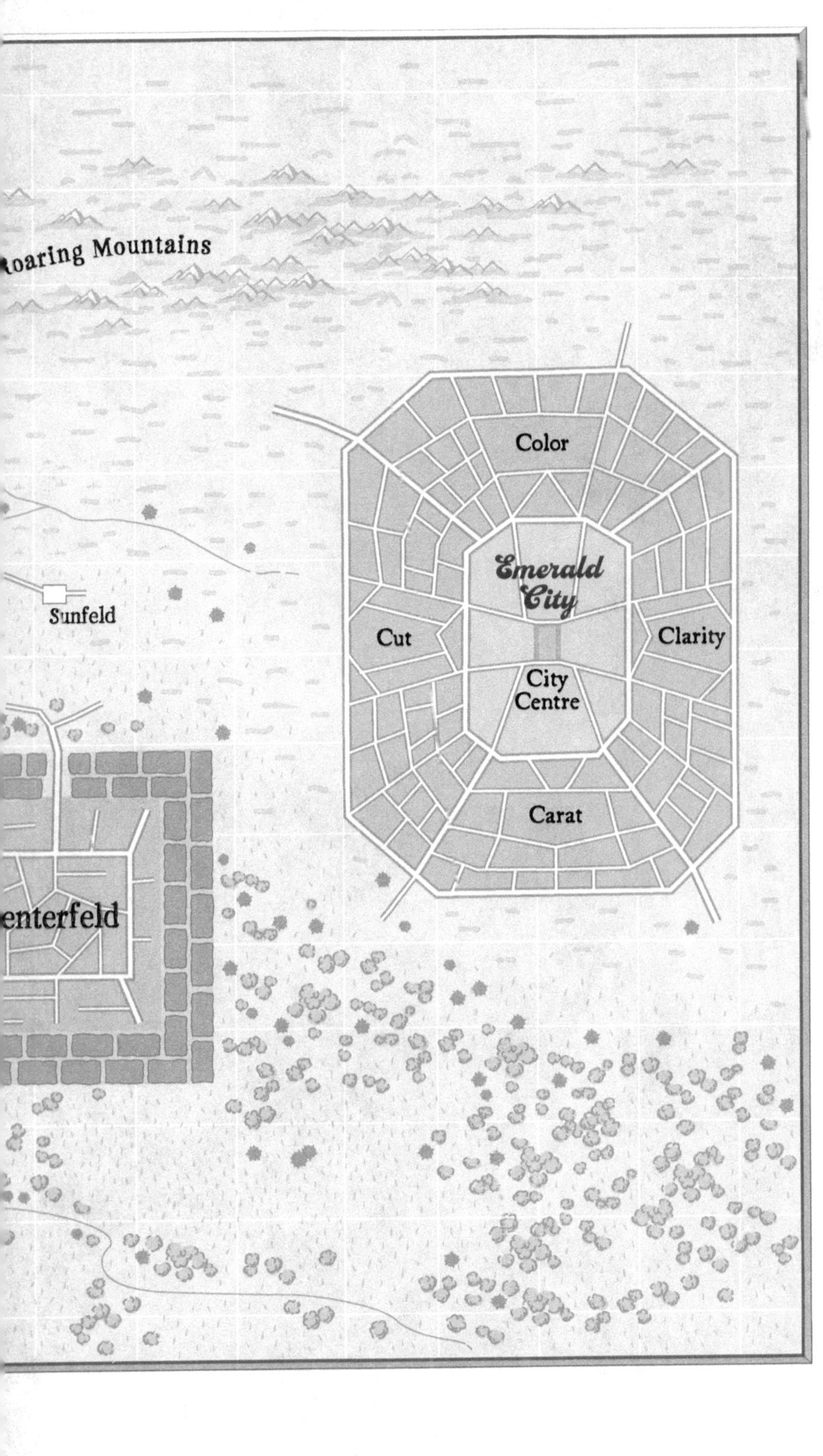

Roaring Mountains
Sunfeld
Centerfeld
Color
Emerald City
Cut
Clarity
City Centre
Carat

DIAMOND CITY CALENDAR

1 - Month of Birth

2 - Month of Love

3 - Month of Loyalty

4 - Month of Shine

5 - Month of Purity

6 - Month of Light

7 - Month of Flare

8 - Month of Innocence

9 - Month of Courage

10 - Month of Strength

11 - Month of Energy

12 - Month of Faith

To Kariany,

For the long drive to see a debut author and the support that's never-ending. My gratitude knows no bounds.

CHAPTER 1

Sick

There was someone outside the window.

Sage had known it way before she opened her eyes. The curtains were drawn, shielding the moonlight, so the room was pitch dark. Only a slither of light escaped through a corner, but it wasn't enough to illuminate the furniture or the stacks of books on her nightstand. Thanks to her searing cramps, Sage didn't leave the bed too often, so she spent most of her time looking at recipes and formulating ideas for pizza flavors. Part of owning a restaurant was learning and knowing how to be creative. She no longer had her nephew, Bram, to help her, but Damian was up for the task even if he couldn't cook to save his life.

Damian was forever banned from the kitchen. After overcooking the eggs (which made Sage gag), turning the oatmeal into slop (which made Nova, the very generous owner of this house, politely ask to be excused), adding way too much sugar to the coffee (which made Candice spit it out), and burning the hash browns (which made Olivia cry), Sage had very gently and sweetly broken the news to him.

"Damian," she had said, "stay the fuck out of the kitchen."

Which, surprisingly, had only made Damian more determined to do better. While Sage read up on everything cheese and dough, he skimmed through cookbooks and watched tutorials. Here in Winterfeld, fabulous chefs knew how to pull together dining masterpieces and sculpt the hell out of blocks of ice. In Winterfeld, where extreme cold thrived all year round thanks to how far north it was, people used what they had to make a living.

Sage wanted to smile, but her focus was on the window. She had Damian's body spooned behind hers, half covering her like a blanket. His arm was around her waist, hand resting on her abdomen where he had been massaging her earlier. The cramps had been searing. Sage's fever had gone down, but she was still so weak. In this state, she wouldn't be able to defend herself or anyone, especially if what was lingering outside the window was a Squid.

The Squids: rumors to many, but real to her. *Lolligo*, their official name, were elusive creatures that didn't like to hang around humans despite how massive and powerful they were. The only reason Sage knew they existed was because she had lived with one for a hundred years. Unfortunately, that was no Samson prowling through the snow.

Sage's heart started a vicious pounding as horror swept through her body. She was so vulnerable here, with her nieces just down the hallway. Thoughts of Samson with her comatose sister over his shoulder plagued her nightmares. Her sister had been stolen, taken, and Sage never doubted that the Squids would be back for her, too. She and Samson were like siblings, but that hadn't stopped him from plotting behind her back and spying on her for a race of monsters whose goals remained unclear.

World domination? Human torture? Evil experiments? No one knew.

Sage turned on the bed to face her soundly-sleeping fiancé. The poor man always described his fitful nights before Sage had come into his life, thanks to nearly dying in the middle of one, so she was careful not to startle him.

"Darling," Sage whispered, caressing his cheek. She heard the shuffling outside, passing the cemetery just a mile from their home. That's where she had fought her sister, where Samson had revealed his true colors. That's where Damian's daughter was buried. The place struck ice into her veins.

Sage kissed Damian's lips. Her thumb passed over the light layer of stubble on his jaw. "Darling, wake up."

Damian stirred, but it was her tongue that got him to wake up. His eyes fluttered, dark with heat, and he purred, "And you call me horny."

"I'm just kissing you."

"In the middle of the night?"

"Why can't I kiss you?"

"With *tongue?*" Damian growled thickly. "It implies that you are in need of me."

"I am," Sage admitted as Damian rolled onto her body. "But you know we can't do anything while I feel like shit. And ..." She sighed with pleasure as Damian nuzzled her neck, "as much as I want to touch you, that's not why I woke you. There's someone outside our window."

"Let them watch."

"This isn't just anyone—I think we're in danger. I can sense that it's not human—it's a Squid."

It didn't take much to arouse Damian, but he did stop to hear her out. He glanced at the worry on her feverish face and then turned his head toward the window. As an Enhanced, a genetically modified human with superior strength, durability, and intelligence, his senses were as acute as hers. When he detected intruders, he braced himself.

"Stay here," he said, reaching over to their nightstand. He opened the drawer and grabbed his pistol. While the gun itself was old-looking, the bullets were laced with Slainium, poison to Squids. Ironically, it was Samson's creation—he had spent years trying to figure out what permanently destroyed a Squid's regenerative cells. Sometimes Sage wondered if it really was ironic ... or intentional.

Had Samson left them with a possible means of winning in a war against Squids? Maybe not. Winterfeld folks were into their cuisine and culture, but they had discovered Slainium, too. They had used it in their weapons against Damian just last year. Sage would never forget what it felt like to be pelted by those bullets, so maybe she was reading too much into Samson's good intentions.

Damian got out of bed and edged toward the window. He parted the curtain to reveal a field of snow. Out here, it didn't matter that it was nearing the month of Shine and spring was supposed to be in full bloom. The ice was multiplying and the trees were dead. Nothing stirred in between those branches except for the Squid that was footsteps away from finding them.

"Don't fight them on your own," Sage whispered worriedly, standing up, too. She touched his arm. "Please."

"I won't," Damian assured her. "I'm going to scout the area and determine if there's a threat." He pulled on some pants, took a coat from the armchair, zipped up his boots, and clipped his hair. He exited through the window and took one last glance at her. "Will you have sex with me when I come back?"

Only Damian would ask that question like a kid who wanted ice cream. Sage wasn't in the mood to be amused, but this was Damian, so she cracked a smile.

"No," Sage said sweetly.

Damian cursed. "Are you really going to make me work for it?"

"Of course I am. And why are we talking about sex when there's a Squid coming?"

"It is a topic of dire importance, darling."

"Sex, Damian? At a time like this?"

"It's good motivation."

Sage grabbed her dagger. "You know what's also motivating?"

Damian shut the window quickly. The bastard was laughing, though. So inappropriate, but he did it so Sage wouldn't worry. It helped until Damian was out of sight, disappearing into the darkness beyond. The lamps along the trail were dim. As soon as he was gone, dread slithered through Sage's veins. She worried about Damian, but she needed to make sure that Nova and the girls were secure.

"There's a what?" Nova whispered from behind her bedroom door, hair messy and eyes laden with sleep.

"We don't know what it is," Sage said. "But Damian went out to check."

It was just a precaution. Nova had plenty of arsenal to defend herself, so Sage wasn't too worried about the house. She peeked into her nieces' room and found the both of them tucked into their separate beds. Asleep? Not Candice, the older one, who was on her phone under the covers.

Fifteen-year-olds had plenty to gossip about, and Candice had her eye on a boy she had met at the festival two weeks ago. Like Sage, she did her share of research whenever she was interested, and her circle of friends had plenty to say about Geoffrey. With a population of ten thousand, Winterfeld didn't hide too many secrets.

Candice noticed Sage at the door and sat up. "Aunt Sage?" she said.

"Just checking up on you—go to sleep."

Which Sage never did, so Candice grew suspicious. She wouldn't do anything dumb, though, so Sage trusted her to stay in the house.

Sage grabbed her coat from the rack. When she pulled it over her shoulders, she noted how much bigger it was than usual. Although she was still muscular, she had lost a lot of size the past month. That meant strength, too, and she wondered how much of a liability she'd be in battle. Her periods were always grueling, but Sage wasn't going to keep pretending that's what it was anymore—at least to herself she wasn't.

She hadn't bled. Store-bought pregnancy tests always came out negative, but Sage wasn't human or Enhanced—she was part Squid—so they probably didn't work on her. Her pregnancy wasn't as traditional as she and Samson had anticipated it would be. Early morning sickness? Bloating? Cravings? Mood swings? None of that.

Sage leaned against the door frame. She touched her abdomen, felt a rumbling there. It wasn't her stomach. She could feel something hard, full of ridges, and it wasn't her muscles, either. What the hell was happening to her?

"God." Sage held her face, fighting the urge to sob. She didn't trust anyone—not Dr. X, not any Enhanced, not any human, and maybe not even Samson, but he was a Squid and knew their anatomy best. He'd know what was happening to her, and if he didn't, he'd figure it out. Plus, he was someone she could trust... right? Only Samson wasn't here right now. Would the Squids outside know where he was?

Sage composed herself and grabbed the shotgun Nova had in the corner. In the woods, anything could crawl out from in between the trees and attack her. For a time, women had gone missing from this town without a trace. Squids had always been the number-one suspects, but now Sage knew for sure. She should have felt confident wielding Slainium bullets, but nothing about this confrontation was certain.

Sage tightened her grip on the gun and slipped outside. The cold slashed her to pieces and the wind enveloped her completely. Her body usually kept her warm, but it was too fucked up to work like it should have. It took nearly ten minutes for her temperature to adapt, and that could have cost Damian his life.

Thankfully, all was quiet. The Roaring Mountains were in the background, peaks as icy as ever. Sage stared at them longer than she should have. A long time ago, they were called the Appalachians. They extended over two thousand miles, with each mountain in the chain averaging over three thousand feet. The highest peak was farther south, in a region that used to be part of the United States.

Five hundred years ago, war had exploded between many enemy nations over politics, territory disputes, and economic status. Worst of all, those nations had employed nuclear weapons to settle their problems, wiping out more than half of humanity in the process.

That's why historians of today had abandoned any names,

trends, or remnants from that time—this was a "new world" now, which they had named Abloudor. Because so much territory and information from before Nuclear Devastation was inaccessible due to radiation, people didn't ask questions. They accepted the new and moved on with their lives.

Although the world of old was dead and gone, their new one had its fair share of challenges. Coincidentally, behind those mountains, was where the esteemed Squids dwelled. At least, that's what the Diamond City officials said and what humans rumored. No one had ever dared to venture that far. Even airships were terrified. What if they hit some magnetic forcefield? What if they were shot down and skinned alive? Or what if they were captured and sold into slavery?

Sage looked out at the stretches of forestry. There was no commotion or signs of struggle, so Damian was probably still creeping through the woods. Sage's senses zeroed in on the cemetery as she loomed closer to it. Just a few weeks ago, she had fought her sister and her sister's pet, Taz, on those grounds. Samson had taken her in Sage's place, so if the Squids were here, that meant they knew there were twin hybrids. But how? Unless Samson had told them . . . Perhaps the Squids had killed Samson for his insubordination and sent these prowlers to finish the job. It made Sage that much more nervous for Damian, who'd be executed on sight.

Despite the horrible cramps in her abdomen, Sage kept her focus as she trudged along the edge of the cemetery, hidden by the trees, then entered the woods. The more ground she covered, the stronger the dread coiling in her chest. As a warrior, she had been trained to keep her focus. Emotions and anxiety had never been an obstacle before, not like it was now. Maybe because she was used to fighting alone and didn't have Damian to worry about. These weren't Enhanced they were fighting.

Sage could feel the Squids' presences just feet away, rustling by a maze of branches. Sage stepped closer, heart pounding out of control, knees quaking just a little bit. Damian was nowhere to be seen.

"... *ilis senisees bilas* ..."

Sage held her breath. They were talking Lolligo. *The other is here,* one of them had said.

Then Sage looked up. Her heart dropped.

Standing atop the highest tree branch was Damian and a girl that Sage didn't recognize. Sage couldn't see her very clearly because Damian had her against the trunk, both hands fisted on either side of her face. The girl was cowering, arms around his back. Briefly, Damian made eye contact with Sage. That's all they needed to communicate: *hide, wait until the coast is clear, and run.*

No fighting. Absolutely no fighting. They wouldn't stand a chance.

Sage crouched, huddling behind a tree. She listened to every word exchanged between the Squids, making sure to memorize it so she could translate it to Damian later. This was a language she was familiar with, so she wasn't sure why hearing it now was making her cry. Sweat gathered along her forehead and neck, fingers shaking against the splintery tree of the bark in front of her. Memories of Samson were fierce, but fear of the unknown, of what she didn't understand, shook her to the core. She had fought Enhanced in the Unification War, had driven corrupt Overseers from their thrones, and united her city without having faced a single Squid. Baby Samson didn't count. Tonight, however, she finally got to confirm her fears.

Squids were real.

There was one standing in front of her, looking right at her. Steps away. Where the hell had he come from? He was as tall as a beanstalk, and as muscular as a bodybuilder.

Damian knew better than to jump in and stir up trouble, especially when he remained undetected, but that didn't stop terror from striking him like lightning. Sage saw him tense up in her peripheral. As if they were tethered to one another, it affected her, too, overwhelming her like a wave and distracting her like a novice facing an opponent for the first time in her life.

Sage took a breath and held it. Life or death. Right now, it was life or death. She had to say something—*do* something—diffuse the situation quickly. This was her territory, goddamn it—these Squids were trespassing. Maybe becoming defensive wasn't the best way to handle this, but that's what instinct told her to do.

"What do you want?" Sage said in Lolligo.

The amber eyes with slits for pupils bore into hers. It felt like she was on an operating table with a surgeon cutting her open from head to foot. Those movements were precise and intricate, unveiling all her innards to the world. It was pure violation.

But Sage didn't back down. Adrenaline filled her like air in a balloon, making her stand up straighter. The cramps in her abdomen subsided. Her body braced itself. She was ready to do whatever it took to save Damian and that mysterious girl in his arms.

The Squid cocked his head, lips peeling back from razor-sharp teeth. His very being vibrated with life, body taut with power. His clothes were loose at the sleeves but tight around his chest and hips, accenting what was a physique meant for war. He looked like a near replica of Samson. To Sage, he was far from a welcoming brother.

"You lived," the Squid said.

"What do you want?" Sage repeated.

The Squid seized her, his powerful fingers like a clamp, and shoved her into the tree. Damian didn't hesitate this time—he drew his gun and fired, throwing the Squid off her. He jumped into the fray, landing in front of Sage to defend her from any rebound, but the Squid didn't move. The amber eyes studied their new opponent before shifting to the bullet wound in his chest.

"Back off," Damian spat.

He was way too confident, so Sage reeled him back to her side. She angled her body toward the Squid, perfectly aware that there were more of them in the distance. Damian was ready for a fight, but Sage wasn't. She knew what the Squids were capable of, how quickly they could cut down their opponents even with Slainium wrecking havoc on their bodies.

Damian got a massive palm to his face, a hit that left him vulnerable to a lethal follow-up, but Sage used her energy to throw the Squid back. She could toss it like a wave, securing a glorious chance to use her shotgun and blow the Squid's head right off his shoulders. Then she grabbed Damian by the waist and jumped into the trees, just as a group of Squids raced into the scene.

Holy shit, holy shit, holy shit.

Sage grabbed the other girl, who was sitting on a branch, traumatized, and flew as quickly as she could through the treetops with Damian in tow.

"Damian, go!" Sage exclaimed, slowing down a bit. "I'll take care of them!"

Damian slowed down, too, a stone-cold expression on his face that said there was no way in hell he was leaving her to take care of anyone on her own. He grabbed her arm and yanked her to his side, but before he could scold her, a massive tentacle struck them from beneath. It destroyed all of the trees in their perimeter, making Damian stumble into a void of snow, dust, and twigs.

"Damian!" Sage snagged onto a nearby branch and seized Damian's wrist. Damian had the girl, who was surprisingly quiet in all this commotion. No average teenager dangled a hundred feet without a scream.

"We're too vulnerable up here!" Damian exclaimed.

No trees—they had to run on ground. So Sage let go, and then they were racing through the snow. Damian threw the girl over his shoulder and weaved through the woods like an athlete. Sage kept up with him, but it wasn't long before the adrenaline dissipated and her breaths got shorter. Cramps cut through her body like knives, making her double over to catch her breath.

"Darling," Damian croaked, coming back for her. "Come on— we're almost there."

Sage wasn't sure what Damian meant by "there" until they reached the cemetery and met the Winterfeld army. No androids— these soldiers were flesh and blood, equipped with the latest weaponry. Missile launchers, bazookas, automatic rifles, and pistols were the least of it—it's what came out of the guns, like Bomb Bullets and Bone Destroyers laced with Slainium, that made them a pain in the ass to fight.

Even with fast regeneration, the Squids knew it wasn't worth the trouble. In fact, they didn't even make it out of the woods. Sensing danger, they stayed far away. Hiding was what they did best. Even when they had been controlling the Overseers in Diamond City's four districts, they had never shown their faces. Just what were they planning?

Right now, Sage didn't care. A few soldiers came forward to extract the mysterious girl from Damian's arms and ask if they were all right. Sage knew what came next—medical care—and she couldn't.

No. She wouldn't go with them. She wouldn't put herself or whatever was growing inside her in jeopardy by surrendering to a bunch of incompetent humans. *Greedy* humans.

"Damian," Sage whispered to him, touching his hand. She got his attention, and he turned to her.

For the first time since she had woken up that night, Sage got a good look at him. Standing under the light of one of the lamps, and soon from the aircrafts scouting the area for danger, she could see the sharpness of his face and the paleness of his skin. He looked so beautiful, even without makeup, and his eyes were always enveloping her with warmth. A few strands of hair blew into his face, but he didn't bother swiping them when Sage was in distress.

"Please take me home."

"Of course, darling." Damian touched her face. "Are you sure you don't need help?"

"No, no help," Sage said quietly. "Just take me home."

No questions. Not until they were alone, so Damian dealt with the soldiers then complied with her request. He scooped her into his arms and trudged across the field back toward Nova's house.

Sage shook violently. Her head was pounding and her abdomen was searing. The colors in her eyes made her throw up once they got home.

Damian was with her as she heaved, holding her hair, rubbing her back, and offering her water when she stopped. He prepared a bath and took it upon himself to strip her. No blood on her underwear, but a stream of it shot right onto the floor as if Sage had just pissed herself.

Sage closed her eyes and clenched her teeth. She grabbed the rail because more colors exploded in her eyes.

Damian didn't make faces or noises—he helped her into the tub and cleaned up the blood with spray and paper towels. He worked with a seriousness that Sage wasn't used to. Perhaps his ex-wife, Ileana, had had her fair share of help from her queasy husband during her periods, but this wasn't a regular menstrual cycle.

Sage was as sick as she had ever been. The Optimum was dying of fever and chills all at once, convulsing in the tub. She was supposed to be Damian's savior, his rock, and now she was crying amidst very dirty water because this wasn't her period. Damian didn't know it, but Sage did.

"Darling." Damian kneeled by the tub. He combed back her hair. "You'll be fine. Just relax."

"God..." Sage croaked, fists in her eyes. "I-I'm so sorry—I-I didn't mean for you to see that—"

"Are you serious right now? This isn't your fault—this is a natural cycle your body goes through. I understand that, and in no way do I think that's indecent or disgusting. *Nothing* about you is disgusting, darling. If anything, my vomit was much more grotesque than a small puddle of blood."

To this day, Damian still underwent withdrawals from that Stars drug he had been addicted to. Sage didn't want to think about it. If her life was coming to an end, at least she could be thankful that Damian was seven months sober.

Damian drained the water and filled the tub anew. He dropped a few eucalyptus bombs inside then prepared a sponge to scrub her. He did, thoroughly. He even pressed his fingers into her vagina, which was still bleeding. The blood was different than it usually was every year at this time—thinner and more aggressive—but Sage didn't say it. She let him rinse her off then carry her out of the tub. He leaned her against the counter as he dried her hair and body.

He went for one of Nova's tampons in the cabinet, and Sage let him put that in, too.

Sage didn't have the strength to speak, so she showed him how much she appreciated him by holding his cheek. Her eyes shined with love, a reflection of what was in his own. Then came the tears.

"I want you to rest now," Damian said to her, wiping them from her cheeks. "Tomorrow morning, we're evacuating Winterfeld and making this a military base. I don't trust so many people near the Squids. I'm taking you and the girls home to Diamond City."

"All right," Sage whispered.

Sage had never felt so weak in her life. That tension, that run, had drained her completely. She must have really looked like shit, even in clean pajamas, because Damian said to her, "I'm worried, darling. This can't be normal, even for a woman's menstrual cycle. Ileana and Phoebe always wanted to tear my head off when they were PMSing, but they still went on about their daily activities."

"It is for me," Sage said as Damian tucked her into bed. That indicated he wouldn't be joining her, probably because he had business to deal with outside.

"I want you to see Dr. X," Damian said.

"There isn't anything he can do for me."

"Maybe there is," Damian pressed. "If we just let him examine you."

"Please don't worry," Sage said. "I want to return to Diamond City with the girls and just take some time off from all of this. But..." When Sage thought about her apartment in the Cut District, the one she used to share with Samson, her stomach coiled into knots. Like a rock in her abdomen, it was a harsh reminder of who was still out there: Samson... and her sister. Sage wanted to cry. And the hardest part was there was nothing she could do about them.

In her delicate state, Sage needed to focus on recovery and establishing normalcy for her nieces. They had been in hiding for six months in Diamond City, then apprehended by the council and given over to Samson. It was a miracle they had done any school-work at all. They had virtual classes to finish now, and then Sage wanted to send them back to brick-and-mortar in the fall. Candice was starting high school and Olivia was starting seventh grade.

"You can stay elsewhere," Damian offered, reading the distress on her face. "In fact, you can stay at the palace in Heart."

Already relieved, Sage breathed out. She nodded, although a small part of her wanted to wait for Samson. But their next encounter wouldn't be anything good, and she had to think of the girls, so she went along with Damian's suggestion.

"Fine," Sage said. She felt Damian's light stubble with a thumb. She liked how it scratched her skin. She hoped he shaved it soon, though. Definitely no darker than this.

"I will help you," Damian said to her. "The girls . . . and your pizza restaurant." He lowered his head and rubbed his nose with hers. "And when we get married, we will move into a house of your choosing. Wherever you want, my love."

"Kiss me."

That was Damian's line, but Sage wanted him to fill her every thought. She wanted to ignore whatever might be on the other side of the Roaring Mountains and relish in her fiancé. His mouth helped accomplish that, his slow sensual takeover of her senses. His kisses were intricate, left Sage's head spinning, and caused heat to envelope her like a blanket. His tongue was everywhere, reminding her of what it felt like to have it between her legs. She matched each stroke and eventually broke into his mouth.

"If you keep kissing me like that, you are going to arouse me," Damian breathed against her lips. "Is that your intention?"

"You're going to have to learn some resistance."

"That will be impossible. I crave you too much, especially since it's been over a month since we've had intercourse."

That was true. The bastard didn't count the blowjobs or hand-jobs Sage gave him whenever he asked for it.

"I want to be inside you," Damian said thickly. "Tongue, fingers, *and* penis. I want to give you pleasure like you give me pleasure."

He slipped a hand inside the covers and stroked her through her shorts. "I don't care about the blood."

"I know, darling." Sage sighed. "But I don't want you to. I feel disgusting and I don't want to associate that with our lovemaking."

"I understand." Damian laid his head on her abdomen. Sage combed his hair, always mesmerized by the silkiness of it.

"When I'm better," Sage whispered to him, "I promise you can ravish me however you want." She didn't want to spoil him, but she had to give him something to look forward to.

Damian's eyes widened. "*However* I want?"

"Don't look so surprised—I'm always flexible. But this time, I'll be even more so."

"From behind," Damian said at once, springing up. "Not anal, though—full-blown vagina. I want your curves and thighs on my lap, tight against my hips. Every single time I thrust into you, I want you to thrust back so that those powerful glutes of yours hit my body and create vibrations. For the first round, I want you sitting up. For the second round, I want you bent over on your hands and knees."

Those angles would destroy her. Sage's body tingled just thinking about them. "Fine," she said. "Whatever you want."

To her shock, Damian had pictures on his phone, hand drawn and digitally rendered. Sage's face blew up with red, the aggressive kind that made her fingers and toes pound. "Seriously?" she chastised him, scrolling through *all* of those sexual positions that Damian wanted to try. The worst part about it was how accurate he drew their faces and bodies. His attention to detail was phenomenal.

"Which one do you want to try?" he asked sultrily.

Sage laughed. Too weak to hold the phone, she let it drop to her chest. Damian would never cease to impress her. "When the hell did you have the time to draw all of this? Or even think of it?"

Damian had been working nonstop with Winterfeld leaders and Diamond City officials the past month. Although so far away, he still kept in touch with Louis and Agathe, Diamond City's new Allseers.

"I started these when I first met you," he replied.

"When we first met?" Sage said, amused. "You mean before we were a couple?"

Damian chuckled. "Yes. I told you I desired you the moment you threw that dagger at my chest. The time we were in my compound, remember?"

"Yes." Sage smiled. Of course she remembered. She and Damian had shared milkshakes and cigars for the first time that night.

"I worked on them most when I was sick with withdrawals," Damian said. "When I wasn't vomiting, I was thinking of your body and what it'd be like against mine."

"You're a sex addict."

"Yes," Damian admitted. "I am. I love good sex, and out of all my lovers, you have been the best. Aside from your hard-as-steel body, you give me those looks that promise misery and death. It turns me the hell on."

Sage smiled lazily. "What 'looks,' exactly?"

Damian had a ton of those drawings, too. He had over a hundred different facial expressions, all of Sage, and there were some she wasn't even aware she made. Like, a puckered side lip when she was annoyed or squinty eyes when she was feeling mischievous.

"Does my lip really do that when I'm annoyed?" Sage asked.

"Yes," Damian said happily. "I'm sure there's a lot you do that you're not aware of. For example: you clench your fists three times when you're getting ready to fight. When you braid your hair, you do an under-and-over maneuver, which is so much harder than over-and-under, darling. Who taught you that?"

Sage's eyes burned with more tears.

"I know," Damian whispered to her. "You miss my penis, don't you?"

Sage burst out laughing. "Shut up!" She smacked him with a pillow.

Damian laughed, too, until there was a knock on the door.

"Sage? My lord?"

The light-heartedness died instantly. Thoughts of Squids and evacuations came racing right back into Sage's head.

"Allow me." Damian kissed Sage's cheek. "I'll answer."

He left the door ajar so Sage could hear him speak. "I'm staying the night with her. I've already given the mayor orders to prepare for evacuation."

Sage waited for Damian, happy he'd hold her through the rest of the night, but she never felt him climb into bed. It took five minutes, even if Sage's mind was racing, for her to succumb to the darkness.

CHAPTER 2

Reina Aulus

When Sage woke up this time, the sun was shining through the curtains. Candice and Olivia were talking in the hallway, exchanging their thoughts on the "scary Lolligo incident" from last night. Sage was glad they had stayed safe in the house and that the Squids hadn't come looking for them. They had already been through so much with Bram and Samson that Sage wanted to lock them up in a bubble and never let them out. It was selfish and borderline abusive, but her girls in the hands of some ugly monsters performing reproductive experiments on their wombs made her want to tear down a wall. It made having children so incredibly stressful. In battle, it was always about Sage's survival . . . in motherhood, it was about that of her children's. Keeping them safe was her job now, and that was difficult to do when she felt so weak.

At the very least, sleep had helped her recover somewhat. Sage could get up and shower without keeling over. She had stopped bleeding, but she used a tampon just in case. After combing out her hair, which was the softest it had ever been in her life thanks to Suave-Suave treatments and Damian's care, Sage left the bathroom.

Now that she wasn't running from Squids, her thoughts lasered in on that mysterious girl Damian had rescued.

Damian was here as promised, but he was in the *kitchen*, standing in front of the stove, doing what Sage had banned him from doing: cooking. It smelled like omelets. Both Candice and Olivia attacked each of his sides, nestling into him like a couple of baby squirrels. The sight was heart-warming as hell. Sage sat in a chair just to watch them. Without their father, the girls latched onto whatever male they could.

Damian was an even better mother, though, serving their food (which he had made sure not to burn this time), preparing their backpacks for whenever they had research projects to conduct for online school, and fixing their appearances. That included makeup and hairdos, crazy ones like the *staircase*, that wound around their heads in intricate braids, or the *trenches*, that left grooves between hair strands that really did look like—well—trenches.

"Aunt Sage, is it true?" Olivia said from the table. "We're leaving Winterfeld?"

A hint of disappointment from both of them. Olivia was vocal while Candice texted away on her phone with a slight pout. Too much traveling and moving in ones so young. No stability. They were both in their favorite band t-shirts, short shorts, and fuzzy socks—right at home. But according to Damian, who served them their breakfast, it was necessary. *Everyone* was moving.

"Geoffrey says he's excited!" Candice exclaimed after learning that her friends would be joining them. "He says he's always wanted to see the palace in Diamond City!"

Sage exhaled a bit in relief. If Geoffrey was happy, then Candice was happy, and then they were all happy. The last thing she wanted was World War 4 in the kitchen.

Damian smirked. "Now Geoffrey will have an opportunity to study nuclear engineering like he wanted."

Candice whipped around. "Wait—you spoke to the Allseers about Geoffrey already?"

"I had to. We have to accommodate all these people. They'll be surveyed when they get to the palace and relocated to the district of their choosing until they're able to find jobs and fend for themselves."

Candice squealed. "Geoffrey is going to be so happy! Thank you, Damian!"

"Whoa—wait." Sage stepped forward. "What's going on?"

"Geoffrey is Candice's boyfriend, darling," Damian said; Candice's face turned a bright red.

"I-it's not official!" Candice stammered. She looked like someone had thrown tomatoes at her face and smeared the juice all over her cheeks. She was dark-skinned to begin with, so that was saying something.

"Come on, Candice," Olivia said slyly. "We all know it."

"No," Sage said slowly, shoving down nervousness. "Not all of us. I thought you were just friends."

Damian snorted. He poured the girls more orange juice. "Please. They hang out every day before dinner and she comes home with a new charm on her bracelet. Those are Soulmate Bracelets, and when the love of your life buys you ten distinct charms, you're supposed to be bonded forever."

At last, Sage noticed the silvery band around Candice's wrist. It was right above the one Sage had made for her a while ago in Diamond City, infused with Slainium. Since Samson's discovery of it, Sage had woven poison with fabric for protection as well as— in some creative instances—attack. While Sage was thankful that Candice and Olivia both wore their bracelets, now she was curious about the new one with a supposed story behind it.

Candice cleared her throat. She really needed a sip of orange juice. "I don't know how you knew that, Damian. Soulmate Bracelets are particular to Winterfeld."

"But it's also one of the greatest love stories of all time."

Sage was lost. Damian puffed up his chest, ready to tell the story.

"Legend has it that the founder of Winterfeld was a widow who had lost her soulmate in a war. She had a bracelet that he had given her, you see, and throughout the rest of her years, she found ten distinct charms that fit it perfectly."

Sage stared. "And?"

Damian wiped his eyes. Candice and Olivia were laughing. "Soften your heart a bit, darling—it's a beautiful story. It's as if her soulmate was communicating with her by giving her the charms."

"How old is Geoffrey?" Sage asked Candice.

Candice stopped her chuckles immediately. She glanced at Damian, as if hoping for his support in what she was about to admit, and answered her aunt truthfully.

"Eighteen."

"No," Sage said at once. "Absolutely not. You're fifteen—"

Damian grabbed Sage's arm and pulled her into the hall. His earnest look halted her protests immediately. When Sage was quiet, despite her breaths of rage, Damian spoke.

"Calm down," he said. "Candice didn't tell you anything because she was afraid you'd react like that."

"How can I not react?!" Sage yelled. "That kid's *three* years older, Damian! Practically an adult with a fully developed penis and testicles, so you know all he wants is sex!"

"Actually, penises and testicles don't stop developing until nineteen or twenty years of age."

Of course Damian was the fucking genital expert. Sage swore she'd strangle him, but she was still in her Candice-boyfriend rampage.

"Regardless of when a penis reaches its maximum *potential*," Sage spat, "what do you think that loser wants? Sex—"

Damian halted her again with that look. "You just called him a loser and you don't know him."

"But you do?"

Damian took a deep breath.

Holy shit. Had Damian met Geoffrey already but not Sage?

"I met him, yes," Damian admitted calmly. "Last week. You were sick in bed, darling, and I didn't want to disturb you. It was a little bit past dinnertime and Candice had not returned from her daily ventures. Thanks to Olivia, I was able to locate her and her group of friends at the ice rink. Although she had texted me, I wanted to confirm that she was telling the truth. Indeed, they were skating, but she and Geoffrey were standing very close to each other. Geoffrey's stance indicated that he had won her as a girlfriend."

Sage was still breathing hard. Her poor brain couldn't process Damian's words fast enough to understand what they meant. All she gleamed from this was "stance" and "girlfriend." How the hell did Damian know these things?

"Candice was very embarrassed," Damian went on. "But I told her there was nothing to be ashamed of. Dating is perfectly acceptable at her age—"

"HE'S EIGHTEEN!"

Damian held up a hand. "I took Geoffrey aside. Actually, we went shopping. You can tell a lot about a man based on the things he buys. He wanted a Sphere Pet—a cute little stuffed animal inside a globe to promote climate conservation—and gloves. Men who wear gloves never make the first move."

"Damian," Sage said patiently, no matter how badly she wanted to choke him now, "*everyone* wears gloves in Winterfeld. It's fucking cold outside!"

"Not everyone," Damian corrected her. "Take a look next time you're outside."

"This is the stupidest thing I've ever heard! 'Men who wear gloves never make the first move'? Where the hell are you getting this from?"

Damian shrugged. "Experience."

"Damian—"

"Give Geoffrey a chance," Damian said earnestly. "Please, Sage."

"I haven't even met him!" she yelled.

"He's a lot like me."

Sage's eyes widened. As images of Damian taking her from behind and riding her like a matador exploded in her head, Damian laughed.

"He's finding himself," Damian said quickly. "He's still learning who he is. While he could use a few pointers in the fashion department, he's brilliant when it comes to his studies. He's living with his grandmother right now and helping support her, so he hasn't been able to finish his education. He can build all sorts of devices and he's some kind of computer genius. At Heart, things might be different for him."

"I don't want them having sex, Damian!" Sage roared. "Candice is too young!"

"I've already spoken to her about the sex. She understands that she has to be responsible, so no intercourse for now. Darling." Damian held Sage's chin to calm her down. Her face was turning red and her breathing was out of control. "Just relax, all right?"

"When were you going to tell me about Geoffrey?" Sage croaked. "Why didn't you tell me?"

"I'm sorry," Damian said. "But I didn't want to be the one to say anything. That was supposed to be Candice, but you've been so sick that we didn't want to add to your worries unless it was necessary. The girls are fine, darling, and you need to concentrate on you."

"D-do they not trust me?"

"It has nothing to do with trust. Candice was going to introduce Geoffrey this weekend, but we got a bit caught up with the Squids and the incident last night. So we'll have to postpone that for a later date." Damian kissed her forehead. "Just take it easy. Candice is not having sex and Geoffrey is very respectable and focused. There is nothing to worry about. If there was, I'd be the first to decapitate Geoffrey and add his head to my collection in Mousafeld."

The last thing Sage wanted to think about was Damian's nasty head display back at his rebel camp, but those thoughts dissipated when Damian embraced her and held her for a few minutes. Sage already knew that Candice and Olivia had eavesdropped on the whole conversation, and the two were awfully quiet from behind that wall. Maybe they were relieved that Sage hadn't blown a gasket. Maybe they were thankful for Damian, who managed his role as their semi step-uncle incredibly well.

Even better than Sage as their aunt.

It was only when the girls were fed and scurried to their room that Damian and Sage finally had a moment to themselves. Now that they weren't discussing boyfriends, Damian could better assess her health. His eyes flashed with relief at her rejuvenated state. Sage doing dishes was a good sign. Last night could have been so much worse.

"The girl we found last night," Damian said, expression hardening a bit. "Her name is Reina Aulus. Human. She was a close friend of Nova's."

"Where is she now?" Sage asked.

"She's currently at a medical facility in Capital Square. They've examined her from head to foot . . . and have determined that she's pregnant."

Sage stopped rinsing the pan. "Pregnant?"

"Indeed. Three months, to be exact, which is how long she's been missing from Winterfeld."

Wait—*pregnant?* That implied Reina had had sex with someone who probably wasn't her boyfriend.

"Where was she?" Sage asked. "I mean, who abducted her?"

Damian shook his head. "We don't know because she doesn't speak. She's traumatized."

If that was the case, and she had been abducted by Squids as they all surmised, then how on earth was she pregnant? In vitro fertilization, maybe, but hadn't Samson said the Squids couldn't impregnate any of the women they captured? So how on earth had they been successful with Reina? And if they were, why had they been so careless to lose her?

"They weren't," Damian answered Sage's raging thoughts. "The girl escaped. It explains why there had been a horde of Squids after her."

A sheer miracle. For that reason, Damian had quite the number of reinforcements around Winterfeld. There were Enhanced everywhere, the strongest warriors in these lands thanks to Squid genetics, from both Mousafeld and Diamond City. Squids were much stronger, but they paled at the thought of being seen or over-whelmed. The ones from last night had completely disappeared.

Even so, Damian made haste with Sage, Candice, and Olivia at his side. Nova and the rest of the town were amidst their own evacuation schedule. Damian's private aircraft was waiting on Nova's front lawn, manned by Justice, a familiar, friendly face.

Handsome and chiseled, Justice was a head-turner. Candice and Olivia appreciated beauty when they saw it, and their stares lingered longer than necessary. He was polite, kneeling at Damian's feet and kissing each of his rings. He would have done the same to Sage if she didn't stop him and opt for a hug instead. She would do without the royal treatment.

"It is nice to see you, my lady," said Justice politely to her. "That you are well after all of the trials the past month."

Which included the brutal attack on Heart by Sage's sister and Taz. Thankfully, the latter was dead, but the first brought up a wave of anxiety and a flurry of concerns without fail. Just where the hell was Wren now? What was Samson using her for?

"It is best we move you to a safer location while you recover your strength."

"Can you keep me updated on Reina's condition?" Sage asked him. "I want to know where she's being moved and how she's coming along."

Justice bowed his head. "Of course."

Sage stepped into the aircraft, her girls close. While she managed to plaster a smile on her face, she couldn't stop thinking about Reina. A human woman who was pregnant ... escaped from Squids ... This was Sage's mother all over again. But the difference between her mother and all of these other women was the survival of her babies.

Her twins.

Sage and Wren. The latter had been sold to science at a young age. Thus, the Enhanced were created. Then, Aurora, Sage's half-sister, had been born.

Sage thought fondly of Aurora and all of their pizza-eating

days, the gossip they'd share under the covers at night, and the extra lunch money they'd make selling *Defenders Unite!* playing cards. Her amazing childhood was a blessing, and the fact she had gotten to actually experience it was a miracle. It made her so very grateful for what she had.

It was the kind of life that Sage wanted for Candice and Olivia. Now that Heart was under Louis and Agathe's control, she was confident that the girls would be safe and could live their teenage years to the fullest: sleepovers, movies, school, projects, and work. The commander of the Diamond City military, Dawson Blackburn, who was also Damian's brother, was in custody, as were a bunch of other soldiers for insubordination against the two sibling Kilstrongs.

The military had sided with the council, who technically had no power unless the Allseer willed it, and that was pure treason. There were, however, exceptions, because the military could have been under threat and acting in self-defense. With Louis and Agathe out of commission, who was the military supposed to have turned to other than the council? The investigation was long, messy, and difficult, especially now that the council was dead and there was no one to testify on their behalf.

Either way, the rightful leaders were on the throne now and Sage could count on them to leave her and her girls alone. They wouldn't be used as a piece of property or leverage against the Squids.

Sage was surprised that Heart was still in one piece after her sister's attack. She saw it from the sky, miles away: a walled metropolis in the center of Diamond City's four districts. The palace had suffered the most damage, but that was already secure and under reconstruction. She never would have thought to see Diamond City working with Damian's rebels or Outskirts forces, people that had been exiled after the Warlord's Rebellion thirty years ago. Sage recognized some familiar faces from Mousafeld, like Turtle, Sailor, Butcher, Clara, and Preacher, who were hanging out by the landing pad. Just a year ago, these four (with the exception of Preacher, maybe) would have gladly seen her head on a platter. Now, they welcomed her like family. So many of the rebels had prophesied ruin under her leadership, but here they were.

Of course, Sage didn't take them lightly. Those Enhanced had been through hell in their exile and they couldn't afford any more screwups. Damian could be aggressive and a bit reckless if left unchecked—Resortfeld's bloody fate was proof of that. To this day, his intentions remained a bit of a mystery—what he *really* wanted from all these conquests—even if he did exhibit some redeeming behaviors. For example, he had given Louis and Agathe their throne and promised not to interfere in their ruling. He and his rebels were muscle only, and that's how Sage wanted it to stay.

"The great Optimum!" Preacher called, raising his hands like a cheerleader. At least he wasn't wearing that quirky mask Claritians liked to wear. The robes were looking clean and spiffy, so someone at the palace was being extra nice to him. No one took their chances on Claritian clergy, just in case they summoned a pantheon of Squids in an angry chant. "Let us thank the Forefathers for her health! For she has granted us entry back into our home territory!"

Turtle rolled his eyes. Short and squat, he had changed his demeanor for the better, so he actually looked Sage in the eye and smiled. Sailor was neutral, but Butcher still had beef. Anyone who messed with his pizza-buddy back in Mousafeld was a public enemy. He just couldn't accept that Dough's pizza sucked. Clara was the female of the trio, and she took her rightful place between the two. Her job was to ease tension and channel the right kind of energy to stem any fighting.

Beyond them, and approaching from across the fields, was Agathe and Louis. And ... wow, did they look royal. White with gold cuffs suited any high-ranking member of this rich family in charge. While Sage was a fan of *The Royal Court*, a TV drama that followed Louis and his life's challenges as a prince on a day-to-day basis, it had been some time since Sage had seen him so ... royal.

Perhaps she had gotten used to the humble house-Louis in Mousafeld, the one Samson had whipped into shape. Reparations and cooking had become his forté, but above all, he had become

Sage's friend. They embraced like ones, too, despite how close by Damian was. Louis was scared shitless of the Warlord, knew damn well who Sage's fiancé was, but this was a moment he had been dreaming of since Sage had gone off to fight her sister.

"Sage." Louis smiled. 115 years old with the face of a young man. Beautiful skin, blond curls, blue eyes, and a charming smile. It wasn't a wonder Sage had been head-over-heels for him. Embarrassingly, she still had posters of him in her room in the Cut District. "You look . . . thin."

"I've lost a few pounds," Sage admitted. "But I'll get them back."

"Any word on Samson?"

Of course Louis would ask. Sage's heart tore in two.

"No," she said. She didn't know if Reina had anything to do with Samson, but that wasn't something she wanted to discuss right now. She had her girls to introduce, and the both of them were absolutely floored they were standing in the same airspace as *the* Prince Louis. Well, Allseer Louis now.

"Whoa!" Olivia squealed with huge cute eyes. Damian had woven some pretty intricate braids into her hair, more so than the ones Agathe had, so she looked like a royal herself. "Are you actually Prince Louis? You're so handsome!"

"Oh." Louis chortled. He rubbed the back of his head, flashing all his pearly white teeth. "Thank you very much."

"I can't believe it's him!" Olivia jumped up and down, smacking her sister's shoulder. "What do you think, Candice?"

Equally starstruck. Like Sage, they were experts at *The Royal Court*, knew what episode Louis had gotten his toenails done for the first time and how many times he had sipped water when attempting the spicy buffalo wing challenge. It was cute and light-hearted fun. Sage only wished the easy interactions would have lasted longer, because then she caught Agathe and Damian in a longer-than-necessary embrace.

Sage's smile fell.

"He knows you're the Optimum. He knows what your blood can do. If he wants you, it's because of that. He wants to create more Enhanced."

Agathe's last words to Sage at the party Damian had thrown in Mousafeld. There, he had unveiled his plans for Louis and Agathe to take the throne in his stead. He had also told everyone whom he planned to marry. In the meantime, Agathe had found her way to Sage to let her in on a few secrets. Damian was not who he pretended to be.

Sage didn't listen, though. Just like she didn't let the way Agathe kissed Damian's cheeks bother her.

Damian was polite and appropriate. His hands never roamed further down than Agathe's shoulders. He didn't push her away or look disgusted when she laid both palms on his chest. He kept his calm, even if Agathe was all high energy around him, as if Sage didn't exist. Of course, Agathe did turn to her eventually.

Agathe looked just as excited as Louis to see her. She was Louis' younger sister, who had never been under the spotlight much. She had been a prisoner in this very palace all her life, gaining freedom and pleasure only when Damian had "rescued" her by killing her father. Now, thanks to Sage, she was one of Diamond City's Allseers with a lot of power in the palm of her hands. While her expression remained friendly, Sage could smell the predatory vibes like a bad odor. Sage smiled regardless.

"You look well, Agathe."

Agathe bowed. Like Louis, she was in royal garbs. All white and gold trims. Sage wondered if Agathe had gotten laid yet. Or maybe she was waiting for Damian to finally get an erection with her. It looked like Agathe had lost some of her baby fat, so maybe she was training, although it was probably more for looks than strength.

Sage tried hard not to snort. Damian wrapped a protective arm around her waist. This was to ward off any of Louis' attentions, but to Agathe, this was a reminder that she didn't have a chance with the Warlord.

Behind the siblings was Sage's good friend, Gertrude. Her heart sank because Gertrude had lost her lover, Little Man, to Wren. The resentment was present in her eyes, a curtain of reservation from that horrible night a month ago. Little Man wasn't the only one—there were dozens of rebels and soldiers who had been slaughtered. Funerals had already been given amidst all the coronations and reconstruction at Heart. The royal mausoleum was tucked in the eastern side of the capital, out of sight but always within reach. Enhanced didn't like to think of death too much, not when their life spans exceeded a hundred years and old age progressed at a turtle's pace.

"But it is good to see you again, though," Turtle said to Sage to cut some of the tension. It was crazy how roles had reversed, how he had been the asshole and Gertrude the savior back in Mousafeld. Now, it was clear he was fighting to keep the air light between two inseparable friends. He didn't stand a chance with Gertrude romantically, but he could try by being the best person he could be. "We've certainly missed you. It's been tough picking up the pieces, but hey—our mission was a success!"

"Indeed," Damian said coldly, drawing Sage even closer to his body. "Because of Sage, the monster is dead and her sister is out of our hands."

In other words: Little Man's death hadn't been her fault. *None of* the deaths had been her fault.

Everyone bowed his or her head, including Louis and Agathe, to acknowledge that. But it didn't lift the mood. Sage's heroism and their success at taking over Diamond City wasn't going to outweigh the losses just because that's the way Damian wanted it to be. Especially not for Gertrude.

Gertrude glared at Sage.

Damian wasn't having any of it, so he steered Sage and the girls away from the black cloud of depression and into Heart. There, more of his loyal followers were waiting: Mega Woman, Eye Candy, and Rockstar. Ironically, these were the three that used to hate Sage the most, but, like Turtle, they were the three that'd do anything for their Warlord.

Like the rest of the rebels, they were all wearing the same white and black uniforms to match the Diamond City military. From above, it'd be impossible to distinguish them from each other. This had to be Agathe and Louis' doing, uniting the two forces into one.

It was nice to see, and it brought tears to Sage's eyes because Little Man wasn't one of them. Who'd play fastball with her now? And while Sage hadn't thought of him too much, looking at the palace from the cobblestone sidewalk reminded her of Gregory.

Her ex-husband was dead.

Sage held her mouth. She closed her eyes to keep the bile down. Was she going to be sick? Was she going to see all that blood and all those guts and all those bodies when she walked in there, with her fucking maniacal sister laughing at the sight of it all? That's where Damian was taking them.

"Worry not, darling," Damian said to her, ignorant of the horrible thoughts in her head. He hadn't been here to see the death and destruction like Sage had. He probably thought she was still upset over Gertrude's coldness. "You won't be interacting with them very much. You're going to live the life you've always wanted, and after we get married, we'll move far away from here."

"Damian says we'll be living in the Color District!" Olivia squeaked with stars in her eyes. "I've always wanted to live there! Maybe I'll become a diva, or a talkshow host, or a nude model!"

Damian loved the Color District. It's where he wanted to have that mega fashion show of his, but it was also a place where he felt himself. As someone from the Clarity District, where Squid fanaticism and Optimum worship could drive anyone crazy, creativity was his escape. That meant he, too, would be taking a break from politics and that's exactly what Sage wanted. It was definitely a step in the right direction.

But this palace thing—Sage couldn't do it.

"Damian," she whispered to him because she didn't want to startle him. "I-I need to use the bathroom."

"Very well," Damian said. He drew his brows, feeling her for a fever with his hand. "Let's get inside and settled in."

"No—I don't want to go in there. Please don't make me go in there." Sage started to hyperventilate.

"Is there something wrong?"

Obviously. No one had ever seen Sage take off for the bathroom so quickly. It was Candice who had to explain that Sage had come a long way with her post traumatic stress disorder, that making pizza and watching *The Royal Court* had filled her head with love and hope, but fighting had reinstated all of it right back in the forefront of her mind.

Sage barreled into the ballroom next to the palace because she knew there was a bathroom there. She had talked to Samson in the corner right outside of it, when Blackburn had invited her to dinner. She had never been inside until now, and her knees had never had the pleasure of touching the sparkling tiles until she was heaving into the toilet.

"Sage!" Damian was right behind her.

"I'm sorry," Sage croaked in between coughs. She tried not to look at the chunks of breakfast swirling around in the bowl. "My God...I-I'm sorry...I-I'm not well...I-I—there was so much blood..."

Damian held her hair and then her body until she calmed down. He didn't let her linger in front of a toilet—when she was done, he flushed. He helped her to the sink and washed her face. He didn't let her go and he didn't talk to her, either. He didn't even ask—he called Mega Woman and told her to move their quarters to elsewhere. There were nice little complexes along the Cut District border they could stay in for now.

"I'm sorry." Damian kissed Sage's forehead. "I didn't know, darling."

"I don't think I did, either," Sage said quietly. "It's just...a lot. A-and Gertrude..."

"She'll be fine. She just needs time. We all do." Damian inspected her face. He must have deemed she looked presentable because he asked if she was ready to go.

If it wasn't the palace, then yes. In fact, the Starlight Complex was out of sight and out of mind from the political traffic in Heart. Sage didn't get to see Louis, Agathe, the new council, or even the aircrafts that came in from trips around the Outskirts—only Damian's rebels and capital security.

Sage appreciated the hospitality and the comfort it brought to Candice and Olivia. An apartment on the top floor was the perfect way to disconnect from stress. While Sage preferred to stay hidden, the girls were at liberty to walk the capital whenever they wanted. Sage went as far as the living room balcony, which she stood in to look out at the blinking lights of the Cut District in the distance. Facing away from Heart was the best remedy for her now. She had Damian at her side to keep an eye on her, but she also understood he had business to take care of. Winterfeld was still relocating its citizens, and they had an important one to keep an eye on.

"I'll come with you," Sage said to him when they were notified that Reina had been transferred to Diamond City one night. This was a whole week later. Candice and Olivia were on a hunt to find their friends from Winterfeld with Mega Woman as an escort. Sightseeing was a plus.

"Are you sure, darling?" Damian asked. He always stripped for bed. "You don't have to."

Sage felt like she did have to, yes. She couldn't ignore Reina and what the pregnancy meant, so she went to visit her with Damian the next day.

Heart had a top-tier medical facility where all the city's best and brightest scientists and doctors worked. They focused their research on the life, growth, and potential of Enhanced, and dabbled in dangerous experiments here and there. Louis had told Sage about them a few times in the past, the council's never-ending quest to replicate Enhanced. Sage would rather not think of it right now.

Reina was there, accompanied by her good friend, Nova, who looked both relieved and frightened at the same time. While Reina was unscathed, it wasn't her physical wellbeing that doctors inquired about—they wanted juicy details about where she had been the past few months and how she had gotten pregnant.

From the view glass, Sage could see the slight roundness of her belly. Doctors were still analyzing the fetus and its state and were reluctant to release any details on it yet.

Not human.

That's what Sage surmised. That's why doctors were so damned baffled. Like Sage's mother, Reina was going to give birth to a hybrid.

Sage rubbed her arms because the cold in this hallway was piercing. She kept a close eye on Reina then slowly studied Nova, who looked like the world was going to end. Perhaps for Reina it was. The Squids from Winterfeld had hinted as much. So many women had died carrying hybrids . . . what Sage didn't understand was how the hell Reina was still alive. Forget the baby—*how had* she escaped the Squids?

That's what Damian was discussing with a doctor down the hall. All of this was way too coincidental and convenient in Sage's opinion. When he was finished with his conversation, Damian stepped over to her and wrapped an arm around her waist.

"What are your thoughts, darling?"

"Samson did this," Sage said.

Damian arched a brow. Sage explained her conversation with the Squids in Lolligo, their lack of a fight, and Reina's too-easy escape. She constructed a satisfactory case, but there was still the question of why? If Samson was working with the Squids, why would he be sending them captives? Sage wished with all of her heart she could ask, and there was that familiar pull of dread again, the longing to see her roommate.

Sage sighed.

"Samson made his choice," Damian stated carefully, knowing how touchy this subject was. "He chose to return to the Squids for whatever mission he has to accomplish. In taking your sister, he has relinquished any responsibility he has to you. Do you understand? You can live the way you've always wanted, Sage."

"You don't think the Squids will try to attack us, do you?" Sage asked quietly.

"That is a very fine possibility, but Diamond City will be ready. Thanks to you, we have allies who care and are willing to defend our freedom. I know that it is in your nature to act, but you told me that you no longer wanted to fight."

Sage wrapped her arms around him. She laid her head on his

chest. She closed her eyes, knowing deep in her heart that that's exactly what she wanted. She wanted to see her pizza restaurant again . . . but then she thought of Bram. And the girls. How she hadn't told them of his death yet.

"You will have to put certain things behind you," Damian said against her head, stroking her hair. "I know what weighs you down—you long for the family that betrayed you. You still don't understand why they did it, but the why no longer matters. For many years after I left Diamond City, I always wondered why the people I loved betrayed me. My first relationship was nothing more than bodily attraction, and I acknowledge that, but my second with David destroyed me. He wanted nothing more than to betray me to the Allseer for all of the glory and attention he could get. I nearly lost my life because of him. Ileana saw me as a tool, too, seducing me and using me to raise a child just to say she dominated me."

Sage clutched his back.

"Promise me that you will try to put this behind you," Damian said to her. "That you trust in Louis and Agathe to make the right decisions when it comes to the safety of our land so you can concentrate on you."

"What if there's something I have to do?"

"Like what? Fight in another war?"

Sage bit her lip.

"Darling." Damian tipped her head up with his fingers. So long and slender like a woman's, but powerful and hard like a man's when they needed to be. Sage looked into his eyes, outlined with black. His skin was white and smooth, a perfect contrast to the darkness of his hair. Today, he was in a gray jacket with gold chains, plain but classy, and still every bit the fearsome Warlord everyone knew him as. Sage never tired of looking at him because there was always something new to discover, some other way of seeing him. "There will always be war," he said softly. "You have lived a long life, and you know that. It is up to you to decide if that is the sort of life you wish to continue living. I will support you in whatever you choose, and I will destroy anyone who attempts to bring you harm."

"I know you will," Sage said quietly. She nestled her head back under his chin and listened to the steady thumping in his chest. Just over a month ago, there had been silence. She was thankful his heart was where it belonged. There was so much rage from his past, and that was normal for everything he had gone through. Damian held himself together so well.

"Why don't we go home?" he suggested. "Let's relax and disconnect for a bit. I found this show we could watch. It's called *The Rainbow in Me*. It's about a straight man who's living in the Color District for the first time in his life. He learns what it's like to be creative and bend the rules I think he falls for his cameraman."

"So he's not straight."

Damian chuckled. "I guess not. Which is why those labels are so useless. Sure, we have preferences, but what's to stop me from falling in love with someone for *them*, regardless of their gender? Isn't that how it should be?"

"You're right."

"It's all in how we raise children and what we force them to believe. Some children carry those 'rules' with them all their lives, but people like me . . . well . . ." Damian sighed. He rested his chin on her head. "I couldn't hide it."

"And yet you're with me. A woman."

"I couldn't help falling in love with you, darling. You see? People are so much more complex than just black or white. That's why I want to see this show—I want to see this man's journey, what opens his eyes, and whom he chooses to marry." Damian chuckled again. "I think the camera guy is cute, but there's a dancer who's especially hot. I swear he's better than any ballerina I've ever seen, the way he floats around on stage like a leaf. Kind of like you when you're fighting."

Sage snorted. "Thanks for comparing me to a ballerina."

"Have you ever seen yourself fight?"

"No."

"Well, that's what you look like. So swift and agile. Just like when you're having sex."

Sage got her fist ready, but Damian jumped back before she made contact. Inappropriate bastard.

"I'll show you 'swift and agile'," Sage snarled.

If only. Sage would have loved to demonstrate her skill to the cackling Damian, but doctors rushed by them in the hall. A trio of them were scurrying to reach Reina's room. "Let's hurry!" they shouted to each other without acknowledging security by the door.

Sage and Damian glanced at each other before taking off, too. They nearly barreled into the view glass to watch Reina squirm and scream on the bed. Nova had been restrained because she wasn't helping in the hysteria department—her cries mingled with Reina's, and the entire room just plunged into chaos. Perhaps doctors could have restored some control if only they had been faster. Or maybe they should have done this hours ago, when they had first received Reina in their care, because it was too late now.

Sage had seen plenty of horror movies in her lifetime. She could argue that some bits of her life had been far scarier than any film she had sat through. She had seen countless deaths, dismemberments, torture sessions, and suicides. But she had never seen anything quite like this.

Reina's belly swelled to the size of a balloon. Something banged against its walls from within, like a vicious worm about to break free from an egg. Something, clearly, had come to life within her because there was an explosion.

If Sage could hear what was going on in the room, she probably would have heard a rip. A crack. More screaming and crying. She didn't need to, though, because the visuals were enough: blood sprayed everyone in the room like a geyser, and out came two alien-looking lifeforms that jumped and landed on the floor with a thump. They squirmed like the oversized maggots they were, eyes slitted, mouth harvesting the sharpest teeth Sage had ever seen.

Like a Squid's, she thought. *Like Samson's.*

Forget science. Fuck the experiments. Security shot the creatures dead, but they didn't silence the commotion.

That escalated.

CHAPTER 3

Back Home

There was only one way to forget something like that. No amount of water or embraces from Damian shook the terrible picture of two alien lifeforms bursting out of a womb from Sage's mind. She saw it over and over, as if it was on repeat. She couldn't answer anyone's questions or engage in any meaningful conversation at the medical facility. Right now, she needed to go home and watch Defenders' Unite!.

It was the only way to escape this hell. It was the only way Sage knew how. She was grateful Candice and Olivia had gone out to see a movie with their group of friends from Winterfeld. As far as they were concerned, Reina didn't exist.

And in this world, Reina didn't. Not anymore. Because the babies she had had inside her had torn out of her like a pair of monsters. Is that what the Squids had meant by not surviving birth? Is that what had happened to all the women in their custody?

Damian stayed with Sage the whole night. He should have stayed at the facility to find out more about Reina's condition, but he probably figured it was futile. The end result, regardless of why hybrids were such parasites, wouldn't change. This wasn't the first failed pregnancy, and it definitely wouldn't be the last.

Eventually, Sage did fall asleep. When she woke up, Damian was standing by the window, gazing out into the horizon. He had a pair of boxers on, as if he had been dressing when the sight of the Cut District had caught his attention.

"Your hair's long," Sage said. It was true: Damian's hair had grown quite a bit from the time she met him. It used to be at his shoulders, but now it was touching his back. Long, black, and silky. So beautiful and soft.

Damian turned to her. His eyes lit up and a small smile graced his lips. "Do you want me to cut it?"

"No," she said. "I love your hair. Reminds me of what I'll never have."

"Your hair is beautiful, too, darling."

"Please." Sage had some nasty pillow hair right now. Yes, it had come a long way thanks to the Suave-Suave treatments, but it'd never be like Damian's. That waterfall of gloss was near impossible to achieve.

"Come here." Damian beckoned her forward. "I'll fix it for you."

Sage got out of bed. She stood in front of the window as Damian picked up a brush. At least her hair was easy to untangle and manage. He tied it into the best braid Sage had ever had, perfectly woven together like stitching on clothes. He put some cream on the top then sprayed it with oil.

"What are you thinking?" Damian asked.

"I'm not," Sage admitted. She ignored the cramps in her abdomen.

"How are you feeling? With your menstrual cycle?"

"Fine." Sage had answered that a bit too quickly. Damian didn't question it, though. The word itself was all he had needed to hear for his next proposition.

"I want to take you to the Cut District," he said. "I think you need a break from all this turmoil. You already did all the fighting, so why do you need to stay here and deal with all the extra stress? You are not a politician nor a doctor."

Sage turned slightly. She looked at him. As pictures of her restaurant came to mind, she asked, "What about the girls?"

"What about them? They can come with us or stay here—whichever they prefer."

"Where are we going to stay, Damian?"

"Don't you have your apartment for now? We can look for another place in the meantime, too."

Sage opened her mouth to argue, but Damian stopped her with a simple hand to her cheek. He gazed into her eyes as he said, "You have to go back at some point. I know that's where you used to live with Samson, but you're not going to abandon it, are you?"

Tears welled in Sage's eyes. "I can't," she croaked. "It's his, too."

"I'll go with you," Damian offered. "And if it's too painful, we'll stay at a hotel. We can stay wherever you feel comfortable. The council already offered to pay for hospitality. I just don't want you around all the hardship here." He kissed her forehead. "You don't want it either, do you?"

Sage wished with all her heart she didn't have to deal with any of this horror. If it were up to her, she'd leave it all behind and pick up her life again, from where she had left off. But that didn't stop her from worrying about Samson, Wren, and the Squids. God, she was so worried . . .

"Tell me what you wish to do," Damian said. "You worry about them, but what can we do? Go after them? Find the Squids? Start another battle and put people's lives at risk?"

Never. How dare he suggest that—

"*You* want to go after them by yourself?"

Sage pursed her lips. She clenched her fists.

"Then let's try to make the best of our situation right now," Damian said to her. "Let's try to move on with our lives, Sage. Then we'll deal with the rest."

He was right. He was so right. Sage played with the signet ring on her finger, the one he had given her in Mousafeld. All participators of the Unification War had one. Sage had given hers to Aurora a long time ago.

Aurora . . . the Frasers . . . Bram . . . Candice and Olivia.

Sage crossed her arms. She rubbed her triceps. She looked down at the rug before speaking another worry.

"I haven't told the girls about Bram. They know he sold them to the council, but they don't know he's dead. I haven't even been to Mousafeld to see his body."

Damian was watching her with an awfully serious look on his face. Sage challenged his gaze by holding it with her own.

"Why would you want to?" Damian finally asked.

"He was my nephew," Sage replied. "Regardless of what he did, I need to pay my respects. Don't tell me you never went to see Ileana?"

"I burned her body myself," Damian said coldly.

"Then let me burn Bram's," Sage retorted.

This conversation was getting ugly. Damian looked a bit frustrated as he finished dressing, buttoning up his shirt and pulling on a pair pants. Sage stood there, watching him, getting ready to send him to hell, but she bit back her words.

Right now, Damian had every right to feel frustrated. He had been through his equal share of hell these past few weeks, so of course Bram was the cherry on top of the cake. Telling the girls was yet another task that'd start up a storm of grief, and Damian was trying so hard to keep their heads above water. Maybe Sage would tell the girls another time, once their lives were a bit more stable.

"Let's go to the Cut District," Sage said as Damian fixed his makeup in the mirror. He smoothed foundation and powdered blush on his skin better than any woman Sage knew. He didn't stop to look at her, but he was listening as he applied eyeliner and green shadow to his lids. "I want to see the restaurant."

And then a whole new wave of nerves began. Not because there might be irreparable vandalism to the restaurant itself, but because it'd bring back a slew of old memories that was as overwhelming as staying at Heart. Homesickness struck Sage hard during breakfast. Now, she couldn't get to Cut fast enough. She'd be returning to the comfortable life she'd left behind, the one she'd abandoned because she wanted to meet Louis and flourish in the palace. Tired of the mundaneness, Sage had ventured out and gotten herself into trouble with the council.

But could she really call this trouble? Could meeting Damian have been worth the effort and heartache, the people secretly plotting to screw her over? Bram had already been planting seeds to catapult himself into Heart's ranks by using her. The thought was more depressing than it was infuriating now. And the answer was yes, it had been worth it.

Damian was worth it.

He was with her every step of the way. He got over his hissy-fit from earlier that morning and played the supportive partner on their way to the Cut District that weekend. He held her hand and assured her they'd be fine. They'd make it work . . . together.

Justice could fly a car the same way he could an aircraft, and he did so effortlessly. Candice and Olivia sat in the front so they could watch. The ride was smooth with no turbulence despite the rain greeting them more aggressively than usual.

Sage was used to it. This was home regardless of the "curse" the Squids had put on the city, the Claritian belief that they'd drown to death one day because of human corruption. Despite the rain, people here hustled to keep their businesses afloat. The towering skyscrapers with all of the blinking lights brought a smile to Sage's face and a twinge to her heart.

The Art Carnival already had its announcements all over the billboards, ready for its fall pass through the Cut District. That's where she had met David and found Damian's heart last year. She wondered if David was still traveling with them.

It looked like the Cut Porcupines were playing the Carat Lions this weekend at the local stadium. Sage couldn't believe she had forgotten about fastball. She always kept up with all the games, and placed her bets here and there depending on the team and its players. While her skills on the court were mediocre, she knew talent when she saw it. And right now, it reminded her of Little Man.

Sage sighed.

In addition to the usual billboards was one Sage hadn't seen in a long time.

ARE YOU COUGHING NONSTOP?

HAS YOUR FEVER BEEN PERSISTENT?

IS THERE BLOOD IN YOUR PHLEGM?

DO YOU HAVE LOSS OF APPETITE AND DRASTIC WEIGHT LOSS?

DON'T HESITATE—CALL YOUR DOCTOR NOW! EARLY RED FEVER

DETECTION CAN SAVE YOUR LIFE!

Red Fever? There had been an outbreak a few years ago in Diamond City. People had fallen sick and dropped like flies all across the districts, until doctors had created an antibiotic to combat it. Since then, cases had decreased. Its origins were unknown despite Allseer Marchello blaming it on Outskirts exposure. Sage was surprised by the resurgence.

"Have you ever heard of Red Fever?" Sage asked Damian, who was busy sending messages on his phone.

"No, darling," he said without looking at her. "What is that?"

"It's a contagious infection that humans get. Like a bad cold. A lot of people die from it."

"That's strange. Has no wondrous medical professional been able to find treatment?"

"They did the first time around," Sage said softly. "But it looks like the contagion is back."

"Perhaps it built resistance," Damian said. "I'm sure doctors will figure out how to stop it."

Sage had donated a lot of money to Red Fever charities. She had immunity to disease, but these poor humans didn't. With Allseer Marchello unwilling to share any physical enhancements with the average population, humans died from the smallest infections, sometimes because of complications. It was needless, but doctors, medical institutions, and pharmaceuticals had to make money somehow. Sage tried hard not to think of how Overseer Callus had treated his people in the Cut District before the Unification War.

Humans had been used as experiments. She'd have to talk to Louis about ensuring that never happened again.

Sage peered at the streets below. They all looked the same, the ones she used to cross every single day. She and Samson had never owned a car, so feet and the cheesy moped had been their modes of transportation. The moped was still in Mousafeld, and Sage would be sure to get that back, too.

Pretty soon, they were flying over Tour the Diamond, a hotspot bar where few brave souls took a shot of Cupid's Arrow. That's where Sage had battled the Cell Destroyer for the first time. Nearly a year ago, but it felt like just yesterday. Sage's life had been so very different . . . She hadn't met Damian, for one. Only heard of him by his nickname, the Warlord. A Diamond City exile that had been feared more than hated.

Just a few more blocks, and Justice used one of the landing stations to descend to street level. From there, he weaved around a few more corners until they arrived at Two for Pizza.

Sage's face was pressed to the glass. Damian had a hand on her shoulder. Candice and Olivia were just as excited as she was.

"Come on, Aunt Sage!" Olivia got out of the car first, followed by her sister. The both of them helped Sage to her feet and dragged her to the front door.

Sage stood there, staring at her restaurant. It was so much smaller than she remembered. She couldn't see anything inside because of the dark tint on the glass. The door and windows were bulletproof, so there wasn't a scratch on them. There was, however, a notice from the Allseer, claiming that the property belonged to the council as of the month of Courage, year 100.

The month Sage and Louis had set out to find Damian on Blackburn's behalf.

Damian snatched the notice before Sage could and crumpled it up. Sage worked on the locks, fingers shaking. She was overreacting way too much. Candice had to help her with the keys then Olivia pulled open the door.

It smelled like dough. All was dark and put away with the chairs stacked on the tables. When Candice turned on the lights, Sage was relieved to see there wasn't any damage by soldiers being spiteful or robbers trying their hand at looting. The walls were smooth, the pizza portraits centered perfectly in their frames. The TV was unscathed and the Diamond City flag perched right next to it wasn't missing a single stitch. The cashier and counter were wiped down, but had still accumulated dust over the months they had fallen into disuse.

"I love what you did with the space, darling," Damian complimented, looking at the walls. "The color combination is perfect."

One side was red and the other white. It'd definitely need a fresh coat soon.

"But I especially love the pepperoni trail." Damian chuckled. "Genius."

Sage's idea. She had pasted ginormous pepperoni on the wall, from the front door all the way to the kitchen. Bram had hated it, but tolerated it in exchange for his obnoxious pizza-man on the back wall. Sage couldn't find it in her to take it down now.

Sage examined the kitchen and the offices next. Those were clean and orderly, too. She stood by Bram's desk, where he had always kept track of their finances. The computer screen had a thin layer of dust. The calendar showed the month of Courage. The Allseer's Private Guard had been using this place as a headquarters, but it looked like they had left as soon as Sage had. Council's orders, perhaps, in case Sage came back and slaughtered them all. Thank God they had packed their shit and left.

"We will make it work, I promise," Damian said to her from the door. He was smiling. "This is the coziest restaurant I've ever been in."

Sage sat down in the chair. She smiled, too. "You're such a sap."

"I'm being honest. Now I want to taste a pizza."

That was going to take some time, but why not? Sage fired up the oven and got started on the dough. Candice and Olivia already knew they had to fetch the yeast, water, and mixing bowl. Damian stood by because he didn't have a clue what he was doing. At the very least, he could measure the flour.

"Don't fuck it up," Sage warned him. "We don't bullshit around here. The measurements have to be exact. This isn't Dough's crappy restaurant."

Damian laughed. "Yes, darling. Whatever you say. And if I misbehave, you can spank me later."

"I'll do more than just spank you."

Damian arched a brow. "Oh?" he purred. "What did you have in mind? I can do a little BDSM if that's what you're suggesting."

"What's 'BDSM'?" Olivia asked.

Sage glared at Damian, who clapped with excitement.

"What?" Olivia insisted.

"I didn't know you were into kink, darling." Damian sashayed over to her, a stupid grin on his face. "And believe it or not, I have some ideas for that, too. I don't mind a bit of roleplaying. You'll play the captor and I'll be the victim. We can use handcuffs and all sorts of chains—"

Sage pointed a knife at him. "One more word, and we'll try the Friday Night Hook-Up Special here and now."

Damian blinked. He knew what that entailed because they had talked about it one night. He subconsciously covered his crotch.

"Candice!" Olivia whined to her sister. "What's BDSM?"

"It's—um . . ." Candice glanced at Sage, who shook her head. This was not for the ears of a thirteen-year-old. "It's an acronym. It stands for 'Boy', 'Drama', 'Sex', and 'Magic.' It's what we use to describe people like Damian."

Damian cackled loudly. "Makes sense."

"Now come on." Candice grabbed Olivia, who was still wondering why "BDSM" had Damian laughing like a maniac and Sage looking like she was about to stab him. "Help me with the dough."

Together, she and Candice kneaded the dough and set it to chill. It was always best to leave overnight, but everyone was hungry. The sauce and cheese were easy to prepare because Sage knew the recipes by heart. Damian looked amazed as Sage sprinkled condiments like a pro, with Candice and Olivia as her little helpers, moving like robots. Those two had earned their keep during the summer.

Then they flattened out the dough, poured the sauce, and scattered the cheese. Damian put whatever toppings he wanted, but he went extra heavy on the pineapples and chocolate bits. He got to pick because he had quieted down and not mentioned BDSM again. Sage was all for rewarding good behavior.

"How about we make the Minefield next time?" Damian suggested as Candice slipped the pizza into the oven.

"What's the 'Minefield'?" Olivia asked.

Damian's creation. It was supposed to feature golden raisins. Sage hadn't given much thought to the menu items yet, but she figured she'd be nice and take his ideas into consideration. The Hippo, which was an explosion of toppings with bananas on top, was still her bestseller.

The four of them took a seat in the corner and talked well into the night. Candice and Olivia wanted to do more sightseeing (which translated to shopping because they knew these streets like the back of their hands), so they asked Justice to go with them. After offering him a few slices of pizza, which he took and said was "so much better than Dough's!", he gave them a ride around the city. The girls loved to visit Diamond Loot, where they found anything from cheap sunglasses to expensive pearl earrings. It was more than just a store—it was a huge, indoor flea market that was dangerous to anyone with a wallet. Sage had given them her credit card and trusted them to use it responsibly.

"Why didn't you give them Louis' card?" Damian asked, standing aside as Sage closed up shop. "That way they can spend all the money they want."

"Louis isn't my sugar daddy," Sage snapped. "While I appreciate his financial help, I'm not an indigent."

Damian laughed. He took her hand as they started toward her apartment on foot. "Do you want me to be your sugar daddy? I'm sorry—I'm sorry!" He cackled at the look of death on her face.

"What's with you today?"

"What?" Damian grinned, his cheeks full and red. "I just think you're incredibly entertaining. And beautiful."

Sage snorted. "I'm glad you're not bored, Mr. BDSM."

Damian cleared his throat. "Did you mean it?"

"What?"

"Do you want to take our sex to the next level?"

"No," Sage said flatly. She cracked a smile, though. The death look wouldn't work if she caved, but she had never seen Damian so silly before. "I'm perfectly happy at the level it's at now. Although I wouldn't mind chaining you up and locking you in a closet for a few days."

"Darling," Damian purred, kissing her hand. "Why so cruel when I've been nothing but good to you?"

Sage chuckled. "I have an evil side."

"Do you now?"

"Especially toward men who need to be put in their places."

"By all means." Damian's eyes turned sultry. "Put me in my place any time."

Sage smacked his ass so hard that Damian jumped. She went for another, but Damian took off like a sprinter. He splashed through puddles to make it a safe distance away, laughing like a crazy drunk. People turned their heads, some looking amused and others annoyed.

Sage didn't bother chasing him. She walked on casually, both hands in her pockets. Damian peered at her from behind a traffic light.

"Walk," she commanded.

Damian blew her a kiss.

Sage grabbed him by the sleeve. She dragged him like she would a dog on a leash. One of the passing women gave her a thumbs up.

From there on out, it grew silent between them. It was drizzling, but neither used an umbrella. Damian's hair and makeup were perfect no matter what, whereas Sage would have frizz soon. Not that she cared about looks right now. She was passing by all the stores she used to see on the way home.

They went in this order: Vivi's Noodles; Nails For Life; Oh, My Lucky Stars! (a smoke shop); Flip-Flop Flop-Flip; Vendors' Corner;

traffic light; Lily Flowers; Tae Kwon Doe (some of those kids were impressive); Swim Time!; We Know You Want a Puppy! (Sage always peered through the window and dreamed of having a pet, but Samson would probably eat it for dinner); The Travel Bug Agency; traffic light; and then her complex, The View, because it was a towering skyscraper over fifty stories high. Sage was thankful she was on the third floor because she hated elevators.

"Wow," Damian said when they got there. He was looking back at the street, though. It hadn't occurred to Sage until just then that this was Damian's first time in the city since his exile thirty years ago.

"It has indeed been a long time." Damian turned to the Hotspot tower in the distance. Only the latest and greatest phone and internet service in Diamond City. "But I never ventured much in the Cut District. Color was always my district of fascination."

"We'll visit there next," Sage promised him.

"Only when you wish to, darling. I understand there is a lot to do here." Damian kissed her hand. "Let's take our time."

Sage pointed at the discount store across the street. "I met Gertrude's sister there the night I chased Taz through the city. I bought a Star Raider toy, and when I showed her my tattoo, she gave me a map to Mousafeld."

Damian arched a brow. "Is that so?"

"She wanted me to join you. I wasn't interested until pizza was at stake."

Damian chuckled. "No hard feelings, darling. You had no idea just how charming and handsome I was at the time. You hadn't met my penis then, either."

Sage pushed him. "Do we always have to talk about your penis?"

"It's an integral part of our relationship."

Sage tackled him straight into a puddle, water splashing everywhere. She might have ruined his nice clothes, but she didn't care. Damian was having too much fun to berate her about it, too.

"Darling," he purred, "save it for the bedroom. I know you're desperate, but let's try to exercise a bit of self-control."

The laughter always relieved so much of Sage's stress. It's why she instigated him. That, and other reasons as well. She wanted him like never before, but the sidewalk definitely wasn't the place.

Reluctantly, Sage got up. When Damian followed, she kissed him. His lips were glossy and wet; it was like sucking on a lollipop. Desire erupted in her belly spreading to the very tips of her fingers and toes. She wanted him to touch her like he always did.

"I want you to make love to me," Sage whispered against his lips. "I want you to touch every part of me."

"I will ravish you," Damian promised her, eyes half-lidded. His irises were shiny, reflecting all the neon colors from the buildings surrounding them. He looked like someone had set him on fire. "Out here or in there. Choose now, but stop with the damn *teasing*." He held her hips still.

"I'm just kissing you."

"We've gone over this before, darling: I have zero tolerance for your sneaky caresses. Just a slight rub"—He held her hips again—"arouses the hell out of me. I swear that if I don't ejaculate, my balls are going to explode."

"That sounds painful." Sage touched them for herself, and Damian cursed out loud. A couple across the street turned their heads.

"Go on," Damian breathed. "Milk me in public, but don't fucking stop."

"I want the bedroom," Sage said innocently.

Damian picked her up and stormed into the complex. They took the stairs to the third floor. Sage inhaled all the familiar scents of this closed hallway: the fresh paint, the potted plants in the corner, and the lingering smell of home. Nostalgia started to swell in her chest, especially when they reached door 312, but Damian served as an immense distraction from Samson's worktable and all of her belongings. Sage was only able to glimpse the clean countertops in the kitchen, the spotless couch in the living area, and the sparkling tiles in the bathroom before Damian reached her room.

"Oh, my." Damian stopped and gasped at all the *Defenders Unite!* merchandise. The most impressive section was the Star Raider display, all of the vintage editions from a hundred years ago. "I knew you were a fan, but I didn't know to this extent." He looked up at the ceiling, the stars there. Then he looked at her.

Sage smiled at him. She was definitely one of *Defenders Unite!*'s biggest fans. How many carried around all four seasons on their body like she did? She had them all in the Portable Projector hanging around her neck. Damian had purchased it for her in thanks for saving his life that day he overdosed in his office. Sage would never forget the night he had given it to her. He had seen her naked for the first time. Sage rolled her eyes and fought back a grin.

"I like it when you smile like that," Damian whispered to her. "I don't see it often."

"Yes, you do," she whispered back. "Every time I'm with you."

Damian caressed her cheek. "Not every time."

"Don't worry—I don't have any daggers on me right now. Only under the mattress. But I think I'll be too distracted to use them tonight."

"Are you sure? What of your menstrual cycle?"

"I . . ." Sage hesitated. She rubbed her abdomen. "I don't have it."

"Take off your clothes, darling."

Damian wasn't asking questions, so neither did Sage. She took off her jacket, her shirt, her boots, and then her pants. When she was in nothing but undergarments, she evaluated her own thinness, how much weight she had lost these past few months. She'd start training again soon.

Damian had seen her naked plenty of times, so he already knew how skinny she was. That didn't matter, though—he touched her anew, starting from her shoulders to her chest. He unclipped her bra, freed her small lumps for breasts, and then pulled down her underwear.

Sage worked on his jacket, sliding it off his shoulders, then unbuttoned his shirt. She pressed a kiss to his chest, right on the scar over his heart, then moved farther down. Soon, his pants, boots, and socks were on the floor.

Naked, they faced each other. This was nothing like Sage had thought it would be after so long, so . . . contained. It was almost as if Damian was in a trance, admiring a fine piece of jewelry that he didn't want to break. Sage was someone he needed to protect. It worked both ways.

Sage embraced him tightly, just like he did her. They stood there like high school sweethearts about to make love for the first time, basking in the warmth of each other's skin, the feel of their bodies so close. Then they stared at each other, devouring the other with eyes alone, that heady look. Sage's heart raced and her stomach twisted into knots. That same fluttery feeling spread into her lower belly and turned into a massive ache. With the head of his penis against her belly button, Sage was going mad with desire.

They kissed slowly and sensually. It was necessary to explore every crevice of the mouth, taste every inch. Damian's hands trailed from her shoulders to her breasts, palms rough and calloused from long days of training. The rings on his fingers were so cold, but felt so good against her hot skin. He rubbed her nipples up and down. He parted from their kiss just to whisper, "I want to hear you moan."

"It doesn't work that way, Damian," Sage said against his lips, hooking a leg around his waist.

Damian used his hands to cup her rear and hoist her onto his body. He took them to bed, settling on the warm thick comforter beneath the glow-in-the-dark stars on the ceiling. After more slow deep kissing and lazy touching, Damian positioned himself at her hips. He was panting, sweating, and trembling a bit.

"I can't delay this any further," he said. "I need you now, darling."

Sage opened her legs some more, but that wasn't enough to accommodate his thickness. After so long, she had forgotten how much he stretched her, the time it took to adjust and allow the pain to subside. Involuntarily, she squeezed him, thighs clamping his waist.

"Fuck!" Damian exclaimed, collapsing onto his elbows. "Darling!"

"What's wrong?" Sage said.

"You are going to annihilate me if you do that." Damian panted wildly. "I-I can hardly keep myself together—you're so damn tight, and I'm going to cum before I even start to thrust."

"Oh, wow." Sage laughed. "Poor baby."

Damian composed himself. He leaned over her and held her hip with a hand, keeping her steady as he started a slow rhythm. It was an up-and-down motion, creating a set of vibrations deep in Sage's womb. It kept their bodies together, trapping the heat between them. That was all it took for Sage to lose herself.

She succumbed to the electricity that shot through her body and the white-hot pleasure that exploded in her belly. That was the end of Damian, too.

He spilled his hot seed into her with a gasp. He was noisy and a bit winded, overwhelmed by how quickly he had climaxed. "I feel like a schoolboy having sex for the first time," he panted.

"You're clearly out of practice," Sage said, chuckling.

"It's you," Damian growled. "You drive me crazy. It's like you suck the soul out of my body through my penis."

"I don't mean to." Sage smiled at him. Her cheeks flushed an even brighter red. She brought him back down to her, kissing his lips. It didn't take very long for Damian to harden again, and then it was round two.

This time went much better than the first. Even so, Damian kept making these hissing sounds, harsh groans that he muffled against her neck as his hands squeezed her rear. Pure ecstasy, Sage quickly realized. Damian was lost to her in those minutes, eyes closed as his thrusts got more aggressive. By the end of it, he had her entire lower body off the bed, legs around his waist like a lasso.

Their love-making didn't become a frenzy, though. There was very little foreplay and touching—they focused on holding each other and reveling in their joined bodies, the thrusts that brought so much pleasure. Sometimes it was Sage on top, and one time they were on their side, facing each other, limbs tangled, hips meeting halfway.

"Damian," Sage panted against his lips, clutching his back with her hand. Her left leg was slung over his waist, giving him full access to her below, but it wasn't enough. "I don't like it."

"Is it not enough for you?" Damian asked.

"No. Lay on your back again." Sage pushed him then straddled him. She sunk onto him, his penis as far up in her as it could go, and thrusted twice before Damian climaxed. She squeezed him without meaning to.

"Stars," Damian groaned, holding his face. "You will be the death of me."

Sage laid on his body and nestled into his chest. They were already tangled in the sheets, so all she had to do was pull them up to her shoulders.

"My sweet Sage." Damian kissed her head. "Are you tired?"

"We just had sex six times. I'm not sure I'll be able to walk tomorrow."

"It looks like someone's in need of *practice*. Is that what you said I needed, too, darling?"

Sage rubbed his nipple with the palm of her hand. "Either that or estrogen shots to lower your libido. You are incredibly horny."

"How can I not be?" Damian grunted with pleasure. "Look at how you touch me. You call me horny, but you are incredibly needy as well."

Sage proved it by wrapping her mouth around his nipple. She sucked on it like she would a bottle, using her cheeks to create a pressure that had Damian bucking his hips. "Wow," she drawled. "Is that all it takes? Look at how hard you are already." She reached in between them to feel his erection, but Damian snatched her hand before her fingers made contact, knowing he'd melt again if she did.

"Give me your breast, darling," he said.

Sage touched her left breast. It wasn't big enough to fill her palm, but it was enough for Damian to play with. Besides, it was her nipple he was interested in. "This one?"

"Yes."

Sage curled back onto his chest. "I'm tired."

Damian made to get up, but Sage held him down. That's how the wrestling started, the twisting in the sheets until Sage was against the headboard with Damian's torso in between her legs. Damian held her ribs as he leaned in and captured one of those nipples in his mouth. He made it a point to suck on her like she had him.

"Look at how they harden for me." Damian flicked her stiff peaks with his tongue. "Just for me. Isn't that right, darling?"

"Yes," Sage panted.

"You have goosebumps all over your skin. Does it feel good when I suckle you like a babe? I know what will make you feel even better." He spread her legs wide, searing her with that intense gaze of his. "Goodness. What does that taste like, I wonder?" He leaned in and dragged his tongue right up her folds, right over her clit.

Sage jumped and hissed. Her body pounded with pleasure, numbing her limbs and drowning out her vision, especially when Damian sucked on her clit with his lips. Sage clutched his head to keep him there, fingers in his hair as he devoured her entirely with his mouth. He thrust his tongue inside, determined to reach every crevice, and he didn't stop until Sage climaxed.

She groaned when she did. She kept swinging her hips against his mouth, too, even after the pleasure subsided. Damian didn't stop licking her, either, as if he was determined to keep going until Sage begged him to stop.

Sage wasn't one to plead nicely, so that wasn't going to happen. Damian's efforts awakened a hidden frenzy within Sage, who found the strength to tackle Damian back on the bed.

"Darling?" he panted, confused as Sage crawled over his body like an animal. "What are you doing?"

The same treatment. It didn't matter how strongly her knees were shaking or how badly Sage wanted to ride his mouth. His lips were extra plump and his tongue was so hot, but Sage exercised control. The payback would be so worth it. She had plenty of experience with his blowjobs, so she knew what set him on fire.

"Darling, no," Damian growled as Sage took the throne between his legs now. Hand on each of his knees, she leaned down and licked the head of his penis. "No teasing . . . please . . ."

It took Sage an entire five minutes to finally use her mouth because tongue didn't count. She took him in as far as she could into her throat without gagging. She could never accommodate him entirely, but it didn't matter. Damian had such little resistance anyway, and a squeeze of his balls had him ejaculating like a water gun.

"STARS!" Damian cried, holding her head as he thrust into her mouth.

The poor thing was a hot mess, collapsing further onto the bed. No longer able to move or tease, Damian lay comatose as Sage settled onto his body, half covering it with her own. They were too exhausted to reach for sheets, so they fell asleep right in the middle of the bed. At some point, Sage rolled onto her side with Damian following onto her back like a blanket. He was heavy, hot, and warm, so he served as her comforter for the night. It was the strangest sleeping position yet.

And yet they woke up like that. At least Sage did some ten hours later in broad daylight. She smiled at Damian's face above her own, his soft breaths fanning her neck. That had been some much-needed sex last night. Sage hoped it'd help satiate his libido some.

"Darling," Sage whispered to him. She kissed his chin. He had shaved yesterday morning. "I'm getting up now. I'll get us some breakfast." She caressed his hand so she wouldn't startle him.

His only acknowledgment was a deep breath. Sage lifted his body and gently laid it on the pillow. She pulled up the sheets to his chest and watched him fall back asleep. He usually searched for her body, but he knew she was close by. Besides, her scent was everywhere and her *Defenders Unite!* collection reminded him of where he was. There was no one here to hurt him . . . to betray him . . .

Sage caressed his silky hair, brushing it back from his face. She kissed his temple. With a deep breath of her own, she got up and nearly fell over.

"Stars," she cursed, steadying the wobble in her legs. She was incredibly sore, but a shower and a few paces around her room alleviated the pain. She forgot all about it when she read the text message from Candice—*Arrived at Heart safely last night*—and stopped by Samson's bedroom.

For a long time, Sage stood by the doorway, staring at the perfectly made bed, the clean dresser tops, and the bare night stands. Samson wasn't one for leaving clutter, and nothing about his decor suggested it had ever been occupied by a person. No personalization . . . no memorabilia . . . just a simple painting that Sage had gifted to him once. It was of a cityscape from the Old World five hundred years ago. The name on the bottom read, *New York City.* Out of all the gifts Sage had ever bought him, this was his favorite.

Slowly, Sage withdrew and stopped by his worktable near the dining room.

There were always towers of trinkets, tools, and metals for all of his online commissions, what Sage teased was the messiest part of the house. Now, remembering all of those inventions, she wondered if they were for Squids infiltrated in the city or for people who truly needed weapons like hunting bows, daggers, and sheaths. It was this very table that had given life to her most treasured sword, the one that Damian had taken for his own. Infused with Slainium, it was deadly to anyone with Cells in their body. In fact, it was in her bedroom where Damian had left it last night amidst stripping.

But now that worktable was bare. The Diamond City military had frequented her apartment a lot last year, so it wouldn't have been wise for Samson to leave any of his weaponry behind. He had left a note, though, one written in Lolligo, indecipherable to anyone that wasn't one. Sage's hand trembled as she read the curves of their strange language.

> The world is a playground. We were part of the game. Still are. Hybrids are valuable, so I took the one that I don't love and gave my Cells to the one I do. Use them wisely, as I have taught you. Hope rests in you and the people you know, the ones you meet. Tyrus and Herman agree, outpost at the place where we parted.

Sage looked up. The writing was cryptic and it took a long time to sink in. She didn't snap out of it until she heard the shower running, indicating that Damian was up.

The world is a playground.

Hope rests in you and the people you know.

Outpost at the place where we parted.

What on earth did that mean?

As Sage prepared some peanut butter and jelly on crackers (the only provisions in the cabinets that hadn't gone bad), she pondered the letter's meaning but couldn't quite figure it out. Did the Squids truly have that much control over them?

When Damian came out of the bathroom and met her in the kitchen, Sage embraced him. She breathed in his wonderful scent, sweet with a hint of spice. Teakwood and lavender. Her arms squeezed him, but it didn't bother Damian one bit. He stroked her hair, lips against her forehead, and asked if all was well with her.

"Look at this." Sage showed him the letter.

Not that Damian could read it, but she translated it for him. The only part she omitted was "gave my Cells to the one I do."

Sage didn't feel anyone—even Damian—needed to know that Samson had injected her with a dose of his Cells as an experiment many years ago. From what they could tell, it had worked. She was already strong as a hybrid, but even stronger now with the Cells of a pure Squid in her veins.

Sage did voice her thoughts on the rest of the letter, then went back to setting the table.

"Tyrus and Herman?" Damian questioned, still studying the curvy handwriting of the Squid language. "Could they be the Squids we ran into at Winterfeld?"

"I don't think so. That was a big group."

"Maybe they're a part of that group? They delivered that girl to us."

Right. Reina hadn't run—she couldn't have escaped from the Squids.

"So what is Samson trying to tell you?" Damian frowned. "That he's joining forces with the 'good' Squids while pretending to follow orders from the evil ones?"

Sage sighed. "Seemingly. If he doesn't pretend, the Squids will execute him, possibly."

"Very well—he's taken your sister. What more does he want? Can't he leave you the fuck alone?"

"It's not him, Damian—it's the Squids. It's only a matter of time before they invade Diamond City—I can sense it."

"We are in full anticipation of that," Damian said steadily. "That's why Heart is going to take care of it—so *you* won't have to."

"I know."

"Darling." Damian wrapped his arms around her waist and kissed her neck. "It's fine. We will take care of it. You just concentrate on you. Here, let's have breakfast and then we can figure out whatever work you need regarding the restaurant."

Right. Sage had bills upon bills to sort through, as well as fines that needed to be paid to Heart before they could reopen. It seemed the council had really doubled down on the restaurant, nitpicking every possible code violation to make staying open impossible. Half of these weren't even valid because all the faucets worked and all the electrical outlets were up to date. Then there were new Red Fever regulations to ensure owners disinfected their restaurants with the appropriate sprays, ones that city officials checked for every week. Bram had taken care of most of these issues, as well as paid for them, but there was still an outstanding balance of five thousand Diamonds laughing in Sage's face.

And without any income, there was no money. Damian assured her that Louis and Agathe would take care of it. Sage had to get her paperwork in order, and that's what she did as Damian made a grocery list for both their refrigerator and the restaurant. There was a lot to do and it wasn't going to happen in one night.

Sage just had to be patient . . . and thankful. She was getting her life together and that's what mattered.

Regardless of what Samson's letter said.

CHAPTER 4

Loyalty

The restaurant was a slow process, and Sage accepted that. What she didn't accept was Samson's apartment as a home to return to every day. It just wasn't the same when she walked through the door, kicked off her boots, and had no one around to scold her. There was no large monster coming out of the kitchen to criticize her or make her dinner, maybe update her on a project he had been working on for a client. The worktable remained plain, and every day that passed made it harder to look at.

A week later, Sage told Damian how she felt. This was supposed to be a new life together, and she wanted to build new memories. While Damian never gave up looking for a place of their own, he and Sage did return to Heart every evening where they joined the rebels for training.

At least, they were supposed to.

Damian had no problem tossing aside his shirt and tying his hair into a bun in all this muggy, summer weather. Spring waned, so the rain got more intense, and so did the heat when the sun came out. Ninety degrees didn't stop anyone from grabbing their practice swords, though. Mega Woman, Turtle, Eye Candy, and Rockstar were here along with some Diamond City soldiers. It was one big group of organized sparring matches on grounds that had seen All-seer Marchello's death. Sage had been standing on the other side of the arena, carefully tucked behind the Private Guard, when she saw Damian for the first time.

"Darling?" Damian called for her when he noticed she wasn't behind him.

"It's fine." Sage gave him the most pathetic smile she had ever plastered across her face. "Go on."

Damian wasn't buying it. In all his shirtless glory, and with sweat already starting to trail down those incredible pecs of his, he returned to her side. "What's wrong?" he asked now that no one else could listen in.

"I-I don't want to train." Sage's eyes burned with tears. She stopped herself from saying, *Without Samson.*

"Why?" Damian said.

Sage shook her head. She looked down at her body, at her thin arms, at her not-so-muscular legs. God, what the hell had happened to her?

"Look at me, darling." Damian held her cheeks gently. "I will be the first to tell you that you don't have to do anything you don't want to. But the Sage I know loves to wield her sword and kick ass. Especially Mega Woman's. She's looking over here, by the way."

Not because Mega Woman wanted a show, but because she was still jealous that Damian and Sage were together. Everyone knew that the black-haired bitch boasted about her sexual relationship with Damian to people willing and unwilling to listen. That annoyed Sage more than it motivated her.

"I'm sorry." Sage covered her face because she didn't want anyone to see her cry. "It's just I feel so goddamned weak . . ."

"But of course you feel weak—you haven't trained in over a month. You've had menstrual cramps and sickness, but that isn't anything new, and you know how quickly you can bounce back."

I'm pregnant, Sage said in her mind because her lips were pursed shut. *I-I'm pregnant.*

"Darling," Damian said worriedly. "Talk to me. Would you like for me to kick Mega Woman's ass and then you can try?"

Sage looked up. Now *that* she wanted to see. "Really?"

"Absolutely. Come." Damian wrapped an arm around her and moved her closer to the arena. There, Turtle, Eye Candy, and Rockstar smirked at the sight of her. They even gave a little bow. Mega Woman's scowl turned ugly. She wasn't going to bow to Sage for anything.

"All right." Damian hopped up the small steps. He drew his sword and pointed it at Mega Woman. "You're up first. Let's see what you've got, woman."

"Is this because Sage is too weak to do it herself?" Mega Woman sneered. She didn't hesitate to draw her sword, too. The three guys started hooting. Half the arena looked over to watch the Warlord in action.

To Sage, there wasn't anything more beautiful. Damian looked good in whatever outfit he chose for the day, but he looked even better when he was blocking strikes, ducking blades, and attacking cold-hearted bitches. He did it with such finesse it was as if he had learned how to fight before he could walk. Sage knew that couldn't be right—if he had grown up in the Clarity District, then he had spent the better part of his childhood with his nose in the books. Sage knew that was Damian's reality, so he must have learned to fight this good when he turned eighteen and joined the resistance against the Overseers.

"Damn it, Damian!" Mega Woman huffed as she blocked another one of Damian's carefully calculated strikes. When he fought, he was never in any rush. Wearing down his opponents was his tactic, Sage realized. That's why, if she had been the one fighting him now, she would have gone for precision over speed. To get the upper hand, Mega Woman needed to throw off his momentum with a hit. That's all it would take, Sage was sure, to win.

Mega Woman swung, utilizing that strategy, but she missed. Damian jumped high into the sky and landed far from her. That was in hopes Mega Woman would take the bait and follow up with a second attack, wasting more energy with all that distance she had to cover to get to him.

No, Sage thought. *Stay back for now. Then go for his right side. He's not expecting you to attack his sword hand.*

When Mega Woman didn't take the bait, Damian reacted how Sage predicated he would: Damian charged her head on. Mega Woman was going to have to block or duck, and the latter was the best choice. Damian didn't hold back when he struck her face with his pommel and broke her nose. Mega Woman howled something vicious, but she didn't let an injury get in the way of the match.

Duck, Sage said in her mind. *Duck!*

Mega Woman did, but she wasn't fast enough to do it a second time. The pain was too much and the blood was gushing down. The three guys were hooting now, a clear distraction, and that was the end of the fight.

Damian extended a hand, but Mega Woman slapped it away.

"I don't need your pity!" she spat angrily.

"Wow," Turtle whistled. "Angry bitch alert."

Rockstar and Eye Candy sniggered. "Giving up already? I mean, you were at it for two minutes."

"Let's see *you* try to beat him!" Mega Woman hopped off the arena. Clearly, she was done with all these bozos. "In fact." She snarled at Sage. "Why don't we get period-girl over there to beat him?"

"Yeah, but that's not fair," Turtle said, crossing his arms. "Sage hasn't trained in a while. And she's sick."

"So?" Mega Woman sneered nastily. "She's the *Optimum*. She can do anything, right?"

Damian smirked. Sage did, too, because being called "period -girl" was so worth it if she got to see Mega Woman storm off. What wasn't worth it was the rest of the training grounds initiating the challenge. It started with a low rumble.

"*Optimum, Optimum, Optimum!*"

Sage's eyes widened.

"OPTIMUM, OPTIMUM, OPTIMUM!"

"Woo!" Turtle clapped and followed everyone's lead. "Come on, Sage! Beat the Warlord!"

Sage clutched the sword at her side. It wasn't even hers—it was a practice one. Hers was in her room. She wasn't used to this.

"OPTIMUM, OPTIMUM, OPTIMUM!"

The crowd wasn't going to let down. And what kind of fool would Sage be if she retreated? She'd be the laughingstock, the "period-girl," and nobody would ever trust her again.

But Sage had to be realistic. What sort of chance did she have against Damian, who was smirking and checking his nails?

"It's up to you, darling." Damian chuckled at her. "But if you think I'm going to let you win because I feel sorry for you, then you're mistaken."

"Asshole," Sage spat. "What happened to Mr. Nice Guy and 'you don't have to do anything you don't want to'?"

Damian shrugged. "You don't. But if you challenge me, then I'm going to take that seriously."

The arrogance. It was one of the qualities she hated in any opponent. Samson always said, "Confidence, not arrogance, is what wins matches." And that's what Sage wanted to prove to Damian.

When Sage stepped onto the arena, everyone froze. A creepy hush blanketed the energy, extinguishing it like a flame from its wick. This was a horrible time, but Louis came out of nowhere and gasped when he saw Sage in the arena.

Had he come here to watch her fight after hearing she had returned to Heart? He always used to watch her fastball practices with Little Man . . .

Damian didn't even notice Louis. He was smiling at Sage with that sultriness in his eyes. "Are you really going to hurt me, darling?"

"I'm going to do more than hurt you if you keep looking at me like that."

"I can't help it. You are so beautiful. I remember watching your breasts whenever you used to spar with the rebels at camp."

"You can watch them all you want," Sage said. "And you'll get a nice view of them when I'm standing over your comatose body."

The entire arena gasped. "*Ooo!*"

Damian laughed. "I see. And while that sounds nice, I can't let that happen. I can, however, have you on the ground with me on top. Isn't that our usual position, anyway?"

"*OOO!*"

"Yes," Sage said. "Before I flip us over and make you climax."

Like a raucous bar crowd, everyone hooted and hollered. They all clapped and yelled as Sage unsheathed her sword and pointed it at Damian.

Damian did the same to her with a smirk on his face and a twinkle in his eye.

They had sparred so many times in the past, but Damian had been going through rough withdrawals, and his stamina hadn't been all there. Now was a different story: he was fast and calculating. Sage would have to be the same until she could get her hits in.

All she needed was one good one, like Damian had done with Mega Woman. Sage had to duck—not block. She didn't have the strength to take it, and she had to conserve what she could for her critical blow. Sage hadn't trained in a while, but fighting was in her blood. She knew it as she stood there, ignoring the crowd and lasering in on her target. Her very beautiful target, but this was her reputation on the line, so she had to stop staring at his abs.

Sage took a deep breath. She didn't need strength to win. She could do this.

Damian readied his stance like he had with Mega Woman. Same pose, same lean, same angle. Sage already knew he was going to charge, and she didn't duck until the very last moment, making him follow through with an attack that hit nothing but air and wasted energy. With a nice view of his torso, Sage put everything she had into an attack of her own.

She hit him so hard with her fist and pummel that she heard a few ribs shatter. Damian staggered, but he rebounded so quickly that Sage hardly had time to dodge. It was clumsy and off balance.

"Don't hurt yourself, darling," Damian cooed. "Are you doing all right there?"

It was hard for Sage to tell if he was hurting or not. All that talk was a mask for the obvious injury to his torso, or was it?

It didn't matter. Damian wasn't going to take it easy on her, no matter what. Maybe if he knew she was pregnant, but he didn't, and he wasn't about to lose in front of every single rebel and Diamond City soldier in attendance. And Louis, for that matter, who watched them spar like a kid watching his favorite superhero beat up the most-hated villain.

"Go, Sage!" he cheered. He was in a white sleeveless shirt with gold pants. He looked ridiculous, actually, but that was Louis. Because his arms were bare, everyone could see his awfully pale skin and the silver-and-coral bracelet he had around his wrist.

Sage couldn't believe it—that was her birthday gift to him last year!

Unconsciously, Sage smiled. She looked back at Damian, who was frowning.

"Quiet now?" Sage taunted.

Of course. Damian hated Louis with a passion. But he wasn't going to let that distract him.

Damian charged at Sage again, this time with a vicious uppercut. Sage dodged and swung out with her blade, just missing him. They exchanged blows for a little bit, but Sage didn't like the vibrations in her arms. Lack of muscle and strength was going to be the end of her, and she couldn't engage like this anymore.

Sage jumped back. She was tiring out fast. The longer she held out, the better the chance she'd be messing up soon. She had to finish this now or Damian was going to win. She knew herself, but she also knew Damian had to be hurting.

His ribs were broken. He had a nasty bruise on his side from a strike he had not anticipated from her. Or maybe he had let her get that hit on purpose? No way. Damian looked way too annoyed right now to have allowed that on purpose.

Go for his right side, her mind reminded her. *He's not expecting an attack on his sword hand.*

He also wasn't expecting her to attack at all. Sage had stayed back the entire match. This was her one and only chance to be the aggressor.

Sage launched across the arena. She did something she had only ever done with Samson: she used her shape-shifting abilities just a smidge. Extending her arm gave her the extra distance she needed to grab Damian's right wrist, hold him tight, swing around his body, and hold the blade to his throat.

Sage held him tightly. Damian didn't resist.

The whole arena stared. So many hadn't even seen what she did. Damian had, though.

When Sage let him go, he whipped around with his nostrils flared. Perhaps he considered it cheating because he looked pretty mad. Or maybe he was shocked that she could shape-shift. Should he really be surprised, though, knowing she was a hybrid? No one was familiar with the extent of their powers.

Sage bowed to him. Then, because she had nothing else to say, she walked off the arena. Louis was the only one clapping like an idiot. It made Sage laugh.

"Wow!" Louis grinned. "You bested the Warlord, Sage! Congrats."

"Thanks. It wasn't easy, though."

"What are you talking about? It was over in like two minutes!"

If Louis didn't stop talking within Damian's earshot, he was going to get beat up. That's why Sage dragged him far from the arena. She could feel Damian's eyes scorching her back. There was so much he wanted to say on both her abilities and her cheating, but he didn't for the sake of maturity in front of his goons.

"I think I had an advantage," Sage said. "I watched his fight with Mega Woman and I used my . . . um . . ." She rubbed her arms. She racked the practice sword as she left the training grounds with Louis.

"Your abilities?" Louis finished gently.

"Yeah."

"Well, they're your abilities. I'd say that's fair game. It's like asking your opponent not to do a double flip because it's his specialty."

"True," Sage said. "But I think Damian will see that as me trying to best him at the cost of cheating. I kinda don't want to be seen that way."

Louis stared at her. "Seriously? Since when?"

Sage looked at him. "What do you mean?"

"Since when do you care about fair or playing by the rules? That guy needed an ass-whooping, and you gave it to him." Louis bowed to her. "Kudos to you. Now, how about a snow cone?"

There was a vendor right outside the training grounds. He got all sorts of customers coming and going, so business was soaring. Plus, his snow cones were not only refreshing, they were ginormous: the shaved ice filled an entire gallon and the syrups were all from natural fruits. Sage always went for blueberry and raspberry. Louis was the only doofus that liked orange.

"Here you go, sir." Louis paid the twenty Diamonds for his and Sage's treats.

"Are you really going to eat all that?" Sage asked.

"Of course! These are the best in all of Diamond City."

Louis dived right into his, and Sage did the same. The ice was just right, silky enough that it was easy to swallow and didn't give her brain freeze. "Thank you."

Louis took her far from the training grounds just in case Damian caught up with them. Either way, Sage had to say she was impressed that Louis had whisked her away like that. Perhaps Louis wasn't such a sniveling coward anymore.

Louis just shrugged. He finally deemed it safe by a pair of government buildings and stopped walking. They did kind of stick out here, though—Sage was in a tank top and shorts, and Louis didn't have sleeves. Nevertheless, he was the Allseer and he still garnered the respect of passing officials.

"I'm the Allseer," he said. "Officially. I can see whoever I want, right? And sure, you're engaged, but we've been through a lot together, and I think we can consider ourselves as friends."

Sage smiled at him. "For sure."

They sat down on a bench. The great thing about not allowing newscasters into the capital was the privacy. Allseer Marchello had been that way, too, although Louis claimed he was more honest with his reports. Red Fever was becoming a pandemic among the human population, but he had his best medical teams researching different treatment options.

"Anything new with Reina?" Sage took a spoonful of ice. She had the perfect blend of blueberry and raspberry, and it was the most delicious snow cone she had ever tasted.

After several autopsies and a quick burial, Nova had put Reina's case to rest. The circumstances of her death were obvious, but there was one detail she and Louis had left out of the spotlight on purpose. It wasn't anything anyone outside their medical circle had to know.

"The babies that grew in her womb," Louis said hesitantly. "They were in cocoons."

Sage furrowed her brows. She hadn't been expecting to hear that. "Cocoons?"

"In addition to the placenta, the fetuses had developed an extra layer of protection." Louis's lips were pinched as he discussed a medical situation no one was familiar with. No one had ever handled Squid fetuses before, not in an Enhanced or human. "Had we removed the cocoons from her body, she would have died. They were stuck to the lining of her womb and the extraction would have caused severe internal bleeding. No human can survive that, except maybe for an Enhanced. But we obviously wouldn't know because we don't have any pregnant Enhanced with Lolligo offspring. As of now, I can't see how anyone can survive a pregnancy like that. "

"My mother did," Sage said quietly. "And then she gave birth to Aurora."

"A miracle," Louis admitted.

Had it been a miracle? Sage knew too little about Squid pregnancies to really label it as such. Maybe because she didn't feel like a miracle at the moment. Sage couldn't have been the only hybrid walking around . . . could she?

Louis shook his head. "What concerns me most is the *why*. Why would the Lolligo allow one of their captives to escape into our lands?"

Sage didn't know. She took another spoonful of ice and syrup into her mouth. There was an announcement on one of the towers that caught her eye. She hadn't traveled this far into the capital yet, so she hadn't seen it until now.

Silver Gears was performing live next weekend? That was Candice and Olivia's favorite band. The girls had t-shirts, pins, notebooks, and even boots with gear patterns on the side. Sage wasn't a fan of shouting in music, and she also didn't see the appeal in painting her whole body silver and styling her hair into a mohawk. It was a fad, and fans took it seriously. The band was especially popular in the Color District, but it looked like Louis—or maybe Agathe—were broadening the capital's horizons a bit. A concert in Heart was sure to inspire a little bit more trust in the government.

Interesting.

Sage wanted to ask about that, but Louis cut in with, "I hope I didn't interrupt your training, but I really wanted a chance to talk to you and invite you to dinner some time. What do you say?"

"I don't see anything wrong with that," Sage said.

"You can bring Candice and Olivia, too."

"But not Damian?" Sage laughed at the look on Louis' face.

"Preferably not," Louis said uncomfortably. "But he is your fiancé, and I can't tell you no."

"Well, we'll see. He'll probably say no anyway."

Louis snorted. "I doubt it. That guy follows you like a lost puppy."

"Good. That means he's behaving." Sage finished her snow cone. "And speaking of lost puppies, anyone on your radar?"

"What does that mean?"

"Are you interested in anyone?"

"No," Louis said, frustrated, "I mean, why are you comparing me to a lost puppy?"

"It's how powerful men like you and Damian should be behaving," Sage said.

Louis sighed, but he no longer sounded annoyed. Actually, he smiled. "You're right. Things would have been different had I followed you around at my birthday party last year, right?"

Probably, although there was no sense in wondering about it now. Sage wished she could do away with the horrid memory of Blackburn trying to rape her, but she might have never met Damian otherwise. Had Louis been the one to seduce her instead, would Sage have lost her pizza restaurant to the council? Would she have been blackmailed into pursuing Damian in the Outskirts?

Probably, Sage thought. *Because it wasn't Louis who sent you . . . it was the council. And they had already known everything about you.*

"I'm not sure they would have," Sage finally replied to Louis. "But why don't we focus on the future?"

Sage hadn't forgotten that Louis' 115th birthday was coming up in the month of Light. If the party was going to be as extravagant as it had been last year, Louis was sure to have his wide pick of women.

Louis quickly struck down that idea with a shake of his head. "Not this time," he said. "I'm going to do something a bit more low key. It's also the anniversary of my father's death. It'll be a day of remembrance."

Sage thought that was rather noble. She certainly hadn't imagined Louis to be the sentimental type. Despite how shitty Allseer Marchello had been, Louis and Agathe still held him with great regard.

Sage had no comment.

Louis, on the other hand, had quite a few praises to sing about his late father. Aside from serving in the Unification War, Marchello had created the Kilstrong dynasty here in Diamond City. Louis acknowledged the harshness and the needless executions, but he also understood that his father had had a lot of enemies. Keeping the four districts together had been no easy feat. Stopping the Enhanced from overthrowing him had been brutal. Thanks to Blackburn and David, they had ousted Damian.

Sage wasn't sure she appreciated Louis defending his father in front of her like that. In no way shape or form did those rebels deserve the torture they had experienced under Marchello. She tried not to take any offense because Louis was seeking her thoughts and feedback. Perhaps he wanted a what-would-you-have-done? perspective from her. Had Damian and the rebels acted up against her rule, would she have captured them and made a spectacle of them in public?

"Would I have torn out their organs on live television and hung them at the capital while I whipped them to near death?" Sage said. "Absolutely not. I would have sat down with them and listened to their concerns. Then I would have evaluated myself and my actions, which a lot of leaders don't like to do, but that's part of the job. This isn't about you and your perfect lifestyle and how much money you're making or stealing—this is about ensuring your people are living their best lives."

"And what if you are doing the right thing?" Louis said. "And rebels just want to take power away from you for themselves?"

"That's different," Sage said. "While I still wouldn't make a show out of torturing anyone, I'd deal with it another way." She narrowed her eyes. "But if you're trying to compare Damian to someone who just wants power for himself, then you're mistaken. Your father was a fucked-up Allseer who persecuted Enhanced because he didn't want any opposition. In the meanwhile, so many people could have benefited from those medical enhancements, but your family kept it all to themselves and their military. Damian wanted your father to share, but Marchello didn't want to hear it."

Louis raised his hand. "I understand that completely and I acknowledge that my father was abusive. I just wanted your insight."

And so, Sage had given it.

But Louis had more questions, so they sat there well into the night, when all the street lamps turned on and the fountain in the center of the capital spewed gold water instead of the standard pink. Caretakers used a special edible powder to make it change colors. Sage had seen that in a *The Royal Court* episode.

"Whatever you need, Sage." Louis took her hand and kissed it. "I'll be here."

"Same," she said.

"Why don't we have dinner next week?"

Sage couldn't say no, so she agreed. But it was times like these she wished she could take a step back from the politics and the love interests. Life was so much easier without the drama and heartache of what was, could have been, and could still be.

Of course, who was Sage to talk? Here she was hanging out with Louis while raging with jealously over Damian and Agathe. If those two were having dinner together, would she have been fine with it?

Sage sighed. Acknowledging her own hypocrisy, she got up to head home. The day's trials spiraled right back into the forefront of her mind and reminded her that Damian was probably raging. That guy was the biggest sore loser on earth, and not only had Sage embarrassed him in front of his own guys, but she had gone out with his arch nemesis.

Then Sage realized something. Why was beating Damian during a stupid sparring match a sin? And why was going out with Louis on a friendly stroll so bad? Sage knew where her loyalties lay, so by the time she made it back to the Starlight Complex, she was ready to defend herself. In fact, she challenged the arrogant bastard to say anything about their fight earlier. Sage was ready for it.

What she wasn't ready for was the smell of pizza. Or a Silver Gears song playing in the background. It was one of their slower ones, but the lyrics were beautiful.

"Darling dear, I'll hold you for an eternity
I'll make you feel my love through the pain and adversity
When the evening shadows and the stars appear
I'll drive away all your fears
When the run rises and the light shines
I'll kiss your lips, our bodies intertwined"

And then there was the showered and nicely-dressed Damian setting the table as if they were at a five-star restaurant. There was a pure white cloth with ceramic plates, silver utensils, stitched napkins, and wine glasses on top. Most eye-catchy of all was the massive bouquet of roses in the center. The biggest Sage had ever seen.

"Darling!" Damian swept her into his arms and kissed her. Sage was all sweaty and nasty whereas he smelled like teakwood and lavender. It was delicious, but Sage couldn't melt into him when she looked like shit.

"What's all this about?" Sage said, head spinning from that kiss.

"I," Damian said royally with a sparkle in his eyes, "have made us dinner. Just for you and me."

Pizza? Sage didn't get it. Damian didn't know how to make pizza. Candice and Olivia had to be behind this—surely, they were hiding in the closet or in the hall somewhere, ready to laugh at the puzzled look on Sage's face—but Sage didn't hear or feel anyone else in the apartment. It looked like the girls were having a late night out with their friends.

"Why don't you get cleaned up?" Damian suggested, holding her face and kissing her lips again. "Then we can eat."

"What's wrong with you?"

"Nothing," Damian said happily. "Why would you think there's something wrong? Can I not make dinner for my beautiful fiancée?"

Sage crossed her arms. "Out with it, Damian. You're upset."

"Why would I be upset, darling?"

"Because I kicked your ass this morning in front of your people. I saw the look on your face then. You were also shocked by what I could do—I know you saw that, too. Well?" Sage braced herself. "Out with it. How you really feel. You're disgusted."

Damian got down on his knees. He held Sage's hips. He looked up at her with the most serious look Sage had ever seen on his face. She even saw a bit of hurt in his eyes, behind all that eyeliner and mascara he had on. God, he was beautiful.

"Why do you continue to accuse me of thinking you're disgusting?" Damian asked quietly. "This isn't the first time. Are you insecure of yourself?"

"Of course I am. I'm the only hybrid among you—I'm the weirdo of the group. Don't you see that?"

"I do, and I understand. But aren't we all unique in our own ways?"

"But no one else is a hybrid," Sage said patiently. "No one else is like me."

"And is anyone else like me? With all my preferences and qualities? Don't you remember in last night's episode of *The Rainbow in Me*, Ralph realized that there is so much more to a person than a label. Whether you're a human, Enhanced, hybrid, or in between doesn't matter. Darling, I know what you are. I've known it for some time now. And as I have told you before: nothing about you is disgusting."

"Y-yeah." Sage cleared her throat. She didn't like how closely Damian was scrutinizing her from this angle. On his knees with his head titled up, he could see her face clearly no matter where she hid it.

"I am quite impressed," Damian went on. "You are a magnificent fighter. Like a ballerina, see?"

"Stop it." Sage bopped him on the head. She was smiling, though. Damian got back to his feet with a chuckle.

"Go on and get cleaned up."

That was Sage's cue for a quick shower. She didn't have time to do anything with her hair so she wrapped it in a bun after a quick towel dry. She threw on a shirt and shorts because she thought it was pointless to dress up nicely in her own apartment. When she stepped out ready to eat because she was starving (the snow cone was nothing), Damian gasped at the sight of her.

Sage froze. "What?"

"No, no, no, darling." He stalked over to her like Samson would. "March right back in that bathroom and untie that bun. You are going to damage your hair like that."

"Are you serious?" Sage breathed. "I'm hungry!"

"March."

"I can dry it later, Damian!"

"And it will be damaged. Then all that hard work we've put into it will be for naught."

So Sage had to hold still in front of the mirror for a whole fifteen minutes as Damian dried her hair like a stylist. She scowled at her reflection, but eased up as time went on. She smiled to herself, but made sure Damian didn't see it.

"There," he said, tying her hair into a fancy ponytail. Sage had no idea what he was doing back there. "Now you're ready."

Sage turned to him. "Anything else I need to fix? Maybe my shirt and shorts, too?"

"No," Damian said sultrily. "That's easy to take off when we're going to have sex."

Sage went for a kick to the groin, but Damian slipped out of the bathroom. With a horrible smile on her face, Sage followed him to the kitchen and finally got to sit down at the table. Her heart softened even more when she was looking at the roses. Beautiful. And then Damian came out with the pie of pizza that looked . . .

Well . . .

Incredible. That was the Hippo from her restaurant. It was all the toppings imaginable—peppers, banana peppers, onions, sausages, pepperoni, anchovies, and olives—with bananas on top. Rick's idea, and it had totally worked. He always used to say people wanted a little bit of everything, and so long as there was sweetness to top it off, well, what could go wrong?

"Did Candice and Olivia help you?" Sage asked as Damian sliced the pizza on the table right in front of her. The bouquet was on the side now.

"No," Damian said happily, working that cutter like a pro. "I watched you very closely at the restaurant the past week. I pay attention when directions are given, darling."

Sage smiled. "Good boy."

"So no spanking tonight?"

"Not so far. Unless you fuck it up."

"No screw-ups today, I promise. I know you will love this."

And Sage did. Shockingly so. The dough was perfectly cooked and crispy, the tomato sauce had just the right amount of salt, and all the condiments were baked to perfection, so Damian had turned down the heat fifteen minutes into cooking time just like Sage had taught him to. After all the insults, slaps on the hand, smack over his head, and flour in his face when he didn't sift it, Damian had finally learned something. The biggest loser in the kitchen was turning into an asset, but Sage wasn't about to admit that out loud. The blush on her cheeks said it all as she ate. Actually, she had eaten more than half the pie already, and each piece was over ten inches in length.

"Wow, darling," Damian cooed as he sipped on his wine. He had his legs crossed as he watched her eat. "Someone is hungry."

"Very. And this is very good, too."

"Is that all I get? Just a 'very good'?"

"Yes."

Damian sighed. "So cruel. But I will impress you one day."

Sage watched him open another bottle of wine. She had hardly touched her glass. She was pregnant, and she didn't like wine all that much anyway. Now, it reminded her of Blackburn. It also reminded her of the time she had found tons of empty bottles in Damian's study back at Mousafeld.

He had overdosed on Cupid's Arrow and Stars. Wine was nothing compared to hardcore drugs like that, but Damian was still very delicate.

"Careful with the alcohol," Sage warned. She didn't want to see him sick again.

"Worry not," Damian said. "Just this bottle and that's it." He beamed at her. "But I appreciate you looking out for me."

Sage had one more slice of pizza to go. "Since when don't I look out for you?"

"I'm a fool, aren't I?"

Sage arched a brow. That comment had caught her a bit off guard. "What?"

Damian wasn't looking at her. He was staring at the table, swirling around the contents of his glass. In the dim kitchen light, he looked like a vampire with that heavy makeup on his face. He made it work, though, because his hair was dark and picked up the right way. His shirt was unbuttoned at the chest and his pants and boots fit deliciously on his legs. Thankfully, Sage couldn't see his lap from where she was sitting.

"I'm a fool for thinking that you're going to cheat on me."

"You are," Sage said. She bit into her pizza. "Just because I'm friends with Louis? Well . . . aren't you friends with Agathe?"

Damian snorted. "No, I'm not 'friends.' We have a professional relationship."

"Right. Well, it shouldn't bother you who my friends are. I mean, unless it's someone who's going to hurt me. But yes, you should know be better than that."

"Can you say it?" Damian asked quietly. "That you love me?"

Perhaps Sage didn't say it enough. She wasn't used to it. With Samson, it was more of a brother/sister relationship and saying "I love you" to Samson would make him snarl like a rabid dog. It was kind of funny, actually. With Bram and her nieces, the love part was already understood. But with Damian . . . maybe he did need a reminder here and there.

"I love you," Sage said sincerely.

"What do you love about me?"

"Your drive. Your persistence. When you want something, you don't stop until you have it." The blush was back, but Sage distracted herself with more pizza. "Even me."

Damian smiled at her. "What else?"

"Balls of steel. And I'm not talking about your physical balls," Sage said quickly as Damian laughed loudly. "Although I like those, too." She cleared her throat. *So stupid*, Sage thought. But whatever— this was a genuine moment that she wasn't going to ruin. She spoke from the heart.

"You're brave. The Allseer exiled you. You didn't give up. You gathered people, searched for more followers in the Outskirts, fought off enemies who couldn't stand the sight of you, and carried on with your mission. Thirty years like that . . ." Sage put the pizza down for a moment. "I can't imagine. The Unification War lasted only one year and I was done. Mentally, I was all fucked up. But nothing seems to bother you."

"That's not true," Damian said quietly. "I was a drug addict. When Ileana betrayed me, I hosted sexual orgies to lose myself because I couldn't deal with reality. I felt like a filthy street rat with no morals. I was nasty to people and made them carry me around in that wretched palanquin."

"Oh, yeah." Sage rolled her eyes. "What an asshole."

"Exactly. So I'm not as noble as you think I am."

"But then I came along and you changed. Why didn't you just treat me like everyone else?"

"I value my penis too much," Damian said, and Sage laughed this time. "I had to behave around you. No choice. Plus, I really wanted to impress you. When I asked you to join me that day you fought Commander in the throne room, I wanted you to be my friend."

"And how long after did you decide you wanted me as a lover?"

"Twenty minutes. When you threw the dagger at my chest in the common room."

They both laughed.

"You are the strongest fucking woman I've ever met," Damian said. "And I'm not sure what it is about you that gives you that strength."

"My skills?" Sage said.

"So why do I get the feeling you'd still be a badass even if you were comatose on a hospital bed? You'd still find a way to win, powers or not."

Sage blinked. She had to admit that even Samson had never said anything like that to her. He had always mentioned outsmarting enemies and never shooting yourself in the foot in battle, but he had never painted a scenario of what Sage could do if she were powerless.

"It's all about survival," Sage said softly. "I've taught Candice and Olivia the same thing. Only they ... well ... they've never had to fight. And I want to keep it that way. I might be strong, but I don't only want to be strong in war. I want to be strong in everyday life, too. I feel like I'm lacking there sometimes. I'm 119 years old, but I can still act like a child. I mean, all the *Defenders Unite!* stuff and all the fairy-tale shit—"

"Darling," Damian said calmly. "What's wrong with liking all that? What's wrong with acting like a child and having aspirations like one? We're near invincible. We're going to live a long time. *Something* has to interest us."

"I suppose." Sage finished her pizza.

"We have a vibrancy for life that humans don't have," Damian said. "And I'd hate to see the hybrid or the Enhanced that becomes bored and commits heinous acts to entertain themselves."

Sage nodded. Damian was right. "But I need to be an example to Candice and Olivia. I need to be their mother now that Bram is dead. And Candice couldn't even tell me about goddamn Geoffrey."

"She would have, Sage. You've just been feeling under the weather, but now you're better. Why don't we take the girls and Geoffrey to the Silver Gears concert next weekend? Take a break from the restaurant and just spend some time with them?"

"How? The concert's probably sold out."

But Sage stopped. Perhaps it was sold out, but that didn't mean it was hopeless. Louis was her friend, after all.

"Use your resources, darling," Damian said with a smirk.

Sage beamed. Right. "I'll ask Louis for VIP access. But wait—do we have to dress up like idiots?"

"Not 'idiots,' darling—it's part of the concert." Damian chuckled. "I am totally putting your hair in a mohawk. You'll look beautiful."

Sage grimaced. At the end, she managed a very painful smile. She looked like she was sniffing garbage.

"Good." Damian finished his wine and got up from the table. He went to the refrigerator and opened it. "I made dessert, but it sounds to me like you're still hungry."

Sage had to admit that training had reignited her appetite. She was shocked that Damian could hear her stomach growling, though. That was convenient.

"Another pizza sounds good to me," Sage said happily.

"Come, darling. Let's make it together."

The only reason that Damian had suggested that was for payback. Sage already saw it coming, so she ducked when he grabbed the bag of flour from the cabinet. He made to throw some in her face but missed. Sage disarmed him quickly, this time without shape-shifting, and he dropped the whole bag to the floor.

Poof.

Flour *everywhere.*

Sage died.

She crumbled to the tiles and shrieked to the heavens. If only she had gotten a video.

Damian sighed. "Now look at what you made me do, darling. My boots are ruined."

"What an idiot!" Sage started drooling. Her sides were hurting, and it wasn't because of the pregnancy.

In fact, she had completely forgotten about it.

CHAPTER 5

The Silver Gears Concert

Next weekend was so last minute for concert tickets that were sold out, but nothing was impossible for Louis. All Sage had to do was go to dinner with him and ask nicely. There wasn't a shred of hesitation over their caviar feast—Louis got on it right away.

"Can I order something else?" Sage asked Louis, unsure of how to feel about those squishy orange eggs. There was an array of them, either on toasted crackers or with creme fraiche, and the saltiness made her gag a bit. Plus, she learned they were harvested from dead sturgeon.

Apparently, those were from a continent across the ocean. Louis had told her that in the Old World, countries like Russia, Iran, and China had been the number-one caviar producers in the fish market. Now that they didn't exist, the only caviar available were the ones stockpiled from before Nuclear Devastation. It was sad to think there was no more, but it was even more depressing to know these eggs had been taken from dead fish. It reminded Sage of Reina.

"Sure," Louis said. He called the waiter over. They were at a high-dining nook accessible only to royals. It was dim with candlelight, so Sage couldn't see the other couples around them. There were wall-to-wall paintings of ocean waves. It was mesmerizing because Sage had never been to a beach. Sage stared at the frosty caps of the waves, wondering what it was like to go surfing.

"Caviar is not for everyone," Louis commented.

"Have you ever wondered what became of those lands across the ocean?" Sage said. "I mean, Diamond City's never dared to venture much into the Outskirts . . . but the ocean is not that far away, is it?"

Louis shook his head. "No. But we've been careful not to interfere with other civilizations that might be out there, and I'm not just talking about the Squids."

Sage arched a brow. "Really?"

"Yes. The last thing we want is to be accused of trespassing and draw attention to ourselves." Louis looked hesitant to admit this, but this was Sage, and he trusted her. "There's a powerhouse city out there called Emerald City. Have you ever heard of them?"

"No," Sage said. She braced herself a bit. "Never. 'Emerald City'?"

"Yes. My father stayed away from them like the plague. You know how isolated he wanted to keep Diamond City from the world." Louis thought for a moment. "There are pros and cons to that, of course. Right now, we're too vulnerable to advertise ourselves, but I do want an Outskirts expedition eventually. Possibly after things have settled down here. Would you be interested in joining us?"

"No," Sage said. And, God, she had answered that awfully fast. While an expedition sounded like fun, like another adventure to get away from the city for a bit, she had too many responsibilities here. She had to see her girls through school, she had to marry Damian, and then . . .

Sage rubbed her abdomen. It was under the table, so Louis couldn't see her. He was too busy smiling at her with his boyish cheeks.

"I understand," Louis said. He looked pretty handsome, too, in his pure white suit with gold buttons and cuffs. "I know you have a lot of responsibilities here. But maybe sometime in the future? I mean, who knows. These kinds of excursions can take hundreds of years."

"Is that how long I have to live?" Sage said. "Hundreds of years?"

"Don't know," Louis said. "But we'll take it step by step. Right now, there are a lot of issues to take care of in Diamond City."

"I've heard people aren't very thrilled that there are two Allseers."

Sage had seen a few political assemblies the past couple of weeks. The Soloists vouched for Louis to take exclusive control, while the Dualists wanted both siblings to rule equally. But the Soloists were gaining momentum because Louis was less in people's faces and delegated more powers to the Overseers. Agathe was an overpowering, controlling bitch.

Sage was biased, so she held her tongue. She wasn't sure why she found satisfaction in kicking Agathe off the throne, but it pleasured her to no end. That's why she didn't offer her views on any group, but it was obvious that people were starting to catch on to Agathe. Surely, there'd be some kind of compromise.

"I know," Louis said shyly. "We're working on it. In the meantime, we both agree that Diamond City needs help in the aesthetics department. So we want to travel each of the districts and 'beautify' them."

"What does that mean?"

"Infrastructure projects, new traffic lights, and better gutters for all the rain. Then we're going to take a survey of which areas need the most renovating and start a campaign to make everything shine. We really want to make this place sparkle like a diamond— no pun intended."

"I guess that's a good thing," Sage said absently. "But then what? What about the people?"

"I, um." Louis rubbed the back of his head. This reminded Sage of the Louis of old, the hesitant one who didn't know the first things about confidence. "Well, fortifying Diamond City is my number-one goal. I want the people to feel confident. I want to eradicate this Red Fever and then start thinking of ways to enhance human lives. Maybe giving them a ton of strength isn't the wisest choice, but something that will make living this life easier. Diseases and debilitation suck."

Sage beamed. She was so happy to hear that.

"I'm glad to see you're looking good," Louis said abruptly. That was an odd change of subject, but it was clear he was done talking about Diamond City. He eyed her shoulders and pecs. "Doing better, I mean. You look strong—and beautiful."

"Average," Sage admitted.

"That's average? You're more ripped than any woman working out for years. And you've only been training for two weeks."

"Thanks for the flattery, but it doesn't count if I'm part Squid, does it?"

"Definitely gives me something to look up to."

"I'm sure you don't need me as an inspiration to get stronger yourself," Sage said. She sniggered a bit. "You have Damian for that."

Louis frowned. "Right. My 'competition,' I suppose."

"You have to admit that Damian has been impressive. He was the feared Warlord in Diamond City a year ago, but he's like your top military general now, isn't he?"

"Yes," Louis said reluctantly. "He's instilled order in our military ever since we took Blackburn into custody. Not only that, he's brought Diamond City and the Outskirts together. Such a union would have been unheard of a year ago. It might have to do with the fact my sister and I are Allseers, but the two sides have stopped fighting and become friends as if all this was one big misunderstanding."

"Do you see how important politics is?" Sage said. "And how that one person can make a difference?"

"Do you want me to be honest?" Louis said. "I think it's you."

"What do you mean?"

"The Warlord—Damian—whatever you call him—behaves because of you. I wonder if he'd be the same person if you weren't around."

"Probably not," Sage said, thinking of what Damian had admitted to her last week. "But what counts is the here and now—not the what-ifs."

Her phone buzzed with a text message from Damian. Sage

rolled her eyes at his naked picture. He was posing in front of the mirror with an impressively erect penis. The message read, *Does it turn you on?* Sage snorted with laughter.

Louis arched a brow. "What?"

Sage gave him her phone. Louis had just sipped more wine, maybe to wash the foul taste of Damian's name out of his mouth, then spit it right back out.

"Stars!" Louis exclaimed as Sage laughed. His face turned red. "Did you have to show me that?!"

"I thought you wanted to see it."

"Not *that!*"

Sage couldn't stop laughing.

"And you honestly like that?" Louis rasped, sounding disgusted. Sage might have enjoyed eating dirt.

"But of course," she said. "He's beautiful. Even you have to admit that much. Plus, he's my fiancé."

"But what's so appealing about him?"

"First and foremost, he cares about me and the girls. He's always looking out for us."

Louis shook his head. He wiped his mouth and suit with a napkin. "The entire military talks about him *all* the time. Even my sister brings him up in every conversation. I just don't get it."

Sage didn't appreciate the sister comment, but Louis was trying to make a point. And Sage did admit that this was a very different Damian from the one she had met at Mousafeld. The thought of him always brought a smile to her face, and his nonstop sexting throughout the day always kept her on her toes.

Slip the phone under your dress and take a picture of your crotch, he messaged her.

Sage typed back, *In public, Damian? In the middle of dinner?*

No one will notice if you're discreet enough.

And why is this necessary now?

I need a screensaver.

Sage laughed loudly.

Louis released a tightly-held air. He looked annoyed that Sage was more amused by Damian, who wasn't even here, than him. He wasn't ready to change the topic, though.

"How are things between you and him?" he asked her. "The wedding, I mean?"

"He's been taking care of the planning," Sage said. "I think. I mean, we've been so busy with the restaurant stuff that I don't think he's had much time to finalize anything. He does want it in the winter, though. He says there's something mystical about getting married in the cold."

"Why? Because the sex is especially good afterward?"

Sage arched a brow. "Jealous much?"

"Yes," Louis admitted. "Very jealous, Sage. You know I like you."

"Actually, I don't. You told me in Mousafeld you wanted to be friends."

"Right," Louis said slowly. "Which indicates that I like you. And given the chance, I would want to get to know you better for the possibility of being something more." Pain crept into his eyes. Eventually, it bogged him down and made him lower his head. "I look back and I wonder where I went wrong. I can't say that I did. We were at Mousafeld for six months, and you and Damian happened so quickly. I was hoping it was just a fling or some military tactic you were using against one another, but apparently I was wrong. You're serious, aren't you?"

"Yes," Sage said. "Damian has been incredibly supportive, especially with the girls and all their interests. He's a better mother than I am, that's for sure."

Louis smiled. But it was forced. "Then I will be here for you as a friend. Whatever you need. And I'll start with those Silver Gears tickets."

It was a done deal, and Sage was forever thankful.

What she wasn't thankful for was the get-up. The weekend rolled around faster than she could blink, and it was time to prepare for silver body paint and black mohawks. Candice and Olivia had done all the shopping they needed to make them all look like part of the Silver Gears family, and they were depending on Damian to execute it flawlessly.

Olivia was up first. Twenty minutes later, and she was all done.

"What the fuck?" Sage croaked.

"Ta-da!" Olivia jumped out of the room with her arms out like a cheerleader. Her skin was all silver, her eyes were black, and her hair was sticking up out of her head in spikes. Twelve inch strands, too, that were as tough as nails thanks to the most powerful hair gel on the market—a hundred Diamonds per 3-ounce bottle. But it wasn't even the money that had Sage's jaw on the floor.

"What do you think, Aunt Sage?" Olivia twirled around in the hallway. "Pretty cool, huh?"

"WHOA!" Candice laughed from behind Sage. She clapped her hands. "Damian, that's INCREDIBLE! Me next, me next!"

"Do you like it, Aunt Sage?"

"Doesn't she look beautiful?" Damian finally came out with his sleeves rolled up and his hands all smudged with silver and black. Sage didn't even want to see the mess in her bedroom. Damian took pictures of his creation then made Olivia pose. While Sage had to admit the little tyke was a natural in front of the camera, she already knew there was no way she was doing this.

No fucking way.

A knock on the door interrupted Sage from her storm of thoughts. Candice rushed to answer it and squealed at who was on the other side.

"Geoffrey!"

Sage stiffened like a statue. She hadn't even seen pictures yet because Candice wanted her to meet Geoffrey in person first. Her nightmares had been plagued by old men with long beards and hairy legs, but Geoffrey was...

Sage's eyes widened.

Nice.

He was a tall slender young man with tight, treated curls. Like Candice and Olivia, he was multiracial because his skin was a bit lighter than a black person's. He had a nice long nose and defined, plump lips. But what really mesmerized Sage was the kindness in his eyes.

There was something else, too . . . but what? Why did he look familiar?

"T-that's her," Geoffrey croaked, without even introducing himself. "T-the Optimum!"

Sage blinked.

"Huge fan," Candice said. "Huge, huge fan, Aunt Sage."

Geoffrey unbuttoned his shirt and showed everyone. He had "Optimum" tattooed across his pecs. His eyes welled with tears, full of pride.

Sage was frozen.

"Aunt Sage, *guess what?*"

Sage looked at Candice, who couldn't fit the grin on her face.

"Do you remember Wyatt?"

No. Who was Wyatt? But wait—

"Your boyfriend from high school," Candice said, and Sage's cheeks flared up.

"Wyatt wasn't my boyfriend!" Sage snapped. "The only boyfriend I had was August, and that's really the only guy I remember clearly."

Damian, of course, was by the doorway, listening in. Olivia was too busy staring at herself in the mirror to take part in the gossip. Damian cleared his throat. "Boyfriend, darling? You never told me."

"That's because Wyatt wasn't my boyfriend!"

"Oh, please, Aunt Sage." Candice rolled her eyes. "We all saw his pictures in your old room at Aurora's house."

Damian arched a brow.

This was getting way out of control.

"I had a crush on him, all right?" Sage said angrily. "But what does this have to do with Geoffrey?"

Geoffrey cleared his throat. With his pecs still out, he said, "That's my great grandfather. He never fought in the Unification War, but he supported the coalition. All my great grandparents did. The next generation also supported ousting Allseer Marchello during the Warlord's Rebellion, but my family had to flee. That's how we wound up in Winterfeld. My whole family was into civil engineering. My parents worked closely with Gavin Craddock, who executed them before the Warlord arrived." Geoffrey sighed. "That's because he knew they'd support him. I've been living and helping my grandmother since."

Sage was mesmerized. It was hard to say no to Geoffrey when he was both a descendant of Wyatt and such an honest young man It seemed Damian had been right about him, after all. Not only that he had a class ring and note from Wyatt to give to her.

"I wanted to give this to you in person," Geoffrey said earnestly. "It's from my great grandfather. He told the family to pass it on to you if we ever had the pleasure of meeting you. He said you loved your city too much to ever leave it. Not a whole lot of people know who the Optimum really is, but Candice told me as soon as she realized that I'm a huge fan."

Geoffrey gave Sage the ring and letter. It was short.

Dear, Optimum,

High school was tough. The Unification War started and so many of us joined the coalition while others stayed back and supported us from the sidelines. It was a year I'd never forget. But it was also a year I learned to fight for what I believed in. Unity, honesty, and fairness. I don't know who you are, but I appreciate all your hard work. For that reason, my family and I will always cherish the city you fought so hard for, even if we have to leave it. I hope you never stop fighting, wherever you are. But I also hope you find peace.

Sincerely,
Wyatt

"Thank you," Sage said quietly to Geoffrey. She looked at the ring. Home of the Cavaliers. It brought back way too many memories, and she was going to start crying.

Sage cleared her throat. She turned to Damian. "You knew? About Wyatt and Geoffrey?"

"I knew they were big fans, yes," Damian said. "But I didn't know Wyatt was your boyfriend, darling."

"He wasn't my boyfriend!" Sage snapped.

"Are you really strong?" Geoffrey asked Sage. "I mean—that's a dumb question—*how* are you so strong? Like how do you jump around and swing a sword like that?"

"I'm still trying to figure that out myself," Damian said.

"You'll find out if you ever dream of laying a hand on Candice," Sage hissed at Geoffrey, waving her finger like a true mother now. "Just because I knew your great grandfather doesn't mean I'm going to take it easy on you or forget that you're three years older than Candice. Absolutely no sex—"

"Sage!" Candice whined.

"—And no sleepovers unless I'm present!"

Damian didn't make any smart-ass remarks. Either he was completely on board with the rules, or he was still thinking about Sage and the list of boyfriends she had never revealed to him.

Geoffrey bowed his head. "Of course, Sage. I will never do anything to harm or make Candice feel uncomfortable. She's a very sweet girl and very focused on her career. She says she wants to be a fighter like you."

Sage's heart stopped beating. It felt like she had a rock in her chest. Her stomach plunged to the very core of the earth. It felt like she was free-falling for hours.

"A fighter?" Sage said.

"I want to enroll in the Diamond City military when I'm eighteen," Candice said happily.

"And I want to be a diva!" Olivia ran out of the bathroom. "Look, Geoffrey! Look at me!"

Sage couldn't take it—she was about to explode.

Thankfully, Candice was too immersed with Geoffrey and Olivia over the upcoming concert to notice her aunt's distress. In fact, Candice was completely oblivious to it.

Sage beelined for the balcony. She needed fresh air or she was going to vomit. This was too much emotion for her right now, and she needed to scream so the world could hear her. She had just managed to shove the sliding glass door aside when Damian grabbed her.

"Damian, no!" Sage croaked to him. "Go tend to the girls! I-I don't want them to see me like this—"

Damian dragged her outside, drew the curtains, and shut the door.

Now, Sage screamed.

She muffled it against Damian's chest. She used his round shoulders and hard back as a punching bag. If she didn't control herself, people were going to think she was committing murder.

"Look at me, darling." Damian held her face to get her to stop this rampage.

"NO!" Sage screamed. "NO FIGHTING! NO FIGHTING, DAMIAN!"

"I know, but listen—"

"NO! Why does she need to be a fighter? So she can be like me, all fucked up in the head? Or dead, like all those people in the palace?"

"Listen to me." Damian tightened his hold on her head. Sage was breathing like a bull, and she had no choice but to look at him. Her nails were digging into Damian's body, but he didn't seem to care about that. He had to say these words to her. "Candice and Olivia both look up to you a lot. A lot, darling. It's only natural they want to be like you, too."

"I DON'T WANT THAT KIND OF LIFE FOR THEM!"

"Listen," Damian said calmly. "You are a parent. You cannot choose what your children will do with their lives—you can only influence them."

"What the fuck does that mean? T-that I didn't influence them—?"

"You're not listening, darling. Yes, you did influence them. You've done incredible things in their life spans. You've run the restaurant and taught them how to defend themselves. They know who you are and what your past entailed, but they don't see the dark side of that because they're still *children*. Candice is only fifteen. Maybe now she has ideas of fighting, but it can change as she goes through high school."

"Who put these ideas in her head?" Sage croaked.

Damian sighed. "I don't know. And sometimes there really isn't anyone else to blame. Who we are or what we grow up to be is inherent and then influenced by outside forces. Blaming someone—even yourself—is not right. It's out of your control. All you can do is hear her out, give your opinion, but ultimately, you need to be supportive. If you tell her no, you will lose her forever."

"I'd rather lose her trust than her life."

"And how are you going to do that? Tie her down to the bed? Lock her in a closet?"

"If it means her life, I'll do anything!"

"Then she really will die," Damian said. "And I think that's an even sadder death than one on the battlefield."

Sage couldn't believe Damian had just said that to her, as if Candice was another soldier, but he didn't let her retort.

"Let's not ruin this night with this kind of talk," Damian said gently. "I'm going back in there to finish everyone's makeup. Right now, there is hope. We've brought the rightful Allseers to the throne and stemmed any future wars. Yes, there are still the Squids, but all has been good so far. We're still alive, and we'll still play our roles as protectors no matter what Candice decides to do. If it comes down to it, I will be the first in the line of fire against any enemy."

Sage's eyes widened.

Damian took her hands and kissed them. "Just take it easy, all right? Everything will be fine, darling."

Damian kissed her lips next. He was gentle and soft, with his hands still holding hers. Sage allowed herself to fall for him. It was the quickest, easiest way to forget about life's troubles. The sun was setting behind them, warming her in all the right places. Sage's hands started to travel up his arms, but then there was a fierce tapping on the window.

"Are you for real?!" Candice exclaimed, her face peering at them from behind the curtain. "Can't you do that later, after the concert? We're going to be late!"

"The lady is calling." Damian chuckled to Sage. "I better get to work. You'll be all right?"

No. But Sage wasn't going to be sour on a night like this. She dried her eyes then went inside.

Candice had already whisked Damian away to the bedroom for round two of horrendous makeup time. It sounded like it was Geoffrey's turn next. Olivia was jumping up and down in the hallway, as giddy as ever.

Sage took a seat on the couch and drew her knees to her chest. She took Wyatt's high school ring out of her pocket. She studied it on her palm, drowning in memories of the past.

Wyatt . . . she had had him in biology class. She remembered when the teacher had paired them up together for a lab. Her heart had skipped multiple beats. But their conversations had never amounted to anything more than coordinating who did what on the report. She remembered it had been on acids and bases. They had worked pretty well together, but no spark. Just a physical attraction, she supposed . . . What would Wyatt say if he knew his lab partner had been the Optimum?

"So, Sage, how do I look?"

Sage looked up and jumped when she saw the modified Geoffrey. A tall silver guy with a black mohawk that looked just like Olivia's older brother.

"Ridiculous," Sage admitted. "But if it's part of the concert, then so be it."

"We're twins now!" Olivia jumped up next to him. "Don't we look cool, Sage?"

Sage sighed. She let herself laugh a little. "Sure."

"Candice is up next, then it's your turn!"

"I'm not doing that," Sage said immediately.

Olivia gasped. Geoffrey blinked.

"But you have to!" Olivia cried. "Or they won't let you in!"

"Please, you think everyone who bought a ticket is going to look like a clown?"

"Yes," they both said at once.

"Sage, you don't understand," Geoffrey said earnestly. "People would give their testicles or tits for a chance to be part of a concert. It's the coolest thing ever!"

"No," Sage grumbled.

"Aww!" Olivia whined. "Why, Aunt Sage?" She got on her knees and peered up into Sage's face. God, she really did look ridiculous with all that makeup. Or maybe Sage was being a bit too harsh— Olivia did look cool, but there was no way on earth Sage was doing it, too. "Please?"

"No, Olivia."

"But you said you were going to the concert!"

"Well, I changed my mind. There's no way on earth I'm putting all that paint on my body—isn't it toxic?"

"This is the non-toxic type," Geoffrey said, as Olivia let out the most piercing wail of all time.

"CANDICE!" she screeched. She scrambled out of the living room to snag her sister. It looked like Damian was only halfway done with her makeup because Candice still had to do her face. The rest of her body was all silver, and the paint must have dried quickly because she was already dressed. It didn't look like clothes smudged any of the gears Damian had painted onto her skin.

Horror crept into Sage's belly. How long would that stuff be on her face? She couldn't open a restaurant like that!

"Aunt Sage?" Candice said. "What's going on?"

If Olivia was letting out piercing wails, then Candice must have thought Sage was having a seizure. Damian must have, too, because he came to her side immediately.

"Are you all right?" he asked her.

"SHE'S NOT GOING TO THE CONCERT, DAMIAN!" Olivia yelled.

"What?" Damian rasped.

Candice started hyperventilating. Geoffrey looked like someone had died.

"Are you kidding me?!" Sage yelled angrily. "Now all of you are going to pressure me into going? I'm not a fucking child—if I don't want to go, I'm staying home!"

"Damian!" Olivia threw herself on him. Tears in her eyes, she choked, "Please convince her! Please!"

"Darling, what's the matter?" Damian asked Sage. He looked genuinely concerned, as if Sage were suffering from some life-threatening disease. "Why don't you want to go?"

"Because I don't want to," Sage snapped. "I don't want to look like an idiot. So please leave me alone."

"I can't believe this, Aunt Sage!" Candice yelled at her. "Why do you have to be such a grouch?! You always used to participate before! This is a once-in-a-lifetime opportunity, and you're going to throw it away?"

"I-it really is, Ms. Sage," Geoffrey said politely. "Besides, we would all look cool together."

"Please, darling." Damian took both her hands and kissed them. His own fingers full of paint, he said, "I will do anything you ask of me after this. It means so much to us. Don't be this way."

Sage glowered at him. She flared her nostrils, breathing like a bull.

"I'll make you another pizza," Damian said. "I'll give you the biggest cunnilingus of your life."

Geoffrey laughed. Candice didn't react. Olivia conveniently stopped her crying to ask, "What's a 'cunnilingus'? And if Aunt Sage is getting a big one, can I have one, too?"

Geoffrey laughed even harder.

Sage wasn't amused. She didn't budge as Damian got down on his knees and kissed her hands again.

"Everyone really wants you to go," Damian said. "*I* really want you to go, darling."

"Are you seriously doing that paint on yourself?"

"Candice will help." Damian's eyes heated. "Unless you want to. That way you can get all the secret spots."

"I'll do it," Geoffrey volunteered. "I don't mind getting the secret spots."

Candice bopped him on the head. Geoffrey's cheeks were aflame even if his skin was all silver. Sage had no idea what was going on.

"Geoffrey thinks that Damian is hot," Olivia announced.

"That's gross!" Sage exclaimed; Damian arched a brow. "Geoffrey is eighteen and Damian is over a hundred!"

"It's not about sexual relations," Damian said. "It's all about appreciating fine looks and bodies."

"And Damian is attractive," Geoffrey said quickly. "Good catch, Sage."

"I swear," Sage snarled at him, "that if you say one more word about Damian's looks, I will staple your lips together! He doesn't need that kind of ego boost!"

Geoffrey cleared his throat and raised his hands. "Yes, ma'am."

"So will you come?" Olivia went back to whiny mode. "Please, Aunt Sage?"

Candice crossed her arms with a scowl. Geoffrey was still grinning like an idiot. Damian started kneading Sage's hands like prayer beads.

Sage sighed. Why did it feel like she was making a huge mistake?

Because she was.

Sage had never painted her whole body before. She had been through plenty of unpleasant experiences—like the time she had shit her pants when doing groceries because the ham Samson had served her had gone bad, or the time she had gotten a ticket for jaywalking because she was in a rush to get to work—but this . . . was different.

Sage hated it. Samson would have made fun of her. But she kept a smile glued on her face because she did it for the sake of her family. She closed her eyes and clenched her fists as Damian spiked up her hair. She grinned nice and big when Damian took a picture of her. She nearly cried because Olivia couldn't stop laughing at her. But at the end of the day, she did it. Candice acknowledged it. Geoffrey gave her a high five. And Damian said he was proud of her.

Of course, Damian looked the best out of all of them. He could wear any costume or any disguise and make it his own. Olivia didn't laugh at him because it was so natural to him that it just wasn't funny. He looked beautiful, even with silver skin, black eyes, and crazy hair.

The five of them took a picture sporting their Silver Gears t-shirts and jeans, and then they were off to the concert.

It didn't occur to Sage that she'd have to walk around like this in public until they joined the rest of the idiots in the arena. That was all the way on the east side of the capital, right next to the Royal Amusement Park, and it seated over 100,000 spectators. At least Sage wouldn't be the only one dressed like this. In fact, there was a long line of weirdoes waiting to get in.

And that was the strange part—what was the hold-up?

"I still say their first album was the best," Geoffrey was saying while waiting in line.

Thanks to their powerful paint, the humidity or leaning against the rails wouldn't ruin their looks. Sage had to admit that they looked the best out of most people.

She saw one woman walking by with flat hair and a simple dress. She was about to exclaim that wasn't fair, when there was a collective gasp from the front of the line.

Immediately, people started backing away from something. Sage had no idea what was going on until someone started shouting, "H-he's collapsed! Oh my God!"

"HE'S SPITTING UP BLOOD!" someone else screamed, and then there was chaos.

"Darling." Damian grabbed Sage's arm. He drew her to his side, as if sensing she was about to investigate and endanger herself. "No. We have to go."

It was instinct to see what the hell was going on, but Sage didn't leave her nieces. She stuck to them and Geoffrey, who was too flabbergasted to say anything. They all held their breaths until security circled them, announcing they had to be isolated and tested for Red Fever.

"What?" Geoffrey breathed. "Red Fever?"

Immediately, security began plucking Enhanced from the line. It was useless to hold people that were immune, so they grabbed them and shoved them as far away from the arena as possible.

"Identification?" They asked the rest of the terrified fans.

"Aunt Sage!" Olivia croaked. "W-what's happening?"

Sage had her ID ready, but she wasn't going to leave her nieces behind. She swore that if that fat-ass security guard named Leo grabbed her like a piece of meat, she'd flip him on his back and slit his throat. Like hell she was leaving her nieces. Damian said nothing from behind her, probably thinking the same.

"Identification, sir?" Leo asked him next.

"I'm Enhanced," he said quickly. "But I request to stay by my family, please—"

"They're not sick!" Sage declared angrily. "Just let them go."

"We don't know that for sure, ma'am," said Leo. "We'll be testing everyone here for the contagion and isolating them immediately before it spreads."

"Come along, sir," said another security guard to Damian, sensing resistance in the line.

"I'm sorry, but I can't leave them!" Damian snapped. "They're just kids!"

"They're in good hands. We'll be examining them and releasing them once they're cleared."

"My ass!" Sage exclaimed. "How do I know you're not going to sell their organs?"

"Ma'am, Red Fever is serious—"

"Then I'm staying with them. My girls are underage, and I'm their guardian—I have a right to know what you're doing to them."

"Aunt Sage!" Olivia cried, wrapping her arms around Sage's waist.

"It's fine, baby," Sage said to her, rubbing her back. "Nothing's going to happen."

"Ma'am." Leo stepped forward. He and his buddy braced themselves. They had already dealt with a few loud-mouthed parents, so this wasn't anything unexpected. "Please step aside."

"I have parental rights," Sage spat. "You can't ask me to leave, asshole."

"Ma'am, this is Red Fever protocol to prevent infection. We cannot allow parents to stay with their children while we search for infected and quarantine them. This is a public safety emergency, and this measure is in place to ensure we maintain control."

"I understand that, sir, but the girls are my responsibility and I am not releasing them to you without my supervision. If this is a public safety emergency, then contact the Allseers and tell them that it's bullshit."

"Ma'am." Buddy-guard grabbed her.

Damian pushed him back. "Hands off, asshole!"

Leo went for Sage, who drew her hidden dagger. Either in her bra or boot, but she always carried one on her body at all times. It was a good thing she did because Leo actually drew his gun and fired at her.

Candice and Olivia screamed. Geoffrey held on to the rails. Sage deflected the bullet with her blade and Damian came from the side to tackle Leo to the ground.

People screamed, and more chaos erupted. A wave of guards ran in to hold the line and investigate the trouble.

Sage and Damian had just disarmed two officers. More guards

were making their way to the scene, and pretty soon the military was upon them. The latter finally recognized the two in crazy paint and beating up authority, and asked the guards to stand down. Sage didn't put her blade away until she made one thing clear.

"If you want to check them, fine," Sage proclaimed for everyone to hear. "But I'm not leaving their sides, damn it! If you want to draw your fucking guns and shoot me, go on, but those are MY CHILDREN!"

To her annoyance, Sage saw Gertrude among the military. Mega Woman, Turtle, Rockstar, and Eye Candy were here, too, so at least they vouched for them and stemmed the violence. Sage didn't care one way or another—she was irritated enough to slam all their faces to the ground.

"Holy shit!" Leo croaked when he found out whom he had drawn a gun on. "That's the Optimum?"

Yes. Dressed as a Silver Gear fan and soothing her crying nieces. Now that identities were confirmed, the guards were able to call for order and continue their protocol or whatever the fuck it was.

Candice and Olivia were glued to Sage's sides. Geoffrey was right behind them, and Damian didn't stray far as he spoke with the military. He kept an eye on them at all times, though.

"What are they going to do to us?" Olivia whispered to Sage. Tears were running down her cheeks.

"They're probably going to make sure you're not infected, is all," Sage said.

"But none of us have been coughing," Candice said. "Or have had fever or anything like that."

"I think this is just a precaution since someone was sick."

Sage hadn't thought the outbreak would reach the capital. With all the health regulations that businesses had to follow, Diamond City had been able to quarantine and treat people accordingly. Symptoms were reported immediately, and the infected were removed from public areas. But it seemed not everyone was honest about what they felt, and now the government was going to have to double down on humans. Sage overheard Damian talking to Mega

Woman, who said, "They're going to start screening people at the entrance to public areas."

Hell. This would be true hell now, because a screening entailed checking IDs and blood if the person was human. Now public areas were going to have to hire health officials to perform the screening, and that meant more money. Sage would have to get one for the restaurant.

Security swept all the Silver Gears fans into the arena, which had already been modified for testing. Tents that had been selling souvenirs were now full of doctors in scrubs. The doctors had these meters that they used to examine people's blood in search of the contagion. Anyone who was clean was immediately taken out through the gift shop of all places. Anyone infected was taken farther into the arena where they were fully examined for symptoms.

Sage didn't like this. She especially didn't like that she was still in all this makeup, but at least she had her dagger. Even if Candice and Olivia were contaminated, a simple exam was no big deal. They'd probably be taken to a medical facility and treated there.

"Are we going to be all right?" Olivia squeaked.

"Of course," Sage said. She kept a tight hold on her girls as they moved up the line. Geoffrey was holding Sage's arm just in case they got attacked by security again.

"What if we're infected?" Olivia asked.

"We're not infected," Candice stated. "We'll be fine, Olive."

Sage turned in search of Damian, who was by the entrance of the arena now. He was still talking to the military, but he kept Sage and the family in his line of sight. He seemed to say, *I'm here, darling.*

When Olivia was up, she started crying. Sage held her head and whispered against her temple, "They're not taking you from me. I swear I'll cut off their heads before they do."

"It's all right, Olive," Candice said bravely. "Show them you're not infected."

Olivia squealed when the doctor pricked her finger. She held her eyes shut as they checked her blood and the light beeped green.

"She's good," said the doctor, dismissing her, but Sage kept her to her side.

"She stays with me, dipshit," Sage snarled. "All right, Candice—go."

Candice gave her hand. She didn't squeak, but Olivia did for her when the doctor took her blood next.

Clean.

Sage exhaled in relief.

"All right, Geoffrey," Candice said, holding the cotton ball to her finger. "Hurry so we can get out of here."

Geoffrey stepped forward. Sage made eye contact with Damian and smiled at him.

He smiled back. He nodded his head. Just one more, and they'd go home. They'd have their own concert, he seemed to say with his eyes alone. Stars, he looked like a god in all that silver and crazy hair. Half of the military was staring at him, wondering if that was the infamous Warlord looking like a punkster, and the other half looked impressed, that the notorious Warlord was a true family man.

Sage wanted to kiss him, but then Candice screamed. She immediately drew her dagger, but there was no one to attack.

She stared at the red light on the meter.

Geoffrey was infected.

CHAPTER 6
Red Fever

"Go with Damian," Sage chanted to the girls. "Go with Damian." Candice and Olivia were too stiff to move. Damian sensed something was horribly wrong, so he ran to them. Was this any other time, Sage would have laughed at how he bulldozed through security guards with all that makeup on his body.

"Geoffrey's sick," Sage said to him. "Damian, please take the girls—I'll go with Geoffrey."

Damian didn't hesitate, but Candice had her fair share of exclamations.

"I'M NOT LEAVING HIM!"

Candice was human, so there was no way she was taking a step past checkpoint. Geoffrey beseeched Sage—"You don't have to stay for me!"—but Sage waved him off.

"Shut up," she spat. "I'm a big girl and you're not my daddy. I make my own decisions. Now march."

Geoffrey was taken into the arena. Ironically, right next to the pit where they were supposed to have been jumping up and down like crazy people. Now there were tents for privacy as doctors examined the contaminated individuals. There, Geoffrey had to strip and sit through an exam with all that paint on his skin. Sage had completely forgotten she still looked like an idiot until she saw herself in a mirror.

This was definitely a day for the books.

"And you are, ma'am?" asked the tall woman doctor. Her name was Dr. Price. She was an Enhanced, worked hand-in-hand with the Allseers and the council, and documented her new patient on her tablet.

"His chaperone," Sage said sourly. Wasn't there a shower she could use? "And your supervisor. If you so much as look at him wrong, I'm going to punch your long nose right into your face."

Dr. Price looked up. She furrowed her brows, glanced at the security guard by the tent door, then turned to Sage again. "Excuse me?"

"Don't look at me—get to work."

"I'm sorry, but who are you?"

"I already told you who I am," Sage spat. "Are you hard of hearing? Or is your IQ just not up to par? Maybe the Allseers should take a closer look at who they're hiring as medical professionals."

"Sage," Geoffrey said nervously. "Please."

"Don't 'please' me nothing—I don't trust any of these assholes. If they could, they'd gladly trap a hybrid like me or my sister and sell our Cells for money or use us for bargaining chips. They're worse than thugs."

Dr. Price opened her mouth to argue, but Sage cut her off.

"Do your job and stop asking questions."

There was something really strange about this Red Fever resurgence. Sage hated to think this way, but desperation sparked her imagination. There was no way Louis or Agathe could be behind it since they had been at Mousafeld the past year, but this could very well be the old council's doing.

They were dead, though. All of them. Wren and Taz had wiped them out, so there was no one to ask about where the hell a fucking germ like Red Fever had gained so much potency.

But wait—Louis and Agathe were the Allseers. Surely they had inherited all the secrets and were perfectly aware of what the old council had done. If that was the case, then Louis and Agathe had to know about the Red Fever's origins. And if they were playing dumb and allowing infection to spread, then what was the purpose? How were they making money on the side or gaining power from all this?

They're going to play the saviors, of course, said the voice in Sage's head. Sage watched Dr. Price examine Geoffrey from head to foot, and she got these little shocks in her body. Dread. Disgust. All of the above.

Poor Wren.

They're going to show Diamond City that they care by making up a problem and finding the solution, Sage continued to think to herself. By the time Dr. Price finished with Geoffrey and sent him off for transportation, Sage swore it was as obvious as two plus two equalled four.

Holy shit. The Red Fever was no accident. It was on *purpose.*

Sage sat quietly in the ambulance. Geoffrey was forever thankful that no one had gotten their throat slit, but now he wanted to hear some words of encouragement.

"Am I going to die?" he asked dismally.

Sage looked at him. She was standing by his gurney, ready to move as soon as they arrived at the medical facility. She shook her head. "No," she said. "No one dies from Red Fever. Well—not many do. It's like catching a bad cold. And you don't even have any symptoms."

"I can get worse."

"They have treatment that will help."

"I don't want to die, Sage."

"Fuck me—stop saying that!" Sage exclaimed. "You're not going to die."

Panic was setting in. Maybe Geoffrey had been in too much shock to realize it before, but he had *Red Fever* and a long road to recovery. One he might not survive. He started laughing nervously as the medics started intravenous fluids.

"S-Sage . . ."

"What?"

"I can't believe this happened," Geoffrey croaked. "But more: I can't believe you actually attacked security and threatened a doctor. A-all while looking like *that*."

The three medics in the ambulance with them looked at her.

Sage rolled her eyes. "What I look like doesn't matter. Sometimes in life you have to fight like hell."

"Is that from firsthand experience?"

"As you just saw. People are going to try to fuck you over, and you have to be ready to defend yourself. I don't care if it's a family member or the Allseer—they take joy in making you feel miserable and causing hysteria. That way they have something to talk about on the news and they can assure people that 'they're on it.'"

Geoffrey gazed at her wondrously. Between Dr. Price and the paramedics, they had touched his chest enough times to warp the paint. Some of his Optimum tattoo showed.

Sage said nothing on the rest of the trip to the medical facility. It was the same one Reina had died in, but a different wing. Sage made sure to stick by Geoffrey's side the whole way through, even when they stripped him and washed all the paint off his body in the shower. Damian's hard work went down the drain. Sage felt a twinge of sadness that their night as a family had gone to hell. But right now, she was still in survival mode and her emotions were locked away tightly. She ignored anyone who asked her questions and threatened security whenever they told her to step back. She still had her dagger, and she could very well be arrested for carrying a weapon in a government building, but she really didn't care. She felt ready to start a whole new war against Louis and Agathe if their stupidity cost this innocent young man his life.

How is he? Damian texted her.

Fine, Sage said. She stood by with her arms crossed as doctors hooked him up to more monitors and started administering medications. One of them with a shiny bald head told her that she was lucky that they had caught Geoffrey in time. Chances were, he'd make it.

"Whoop-de-fucking-do," Sage mumbled.

The girls are safe. We washed up and had some dinner. They feel relieved that you're in charge over there. I'll come see you as soon as they get to bed.

There was no way Candice and Olivia were going to sleep. Nor were they going to allow Damian to come to the facility by himself. That's why, when Damian arrived the next morning, the girls were waiting outside with Justice as an escort. They weren't moving until they had an update from the only two people they trusted right now.

Suddenly, Damian roared with laughter.

Sage jumped in her chair. She had been half asleep, and now she was looking at Damian—showered and clean with silky hair, normal makeup, and leather clothes—turning red in the face. Confused, Sage looked to Geoffrey, who was laughing, too. Even the two idiot security guards in the hall were shaking their heads at each other.

"What?" Sage said.

"Darling," Damian choked. "Are you seriously still in all that makeup?"

"Are you for real?" Sage got to her feet. "Is that what you're laughing at?!"

"It is pretty funny," Geoffrey admitted. "I mean, only you can pull off that look in one of the most serious facilities in Heart."

"What was I supposed to do? I was babysitting the whole damn night! Now that Mr. Hilarious is here, I can take a shower."

Damian had some clothes for her in a bag, but he must have thought she'd clean up by now. Sage grabbed the bag from his hand and ignored his puckered lips on the way to the bathroom.

"No kiss for me, darling?"

Sage slammed the door closed for an answer to that. She was being a bitch right now, but she was cranky and irritable. On top of it all, she was worried.

What if Geoffrey wasn't really sick? What if this place was going to make him sick? What if they had picked him on purpose for one big experiment? Louis had known Sage was going to the concert . . . so what if this was on purpose?

With the water, four bottles of body wash, and ten bottles of shampoo, Sage got all the gook off her body. She was finally back to normal, but the anger hadn't subsided one bit. She combed her hair, wrapped it in that bun Damian was sure to give her hell for, and exited the bathroom.

Sage was back in the hall, and that's where she saw Damian and Nova having a conversation. Her heart swelled.

As if Damian had picked up on her concerns, he was demanding of Nova the same answers that Sage wanted from every damn doctor here. It seemed Damian was skeptical of all this, too.

"Why do I continue to hear about this sickness?" he asked Nova. "We are in the goddamn twenty-third century, and you're telling me—or expect me to believe—that doctors are clueless on how to eradicate this contagion?"

"We did before," Nova said patiently. She looked so petite compared to Damian, all in white with her blond hair in a ponytail. So small and fragile, the girl that would be trampled on a college campus in the hallway. But Sage had learned not to underestimate her, especially since she was the brains behind Winterfeld's defense systems. "But this is a new strain that requires a lot of testing. Many of the quarantined patients will be cured and ready to go, but other cases won't be so simple."

Was that so? Sage glanced at Geoffrey through the view glass. He was on his phone. He was probably texting Candice. And what were the chances that Geoffrey would be one of the ones to die or be detained? If that happened, Sage would know this was all a farce.

"That boy better recover quickly," Damian said seriously. "So you and all those big-brained doctors better figure this out."

Damian looked up when he noticed Sage.

"Damian," Sage said without saying a word to Nova. "Can you keep an eye on Geoffrey? I want to check on the girls."

"Very well."

Sage took the back exit just down the hall. In a matter of steps, she was outside under the rays of a new sun. She smiled when she spotted Candice and Olivia by one of the benches, but gasped when she noticed Agathe standing right next to them.

Sage didn't believe in spiritual possessions. But she did believe there were evil influences that changed moods and behaviors, and Agathe was one of them.

In an instant, Sage went on autopilot. Her mind, her instincts—whatever controlled her body then—took over all her motor functions. Her actions from then on out weren't planned or thought through—they just happened. This had happened to Sage on multiple occasions in the past, particularly when her life was in danger or one of her loved ones was under duress, and so far, they were never wrong.

Sage got to Candice and Olivia. Like a mother eagle to her babies, she wrapped an arm around each of them. She froze at the vicious look on Agathe's face, as if Agathe had just ripped her prey into tiny pieces. The bitch wasn't fast enough to hide it, either.

"Oh, Sage." Agathe cleared her throat. She plastered that smile that Sage knew now was fake back onto her face. "There you are. Louis and I came by to see how the infected were doing. I heard it was quite traumatic last night."

Something was wrong. Agathe had said or done something that she was trying to hide—Sage smelled it. Her girls were uncomfortably stiff in her grip, too, as if they had just found out Geoffrey was dead.

"So much that you got a bit riled up."

"Trust me," Sage said. "If someone was about to take away your children, you'd do the same."

Agathe nodded her head. She had those ugly braids in her hair. Whoever had done them really sucked. There was something off about her robes, too. White and gold just didn't suit her. Louis looked much more royal, waving his hand at everyone he crossed on the way to the facility. The grounds were beautiful with the bushes trimmed and the magnolias in full bloom, but this was nothing short of hell for Sage right now.

"That's right," Agathe said, eyes narrowed. "Their father is dead, so auntie has to step up to the plate. But I know you're already an amazing mother, Sage. You would give your life for them, wouldn't you?"

Candice was shaking. Unlike last night, silent tears were streaming down Olivia's face.

"I'm sorry," Agathe said quickly to the trio. "I thought they knew already, Sage—I swear I did!"

Sage said nothing. She couldn't. This was all her fucking fault for not having told Candice and Olivia anything about Bram before. And as much as Sage was starting to really hate Agathe, Agathe wasn't really in the wrong . . . was she? She had been having a pleasant conversation with the girls . . . hadn't she? And, naturally, Bram had come up in that conversation . . . right?

Sage didn't know what made her do it, but she looked up. She found Justice next to his car by the sidewalk. She saw his face.

Handsome and stoic. But his eyes came to life when they met hers. The flash in them spoke lengths about the sort of conversation the girls had had with the female Allseer. All was not as it seemed.

"Sage!" Louis said happily, bouncing right into their circle. "There you are. How are you—?"

"I want you to listen very closely," Sage said quietly. She had cut Louis off, but she was looking at Agathe. Maybe this was for Louis, too, but this was more for the bitch who looked like a goddamn rattlesnake. "Are you listening?" she asked them. "Because I'm only going to say this once. You will *not* fuck around with me or my family. You will not talk or try to influence them in any way. They are not your pawns for whatever sick games you're playing."

Agathe blinked innocently. "What are you talking about, Sage?"

"You know exactly what I'm talking about. You might have been locked away in the palace all your life, but you're not an idiot. You know exactly what you want and how to get it. At the end of the day, behind your pretty faces—Louis', because I think you're an ugly bitch—you're heartless politicians."

Agathe's face contorted.

"S-Sage!" Louis croaked. "I don't understand—?"

"Yes, you do," Sage snarled. "Red Fever? Are you kidding me? Find out how to get rid of it because I swear if something happens to Geoffrey I'm coming after both your heads."

"Is that a threat?" Agathe asked quietly. She was clenching her fists by her sides. "Haven't you caused enough trouble already? Disarming two guards? Threatening my doctors? You're becoming quite the menace to Diamond City, Sage. You and your handsome fiancé."

"I think you've forgotten who I am," Sage said, equally quiet. "And what I can do. I unified this city. I lived with a Squid for over a hundred years, whose Cells run through my veins. I can wipe that ugly smirk off your face in the blink of an eye. Would like to see me do it?"

Louis stepped forward. "Sage, that's enough. I don't know what's going on, but what's with all the accusations? Why are you making it sound like Red Fever is our fault—?"

"Stay away from me!" Sage snapped at him. She grabbed her girls and pulled them away from the two royals. She semi shoved them into Justice's chest, who ushered them into the car without resistance. Candice and Olivia were way too shaken up to complain. Just what on earth had Agathe said to them?

"Sage?"

Sage looked up as soon as she heard her name. The very person she wanted to see came stalking out of the building. It was as if Damian could sense her distress from wherever he was on the planet. Her heart softened because she knew that if anyone could get through to the girls, it was him.

"Well, hello, Mr. Warlord." Agathe nearly purred. "I heard you were here, too, checking up on Candice's boyfriend. I didn't know you could be such a family man." She had the balls to put her hands on Damian's chest, but Damian quickly pried her off him. As if she was just another starstruck tramp, Damian brushed right past her and reached Sage's side.

Sage had never felt such pleasure in her life. She had never wanted to kiss Damian more than she did now, after rejecting Agathe right in her face. Damian didn't even look at Louis as he held Sage's cheek, checked her expression, assessed what sort of words had been exchanged in his absence, and turned to the culprit.

He glared at Louis and Agathe.

"I don't like this," Sage croaked to him. "I-I don't like this at all."

"Don't worry," Damian said. He held her tightly. "I trust Nova, who will figure out a way to make Geoffrey and the others better. If this is truly the Allseers' doing, then they'll be losing some of their arsenal soon."

"WHAT ARE YOU TALKING ABOUT?!" Louis roared. "This is not 'my' doing or my sister's!"

"It doesn't matter," Damian sneered at him. "Because Red Fever will be eradicated soon enough. If it was part of some corrupt plan for more control or human extermination, then it's moot. And if Nova winds up dead by poisoning, I'll know exactly who to blame." He turned to Sage. "Come along, darling—"

"Damian." Sage was nearly in tears. She really didn't know how to get in that car now and face the girls. She hung her head in shame. "T-they know . . ."

"Come."

"No, they know about Bram—Agathe told them!"

"Come," Damian said again. He kissed her forehead. "We'll talk to them."

Sage's hand in his, Damian led her to the car. He put her in the backseat next to a sobbing Olivia and got in the front next to Justice. Justice didn't waste any time getting them the hell out of there. Candice and Olivia didn't seem very inclined to use their vocal cords, so Sage started.

"I was going to tell you," she said earnestly. "But I didn't because of the Squids, the move to here, and the restaurant. There was too much going on."

"And you decided not to tell us?" Candice interjected fiercely. "Because it's not important to know our father is dead?"

"I said I was going to tell you, not that I wasn't. There is a time and place for everything, Candice, and I didn't want to jeopardize your emotional health. Can you try to understand that?"

"Who killed him?" Candice said.

"He killed himself," Justice said.

Sage was surprised to hear him speak. Perhaps Justice had not been very thrilled with Agathe's brutal approach of the subject, either. Or had there been words that revealed more than just an untimely death?

"We found him in his cell shortly after the Warlord took off to search for Sage," Justice went on.

"You weren't even there!" Candice exclaimed. "How do you know that's what happened?! Dad wouldn't kill himself like that!"

"While it is true that I wasn't at Mousafeld at the time because I had accompanied Sage to the capital, I am always in communication with the other rebels, who did see what happened. And this is coming from more than one eyewitness account."

"How do you know you can trust them?"

"I have been on the run for so long, betrayed by so many in the past, that I know exactly who I can and cannot trust," Justice said. "If it wasn't for the rebels at Mousafeld, I would have been dead. While I don't usually gloat, I feel I have developed a sixth sense for people. And if there are two people I can trust with my life, it is Cushion, who were there when your father was discovered, and the Warlord."

Sage wasn't sure what to call the feeling that seeped into her like a cracked egg, but it had to be some sort of relief. At the same time, she found it strange that Justice was declaring his loyalty like that. Just what the fuck had Agathe said?

"And now that I've gotten to know her, I trust Sage as well," Justice said to a panting Candice. Olivia had curled into herself, head to knees. She had probably stopped listening. "She will do anything to ensure your safety, as she has proven today. She didn't tell you about Bram for all the right reasons. She wanted you to disconnect from the evils of this world and have fun. She's allowed you to roam the capital, build friendships, and even went as far as to accompany

Geoffrey to the medical facility. Please don't be upset with her."

"How do I know you're not in on this, too?" Candice snarled. "That you're not covering up for Damian?"

Sage's eyes widened. Wait, Damian—?

Damian raised a hand to stop her. It was as if he knew exactly where this was going and how Sage was going to react to it. He didn't let her speak because it was his turn now.

"I know my reputation precedes me," Damian said softly. "But why on earth would I kill Bram? Because he betrayed Sage? I would never make that decision on my own. *Ever*. Sage and I have been a couple for nearly a year now, and I have never acted without permission or consulting with her first."

Candice had no comeback for that one. She dried the last tears from her eyes and quieted down. By some miracle, perhaps, Sage had been successful in calming her down.

When they arrived at their complex, Candice and Olivia got out of the car without saying a word. They thanked Justice and marched into the lobby, right past a waiting Mega Woman.

Sage embraced Justice. She thanked him for his words. Damian came up behind him and patted his shoulder.

"Take the day, will you?" Damian said to him as Sage trudged up to the lobby next.

"Everything all right, Optimum?" Mega Woman asked her.

"Other than a shitty concert and a shitty night, sure," Sage said curtly. There was so much more to it than that, she wanted to say, because now she was worried about Louis and Agathe. Could they really be behind the Red Fever?

Damian stayed behind to chat and possibly raise awareness of their rising problem to his rebels, so Sage went in by herself. Candice and Olivia were in their rooms, so it was just her in the living room. She sat on the couch next to Wyatt's letter and ring. She studied both again, as if she were seeing them for the first time.

I hope you never stop fighting, wherever you are. But I also hope you find peace.

Sage caressed her abdomen.

"The babies that grew in her womb were in cocoons."

Sage grew cold with fear.

"I don't trust any of these assholes. If they could, they'd gladly trap a hybrid like me or my sister and sell our Cells for money or use us for bargaining chips. They're worse than thugs."

Sage jumped when she heard someone at the door. It was Damian with two bouquets of roses. Sage couldn't believe he had come up here to seduce her now of all times, but then she saw him step into the kitchen. Curious, Sage got up.

"There you are, darling," Damian said. He had the bouquets on the counter. He was cutting the tips and preparing two vases. Strangely, he didn't fill them with water—he opened a can of soda.

Sage stared. "What on earth are you doing?"

"Don't you know? Soda makes them last longer."

Sage laughed. "What?"

"It was one of my science fair projects in school," Damian said happily.

Sage crossed her arms and leaned against the doorway. With the roses ready to go, Damian sat at the table and wrote two cards by hand. At long last, Sage understood exactly what he was doing.

"For Candice and Olivia," Damian said softly. "And my condolences for their loss. I can't imagine what it's like to lose a parent you love. I am very thankful for Cushion, who is the best mother in the world . . . and while I did have a father, I hated him with a passion. So I always think of what I would do if I lost my mother instead, and it hurts a lot."

"You lost Ileana and Phoebe," Sage said quietly.

"Yes. But Ileana was a traitorous bitch and Phoebe didn't trust me. She put her trust into that disgusting bastard from Winterfeld, and it got her killed in the end."

Damian was silent for an uncomfortable moment. It wasn't often that he spoke of Ileana and Phoebe. It was a trauma he had a hard time letting go of. Ileana had betrayed him to a band of thieves in the middle of the night. Phoebe . . . well . . . Sage didn't know what had happened there. But, apparently, according to Nova, Phoebe had blamed Damian for killing Ileana. Had called him a monster for doing so.

Sage wasn't sure what she called it. But if anyone tried killing her in the middle of the night, she'd definitely be retaliating with a dagger.

"It's different losing a parent, someone who is supposed to love you," Damian finally said. He continued writing the letters. "I know that Bram betrayed them, too, to the council for glory. But it still hurts, especially in ones as young as them. You and I are more seasoned to handle the ugly. They are so innocent."

Damian folded the letters and stuffed them into their envelopes. He wrote each of the girls' names on them. Then he took the bouquets and placed them in front of their bedroom doors. He kneeled on the floor to make sure they were just right.

"You didn't have to do that," Sage said.

Damian looked up at her.

"You didn't have to do any of this. This concert stuff, me, Geoffrey—any of it."

"What do you mean, Sage?" Damian asked quietly.

"You have what you want, don't you?" Sage dared to ask. "What you wanted when I walked into your camp? You're finally back in Diamond City. Why do you trouble yourself with all this family stuff?"

"Is that what you call it? 'Troubling' myself?" Damian got to his feet. He looked her in the eye. "None of this is 'trouble,' Sage. This—everything I'm doing—I do for the sake of my family. You, from the moment we became a couple, are my family. Why do you still talk to me as if I'm a stranger?"

"Because it still feels too good to be true!" Sage exclaimed.

At long last, she had said it. The cancer eating away at her, the thoughts that kept her up at night—was Damian playing games with her? Was he pretending? Or did he truly love her? The longer she stayed with him, the more she believed the latter. She gave a small sob.

"Darling," Damian said softly. "What do I have to do to convince you that I love you? Perhaps more time? And easing your insecurities when they surface?"

"I'm sorry." Sage dabbed at her eyes. "This isn't fair to you, and I'm sorry." She turned around and walked into the living room. She liked it there because there was a balcony. If life got too tough, she could always jump and fly. But Damian kept pulling her back in. He reeled her into his chest.

"We haven't had our wedding vows yet," Damian said against her temple. "But I'll go ahead and say them now. I vow to always be by your side and protect you. To love you and cherish you no matter what happens."

"Do you love me?" Sage whispered against his shirt. "I want to hear you say it."

"I love you," he said.

"Why do you love me?"

"Because you're an incredible soul, darling," Damian said as Sage's eyes welled with more tears. "You are the strongest woman I've ever met. You always put your family above yourself. You nearly knifed that security guard, and I heard you gave those doctors hell. Dr. Price was yelling about you. I heard her in one of the conference rooms."

"What?" Sage raised her head. "Seriously?"

Damian chuckled. "I would have peed myself, too."

"She peed herself?"

Damian laughed. "Apparently. She said she never wanted you around her again. And, of course, you were still in disguise, so you looked a bit unhinged." He sighed pleasurably. "I find that incredibly sexy. When I saw you in Geoffrey's room in all that black and silver, it really turned me on."

"Damian, I looked fucking ridiculous."

"You were so hot, darling." Damian ran a hand through her hair. "The mohawk suits you. We should consider it for the future."

Sage glared at him. "No."

"Not even if we're role-playing in bed?" Damian asked. "You can be a punkster, and I'll be your drum set. You can bang me as hard as you want."

Sage smacked his shoulder, but that didn't loosen Damian's hold. He chuckled.

"I'd rather you smack other places, darling. Would you like me to turn around for you?"

"Why are you so inappropriate?" Sage said.

"You wouldn't want me any other way."

Sage smiled. That was so true.

Sage ran her fingers through his hair. She brought his head down for a kiss. She had yet to give him one today. Now that they weren't battling doctors and Allseers, it was so much easier to concentrate on loving him. It was quiet here, too, with the sun setting outside.

"Put your tongue in my mouth," Damian whispered against her lips, and Sage really did smack his ass this time.

"I put my tongue in your mouth when I'm ready," Sage scolded him. "Not the other way around—"

Sage stopped when she heard Candice's door open. Olivia's, too. They must have seen the flowers because there was a pause. A few moments later, Candice came out, saying, "I'm going out." No indication as to where, but Sage didn't ask. Mega Woman would escort her.

"Damian." Olivia ran out of her room. Actually, she jumped into his arms and wrapped her legs around his waist. She sobbed. "T-thank you for the letter!"

"It's all right, darling." Damian kissed her head. "Everything will be fine. You'll see."

As they had their moment, Sage edged toward the hall. She wondered if Candice had read Damian's letter, too. While the bouquet was no longer on the floor, her heart tore into pieces when she noticed the garbage can in the corner of the room. From this angle, she could see Damian's letter on top of the discarded roses.

Candice

Unopened.

CHAPTER 7

Opening Day

As Geoffrey's health improved in the following weeks, Sage admitted that family life did, too. Candice was no longer as hostile toward Damian and Sage about Bram's death. Either she had accepted it, or Olivia was doing a great job of convincing her that their new foster parents were people to trust—not condemn.

Olivia had always had a sweet spot for Damian, but ever since that letter, she never left his side. They made breakfast together, folded clothes together, and cleaned the apartment together. When Damian wasn't away on business with the Allseers or coordinating defense strategies with the military, they went shopping together. At night, they'd talk about boys for hours. Sometimes, Sage spied Damian lying next to her on the bed, arms crossed behind his head, as he gave her some pointers and signs to look for in male counterparts.

"Boys are usually shy around their love interests and will say nothing," Damian said. "But you can tell because they avoid you. They are very insecure about themselves until they're ready to voice their feelings."

So Olivia liked a boy now? According to Damian, no. But that didn't stop her curiosity, or her wondering if she liked girls instead. She asked Damian which one she should go for, but Damian shook his head.

"That's not up to me to decide," Damian said. "You go with what your heart tells you."

Sage was so thankful for Damian because she wasn't alone in educating Olivia about the woes of adolescence and menstrual cycles. It didn't matter how many nieces Sage cycled through in her life—the talk about "bleeding from your private parts" wasn't bad, but the first time it happened was a mixed bag of emotions. Sage had experienced a shrug of shoulders to all-out bawling in her family. In Olivia's case, she got her first period one night when Sage and Damian were already asleep.

"Aunt Sage?" Olivia gave a coy little knock on the door. "Damian?"

Honestly, Sage hadn't heard it. Not until minutes later, when Olivia grew bolder with her cry. "A-Aunt Sage!"

Sage jumped. She was on Damian's back, hair everywhere, and completely startled. Without hesitation, she reached for the dagger in her nightstand and Damian grabbed his pistol from the drawer. She thought intruder, but it wasn't that at all.

"I-I think I got my period!" Olivia stammered.

Sage scrambled off the bed. She pulled on a shirt and threw a pair of pants at Damian. Still in underwear, she rushed out of the room and swept her little niece into her arms. "Show me," she said.

Olivia took Sage to her room. Candice remained idle in hers, either sleeping or texting without a clue that her sister had officially entered womanhood. Sage wanted a confirmation first, and Olivia showed her the bloodstains on the bed. Then she pulled down her pants and underwear, and there were no doubts.

There was a loud *pop!* that made Sage curse and Olivia scream. But the scream wasn't one of fear—not when Damian was waving around a sizzling champagne bottle with a stupid grin.

"Congratulations!" he chortled. "You are officially a woman now!"

Sage sighed. "Really, Damian? Champagne?"

"Why not? I say this calls for a celebration! It's not every day a girl gets her first period."

Damian had glasses for everyone, even Candice, who scrambled out of her bed at last to inquire about the noise. That's when Olivia, still without undergarments, twirled around her sister and exclaimed, "I got my period! I can use a pad now!"

Sage laughed. Olivia made it sound like so much fun. Was it, though? For some human females, it was hell. For Sage, it was worse than hell. That's why she was grateful that neither Candice nor Olivia experienced the periods she got.

Which reminded Sage: she hadn't gotten hers this year.

Candice had to show Olivia how to put the pad on her underwear. "You change it every three hours or so," she said to her. "Or else it can leak and—er—stain your clothes."

"Didn't it happen to you that time you had to present your geography project in sixth grade?" Olivia asked.

Sage remembered that day. Candice had called her right after school, crying.

"Do you remember when you got your first period?" Damian asked Sage, sipping champagne now.

"Yeah," Sage said. "Although I knew about it, it was so painful I thought I was dying. I got it right after a track meet in middle school. My mother had just picked me up, and Aurora noticed the stain in my pants. Kind of embarrassing, actually."

Damian arched a brow. "You were in track, darling?"

"Fastest in my class." Sage blushed some. She gave her champagne to Candice, and then Damian poured one for Olivia.

Olivia gasped. "I can, Aunt Sage?"

"Sure." Sage cleared her throat. "According to Damian, you're a woman now. So why not enjoy a drink, too?"

"Does that mean I can have babies?"

"Yes," Damian said at once. "Although, technically, you can't get pregnant during or right after your period. You're most fertile 12-14 days before your period starts, when you start ovulating.

'Ovulating' is a fancy word for when an egg is released from one of your ovaries. Did you know you are born with all the eggs you will release in your lifetime? At the time of birth, it's about two million, but it decreases by 10,000 each month before puberty."

"Oh ..." Olivia looked wondrous. "So how many eggs do I have now?"

"Around 300,000, but the numbers continue to drop as you age."

"And once I run out, I can't get any more?"

"Well, there are ways," Damian said. "There is, for example, in vitro fertilization where you are given another woman's eggs. This is mostly for women who can't conceive naturally or are too old to conceive."

"Does it hurt?" Olivia asked curiously. "To get another woman's eggs?"

"It depends on the woman, but discomfort can range from cramps to abdominal pressure."

"Ever considered gynecology, Damian?" Sage asked with a snort. "I think you know more about women than some doctors."

"Actually." Damian blushed a bit. "I was always interested in urology."

Right. The genital expert here.

"What's urology?" Olivia asked.

"For penises, Olivia." Sage rolled her eyes and Candice laughed.

"But men don't bleed, do they?"

"No, they have other problems. Like, if they can't perform during sex, then their whole world comes crashing down. Or if they can't pleasure their lovers, they become losers."

Damian cleared his throat. "You're not implying me, are you, darling?"

Sage shrugged, and that made Candice laugh harder. Olivia still had more questions.

"So now that I can have babies, how do I make sure I don't get pregnant?"

"You must abstain from sex or take contraceptives to avoid pregnancy," Damian said, still looking at Sage with a worried expression on his face. Sage wondered if it was truly about his sexual performance or the fact she hadn't bled this year. "When you're dating, of course."

"But what if I like girls?"

"Then you don't have to worry!" Damian said brightly.

"But no sex." Sage wagged her finger at Olivia. "Until you're eighteen or older. Understand?"

Olivia sighed. "Yes, Aunt Sage."

That night, no one went to sleep. They stayed up drinking champagne until morning came.

Sage didn't drink, though. She was pretty quiet, too, thankful that Damian and Olivia kept the conversation going without stop. Amazingly, they were still discussing reproduction, with Candice pitching in once in a while. Then Olivia asked about Enhanced women. Although Enhanced women lived longer, they still had a limited number of eggs. Sage knew it was only a matter of time before the conversation took that dreaded turn.

"But what about hybrids like Aunt Sage?" Olivia asked. "She only gets her period once a year! So how many eggs does she have left?"

"No one knows," Damian said happily. He opened a second bottle of champagne. "Hybrids haven't been studied yet." He served everyone another glass.

Sage wanted to scold him, but she didn't want to ruin the night. Eventually, Candice and Olivia got a bit tipsy and went straight to bed. Damian, on the other hand, practically finished the bottle himself. At least, those were his intentions until Sage confiscated it.

"That's enough," she said, now that the girls were out of earshot. "You're going to make yourself sick. You can't down so much alcohol when you're not used to it anymore. Get it?"

Damian sighed. He leaned back in his chair. "You're right, darling."

Sage didn't cap the bottle—she dumped it in the sink.

Damian gasped. "That's perfectly good champagne!"

"It's served its course," Sage said bitterly. "And I wouldn't want you tempted."

Damian didn't protest. Instead, he got up and walked over to her. He wrapped his arms around her waist. He laid his head on her back and sighed with content. "Darling … have you taken a pregnancy test?"

Sage froze. Damian must have felt her stiffen, for sure. That concerned him because he straightened up and pressed her for more.

"You told me you haven't gotten your period," Damian said. "Yet you were sick in Winterfeld."

Sage turned to him. She looked him in the face and whispered, "I've taken multiple tests. They all come out negative."

"I see," Damian said quietly. He held her cheek. "But you are not human. I imagine it wouldn't work the same. Have you felt different?"

Sage held her abdomen. She shook her head. "No. Other than the sickness and fatigue, but … not anymore."

Damian got on his knees. He held her hips. Face level with her flat belly, he leaned forward and pressed a kiss to it. "I understand you don't trust any of these doctors," he said. "I don't trust them, either. But if you feel you need a medical professional, then we'll go to Dr. X in Mousafeld."

Sage made a face. "That weirdo?"

Damian chuckled. "A weirdo, yes, but I trust him with my life. Sage, I don't want you to be afraid. If you are pregnant … and I know you're taking precautions just in case you are … well …" His eyes welled with tears. "I would be the happiest man in this universe."

Sage's eyes welled with tears, too. She didn't want to cry, but her emotions were a bit out of whack after Olivia's first period and the possibility that she was, indeed, pregnant. She just didn't know for sure. Couldn't know, nor understand if what she felt inside her was human …

Or monster.

Damian pressed his ear to her abdomen for a listen. But there was nothing to hear. If Sage was pregnant, she'd be eight weeks. Four weeks here, and four weeks in Winterfeld, when she had missed her period. It was still early for a heartbeat, but that was the thing …

"The babies that grew in her womb were in cocoons."

There wouldn't be heartbeats. There would only be dead silence because her babies were inside cocoons.

"They would be like Reina's," Damian said softly.

His words took Sage by surprise. Out of all the topics they had discussed since moving to Heart, Nova's findings on Reina hadn't been one of them. It seemed Damian and Nova really were close.

"I heard about the cocoons," Damian confirmed. "I think it was a surprise to all of us. No one expected a Squid pregnancy to generate such a thing."

"Do you think it was how I was born?" Sage whispered. "And how our babies will be born?"

Damian looked up at her. He gazed into her eyes with a seriousness in his own as he said, "And so what if they are, darling?"

"What if they become monsters?"

"Are you a monster?"

Right. Sage wasn't a monster. She was a hybrid. Reina had been human.

But so had Sage's mother . . . right?

"Are you hungry?" Damian asked, and Sage blushed.

"Maybe a little." She bopped him on the head, and he laughed.

"Then I'll make us a pizza." Damian got back on his feet and kissed her. He said nothing else about the potential pregnancy as he gathered ingredients from the refrigerator.

As for Sage, she did feel better. She smiled to herself knowing that she had Damian's support . . . although that had never been her worry. It wasn't so much his support, but his trust. That's what Sage worried about.

Why, though? Damian had never done anything to hurt or betray her.

But Agathe had. And that devious bitch wasn't all talk, either.

Regardless, those were thoughts that quickly dissipated when other issues took root in Sage's mind. Geoffrey and his recovery, for example, were always at the forefront. Sage spoke to Nova about any upcoming treatments, and there was good news to go around:

doctors were administering a brand new but effective antibiotic that was supposed to isolate and target the contagion. Nova called it a "Mega Antibody", or "MA" for short.

And not only did it do away with Red Fever, but it was supposed to enhance the recipient's immunity. Not that Geoffrey would become an Enhanced or anything like that, but he'd be cured and even stronger than before. While he wasn't exhibiting any Red Fever symptoms, Nova wanted him and the other hundred or so patients from the Silver Gears concert under strict observation. The Mega Antibody was too new and too raw to be trusted.

If Damian trusted Nova, then Sage did, too. That meant she could rest a bit easier when it came to Red Fever, although she still had to hire a medical professional to test customers at her restaurant. That was thanks to the Allseers, whom Sage avoided like the plague.

To her slight annoyance, Louis still came out to watch her train in the evenings. And while these were friendly matches against Damian, Mega Woman, Turtle, Eye Candy, and Rockstar, he still cheered her on.

Sage was skeptical as hell of the sibling Allseers, but she did know that Nova and Geoffrey were still alive and there was hope for the human population of Diamond City. That's why she gave in. A little. Instead of ignoring Louis, she smiled at him before racking her sword and returning to her apartment.

The strain was obvious, but Sage wasn't dropping her guard around anyone. Plus, she had Gertrude lurking in the corners like an overgrown bat. Once in a while, Gertrude even accompanied the girls around the capital for protection, when Justice and Mega Woman couldn't make it.

Sage hated it. Sometimes, she got the sneaking suspicion that they were conspiring behind her back. Damian would say that was all paranoia, because what sort of backstabbing schemes could anyone plan around the military?

Damian's brother, Blackburn, was still in custody. Thanks to Agathe, who had appointed judges to oversee the trials, he'd get a fair hearing and ruling. The more Sage thought about it, the more she wondered if Blackburn would be punished for his ... what, exactly? Torturing Damian? Hadn't that been the Allseer's will? Blackmailing Sage? Hadn't that been the council's will? Hadn't Blackburn just been following orders?

Sage grew weary. The restaurant, the military trials, Gertrude, the girls, Reina, and now all these Red Fever cases stressed the hell out of her. But she did have a small light at the end of the tunnel.

"Does Gertrude talk shit about me?" she asked Olivia one night after dinner.

"No," Olivia replied honestly. "She asks how you're doing. She asks about you all the time."

The month of Light was here in no time at all, and Sage could hardly believe it. Summer was her favorite season after winter because it meant spending time with her nieces on their break from school. It wasn't always all work at the restaurant, either— they went to water parks, museums, and scoured the Cut District for the best ice cream when they could. They usually left Bram doing all the work.

This year, though, the month of Light signified something different for Sage. The first was opening day at Two for Pizza, and Sage could hardly contain herself.

Damian and the girls were right by her side when it happened. Sage nearly exploded with happiness. It was the moment she had fought so hard for since Blackburn had taken her business and shut it down. Any thoughts of Squids and Reina dissipated like the wind. Geoffrey couldn't be here with her, but he was on Candice's video call.

Candice had her phone clipped on her belt like a body camera. That way, Geoffrey could see everything she saw. He spoke sometimes, too. "Wow, that's a nice-looking restaurant! Good luck!"

Candice and Olivia both had strained smiles on their faces. While there was always a bit of reservation in Candice since the

Agathe incident, she and her sister looked more tense than usual. The pizzeria certainly brought back memories of their father.

Even so, the girls weren't going to ruin Sage's moment of glory amidst *hundreds* of Cut District customers. The signs and banners some of them were holding all said *Give Us Pizza Now!* Everyone missed the comfort and simplicity of affordable gourmet pizza for lunch and dinner. There was so much to do and so many people to tend to that there wasn't time to bicker. The girls had pizzas to deliver and kitchen personnel to assist.

Damian, on the other hand, had customers to greet amidst annoying Red Fever checks. He had a flirty, easygoing way with people that astounded Sage. Today, he wasn't the vicious Warlord that cut down his enemies and tortured prisoners—he was an everyday citizen helping his wife succeed in the business world. No one knew who he truly was and what he had done to return to his city, not with his simple button-down, slacks, and boots. He looked every bit the Color District model, and it certainly encouraged young women (and men) to flirt back, to feel at ease, and to feel loved. One woman even swooned at the sight of him, making Sage roll her eyes. Another man kissed his hand. Damian winked at him. The cherry on top of the cake was when he kissed the doctor taking people's blood sample on the cheek.

The doctor jumped so high that he toppled off his stool. But the whole street was roaring with laughter, and even more customers flocked to the restaurant to see what was going on. More: they wanted a glimpse of Damian's beauty and how he got someone's face to turn the color of a tomato.

"Wow." Olivia marveled at what she was seeing from behind the register as Sage headed into the kitchen. "People really love him."

Flirty bastard, but Sage wouldn't have him any other way. Damian carried the restaurant the entire day, tending to customers and helping servers when things got crazy. It wasn't until closing time and the clean-up crew was wiping down floors that Damian swept Sage into his arms and pinned her against the wall, right next to the pizza tapestry.

"Damian!" Sage laughed as Damian kissed and licked her lips like a crazy dog. He held her legs and wrapped them around his waist as if he was about to hump her. He would have, too, if Sage didn't climb off of his body and push him back. "Not in public!"

"Why not?" he murmured, eyes ablaze. "Miriam doesn't mind a show. And neither does Jade."

Miriam scowled in her usual fashion as she mopped up the tiles. Jade was beet-red, trying hard to concentrate on wiping down the tables.

"Down," Sage commanded. "Before Candice and Olivia see you misbehaving. They'll think you're a sex fiend."

"And I am, darling," Damian purred. "I'm not ashamed of it. The question is: do they know *you're* a sex fiend as well?"

"I'm not."

"Please. I'm sure you're wet for me already."

Jade coughed loudly. Miriam continued mopping.

"That's because you instigate me," Sage hissed in his face, cheeks burning. "And we already went over this: you're damn irresistible. But unlike you, I can control myself until tonight—"

And then Sage remembered. She had completely forgotten that Damian was leaving today for the Color District to meet up with the wedding planner, Arian. It was to go over the itinerary for their wedding in the winter. That included a full tour of the entire district for the perfect venue, a thorough analysis of all the themes, color schemes, and costumes available, and an interview with all the chefs Damian wanted at the reception.

Darkness swept over Sage's mood. She really didn't want Damian to go. She would have accompanied him on this trip, but she had to stay here for the restaurant. The first few weeks were always the busiest, and Damian insisted that the wedding was a surprise. He didn't want her nosing into the extravagant plans he was coordinating for that day.

So they parted outside. It was starting to sprinkle, but Sage didn't care about the rain. She had her arms around Damian's neck with a quiet Candice and Olivia watching in the background.

"Two weeks is too long," Sage whispered into his hair.

"I know, darling. But coordination is vital." Damian held her face, forcing her to look at him. Into those dark eyes that twinkled with life. It was a twinkle that hadn't been there before. This was a Damian full of energy and vigor, but that didn't make it any easier to let him go.

Sage wasn't sure what was wrong with her, but her eyes stung with tears. The thought of losing him for two weeks was overwhelming. Her very soul cried for him and her body ached horribly. Maybe she was in some kind of frenzy, a feeling she had never experienced with Gregory. With him, their relationship had been mediocre. With Damian, it was so much more.

Or maybe this was the pregnancy. The hormones. They told her that having Damian so far away was dangerous for him and her. This was about survival.

"There's always phone sex," Damian teased.

"Why does it always have to be about sex?" Sage wiped at her eyes.

"Isn't that what it boils down to?"

Sage squeezed his balls, making Damian jump and hit the lamp post.

"Hey!" he huffed. "Those are sensitive!"

Olivia laughed. Candice crossed her arms, but she didn't smile. Geoffrey was still on video call, and he was grinning.

Sage shook her head. "I don't want you to go. I want you close to me. I have a horrible feeling in my gut."

She truly did. It was like facing an opponent and sensing they were hiding a weapon behind their back. Sage couldn't see it, but she knew it was there. Why did this two-week trip in the Color District feel like the biggest trap imaginable?

Damian embraced her again, despite his aching groin. "I'll come back every night, then," he said. "Just to see you."

Relief exploded in Sage's chest. A little. Until she realized that an ambush could happen during the day, too.

"I know that you are possessive of me," Damian cooed in her

ear, but he was serious when he added, "And I think it's for a reason. Instinct, possibly. Although I will admit that I'd throw a shit-show if you were to leave, too. The only reason I thought of leaving for a bit is because I want to surprise you, darling. To make our wedding day special."

"I know," Sage said quietly against his chest.

"Then I'll be back tomorrow night as promised." Damian held her chin. He tilted her head up. "Now lick me."

"I'm not a dog."

"Pretend."

"I'm going to squeeze your balls again."

"Can't you save it for the bedroom, where you can do more than just squeeze them?"

Sage laughed. She rubbed her abdomen with a hand. If she pressed hard enough, she could feel the cocoons. They were inside her.

"All right, darling?" Damian kissed her forehead and nipped her nose.

Sage had a hard time stepping back, but she had to. Damian already had his personal chauffeur at the end of the street, and he got in the car with one final look at her. Sage had her girls close by, crestfallen now that she wouldn't see Damian again until tomorrow.

"You should be excited!" Olivia chirped. "It's for the wedding, Aunt Sage. Right, Candice?"

Candice said nothing. Better that than insults, Sage supposed. Candice kept her thoughts to herself because she saw how depressed Sage got. When they returned to Heart, Sage's mood plummeted to the planet's core. She was in tears by the time Justice pulled up to the complex.

"Aunt Sage?" Olivia said worriedly, watching Sage wipe her eyes in the kitchen.

"I-I'm sorry," Sage croaked, ashamed of her emotional display. It wasn't a cry for attention—the girls knew that. That's why they suspected there was something horribly wrong.

Sage sat at the table and hid her face in her arms, shoulders trembling. She had no damn clue why she couldn't control her tears, but it was bad. Without Damian, she felt alone, miserable, and vulnerable. Candice was a comfort to her as Olivia got Damian on the phone. This was clearly not normal behavior.

"Darling, what's going on?" he asked her sincerely.

"I don't know," Sage said weakly. "I feel so bad. I have a horrible ache in my chest."

"I am starting to worry about you. Are you coming down with something?"

"I don't think so. I've never gotten sick. Outside of my period month, anyway."

"It could be anxiety, so why don't you take a shower and try to relax? It's been a long emotional day, and I know you're upset about me leaving."

"Come back to me," Sage whispered. "I want you close."

"And you will have me, but I can't exactly turn back now," Damian said. "I will return tomorrow as promised. I want you to do as I say and get in the shower. Don't hang up because I want to hear you."

"Damian, please listen to me this once. We can do the wedding plans another day—Geoffrey said he'd be willing to manage the restaurant when he gets out of quarantine—and we can go to Color then."

Damian was uncharacteristically quiet. Sage had never dealt with his silence, so she wasn't sure what it meant. Probably nothing good.

"I want it to be a surprise," he said at last. He was fighting to sound patient—Sage could hear the strain in his voice. "I really do. Can you seriously not control yourself for a day while I do this? I am going to see you tomorrow night."

"I'm not sure you're listening," Sage said. "I think you're in danger."

Damian snorted. "In danger? From what?"

"I don't know. But I have a really bad feeling, and I usually don't get this way unless there's an ambush."

"Sage, this is ridiculous. What ambush? I am around council members and military all day in Heart. I am going to Color for a damn wedding—not politics."

Exactly. It was in Color. Isolated.

Sage massaged her temple. Olivia rubbed her shoulder.

"Can you just trust me?" Sage said. "I wouldn't be asking if I didn't feel something was truly wrong."

"Darling, we can't go based off of 'feelings.' I believe you are upset because I am not there holding your hand—"

"Damian, I am telling you that there is an ambush. I'm not calling you to come back because I want you to hold my fucking hand—I have my nieces here for that."

"I can take care of myself, Sage," Damian said coldly. "I appreciate the heads up about whatever ambush lies in waiting for me, but I know what I'm doing."

Sage hung up the phone. She did so because there was no getting through to Damian at the moment. He wasn't going to listen to her, and Sage would rather save her strength. Emotionally, she was crumbling. Not just because Damian was absent, but because he had sounded . . . defensive.

Wedding plans? They could do that at any time. Damian wouldn't have had any problem turning back around and returning to her. But it was clear he wanted to do something in the Color District. Perhaps something that didn't have anything to do with the wedding.

"Aunt Sage?" Olivia said worriedly.

Candice remained by the doorway, arms crossed. She had a hard look on her face, as if she was angry at the world. Specifically, she was annoyed with Sage, who didn't care about what anyone else thought right now.

Sage took a shower. She made sure to scrub her body thoroughly, all over her restored muscles thanks to her training the past month. Despite the pregnancy and the cramps in her abdomen every once in a while, she felt strong. Her mind was also clear.

Damian was up to something.

Sage threw on a tank top and some shorts. It wasn't so much her desire for sex that depressed her—it was that sense of foreboding. Whether it was Damian or what was waiting for him in the Color District, Sage didn't know.

"Aunt Sage?" Olivia tapped on the door. "It's Damian. He wants to talk to you."

"Tell him I have nothing else to say to him," Sage said. "Take a shower and go to bed, sweetheart."

Olivia hesitated. But eventually, she withdrew.

Sage didn't have her phone, so she didn't have to worry about ignoring Damian's calls all night. She hated to be this way, but if her speculations were correct, then she knew two things with certainty:

Damian wasn't coming back tonight, no matter what Sage said to him. And he was at the Color District for more than just wedding plans. It was so damn obvious to Sage.

So Sage didn't sleep that night. A cold hard truth was seeping into her veins like a disease. It was infecting her from the inside out, destroying the false reality she had thought she was living in. The empty space on the bed behind her proved this had all been a farce. All their nice days and times together had been fake. Pretend. Agathe's words from so many months ago didn't leave any doubts when it came to that.

"He knows you're the Optimum. He knows what your blood can do. If he wants you, it's because of that. He wants to create more Enhanced."

Sage sat up slowly. She eyed the cold pillow that had never seen a head last night. She listened closely for a shower going in the bathroom, but there wasn't a sound. Candice and Olivia were chatting softly in the kitchen. Damian wasn't here to cook, so they had Fruity Tarts to munch on. Not the healthiest, but they tasted incredible.

"Aunt Sage!" Olivia greeted her with a hug and smile. Like her sister, she was in a white and gold uniform, the Royal Academy's colors. Both she and Candice were taking summer courses to catch up with their credits. The official school year was due to start in the fall. "How are you?"

"Fine," Sage said. She took a deep breath. "Damian's not back, is he?"

Olivia blinked. Candice remained stone-faced.

"Was he supposed to come back?" Olivia said. The braids in her hair were loose and a bit messy because Damian hadn't done them. Neither she nor Candice had anywhere near the skill he had. "I thought he was coming back later tonight."

"Yes, but there's something going on with him." Sage picked up her phone from the table. She had over thirty missed calls from Damian. The last one was at three in the morning. When she tried calling him now, it went straight to voicemail, so instinct told her one thing.

Damian had been kidnapped.

But by whom?

As dread bubbled in Sage's chest like nasty slop, one answer struck her hard.

Agathe.

If Damian was missing, then someone had taken him, someone who knew that he was the Warlord from Mousafeld. It came to Sage so quickly that she marveled at how she hadn't become a private investigator. Without so much as brushing her hair, Sage threw on a pair of pants and a coat. Then she stuffed her wallet into her pocket and strapped her sword to her belt. She had a backpack, too, stuffed with extra weapons and emergency supplies. This was all she'd need.

"Aunt Sage." Candice stepped away from the counter. She spoke in her most authoritative tone, as if she was taking care of a young child. She approached Sage with her brows drawn, an unpleasant twist to her scowl as if Sage were rushing out to meet her troublesome boyfriend. "Please stop. Where do you think you're going?"

"I'm going to find Damian," Sage said steadily. "He's been kidnapped."

"How on earth do you know that? He's supposed to be in the Color District until tonight."

"I had a feeling something was wrong, and it seems I was right. I just tried calling him now, but he doesn't answer."

"Maybe he doesn't want to be bothered."

Sage stared. That didn't sound right. Plus, Candice was behaving too coldly. Sage didn't want to acknowledge the reason behind Candice's attitude, so she addressed the heinous statement instead.

"Damian's a lot of things, but he has never felt 'bothered' by me."

"Can't you just leave him alone for Stars' sakes?" Candice spat. "Give him a chance to come back! You've literally been on his ass since you moved in together, to the point that he doesn't have a chance to breathe! He can't even complete the wedding plans without you crying over him. I don't know if you've realized it, but you've become such a clingy bitch, Sage."

Those words rang harsher than glass breaking.

Clingy bitch.

They hung foully in the air like a bad odor. They never left the room, sucking the oxygen out of every living person and making it hard to breathe.

Sage braced herself. It was instinct, a reaction to being insulted. Confronting her niece was part of being a parent, even if the words stung like a hornet's bite.

"Is that what you think I am?" Sage asked quietly. "A 'clingy bitch'? Because I'm on top of my family—including Damian now—and looking out for them?"

Candice shook her head. "It's not like you."

"That has *always* been me, Candice, and you know it. It's always me sticking out my neck, and I'm not complaining because I know it's what I have to do to protect the ones I love. Do you have any goddamn idea how many vipers are out there, especially that bitch, Agathe, who wants to manipulate the hell out of all of us?"

"You're always blaming Agathe," Candice said angrily. "But she hasn't done anything wrong! Are you mad because she told us about dad? That was your responsibility!"

"Fine, and I have already admitted I was wrong. But how dare she blame Damian for something he didn't do."

"He killed Poppa!" Candice exclaimed. "How can you possibly love him or fight for him—"

"AND DO YOU HAVE ANY PROOF OF THAT?!" Sage shouted, shushing the entire room. The ice maker in the freezer grumbled loudly. "Do you have any proof that it was *Damian* who killed Bram when it was a reported suicide? Who the hell is feeding you these lies? Oh, let me guess. Agathe."

"Lies?" Candice said. "Isn't it the truth?"

"Bram committed suicide, but that wasn't Damian's fault! We've already talked about this—"

"I don't trust him." Candice dabbed at her eyes, but maintained her glower. This wasn't a statement up for debate. "Poppa didn't commit suicide," she said. "He would never do that. *Damian* killed him. He killed him to get him out of the way, either on a revenge quest for you or to limit your allies."

There was still no proof. Even after the spiel from Justice and the heartfelt flowers from Damian, Candice didn't give two shits about Damian's innocence. It angered Sage that Candice would continue to condemn him like that. Perhaps Bram had betrayed them, but that didn't give anyone the right to end his life, and Damian of all people knew that. Blaming him for that was a huge insult.

Candice, however, couldn't take reality. She stormed out of the apartment in both frustration and anger. Sage remained standing there like an idiot, unsure of how to look Olivia in the face after that exchange with her sister.

"Did Gertrude tell you this?" Sage asked her quietly.

Olivia shook her head. The sorrow in her eyes said that she didn't believe the accusations either, but she couldn't know for sure without proof.

"Agathe."

Little by little, the tornado of dread grew in Sage's chest, making her dizzy. It got so turbulent that it interfered with her heart rate and breathing. It was horrible, but Sage's eyes started another fierce burn as her hands clenched into fists.

Damian. Always the monster. And now he was missing.

Sage didn't stop to cry or throw a tantrum. She knew Olivia could take care of herself, so she stomped out of the apartment. Like always, Justice was standing by the door, but he looked a little con-fused by how Candice had stormed down the hallway. He had Mega Woman to intercept her in the lobby. Right now, Sage didn't care about their tight security because it very obviously hadn't worked.

"Sage?" Justice said, on the phone with someone whom he put on hold. Was it Gertrude? "What's going on?"

"Haven't you heard?" Sage said tightly. "The Warlord's missing. And I think I know who took him."

CHAPTER 8

Lover

When times were desperate and Damian was in danger, Sage didn't stick around to ask questions like "Where's Agathe?" There were only two places the female Allseer could be: her quarters in the palace, preparing for meetings or entertaining guests from the districts, or the Color District, intercepting what she truly wanted. The more Sage thought about it, the more her heart sank.

"Give me the keys." Sage held out her hand to Justice. She was marching toward the parking lot. Justice's car was in the far east corner, but Sage's legs were long enough to make it there in just a few strides. "Give me the keys right now."

"S-Sage—?"

Sage drew her sword and pointed it at Justice's neck. She swore that if she had to impale him and yank the keys from his lifeless fingers that she would. "Give them to me right fucking now."

Justice handed them over. His handsome face was screwed up in agony, and not just because Sage would have killed him without much thought, but because his beloved leader was missing?

"I-I thought he was with Arian," Justice said. "My lady, please think this through—he stayed in the Color District for wedding plans."

"Sure." Sage got in the car. "But the problem is other people have plans for him, too. And if he's not picking up the phone no matter how many times I call him back, something is wrong."

"Perhaps he is sleeping?"

"I sleep with that man every night," Sage snarled. "And he jumps every time one of his phones goes off, which is why I have to personally silence them or shut them down myself. Don't tell me that sleep is the reason he doesn't pick up the damn phone, especially when he was trying to call me all night!"

"Perhaps he got caught up?"

Sage didn't have the energy to argue. Right now, she needed it to concentrate, so she ignored the rest of Justice's hopeless excuses and started the ignition.

Then she was racing out of the lot, swerving down the street until she got to an ascension station and shot five thousand feet into the air. She was no Speed Star like her dear Rick, but her instincts were excellent and they navigated the airways well. She had GPS to help her find the Color Dome, one of the Color District's iconic landmarks, and the place where Damian was allegedly making plans for the wedding.

Sage saw it from miles away. Its stained glass reflected a scope of colors when the sun was shining directly on it. It happened rarely because of all the rain, but when it did, it was the perfect Color District icon. Sage had been there once, would have loved to marry Damian there if that's where his heart had been set, but right now that giant kaleidoscope was hell here on earth. True hell, not the ones the Squids, according to the council, imposed on them.

Arian. Arian. Arian.

God, why hadn't Sage seen this sooner? Arian was Agathe's personal event planner, promoted once she had become the Allseer, and tasked with organizing this wedding of a lifetime between a revered exile and a half Squid. Of course, Agathe had no intention of letting that happen—not with the way she was eyeballing the

Warlord like a bloody piece of fucking meat. The only question was: how had they restrained him? Damian was no pushover in combat, and he certainly wouldn't have allowed people to capture him so easily, would he?

In the far recesses of her mind, Sage allowed doubt to wriggle its way in. It presented her with a number of scenarios. Maybe Damian had spent the whole night partying with his people, with the district he loved so much. Maybe he had ditched the "clingy bitch" and performed orgies with partners far more attractive than her. Was that why Damian had sounded so annoyed when Sage asked him to come back? This was his time to do more than just plan a wedding—this was his time to be free.

But Sage couldn't believe that. She couldn't believe that Damian would ever do that to her, not with the way he had been talking to her, soothing her, expressing his love and desire to comfort her no matter what.

"We haven't had our wedding vows yet, but I'll go ahead and say them now. I vow to always be by your side and protect you. To love you and cherish you no matter what happens."

Damian wouldn't have ditched her. One of his greatest qualities was his loyalty. Sage knew that no matter what these other assholes tried to tell her.

When Sage raced through the Color District border, she felt like she was flying in a very brilliant collage, a mishmash of colors that shouldn't have worked together but did. All the buildings had their own flare: some glittered like divas on stage, some played music that entertained blocks, some projected 3-D images all along its walls, and some featured different designs on an endless loop. Sage had forgotten how easily she could lose herself in these streets with all the shops, stages, and restaurants. It wasn't all about the fashion—some of the city's greatest chefs lived here. One time, Sage had eaten ice cream in the shape of Heart's palace.

No trembling. No crying.

It didn't matter how aggressively her mind conjured up images of she and Damian touring the district, doing everything and anything it had to offer. What their honeymoon would have been like in different outfits every hour of the day, living life the way they deserved to after so many years of fighting and heartache.

No one is going to take that away from me.

Sage clenched her teeth. Her trembling hands squeezed the steering controls so tightly that she dented them. The adrenaline was twice as hot as it had been when Wren and Taz attacked the capital, because now it was her fucking fiancé on the line and no jealous bitch was going to take him from her.

"Sage, please," Justice croaked to her. "Stay calm."

But Justice wasn't very calm, either. He was scared shitless of the possibility that the Allseers were conspiring behind their backs after all, the truce between Diamond City and its rebels be damned. The fear permeated the cabin like a bad stink, fueling Sage's anxiety further. Flashing colors didn't soothe any of them, and that Color Dome just a few more miles away portrayed certain death.

Death of Sage's future.

Beautiful, yes. The architecture was fantastic and intricate with its curvy pillars all meeting at the building's peak. The attendants in multi-colored suits were like crayons with heads, arms, and legs, running every which way to tend to tourists and important district officials alike. Overseer Casanova was known for his routine visits and extravagant shows in the Center Theatre, where the dome opened up to project its colors onto the night sky as performers went all out on stage.

Beautiful, yes. If it hadn't become her fiancé's prison. If Sage hadn't been about to engage in the battle of a lifetime with her entire future at stake.

Sage should have never come back to Diamond City, she realized too late. She had chosen this city over Damian, and that had been her mistake: seeking a life that she no longer deserved. God, how she loved her pizza restaurant, but she hated politics and manipulation even more.

She hated how security tried to stop her as she strode in through the front doors without an invitation, identification, or valid reason for being there other than to see Damian. Would future bride be enough?

"I'm getting married here." Sage waved Damian's appointment with Arian in the guards' faces. They were in all green, including their skin. It was bothering the hell out of her now, like she really was talking to a pack of crayons without a brain. "And I need to see my fiancé, who's apparently stayed the night."

The guards weren't going to give her a hard time now. While they seemed reluctant, they also got a call from some higher-ups that Sage was expected. She and whatever other rebel had tagged along with her.

No time to think. Sage's mission was to rescue Damian and get the hell out of here. She didn't let any other wayward thoughts enter her head to distract her. Samson had taught her better than that. That's what allowed her to focus, keep her gaze straight as the guards led her to a hallway on the right, one that circled around the theatre in the center.

The rugs were red and plush, absorbing the heaviness of Sage's boots with every step she took. She had Slainium bracelets on her wrist, Damian's sword at her belt, a few daggers in her jacket, and a gun strapped to her leg. No guard was brave enough to take the Optimum's weapons away, or this would turn ugly very quickly. Sage suspected that whoever was waiting for her was more interested in conversation than a bloodbath. Pretty soon, she found out why.

What Sage saw next was so much more painful. It was a sharp-as-fuck sword straight through her chest, destroying her sternum and puncturing a lung so that it filled up with liquid quickly and choked the hell out of her. Goddamn, that's what it felt like. Water rising up from her feet to the very last strand of hair on her head. In seconds, she'd run out of air and then she'd drown. That's what the enemy wanted.

To Agathe, this was a dream come true. What demented man or woman wouldn't dream of having a semi-comatose Damian sprawled on a chair without a clue where he was? Arian couldn't stop staring. With an erection that he didn't even bother to hide, he was probably wondering when it'd be his turn to ride one of the prettiest men he had ever seen. Agathe sure wasn't wasting any time, knees on either side of Damian's hips, lips all over his, hand in his hair as she held him to her and sucked his soul right through his mouth. Damian's hands were on her hips, his pants unbuttoned but not pushed all the way down. For Agathe, dry-humping a semi-erect penis was enough. And apparently, so was raping a drugged-up man.

Sage whipped out her gun so fast that she would have shot Agathe if it hadn't been for Justice. Yes, the fucker actually grabbed her and stopped her from attacking the bitch on top of her fiancé— man, did he have balls. Or maybe it was Sage who had balls because she stabbed her own comrade with her sword and then flung a dagger at Agathe, who wasn't going to stop until she climaxed. That's what Arian was there to do: engage Sage, stop the dagger in midair, and allow Agathe to finish her ride. She did so quickly.

"Oh, Stars…" Agathe panted, still swinging her hips against Damian's. She let go of his lips to throw her head back. While she was at it, she lifted her shirt so he could suckle her breasts.

Damian did. He captured a nipple in his mouth and gave a lazy suck. But Sage saw his eyes and she knew there was something wrong. That haze was awfully familiar, and it wasn't long until the vomit frenzy commenced.

Cupid's Arrow.

Now Sage finally noticed the bottles of liquor on the table with a few smashed ones on the floor. Agathe and Arian must have forced Damian to drink all that.

"Now, now, Sage," Arian said, with her dagger in his hand. "Let's not act rashly here—"

Sage's sword in Arian's chest, abdomen, and thigh incapacitated him immediately. Sage's arm around his neck choked him and the pathetic life all of Wren's Cells had given him. It also made him a hostage in the face of the military that flooded the room to defend their precious Allseer. But what truly had him screaming was his penis on the floor, when Sage sliced it right off like a sausage on a cutting board.

"Don't shoot." Agathe waved at her soldiers. She got off Damian, looking annoyed at all the bile on her dress. She had to wipe it off because servants were too petrified to move. She gritted her teeth, covered up her naked breasts, and fixed what she could of herself. "We don't want to kill her."

"Let him go," Sage said, still holding Arian to her chest. She kept her eye on Damian, who threw up some more.

God, after all the rehabilitation he had been through ... Now, he'd have to start all over again. Traces of Stars in Cupid's Arrow were minimal, but there. Any amount of it would set him back a lot. Somewhere in his foggy brain, he knew it, too. But that wasn't why a veil of shame fell over his face like a curtain. It was like a waterfall starting from his head all the way down to his toes. It pulled him down into an abyss, especially when he looked at Sage and made eye contact at last.

Damian had heard and felt *everything.* And he had been helpless to defend himself. All because he didn't have a shred of resistance when it came to Cupid's Arrow. Not after so many months of sobriety. He wasn't strong like Sage was.

These tiny moments felt like hours. Sage communicated with her eyes, indicating to Damian that that wasn't true. The addiction had destroyed his body, which had yet to fully recover, and Agathe knew that. Exploited it. That's why she was so high and mighty now, prancing around like a ballerina on stage, the spotlight on her. The bile, perhaps, was her trophy.

"I'm not letting him go," Agathe said sincerely. "He's mine, Sage. When he stepped into Diamond City, he came for me—not you. He took *me,* not you. Even now, look at him. He came here of his own free will, had a few drinks with me and Arian, and chatted about the wedding. I was very sincere with him, so I asked why he was marrying you." She scowled. Her face wrinkled up, as if she had stuck her head inside a litter box and taken a whiff. "I think he told me the truth. He wants to bed you and have babies, strong hybrids that can survive in a host until they're ready to be extracted and used for battle. It's the only chance we'll stand against the Lolligo. Am I wrong?"

Arian slumped in Sage's arms. He was dead. Not so much because blood was spurting out of his dick, but because the Slainium had already run its course and eaten up his Cells. Sage didn't dare drop him, though. She wasn't going to twitch amidst this intensity.

"I swear to God," Sage whispered. "That if you don't let Damian go, I am going to cut off your head and staple it to the wall by its hair. Then I'm going to do the same to all your friends who are pointing their guns at me. How fucking dare you, Agathe."

Agathe blinked her large eyes. "Sage, how can you say that? Damian was the one who came here!"

"He didn't come here to have sex with you."

"He did! I swear it—he came here of his own will to talk to *us*! Why can't you believe it? Because you think he's loyal to you? Haven't I been telling you this all along—he doesn't want you for you— he wants you because he wants your children."

"He didn't come here to have sex with you," Sage said.

Agathe laughed. "Please." She served herself a glass of wine from their table of liquor. Sage recognized the bottle instantly.

Dated year one, for the very first year Diamond City had unified its districts, with glittery smooth contents? That was not wine. That was strong-as-hell Cupid's Arrow.

That was Blackburn's stash.

"You are so delusional, Sage," Agathe went on with a chortle. The head of Arian's penis might have been part of the carpet. "I guess I can sort of understand—the Warlord is so very charming. Handsome. And the sex . . . well, we haven't even had intercourse yet. You just had to ruin everything."

"Give him to me."

Agathe nodded at Damian. "Then let him get up and take you away if he really wants you."

"Give him to me."

Agathe was waiting for Damian, but that only made Sage angrier.

"GIVE HIM TO ME, AGATHE!" Sage exclaimed. "Right fucking now, damn it! You think he's going to get up after you poisoned him?! Like he has a choice in any of this?"

"I didn't poison him!" Agathe yelled. "Stars! Can someone pull up the damn footage from this place so that she can believe me—Damian came here of his own will!"

Sage still didn't let go of Arian, even though he was dead. As some of the attendants in the room ran to fetch the desired footage, she kept her eyes on Agathe, trying so hard not to glance at Damian, who kept throwing up all over himself. She felt her heart breaking with every minute that passed, because a small piece of her actually believed the bitch who told her that Damian had come here willingly. Not only to discuss wedding plans, but to down a few drinks and engage in some wild sex with whomever he could. But why?

Why Agathe if he couldn't get his dick up with her? Why would he have sex with her just because, all to betray Sage, someone he claimed he loved? That's the part that didn't click in Sage's head—and that's what made her believe that this was one horrible set-up.

One of the attendants stepped up to Sage with a screen. On it was footage from last night, midnight, about half an hour after Sage had fallen asleep. This was the view of the courtyard, in which the taxi had pulled up on the driveway and opened its back door to let Damian out. She saw him walking—not in handcuffs, not with a gun to his head, and not with a blade to his throat—toward the building. Then the view shifted to the lobby, and there was Damian again, accompanied by Arian, who had been waiting for him at the entrance. Then the two of them strolled down the hall to this very room, where Damian had taken a seat in the chair and served himself a few drinks, Agathe an appropriate distance away.

At this point, Sage didn't want to see any more. She had already caught the tail-end of what excessive drinking had led up to, and she surmised that's why tears welled in Damian's eyes.

They trailed slowly over his cheeks. His fingers twitched on the armrests. His shirt and pants remained half buttoned, with not a whole lot of skin to see. Agathe hadn't made it that far.

"Well, Warlord?" Agathe said lazily, sipping her wine. "Aren't you going to say anything before Sage kills me on a false accusation?"

Damian couldn't speak. Or he chose not to. Right now, he needed a hospital, but Sage wasn't sure she had the will or the determination to take him there. Not when she felt a squirm in her belly, and a sharp pain attacked her side. It was enough to put a picture in her head, one of a worm wriggling around its cocoon. Soon, it'd hatch into a butterfly. One she'd have to protect with her life.

"It's not a false accusation," Sage said steadily. "As far as I'm concerned, having sex with someone who's under the influence is rape. He didn't have a choice."

"But he did!" Agathe yelled. "And the main witness is dead on the floor! Stars, Sage, I sat on his lap and he kissed me because he wanted to show me how! Then he told me I could hump him, and so long as there was no penetration, it wouldn't be cheating—"

Sage pushed Arian to the floor. His body slumped in a pool of its own blood. Somewhere behind her, Justice was still choking on himself. He had a large amount of Slainium to pump out of his body, but he wanted to see this too much to leave.

"You!" Agathe snapped her fingers at one of the servants. "Right it was willing? The Warlord gave me permission!"

The servant, who was still staring at the dead body of someone she used to tend to, nodded. "Y-yes, Allseer. It is true."

Maybe if Sage saw the rest of the footage, she could confirm that Agathe was telling the truth. But there was still something so horribly wrong with this set-up. Was there a reason why Damian wasn't saying anything? Why wasn't he defending himself?

Because he can't defend himself, you idiot! said a voice in Sage's head. *It's all fucking true!*

"It's not true!" Justice choked from the floor. He had to get help and fast, but he had to say this first. "The Warlord would *never* betray you, Sage! This is a set-up! They got you all the way out here because they want to kill you!"

"Shut up!" Agathe spat. "I don't want to kill her—we need her!"

"Any plans they have for you would be worse than death!" Justice exclaimed.

Clearly. Sage had already known and accepted her fate in Diamond City. Staying here was no longer an option for her, but she wasn't worried about that. It was always her family and friends—the girls and the rebels—who'd have to fend for themselves. How much power did Louis have over his sister? Was he anywhere near as cunning as she was to keep control of the city?

Sage got chills whenever she remembered the Agathe from Mousafeld, the one who had been homebound in a cottage while the Warlord went off on dangerous missions. Sage remembered the conversation in which Agathe had claimed the Warlord was evil for wanting to spread power. Sage remembered the tears that had spilled from Agathe's eyes as she confessed that her father had wanted Sage for reproduction. Perhaps Agathe had not had much say in Sage's fate back then, but she was the Allseer now and power changed everything. Enhanced weren't enough to fight the Squids, but hybrids would be. Sage got to show them why.

Right now, Sage had to put her family in the hands of a few trusted individuals. She had to believe that Louis was genuine enough to fight for what was right, and that everyone she cared for would be safe somehow. Sage had her own fair share of trials and tribulations to face. Living in the Outskirts was dangerous, especially with how much more aggressive the Squids were lately. Besides, Agathe wanted Sage—not her family. What good would hostages do her if she couldn't locate Sage?

"S-Sa . . . ge . . ." Damian croaked.

I'm not sure what to believe. Sage closed her eyes. *I don't understand why you drank Cupid's Arrow. Why you allowed Agathe to have sex with you. Either way, if I show them that I care about you, they'll use you against me. I have to pretend that I believe them.*

Sage opened her eyes. She held his gaze. Ever so slowly, she dropped it to her abdomen. It was as flat as a board, but there was life within. More than one, she felt.

Damian's eyes widened. His fingers curled over the armrests, clenching it, as he sought the power to get to his feet. But Sage had already turned around, picked up Justice, and stepped out of the room.

"Sage!" Agathe exclaimed. "Where do you think you're going?"

Sage had to get to the car.

"Do you think you can just walk in here and cause a scene? Kill Arian, Color's most influential designer, and just *leave*?"

Keep going. Keep walking.

"SAGE!" Agathe exclaimed with as much power as she could muster, bursting into the hall with Damian's vomit for all to see. "DON'T MAKE ME SHOOT!"

"Sage!" Justice croaked. "F-Forefathers—leave me! Leave me, damn it!"

"Seize her!" Agathe shrieked to the militants and guards around her—anyone that would listen. "SEIZE HER NOW!"

Sage threw Justice over her shoulder and ran. Gunshots erupted all around her, so Sage fired her arm toward the ceiling. It stretched into a massive tentacle that she used to tie around one of the chandeliers. Like a slingshot, Sage jumped into the air, over most of the bullets and energy waves, and landed in front of the double doors. From there, she ran to her car still in the driveway, using her body as a shield to spare Justice any more Slainium, and clambered into the front seat. She threw Justice to the passenger side, started the ignition, and pressed the ascension button so quickly that their eardrums nearly burst from the sudden change in altitude.

"Sage!" Justice choked. "They're coming for us!"

Yes, they were. All of Agathe's lackeys, who had seen Sage kill Arian as well as escape the dome in a hurry, were after her now, and they weren't going to spare any ammunition. This wasn't a runaway lover they were hunting down—this was the most dangerous being in all of Diamond City—and she had just shown everyone there was more to her physique than super strength and speed.

Justice wasn't strong enough to bring it up now. Plus, it wasn't appropriate when they were soaring through the air and Sage was driving this thing from side to side as if she were playing a simulator at a movie theatre. Alien Planet was the only game she had been able to beat her nieces at.

As Sage drove, she picked up her phone. "Justice, please call Gertrude and tell her what happened. Tell her not to panic. There's a chance Agathe will go after the rebels if she feels she can't control them, but I think as long as Damian cooperates, they'll be safe."

"He won't cooperate!" Justice croaked. "Sage, don't you know? He loves you! H-he didn't do this!"

Maybe not, but he had certainly dug himself into a hole by visiting the Color Dome. Then again, could any of them have predicted an innocent visit becoming a life-or-death situation?

I did, Sage thought to herself. *I felt it.*

Sage had told him there was an ambush. She had seen the viciousness in Agathe's eyes that day at the medical facility. She had known Agathe was going to try something, and Damian hadn't listened to her.

Why hadn't he listened to her?

Candice had called her a "clingy bitch" who couldn't go a few hours without holding her teddy bear. Damian must have been upset at the thought of ditching his wedding plans and returning home to coddle her.

Maybe. But now the situation was so much worse. Losing Damian forever set Sage's soul on fire, and it hurt. It felt like bad acid reflux that shot up her esophagus and dribbled over her chin. Sage had to wipe her mouth as she got Candice on the phone and said, "Stay close to Gertrude and look after your sister. Do you hear me?"

"Aunt Sage?" Candice panted. "What's going on?"

Sage wasn't going to say. Right now, she was so fucking confused that she didn't know up from down. She felt like this was one grand scheme—that even if Damian had drank Cupid's Arrow and had had sex with Agathe of his own free will, that this was all done on purpose. Perhaps Damian had already known that she was pregnant, and luring her to the Color Dome had been his way of finally capturing her.

"Sage!" Justice wailed as Sage took a sudden dive, from ten thousand feet in the air to street level. Weaving in between buildings was her only shot of making it out of the city in one piece. Before Heart could mobilize its heavy-duty forces, Sage was zooming into the Circular Forest and crashing into branches galore. Each one of them smacked the windshield and scraped the sides, whittling her car into trash that didn't go much farther. It all ended when she crashed headfirst into a protruding branch and got bark through her brain.

"Sage!"

Her surroundings were blurry. The smoke from the airbags stunk so badly. The ringing in her ears got louder.

"Sage!"

Justice grabbed her arm—Sage felt it. He pushed her head back and yanked out the branch. He snapped it, freeing her somewhat. He didn't care about being careful because he already knew this was a flesh wound for her and the military was right on their asses. He had to be quick about lifting her body and escaping through the forest, covering as much ground as possible before collapsing from exhaustion.

Justice was dying. His handsome face looked like that of a corpse's, all sucked up and dry as the last of his Cells faded. His true age and disposition showed so clearly, and it was one of the saddest ways to die. All the borrowed years caught up to him in those moments, and he seemed to accept this was his end because he didn't move.

"Sage," he whispered as Sage got on her knees and grabbed a dagger. "There's something I have to tell you."

"You don't have to tell me anything right now." Sage sliced her wrist open. It was the quickest way to get blood into Justice's body, so she pressed her arm against his mouth, silencing him, and let it fill him with life.

Sage tried not to look at the stab wound on his side. She certainly hadn't meant to do that, but she couldn't blame herself. She had lashed out in anger, a reaction to the worst sight she had ever seen in her life. The very thought of Agathe humping Damian made tears burn her eyes, and she actually let them fall as Justice sucked on her blood like a madman.

This was temporary. Sage's Cells would save him until the Slainium destroyed them, too. Then Justice would need more blood to replenish them. That was fine. Sage could survive doing this so long as Justice did. Somehow, they'd have to get the Slainium pumped out of his body. Dr. X was so far away, but Sage was resourceful.

Mousafeld was way south, hundreds of miles from here. Further north was the base of the Roaring Mountains. If Sage could make it back to Winterfeld, perhaps she'd stand a chance of finding Tyrus and Herman, the only two Squids that she could trust, according to Samson. Maybe they had a way of extracting the Slainium, too.

"Sage . . ."

Justice had stopped drinking.

Sage gasped. Why?

She noticed the blood had failed to bring back the youth he had lost in those moments of near-death. His hair was still dark, but there were hints of grey; his face was wrinkled, with dark blotches in some places. He had aged tremendously in a short time, and no amount of Cells would reverse the damage. Justice didn't care about that, though. He was looking at her in earnest, as if he truly were about to die soon and had a limited amount of time to recite his final words.

"It's not going to work," he whispered.

Sage blinked. What?

Justice took a deep breath. When he exhaled, Sage could hear every bone rattle inside him. He deflated like a balloon, as if the life were continuing to seep out of him through a hole.

"Take care of your children," he said. "They don't deserve to be soldiers in this war."

"Justice." Sage sliced her wrist again. "More blood—here—"

Justice declined her wrist. He shook his head at her. "It won't do any good. Please ... don't waste your strength."

"Justice—"

"My name is Humberto."

"Drink more of my fucking blood, damn it!" Sage yelled.

But Justice refused. He shook his head and turned away. He took another raggedy breath and said, "My family—we come from a long line of warriors. From before the Lolligo invasion. From before there were Lolligo at all."

Sage held her breath. She didn't want to miss a single word.

"Sanchez," he whispered weakly. "That's my family name. All my ancestors never stopped telling the story of how we fought for our country's independence. Have you ever heard of Mexico? In Central America?"

Sage had, but this wasn't the time to talk about history—

"We fought against this country called Spain from across the ocean and liberated our people in 1821. I-I remember that year for some reason—I've never forgotten—and then there was 1846, the Mexican-American War, and then the defeat of Santa Anna, a horrible dictator, and then a civil war—"

"Can you stop?!" Sage exclaimed.

Justice exhaled. "There's more to this life ... than just this. Diamond City, Allseers, and Lolligo. There's a whole history of people, Sage. We have to make sure we don't forget. I don't have any children ... but please remember me."

"I-I will," Sage croaked.

Justice kissed her bloody hand. "I love you, Sage. And I was a fool for never telling you how much I admired your bravery. I couldn't get in the Warlord's way. Trust him, Sage. You know he loves you, too."

Right now, Sage didn't know how any of this was love. She didn't know anything past this pain. She cried for Justice, and it hurt so damn bad.

So far, worse than anything she had ever felt before.

CHAPTER 9

Survival

Sage prayed. She didn't do it often, and never to the Squids. Once in a while, she asked God for help and guidance.

Having lived over a hundred years and fought in so many battles, Sage often wondered if this had all been planned by a higher being. Was there some kind of deity watching from above, judging their actions and values?

Sage didn't know. She liked to believe it, because she refused to bow to anyone here on earth. There had to be someone or something better out there, an entity who had a ton more power than any human or Enhanced did, who was kind enough to allow them freewill and offer them solace in times of need, and who was sentient enough to feel disappointment whenever someone strayed from the path of righteousness.

And Sage was that someone right now. She had gotten Humberto killed. She had been acting so rashly and selfishly lately, and it wasn't like her at all. Samson would be so disappointed. Maybe love was making her reckless. Or maybe it was the pregnancy.

Sage clutched her abdomen. Whenever she did, Reina popped into her mind. The snapping bones and the squeals. The blood.

Sage sat by Humberto's grave for some time. Days, maybe. She fell into a meditative state, between prayer and nightmares of what her babies might look like. Exhaustion was a key factor, too. She didn't move because she didn't have to. There was water and a few Fruity Tarts in the car, but Sage didn't get up until she had the will to.

Her legs shook like crazy. Her breaths were painfully tight, as if she had run a marathon. Her steps were unsteady until she calmed herself. She ate, pulled on a spare jacket from the backseat, and grabbed her backpack. She crushed her phone with an easy squeeze of her hand and threw it on the ground. She had lost signal a long time ago, but she still didn't want to leave any traces of her whereabouts. She had her sword, guns, and daggers, too. Hopefully, she wouldn't be needing them. She had to travel north then follow the Roaring Mountains to Winterfeld. There, she expected to find the Squids.

A trek through the Circular Forest took about three days. Sage was fit and savvy enough to survive the plummeting temperatures at night and any animals that happened across her camp. She no longer feared the Twig Man because it reminded her of Samson. It hurt so much more than it scared her.

Most of all, though, Sage thought of Damian. She wondered where he was right now and if he was barreling through the Circular Forest looking for her. He and Agathe shared a common purpose, so they were probably working together to achieve it. Sage knew it was the only reason Damian was a free man today: no one underestimated the Warlord's ability to claim what was his, and when Sage was the target, there was no one better for the job. Whether or not his interests truly included Agathe didn't matter to Sage anymore. She only cared about his well-being and liberty. Perhaps an endless search for her would save his life in the long run—it'd keep him in Agathe's good graces.

Sage weaved through the forest with caution. Once in a while, aircrafts zoomed overhead or a search squad got a bit too close for Sage's comfort. She kept still or to the shadows until it was clear.

She could hold her breath or quiet her vitals until she completely blended in with the silence. Out here, she was comfortable until she reached the last line of trees.

She looked out at the endless blankets of snow that led to the Roaring Mountains in the distance. So far north, it didn't matter that it was summer. A check of the skies told her that there weren't any aircrafts on the lookout. There weren't any clouds, either. Sage looked behind her, listening for movement. It had been five days since her escape from Diamond City, so someone had probably found her trashed car by now. Maybe even Humberto's grave. She had written his name with the pebbles she'd clawed out of the ground.

Then Sage ran. Her boots were high enough that she could glide through the snow without freezing her toes off. Plus, her body temperature adjusted quickly. A sprint out here was like one around the track at her gym.

One time, Samson had made her run for a day straight. Anything more than six hours was a nightmare, but Samson would cut off a limb if she stopped. He knew how to make it grueling, far worse than any annoying side stitch or muscle cramp.

That's what Sage thought of as she traversed the Outskirts: Samson and his coaching, his brutal but helpful ways of making her stronger and prepared for situations like this, where she had nothing but her legs for survival.

Twelve hours later, Sage stopped for some rest in a rundown tractor barn. The trails out here were gone, and the farms were abandoned. There was nothing but white, and Sage wasn't sure she was close to Winterfeld yet.

That was fine. Sage still had plenty of Fruity Tarts and water for a week, if she rationed everything appropriately. She got a fire going then took a walk around the inside of the barn. There were stalls for horses and a pen for sheep. A hole in the roof let some snow blow in. The wind whistled, but Sage heard noises. Miles away, but they were there.

Sage grabbed her sword and peered outside. She could see

nothing past the darkness. It wasn't movement she looked for, though—it was sound. There was definitely something happening close by, but far enough to deem this place safe. For now.

Then, slowly, with every passing second, Sage realized something. A cold, harsh realization dawned on her.

There must have been a village or town close by. Possibly, also abandoned. But why? What had driven the people away? Sage had never been this far west of Winterfeld, so she didn't have a clue what was out there, but instinct played a vital role in keeping the dangers of where she was alive. Diamond City's lack of Outskirts exploration was always because of the Squids. Nova had told her so many times that women went missing too often. And the Squids that had been lurking in the woods that night in Winterfeld? They had to have come from somewhere . . . and not all of them were friendly.

Sage tightened her grip around her sword. Go through or around the town? No movement, no vehicles, but there was sound. Shuffling. Groans. Creaks.

"Damn it," she cursed, more at her own recklessness than at the danger that was out there. She couldn't turn away because answers to her billion questions about the Squids were too alluring. Confronting Squids was stupid, but there weren't any nearby. Only what they had left behind. That much, Sage knew.

Steeling her resolve, Sage started her trek toward the abandoned town she still couldn't see. It didn't take long to find the source of the noise she had detected: a four-legged figure was running right at her. This was no wolf or bear—at least not any that Sage had ever seen in her life—this was a monster.

Pink and fleshy with legs the size of tree trunks and body as slick as a bloodhound's. Its eyes were amber, glowing in the darkness, and its snout housed a series of teeth that could cut through steel like an impenetrable blade. Blood and saliva dribbled everywhere, an indication that it hadn't been long since its last meal, and it was here for another course. Sage noticed small tits in its underbelly, so this was a female, whatever-it-was.

The roars that left this monster's throat were powerful. They didn't just shake the ground—they rattled Sage's bones, throwing off her concentration. The smell from this monster hit Sage in the nose, too—coppery and pungent, like a corpse left to ferment in the sun. This thing was very much alive, though, and she tried her hand at meal number two by lunging for Sage's throat.

Sage ducked, slashed the monster across the face, and tumbled out of harm's reach. The monster sprouted two thick tentacles from her back, slimy and gross, that she used to swat at Sage from a distance. Sage sliced them both in half, making the monster whimper, and drove forward for the kill only to stop last moment.

That's because the monster was on her side, panting. She could regenerate her tentacles, so that wasn't why she was out of breath. It took a certain scent for Sage to realize that this beast was pregnant.

Sage sighed. She lowered her sword and sheathed it. No matter how ugly and aggressive this thing was, Sage didn't have the heart to end her life now. With a glare of her own at the amber eyes gazing at her, she turned around and walked away. Dumbass, giving her back, but there was no way she'd sleep at night with that guilty conscious.

"You're about to have pups," Sage said out loud. It's not like the monster could understand her, but she said it anyway. Fair warning. "Best not to go attacking strangers that can kill you quickly. Assess your opponents better next time."

The beast whimpered. Was that an admission of her mistake? Probably. How many stragglers out here were powerful Squid hybrids?

With the beast no longer a threat, Sage grew more wary of the town she had come from. Clearly, it was a place that this monster had claimed as her territory for pup-bearing. Sage didn't look back, but she felt the amber eyes scouring her, unsure if they exuded anger, frustration, gratefulness, or all of the above. She didn't intend to destroy any habitat, but she quickly changed her mind when she finally reached that elusive town even Damian hadn't pinpointed on his Outskirts map.

It was a town visibly less advanced than ones like Winterfeld or Wolfeld. Like the barn, buildings were either wood or concrete. Street lamps had failed to pass the test of time, either broken or rusted from everlasting snow. Streets were overrun by weeds and cracked in a lot of places. Cars couldn't fly thousands of feet in the air like the ones from Diamond City—they were lucky to have ever run at all. Towns out here were pretty self-sufficient, but some were more equipped than others.

And some were better prepared for invasion than others.

And there was a price to pay if they weren't.

Corpses everywhere. All women. In houses, stores, restaurants, and offices that had become makeshift labs from hell. The Squids clearly hadn't cared for aesthetics when their objective was reproduction. When the women in this town had failed to deliver, they had taken their experiments elsewhere without a single look back.

What the fuck.

Sage threw up in the snow. There was no one around but the beast, who took a seat near the electronics store, to watch the intruder make an even bigger mess of this place. Perhaps the monster had been tailing Squids until she got pregnant and decided to stay somewhere secluded for birthing.

As desensitized as certain animals were, how could anyone or anything hope to give birth in a place where every womb was broken and every child was dead? Either shot down, cut in half, or completely stillbirth from lack of a suitable placenta?

"God!" Sage sobbed, clutching her head. "Please, God! Please!"

Please what?

"Please t-take these women . . . t-take care . . . Oh, God . . ." Sage sobbed some more.

She had to be honest with herself: these women and all these children were dead.

"Don't let this be me . . . p-please don't let this be me . . ."

The smell was too much. Paired with the sight of wide-open abdomens and skeletal corpses with faces frozen in time, Sage had to run. She tripped over herself on the way out, making a big-ass target of herself in the face of the monster still watching her from her spot near the store.

That town was too much—too goddamned much. What if that had been Candice and Olivia? What the fuck would Sage have done if Samson hadn't saved them?

Sage sobbed some more. She fell face forward on the snow, bawling for the entire Outskirts to hear. She screamed for Samson because he was the only one who could help her now.

Or could he? What sort of help were these Squids giving these women? They were all dead!

"Yo!"

Sage didn't hear someone calling her until she noticed a snow-mobile with a woman on top barreling across the Outskirts.

"Are you well?!" cried the woman, waving her arms like a crazy person.

"Sonia!" scolded another woman on a second snowmobile, coming up behind her partner. They were both Enhanced. Not only could Sage smell it, but no human was brave enough to wander the Outskirts on their own like that. "What the fuck are you doing— don't talk to her!"

"Dude, she's lost! And crying in the snow! She's probably seen Hellfeld and thinks it's hopeless, so chill out, L. No pun intended."

"We don't know what she is!" L cried above the humming of her engine. "What if she's a Squid?"

"Squid?" Sonia snorted. She wasn't afraid, and she proved it by climbing off the vehicle and raising her goggles. She had a nose piercing and a few lip rings. Her skin was white and splotchy in some places from the cold. This woman was used to this weather, though—Sage had a feeling that she rode that snowmobile on both snow and land. "Please. She's one of the hottest women I've ever seen—no offense, babe."

L rolled her eyes, but was cautious enough not to hop off her snowmobile. She watched from a distance as Sonia stepped over to Sage.

The moment Sonia got too close, the monster from Hellfeld let out a roar and jumped forward. Actually, it lunged at Sonia, so Sage threw out her arms and captured the beast in a tight headlock. A snapping jaw said she would have torn Sonia's throat out.

"Whoa—fuck!" Sonia cried, scrambling back. "What the hell is *that?!*"

"Get back!" L raised her rifle, possibly loaded with Slainium bullets. It didn't seem like these women were unprepared if they were ravaging fields all day long. L got ready to shoot—

"Stop!" Sage raised a hand. "Stop, please—don't shoot—s-sorry!" She kept the monster back, getting a good whiff of the blood, sweat, and a strange glossy mucous that covered her entire body. "Would you stop?!" she scolded the beast, who whimpered and stopped squirming instantly. Once again, Sage could have snapped her neck. In choosing not to, Sage got the beast to back down.

"Whoa," Sonia breathed in awe. "Is that Fido?"

Sage blinked. "Fido?"

"Yeah. Your dog." Even Sonia didn't believe her own question. But out here, with a town full of dead women, anything was possible.

"It's—*she's*—not my dog." Sage cleared her throat. She finally let go of the monster, who sat down on her haunches and closed her jaw. The amber eyes pierced Sonia's and then L's. Was she examining these people? "I found her hanging around that town. She's pregnant."

"Oh, wonderful," L sang, waving her hands. "Pregnant, so she's going to give birth to more mutant freaks. Nice."

Sonia shushed her and turned back to Sage. "Are you hurt?"

"I'm devastated," Sage admitted, still kneeling on the snow. She really didn't have the strength to get up at the moment.

"Yeah." Sonia scowled. "L and I don't drive through these parts often. They always give me the creeps. Reminds us of why we have to be careful."

"So you're from around here?"

"Centerfeld," Sonia said. "Largest town in the Outskirts. We've become a force twenty thousand strong now."

Twenty thousand? Damian would have salivated for numbers like that. Sage was inclined to ask if the Warlord had ever paid them a visit, but Sonia beat her to another question.

"And where are you from?"

"Diamond City," Sage said curtly. "I escaped." She got to her feet. "I'm out here looking for a friend who lives by Winterfeld."

Sonia arched a brow. Her partner waited patiently on the snowmobile. "Maybe not such a good idea to be wandering around here by yourself? Or without a vehicle? I mean, you said you 'escaped', because I figured that Diamond City wouldn't let its residents just waltz into the unknown."

"That's right." Sage didn't mean to be so curt, and it would be a good idea to follow the couple to wherever this Centerfeld was, but there was no way she could go anywhere without resolving the shit-show of dead women in Hellfeld. Sage learned that the town's true name was Smallfeld. Indeed, the most vulnerable.

"Whoa, wait!" Sonia trudged through the snow after Sage; she jumped when Fido growled at her. "Y-you're going back there? To *bury* them?"

It took too much energy to say it, so Sage nodded. There was no way she could leave corpses out in the open to rot and freeze all at once, without dignity or acknowledging that they had every right to be honored in death. Sonia glanced at L, who shook her head vehemently and mouthed *No!* to her very air-headed partner. Not only was it nasty digging up bodies, but it'd make them sitting ducks. As for Sage, she didn't really care.

This became a moral test for Sonia, who hesitated. Her partner was already revving up the engine, but Sonia made no moves to get back on her snowmobile. Ever so slowly, she inched toward Sage, hesitantly asking, "Would you like some help?"

"Are you stupid?!" L exclaimed. "Crazy? Sonia, I always knew you were a dunce, but this is a new low."

"I know, but—"

"If you *know*, then don't do it! Quit thinking about it like a goddamned idiot and let's just get the fuck out of here!"

Sonia sighed. She stood there for a long time, watching Sage's retreat to Smallfeld. Ultimately, Sonia didn't abandon her.

"Are you fucking kidding me?" L got off her snowmobile, maybe to yank Sonia into the trunk and drive her the hell out of there. "Now I have to babysit, too?"

Sage looked over her shoulder. L seized Sonia's arm, but physical contact was the last straw—Sonia turned away, roughly dislodging L's hand.

"Sonia, what—?"

"Shut up," Sonia said. "Shut up, L. You go back, yeah? I'm staying here with..." She very quickly realized that she didn't even know Sage's name. She waited for Sage to give it, but Sage was far away enough to pretend that she hadn't heard her.

In Smallfeld, something as trivial as a name became unimportant. All these poor women who had been deviled in the worst way possible looked like they had been filleted with their guts hanging out. It was time to get to work.

Sage grabbed a shovel from a hardware store. She came out, feeling a bit overwhelmed at the sheer amount of labor and time this was going to take, but she wouldn't be able to move on with her life if she didn't do this. Sage grabbed a few bodies on her trek to the field next door. She was surprised to find Fido already digging into the ground with her ultra powerful front claws.

Sage watched, impressed. It took Fido just minutes to open up a hole big enough to fit a body. Sage ditched the shovel and focused on carrying the corpses instead.

The first woman was a teenager. Sage could tell because of her round eyes and cheeks, girlish features that would never fully mature now that she was dead. This was so much harder than Sage was ready for, and it took a lot longer to transport the body than it should have. Seventy pounds should have been like carrying a coin, yet Sage collapsed at the grave site. She pulled her knees up to her chest and stuck her face where no one could see it.

Inside, her heart longed for Damian. So much that it hurt. Sage wanted to feel his arms around her, and his kisses on her neck and pretty much everywhere on her body. She missed his glittery black eyes and devious smile, always with sex in mind. It was obnoxious and inappropriate, but so very entertaining. He always made her laugh with his stupid remarks.

And maybe that was the problem. Damian had gotten too cocky, thinking he could resist Cupid's Arrow and Agathe's advances all at once. Sage knew that sex with Agathe had never been his intention, but how would he redeem himself after that screw-up? Sage didn't see herself dealing with it when there were so many other problems to pour her energy into. Perhaps Candice was right and Sage had become a "clingy bitch." Weak. Pitiful. Samson would be so disappointed in her.

"Um . . . hey."

A warm hand on Sage's shoulder. Sonia kneeled beside her.

"You don't have to do this alone," she said. "I can help. L can, too, even if she's being a bit of a bitch right now. She's here."

Sage clutched her knees tighter. "Thank you."

Sonia didn't hesitate: she got up and entered the town. She grabbed her partner by the wrist and dragged her along for the ride.

For some time, Sage didn't move from her spot. She didn't have the strength to do anything at the moment. Fido never stopped digging, although she did come over to lick Sage's knuckles every once in a while.

"That ring on your finger," Sonia said after depositing another body in its hole. "It has the Diamond City insignia. Did you fight in the Unification War?"

Sage was impressed that Sonia would know this was a ring from that war. Not a whole lot of people did, much less ones in the Outskirts. At last, she raised her head a little to look at the ring Damian had put on her finger. It fit her perfectly because Damian's fingers were even more slender than hers. She eyed the red ruby at different angles before wiping her face and taking a deep breath.

"I did," Sage said truthfully. "Although this ring belongs to my . . . fiancé."

Sage smacked her lips. Her tongue. It felt odd saying that,

forced. Sonia picked up on every detail as L came around with another body, bitching at the top of her lungs, "Now I'm the one doing all the work? Are you for real?"

"Did something happen?" Sonia asked Sage innocently. "I mean, is that why you ran away from Diamond City?"

To her, it was probably a wild guess, but she was right.

Sage nodded. "One of the reasons."

"I'm not sure what he did, but if it drove you to run away from the city, then it must have been bad."

It wasn't him, Sage wanted to say. *It was Agathe.*

But . . . was it? Did Sage really give two shits about Agathe and her sexual fantasies?

Yes. Yes, very much so. Sage was pregnant, after all—had Candice and Olivia and the rebels to defend—and Agathe was on a mission to claim Damian. That meant using whoever she could to get to him.

But making excuses was Sage's way of shoving down the God-awful truth: Agathe wasn't the only reason Sage had run. Agathe or not, military wanting to seize her babies or not, she just couldn't look Damian in the face after what he had done, what he had allowed Agathe to do to him.

Sage closed her eyes. Tears welled inside them. Fido whimpered and licked her face gently.

"Is she crying?" L said loudly. "Did you make her cry, Sonia?"

"Not me!" Sonia exclaimed. "Her asshole boyfriend, kind of like you every other day! So goddamn insensitive to everyone's feelings!"

That's right . . . insensitive. Because Sage had wanted Damian to come home, and he had totally ignored her. Brushed her off. Hadn't considered her warning of an ambush at all. Hadn't cared about her feelings or her requests. Had thought of her as a "clingy bitch."

Fuck that. Samson had taught her better than that.

The only way to get these horrible thoughts out of her head was to get up and walk around, so Sage did. She headed back into town where there was still so much work to do. She shut down her feelings and focused on her task. It took the rest of the day to put about half of the women here in the ground, and Sage counted three hundred holes so far. Fido was busy covering them with snow and dirt.

"Oh, great." L waved her hands. "It's nighttime. Now we're stuck out here in the dark."

"Relax." Sonia got two sticks and rubbed them together. She started a fire pretty quickly. "We'll be fine out here. Squids aren't going to come looking for a bunch of old corpses."

"Here." Sage had found some jerky and chips at a convenience store. She had blankets and sleeping bags, too.

"This is insane!" L hissed. "Are we actually camping out here?"

Sonia tore off L's goggles and beanie. She revealed a head of beautiful black hair, half of it shaved. L's eyes were as narrow and intense as Damian's, the sign of a true fighter. The two started bickering with each other about indecency.

"It's fucking cold!" L whined, snatching back her hat. "Seriously, Sonia?"

"*Relax*," Sonia said, taking off her own beanie. She had short, messy blonde hair that would probably need a shower and some conditioner to tame. Despite how cold it was out here, she had worked up a sweat. Now it was time to sit by the fire, eat some jerky, and sleep next to a bunch of dead women.

Sage couldn't stop thinking of the ones still left in the cold, and that's why she didn't get any sleep that night. Other than looking out for intruders, Sage's mind was way too wired and the thick smell of rot coming from the town burned her nostrils. She stayed by the fire, kept it alive, and just stared at the night sky when her thoughts got the better of her.

"... Thinking of him?"

Sage didn't turn her head. Sonia was in a sleeping bag right next to her. L snored away from the other side of camp. For someone who had been yelling about risk, she sure slept like a baby. Sage envied her a bit, knowing that some disconnect would be good for her mental state. She just couldn't sleep, though. Not without Damian.

"I am," Sage admitted. She played with the ring on her finger again. "I am . . ."

"Want to talk about it?" Sonia offered.

"No."

All Sage wanted to do was finish digging. It took her, Sonia, and L another two whole days to carry and bury the rest of the bodies in Smallfeld. They scoured every corner until there was nothing but bloodstains and debris left.

The homes were the hardest part for Sage. The family pictures of the women who had been used for a Squid's nasty experiments were depressing as hell. At times, it wasn't even the thought of the grisly fate that had awaited each of those smiling families—it was the reminder of what Sage could never have.

A loving husband and children. The pizza shop. Candice and Olivia, who thought she was a "clingy bitch," who no longer saw their aunt as strong and independent. God, how it hurt.

"Are you fucking kidding me?" L yelled at Sonia. They were right outside the town, fighting yet again. "Damn it, Sonia, why do you always pull this shit on me? It's like you're doing it on purpose to get away from me!"

"Maybe I am!" Sonia yelled. "God, why do you have to bitch and complain about everything?"

"Because the things you do are *dangerous*! Didn't I already tell you that I don't trust her? No one walks around here by themselves, much less a woman!"

"Have you seen the muscles on her body? She's a beast!"

"Exactly, so I don't trust her."

"Well, I do," Sonia snapped. "No Squid would think to bury any of those poor people, so I'm following her—"

When Sage got closer, approaching the couple after that final walk through the town, they dropped their arguing. Sort of.

"Do what you want," L snarled at Sonia, marching toward her parked snowmobile in the distance. "But I'm done with you."

Fido growled from behind Sage's leg. Sonia turned to Sage with an air of determination, ignoring L, who revved her engine and took off. "Bitch," Sonia mumbled. The worst part about all this was that traveling with Sage was a pretty bad idea.

"You can't come with me," Sage said flatly. "It's too dangerous."

Sonia's eyes widened. *Too dangerous for me, but not you?* was what she was probably thinking, but Sage didn't bother clarifying. This was taking too much energy as it was. Sage started for her backpack at the barn.

"Wait," Sonia said. "Where are you going?"

Sage stopped. Abruptly. That's because she swore she had heard something, and a second was what she needed to confirm that she was right. There was movement coming from Diamond City's direction, heading right toward them. The hum in the air said that it was an aircraft, but whose was a mystery, one Sage didn't care to solve right now. Her goal was Tyrus and Herman and no one else. So she turned around, grabbed Sonia by the wrist, and jumped onto the snowmobile. Fido didn't need a motor to speed through tundras, because she kept up the entire time.

Sage slammed on the energy pedal full throttle. She sped through the Outskirts like she never had before, snow flying into her face. Sonia cried out and covered her eyes with her goggles. She didn't have her beanie, so her hair stuck up everywhere.

"Where are we going?!" she croaked. "Sage!"

"Someone's there."

"W-what if it's Diamond City? We should tell them about Smallfeld—"

"They'll figure it out," Sage said over the rush. "We can't afford to be caught by them."

"Is it your boyfriend?"

"Don't know."

"Sage," Sonia croaked with her swollen cheeks and splotchy skin, "are you a fugitive?"

"Yes," Sage replied. There was no sense in keeping that a secret anymore. It was obvious that Sage was avoiding Diamond City at all costs, and it wasn't because of a fight with her boyfriend. It didn't matter if Sonia knew it or not, either—Sage didn't plan on keeping her around for long. She just needed the snowmobile to get as far away from Smallfeld as she could, then she'd send Sonia on her way.

At least, that was the plan. And pretty soon, Sage found out it wasn't going to happen the way she pictured it in her head. She should have been able to cover a bit more ground before being shot off the snowmobile, struck in the shoulder with a blinding laser that cut her ligaments and burned what it touched. For a moment, Sage blacked out. She tumbled to the ground hard, and then she heard growls from Fido and screams from Sonia.

Sage leaned on an elbow as her injury healed itself. The damage was extensive and it was going to take a while to mend, but at least Fido was holding her own.

"Sage!" Sonia cried, waving at her. "C-come—come! We have to go!"

There was a seven-foot Squid right in front of them, and he blew Fido to bloody pieces.

CHAPTER 10

The Squid Troupe

Fuck.

Holy *fuck*.

The booms from that gun were deafening. The damage was devastating. Fido's body was all over the snow, guts and blood splattered everywhere. Squids didn't care about who was human or Enhanced, so Sonia would have been next, but Sage was ready for a fight.

The rumors were true. The Squids were real. This was Sage's third run-in with one after Samson and Winterfeld, but she still had a hard time believing it. She still couldn't internalize it. That might have been why she couldn't balance herself or concentrate. The massive Squid was damn close to getting another shot at her.

In a battle like this one, in which Sage knew she was physically inferior to her opponent, her objective was to take the weapon. Her Slainium sword could cause some damage and win her that momentum she needed to get the gun, but Sage was going to have to be quick and precise. She was going to have to ignore Fido's twitching limbs on the ground and Sonia's fierce cries. If she wanted to survive, she had to take out this Squid.

And run.

The snowmobile, her mind said. Sage's eyes made an involuntary glance at it. Taking that vehicle meant putting Sonia's life in danger. The Squid would follow and shoot more lasers. But letting Sonia escape by herself meant putting Sage's in peril. There'd be no other way for Sage to escape unless she could hijack the aircraft still making its way to her. That was too crazy, though, and Sage wasn't feeling very lucky at the moment.

No, if she grabbed the snowmobile and acted quickly, she could escape with Sonia and still make it to Herman and Tyrus. That was going to be her best option here.

This Squid didn't stop to speak or look surprised by Sage's quick regeneration—he fired his laser gun again. Similar to Diamond City's, but twice as potent. Sage dodged those blows as if she was training face-to-face with Samson. It was he who had taught her how to combat Squids, what to look for, and it didn't seem this one was very prepared for physical combat. Maybe he had never needed to use it out here, especially not against a human-looking female.

Sage quickly proved that she was anything but. She was swift enough to skewer the Squid through the head with her sword, a precise throw that had caught him off guard, and snatch the gun with a tentacle. She held on to the weapon tightly, one hand around the barrel and another around the handle. Finger to trigger, she squeezed and blasted the hell out of that Squid. It might have been overkill, but Sage wasn't about to take any chances. With a dose of Slainium in his body and a splatter of guts everywhere, the Squid drowned in a mangled heap of gore. Sage took back her sword and kept the gun, which she handed to Sonia.

"G-God . . ." Sonia croaked, dropping the gun because her hands were shaking too much. "S-Sage . . ."

Fido's body was twitching. Slowly, tendrils were whipping out of dismembered limbs to join back together. Her round belly was somewhere in the distance, and it'd be a sheer miracle if the pups were still alive in there. Perhaps they were, but bringing them along would only be a liability. Sage and Sonia had to go.

Sword in its sheath, Sage jumped back onto the snowmobile.

Sonia clutched the gun as Sage revved the engine and took off again, this time braced for any more Squids nearby. Just when she thought she was in the clear, she realized she was flying right into a *group* of them. Before they were even in sight, Sage looked over her shoulder at Sonia.

"We're not going to escape," Sage said. "So you'll take the snowmobile and drive back. If you run into anyone from Diamond City, tell them that the Squids are in the Outskirts." She nodded at the gun. "That might come in handy."

"SAGE!" Sonia screamed as Sage leapt off the snowmobile like springing from a diving board. It might have been impressive if she weren't jumping to her death. Sonia had very little time to make up her mind and get the hell out of there, and in this life-or-death situation, she did the right thing.

Against this band of Squids, Sage only had her sword. Damian's sword, actually, since the bastard still had hers. Her palms started an immediate sweat, making the hilt slick between her hands.

This was the end for her. These weren't the Squids that were going to help her—these were the ones that were going to throw her in that massive cage on skids, already housing a handful of victims from the Outskirts. Sage couldn't tell what made them so special— she was busy looking at the towering Squids with muscles the size of boulders and teeth like that of a Great White's.

She had never been to the ocean, but she had seen old books in the Clarity District about places with a lot of water. They had pages worth of various sea life—all kinds of creatures that were creepy as hell to look at—like the Anglerfish. But Sage especially remembered the sharks because there was this massive prehistoric one that could swallow people whole. These Squids had to be descendants, because their mouths and teeth were big enough to make a dent in anything they chomped on.

Their armor was just as intimidating. It was nothing like the Diamond City military's uniform—all white with black trims for beauty—or even the police's—slick, thin armor for protection— those were thick and reflective. Both lasers and bullets would bounce right off it. The more Sage studied what she was up against, the more she realized her chances of winning were nonexistent. There weren't any creases in the armor, no weak points. She didn't doubt that a direct hit would throw her right back on her ass, maybe even break a few bones.

This was not a good idea. Fighting them was committing suicide. But there was no other way past them. There was no other way to distract them than to try her hand against Squids that were far from Samson's caliber—these were more . . . brutish.

They jeered at her with their dagger teeth, licked their puffy lips in wanting, and hooted at her as if she were a prostitute. Their amber eyes flashed as their minds imagined what lay beneath her clothes. Pretty soon, one of them realized that she wasn't a stupid human who had run away from home.

"She's weird," said the biggest Squid of the five, the huge one that towered nearly ten feet. Like all Squids, he spoke in their native tongue. But Sage had never heard a dialect quite like that one . . . then again, she and Samson had learned Lolligo from a children's book and filled in the blanks themselves. Perhaps if Sage spoke, she'd sound weird to them, too.

Sage didn't, though. She kept her distance, hoping this distraction was enough for Sonia to make it a safe distance from the troupe. There was always the possibility of more Squids. The one they had fought earlier was not from this group.

"There's no way she's human," said the Squid with what looked like thumb tacks across his brow. "No human is that brave to stand there with a measly sword."

They don't know what you are, Sage thought to herself as she held her ground, braced for battle. *They don't know there's another hybrid aside from Wren out here . . . and that you understand them.*

Right. Maybe Sage could stall a bit more. Or maybe there was a way past them and onto their vehicle. The women in the cage were all connected to a bigger, fancier snowmobile that hovered a few inches off the ground. It didn't have skis like Sonia and L's did. Whatever Squid was manning the controls got out to see what the delay was, and he didn't look very happy. Like his cohort, he had those thumb tacks across his forehead and down his cheeks like a trail of tears.

"Hurry it up!" he barked at them. "Prime forgive me, but what are you idiots waiting for?"

Prime?

"She's not human!" shouted Ten-Foot-Squid. "Don't you feel it?"

Driver-Squid took a good look at Sage. He scowled even more, and it looked like a grimace now. "For Prime's sake, just take her already. Human or not, she's a scrawny female with boobs and a vagina—what the fuck can she do?"

"If she's a hybrid, sir, we want to sell her," said a reddish-looking Squid, the ugliest freak Sage had ever seen in her life. He looked like he had gotten too much sun and burned himself. There were monstrous boils on his face that Sage suspected had more to do with looks and trends than a disease. But then she saw them burst and these white worms poked out their heads.

Fear struck Sage in the heart. For a few seconds, her surroundings turned blurry and her breaths were so ragged that oxygen wasn't making it to her brain. For the first time in her life, in this instant before death, she felt a massive squirming in her abdomen, the two lives writhing in her belly, nestling into their cocoons.

Sage lost her composure. She actually faltered, although the Squids were too busy arguing with each other to notice. They were so disgusting. This was so disgusting. Sage's confidence plummeted. She would have thrown up, but she heard something invaluable that made her hold all the bile in.

"Hybrids fight to the death," Boil-Squid said. "It's just that those five were easy pickings."

Sage looked up at the women in the cage. Actually, they were sprawled all over the floor, unconscious. They didn't have clothes on, as if the Squids didn't believe in shielding them from below-freezing temperatures. Perhaps it was a form of restraining them. Not that it would take much—those women didn't look very nourished, and Sage wasn't sure she believed they were hybrids.

Maybe because the light in their eyes had gone out. The determination that Sage carried didn't exist inside them, so they looked weak and sickly. This was everything Samson had trained her not to be in the face of Squids.

"Not 'easy'," spat Ten-Foot-Squid. "One of them nearly broke my neck! She shoved a dagger right through my armor!"

The other Squids snorted.

Sage couldn't see it, but she pictured the crack behind Ten-Foot-Squid's neck. Vulnerable.

"That's why you shouldn't underestimate hybrids," Thumb-Tack-Squid said. "They're all just as powerful as the other. Some just haven't had enough training."

What the hell were they talking about? There were *more* hybrids?

"Like this one." Boil-Squid stepped forward. "The confidence. The *power*. Do you think Samson fooled us?"

Samson?

"How?" Ten-Foot-Squid said. "He brought back a hybrid like he said."

"Yes, but she was so primitive. I don't know—nasty, like an animal. This one's kind of beautiful. I mean, look at her hair, all groomed and shit, and clothes, like she cares about how she looks. Her eyes aren't amber, either, and she hasn't flashed her teeth at us like an animal."

There were a lot of words that Sage hadn't understood in that declaration, but she did catch on to a few: "primitive," "nasty," "groomed," and "animal." She very quickly realized that they were talking about her sister, but they were also implying there were more hybrids. More that they were aware of.

But how? All those women in Smallfeld and other towns were dead. Any attempts at reproduction were a complete and utter failure. So if there were more hybrids out there, who had given birth to them?

Sage tightened her grip on the sword again. She didn't make any sudden moves because she wanted to draw this out as much as she could. The Squids were still arguing with each other, in complete disregard of their opponent. They had done away with other opposition easily, so one girl with a sword wasn't going to deter them in the slightest. Driver-Squid grew impatient, though, and he rounded up his quintuplets and ordered them to finish the job.

"Hurry up and get her." he barked. "Fools!"

Ten-Foot-Squid. Dagger. Neck. Why hadn't that massive Squid been able to defend himself against a measly hybrid? Cocky? Or were these Squids a bit out of their element in the cold? Perhaps they weren't used to it, or maybe this was their first mission and their muscles were stiff and not so supple. They couldn't move like they usually did, especially with armor that covered them from neck to foot. They relied on their laser guns and completely underestimated Sage's ability to move like a bullet herself. God, the amount of training Samson had put her through, the endless flurry of limbs she had gotten in her face when she was seconds away from unconsciousness, and the number of bones he had broken in her body never let her forget the consequences if she fucked it up.

No fuck-ups. Not here. Lasers at this distance were easy enough to dodge. But like the previous Squid, these dunderheads didn't have a clue that she could shape-shift as readily as they could.

Samson. Thanks to Samson. He had given her so much—more than these Squids knew. He had fed her, trained her, given her his Cells, and experimented with her abilities to produce the most capable Sage imaginable. That had been Sage's reward for saving him from the Clarity District during the Unification War.

Or had she really saved him? Hadn't domination been the Squids' plan all along? Hadn't Sage facilitated that by saving Samson's life and allowing him to carry through with his plans?

No time to think about that now. The Squids all thought Wren was Samson's only test subject. They hadn't a damn clue what they were looking at right now.

Sage had to play her cards right. Quick movements saved her a painful hit from one of those lasers, but did absolutely nothing to give her the upper hand. Her next move had to be critical, executed flawlessly, or these Squids were going to rally and overwhelm her. So what should she do?

She could attack them head on. She could flash a series of tentacles in their faces and catch them off guard. They'd rebound quickly, though.

She could run around them. She was fast enough to keep dodging lasers and anything else they shot at her. But would she be able to get any closer to them? What would be the point?

She could jump over them and get into that snowmobile. She could drive herself and those women the hell out of here. But could these Squids catch her? The six of them were more than capable of trapping her.

She could distract them. She could put on a show with her shape-shifting, catch their attention, and then target Ten-Foot-Squid in the middle there with his broken armor. If she could snag *him* and use him as a shield, then maybe she'd stand a chance of getting out of here. But—oh, God—how was she going to get in the snow-mobile and leave with him in her clutches? The risks were too high, and Sage didn't feel confident enough to execute that move.

Sage had to do a combination of all four. There was no time to think about each step individually, so she had to go with what her instincts told her to do first. Her brain took over all bodily functions, ignoring anything her mind said, and made her act in a semi desperate way.

Sage threw her sword. Not at the Squids, though—somewhere off to the right where it hit nothing but snow. It stabbed the ground with its hilt up in the air. These Squids were tense enough to follow every bit of movement, so all six pairs of eyes swiveled and followed the sword's path.

So they totally missed when Sage grew a massive blade from her right arm. Flesh and muscle twined around it in support, supplying it with all the blood and oxygen it needed to keep its form. Sage had been shape-shifting for so long that this was as easy as clenching her fist. It had to be if her next move was going to work.

She shifted her left arm into a thin tentacle and lassoed Ten-

Foot-Squid around the neck. So fast, that by the time the other five Squids realized their comrade was being choked to death, Sage was already swinging into his face, maneuvering around his big-as-hell body, and striking him in the sweet spot of his cracked armor. The blade burst out the other side of his neck. Blood sprayed all over the snow, wetting Sage's hand. That's when the other Squids retaliated, fully aware that they were under attack by a rabid hybrid.

Sage didn't need her tentacle anymore, so she changed it back into a hand and grabbed Ten-Foot-Squid's gun from its holster on his hip. She fired at Driver-Squid, Boil-Squid, and Thumbtack-Squid in the face, then used her captive's body to block the lasers from the two Squids on her right. One was blue-eyed and the other couldn't stop drooling. While the saliva didn't penetrate through armor, it hissed when it dribbled onto the snow. Sage threw her captive right at them, with enough force that it knocked them both off their feet

This was it: Sage had moments to swing into the snowmobile and she did. She slammed the door shut, thankful for whatever shatter-proof window blocked those lasers, and slammed on the go-pedal. She didn't know what kind of energy powered this thing, but she blasted right out of the area with the captured women in tow.

"DAMN IT!" Driver-Squid screeched at the top of his lungs. The force of his voice shook the entire grounds. "GET HER, DAMN IT! GET HER!"

Sage never forgot about the vulnerable women in the cage behind her. They were an open target, but they were also valuable to the five pursuing Squids. They weren't about to jeopardize big bucks for their rare captures, so they had to run to catch up to the snowmobile.

And holy shit—could they *run.*

They looked like gods thundering across the tundra. Sage wasn't going to make it. Another mile, and they'd be on her ass.

She threw the controls to the right, and the snowmobile nearly tipped over as it circled around the Squids. Her sudden shift in direction threw them off again, so they stopped to watch her drive right to her sword in the distance. Sage pressed the go-pedal then set autopilot as she kicked open the door and grabbed her fiancé's sword right out of the ground. Damian entered her thoughts, and perhaps he was good luck after all. His sword in hand, Sage climbed to the top of the snowmobile.

The wind cut her from behind and blew her hair forward. Thankfully, it was in a braid and stayed out of her face. She could see the women sprawled in the cage in front of her, all of them thin and malnourished from hours of trying to stay warm and lack of food. From up here and so close, Sage noticed that they all looked the same: their faces were identical, and not just because they were emaciated, but because they had similar features.

With the snowmobile zooming across the Outskirts, Sage jumped onto the cage and crawled to the back end of it. She found the Squids quickly catching up to her again. This time, when Sage threw her sword, she didn't miss.

The blade struck Thumbtack-Squid through the face and skewered him to the snow. With another comrade down, the four Squids stopped and gasped. Another moment of hesitation, and Sage had another huge advantage to exploit: she grabbed one of the bars of the cage, jumped fifty feet into the air—her arm stretching like a rope—and landed an ideal distance from her opponents. Enough for Sage to perform the most powerful swing in her life—one that would make Little Man proud on the fastball court—and slam the entire snowmobile right into those four monsters.

Sage kept a tight hold on the cage and let the snowmobile do all the work. She sent the four flying into the air like bullets. As they careened across the Outskirts, Sage used her left hand to grab her sword from the twitching Thumbtack-Squid. She set her sights on the sky and braced herself.

Four left. They had been whacked by their own snowmobile, so they weren't expecting the sword again. Sage was precise enough to throw it a third time and hit Blue-Eyed-Squid through the face. The other three grabbed their lasers as they flipped back to the ground, but they should have known that guns weren't going to work because they had already tried it before. Desperation set in—and so did fear—when three of their comrades were down. Sage knew that head-to-head combat was futile, but she still had a few tricks that would catch them off guard again.

"SHOOT HER!" screamed Driver-Squid. "DAMN IT, YOU FOOLS—WHY CAN'T YOU GET HER?! USE THE INK!"

Ink?

Drool-Squid had what looked like a pellet of black slime. Sage didn't have a clue what that was, but she made sure to avoid it at all costs. The Squids still hadn't caught on to the fact that she could understand them, and "ink" was enough to paint a very vivid picture in her mind. Whatever that ink was, it must have killed opponents, because Drool-Squid was hesitant to use it.

"But what about the money—?"

"Forget the money!" Driver-Squid exclaimed. "She'll kill us before we see a single coin!"

More hesitation from Drool-Squid, and that's the only reason Sage was able to get so close to him. Perhaps this would have been Drool-Squid's chance to capture her in the ink, if he had been fast enough to throw it at her. Well, he did throw it, but Sage caught it before the pellet broke and all that thick goo spilled out. She ducked when Drool-Squid swung at her, grabbed a dagger from his belt, and shoved it up his nose. No Slainium, so he'd be back in action within minutes, but he did loosen his hold around his laser gun, which Sage grabbed and used to blast Boil-Squid in the face.

The worms shot out of their homes to attack her, but Sage jumped feet away from them. God only knew what those worms did inside a body, but they didn't last long in the snow. They were dead before they could think about returning to their host.

Driver-Squid screamed. He used his gun to shoot at Sage until it ran out of energy. Useless. He realized that, so with great heaving pants, he roared. "YOU WANT TO PLAY, GIRL?! LET'S PLAY!"

He ripped off his armor as if he was taking off a one-piece, and now he was stark naked. Sage understood that the armor stopped the Squids from shape-shifting. It was too cold to pull such stunts, but this bastard was desperate enough to do anything to stop her. Sage kept an eye on Drool-Squid and Boil-Squid, who weren't going to jump in any time soon. Still, Sage had to end this quickly if she was going to escape with her life.

Driver-Squid expanded to five times his size. He got so big that Sage knew there'd be no penetrating that body with her weapons. Samson had done this a few times in their sparring sessions. This was a lesson in using your head more than brute strength, which was the only reason Sage was still alive right now. She had to do it one more time, and she considered her options.

There weren't many.

The cramps in her abdomen made her see stars. Those two little lives were coming to life in the worst of times, but this was yet another pain Sage was going to have to ignore. If she wanted to save them, she had to defeat this massive Squid her way. Thankfully, she didn't have to do much maneuvering or she might have passed out.

With both claw-like hands, Driver-Squid picked her right off the ground. His entire body lifted with relief that he had caught her at last, a slack grin on his face as the amber eyes the size of cable dishes lit with glee.

"FOOLISH GIRL!" he yelled in her face. He stank of blood and rot, as if he had been eating corpses all day. Maybe he had. "I AM GOING TO EAT YOU!"

"Then eat me," Sage said in Lolligo.

Driver-Squid stopped. Her Lolligo was a bit different than his, but he still understood the garbled words she had spoken, and his eyes widened. More importantly, his mouth opened, and Sage spit right into it.

Not her saliva—the black pellet. Maybe that's why her words in Lolligo had come out garbled.

Somewhere in that flinch, Driver-Squid had crushed the pellet in his throat and swallowed it and its slimy contents. He seemed to already know what was about to happen, so he dropped her as he roared into the sky. It was dark out now, and three of his friends were dead, so the only ones witness to his horrifically grimy demise were the two that were starting to come back to life.

Driver-Squid's entire body started convulsing. He screamed in agony as that slime expanded from within, bursting from his eyes, nostrils, and mouth. It broke through pores, too, quickly taking over everything it touched. It didn't take long to cover him in its inky texture and silence him forever. With no more life to feed on, it quickly died, too.

Sage turned to the last two Squids. They scrambled back from her, making a run for it across the Outskirts. *Never turn your back* was the first rule Sage had learned in combat. She picked up Driver-Squid's discarded laser gun on the way. Two blasts to the head each, and they were down for the count again.

Sage ripped off two of her Slainium-laced bracelets. She used one to choke the hell out of Boil-Squid, making sure that it pierced his throat and delivered a good dose of Slainium to his blood. Then she turned to Drool-Squid, who vomited all over himself.

"Prime help me!" Drool-Squid croaked as his own bodily fluids melted the snow around him. The smell was atrocious. "Please, no! Please don't!"

"Please don't what?" Sage said in Lolligo. "Kill you like you were going to kill me? Or them?" She waved at the unconscious women in the cage. "Don't deny that's what you were going to do. Your mistake was underestimating me and taking me for granted. Oops, right?"

"Please don't—"

Fido bounded out of nowhere and clamped her powerful jaws on Drool-Squid's head. She tore it right off, thrashing back and forth for the kill she couldn't deliver. Not without Slainium or that black slime.

So Sage plunged her bracelet right into Drool-Squid's chest. It was malleable enough to use as a small dagger, and it did the trick here. It would take a while for death to set in, if it did at all, but Sage knew these Squids wouldn't be bothering her for a while. At least,

Driver-Squid would never see the light of day.

As Sage trudged over to her sword still holding Blue-Eyed-Squid to the ground, Fido let go of the head and bumbled after her. Surprisingly, she was still in one piece, muscles expanding and contracting as she moved. She jumped up and down, tentacles sprouting out of her neck and waving back and forth, as she tried to tell Sage something, but Sage already knew.

She grabbed her sword and turned to face the landing aircraft in the distance. The ramp wasn't even out and Damian was racing onto the snow right for her.

CHAPTER 11

Farewell, Love

There were six dead Squids. One had grown to the size of a Cthulhu monster. One was headless. One had been choked to death. And three had been skewered like shish-kabobs through the head. Their snowmobile was some ways away, with women still trapped in the back.

But Damian didn't care. He ran past all the gore, maneuvering through the snow as if he were on an obstacle course. His boots were high up to his knees and his coat was flying all over the place. The button-up shirt beneath it was the same one Agathe had fondled when she rode him hard a few nights ago. That meant he had chased after Sage immediately. His hair was always beautiful, but it was loose and messy. He hadn't brushed it or tied it into a bun like he usually did when he was getting ready to fight. The age on his face was showing a bit, too. Stress, perhaps? Grief, maybe? Or the Cupid's Arrow relapse? All the above.

"SAGE!" Damian made it pretty close, but he stopped when Fido jumped in.

Fido barked like never before. Her face turned all red, snout growing more monstrous than it already was. More teeth grew in the space, ready to tear into someone she deemed an enemy.

Damian was.

Sage didn't put away her sword. She kept it in her hand as she faced him and the crew rushing out of the ship. All the familiars were here: Gertrude, Mega Woman, Turtle, Eye Candy, Rockstar, Dough, Butcher, Clara, Sailor, Preacher, and a few others Sage didn't see very well. She did spot Sonia, though, who must have intercepted Damian on the way here.

Everyone had come out to rescue her except for Justice. Not that he would have made a difference. His dying breaths had been dedicated to Damian's innocence, but so had Commander's, and he was dead, too. They had all sworn by Damian's virtuous morals. Sage, not so much anymore.

"Praise the Forefathers!" Preacher cried. "The Lolligo are dead!"

Yes. Everyone was busy scanning the grounds now, the bodies and guts all over the place. Pieces they had never seen before in a human, big bulky muscles capable of breaking them in half. They settled on the snowmobile some feet away, the unconscious women all curled on the floor of their cage. No one had to command help, but they didn't move unless their Warlord told them to.

Or unless their precious Allseer commanded it. Agathe and her cronies were here to ensure Sage made it back to Diamond City in one piece. The last thing they needed was two lovebirds eloping for months, having babies, and then coming back with even more rebels to raid the palace. Diamond City's defenses were shaky enough as it was.

Sage understood that Damian had no control over what Agathe chose to do, but how fucking dare he show up here with her.

How *fucking* dare he.

"Sage," Damian said calmly, ignoring Fido's vicious snarls. He drew his sword—*her* sword—but only for defense. Sage wasn't sure if Fido would lunge for a killing blow. She wasn't sure if she'd stop her, either. "Please." He raised his hands. "It's fine. We're not here to attack you. Or fight."

Sage glanced at Agathe. Her black-striped militants pointing their guns at her would have fooled her. But again, Damian had no control over that. He came closer, but Fido grew more aggressive. She grew a second head with teeth more ravenous than the first. More tentacles erupted out of her body. If that wasn't enough to scare Damian off, then nothing would. It seemed she, too, was waiting for Sage's instructions before making a move.

"You have some nerve coming here, Damian," Sage said quietly.

" 'Some nerve'?" Damian repeated, equally quiet. It was hard to hear him above Fido's growls, but she quieted down some. "Some nerve for rescuing my wife?" His eyes traveled down to her abdomen. *And our children*, he seemed to say with his expression because the last thing they all needed was Agathe finding out Sage was pregnant. Or did she already know?

"You didn't 'rescue' me," Sage said. "I've never needed rescuing, especially not from you. And I'm not your wife. Thank God for it because I'd hate to see what you would do if we were married."

"What on earth are you talking about?"

"How many people would you choose to have intercourse with?" Sage said. "Oh, but it's not intercourse so long as there's no penetration, right?"

"Sage—"

Fido lunged. She knocked Damian to the ground with her front paws then took two huge bites out of his neck and chest with her teeth. Damian flung her off as his rebels opened fire; Fido swatted all the bullets away with her tentacles. She stepped back, not attacking, because another bite would kill Damian, and there was still a lot more Sage had to say to her ex-fiancé.

Blood spurting out between his fingers, Damian got back to his feet. He didn't seem to care that his wounds were raw and wide open. He shooed back Mega Woman and Gertrude and didn't allow any of his rebels to get any closer. His eyes filled with tears as he gazed upon Sage with the horrifying realization that she was more than mad.

She no longer trusted him.

It must have been Damian's every waking nightmare. If he had gotten any sleep, that was, for the circles under his eyes were big. Sage should have felt pity, but her emotions were a bit clouded at the moment thanks to that fight against the Squids. She was still shaking, adrenaline still pumping, from facing monsters twice her size. Samson didn't count.

"Sage," Damian croaked. His wounds were starting to heal. They weren't why he was having a hard time talking, though. "Sage, that wasn't me. I-I never gave her permission—"

"So she raped you."

"I was drunk!" Damian sputtered. "I was fucking drunk from that goddamned drink that I should have never had! Sage, I'm sorry—I didn't mean for that to happen! I wanted to turn back and comfort you that night, but I also wanted to get our wedding plans started—I-I wanted to surprise you—"

Sage held up a hand. "I don't want to talk about this right now, Damian. I didn't mean to be a clingy bitch, but that didn't give you the fucking right to take risks and drink a goddamned drink you were supposed to stay away from. Did all those months vomiting your stomach out mean nothing to you, you bastard? You threw it away just like that, because you thought you were macho enough to handle it?"

"I made a mistake," Damian croaked.

"This wasn't a fucking mistake," Sage spat. "You knew exactly what the fuck you were doing, asshole—the Damian I know would have turned back the moment I suspected there'd be an ambush. Do you know why? Because that ugly bitch on her throne over there has been grinning at you like a hyena ever since we returned from Diamond City. And so I pondered and wondered why you chose to ignore me, and now it makes sense."

Sage gritted her teeth. "You were ready to mate with Agathe because she's the Allseer and that's what you want, isn't it? More power? Why not become her concubine and show her what it's like when a true man eats her pussy out?"

Damian looked like Sage had just punched him in the face. Her words were ten times worse.

"YOU USED ME!" Sage roared. "YOU USED ME! YOU NEVER REALLY LOVED ME—YOU USED ME TO CREATE BABIES! THIS WAS YOUR AND AGATHE'S PLAN ALL ALONG!"

The rebels were frozen stiff. Gertrude and Mega Woman were stunned. Agathe had an intense look on her face, but the smallest of smirks curled her lips.

"Sage," Damian croaked weakly. "W-what on earth are you talking about? I-I never planned *anything* with Agathe—where on earth did you get such ideas?"

Sage threw his sword at his feet. This whole scheme was so obvious to her now that she felt like a dumbass for not having seen it sooner. For not realizing that this had been Damian and Agathe's plan from the beginning: to woo Sage and create hybrids, strong children to combat the Squids. Clearly, ones of Sage's caliber could take them down like fish in a barrel. All Damian had to do was make a ton of them, dump Sage, then co-rule with Agathe, Louis be damned, too.

"Sage, no." Gertrude stepped forward. "None of what you said is true—no way—"

"SHUT THE FUCK UP!" Sage barked at her, louder than any howl Fido was capable of. "Shut the fuck up, you traitorous bitch, blaming me for every damn thing that went wrong in your life! You blamed *me* for Little Man's death—*how dare you*! Well, you won't have to worry about that anymore, because I'll be out of your hair forever."

Damian braced himself. He sensed Sage was done here, so he ran after her. Fido jumped in, but this time Damian retaliated with a vicious slash of his sword. Not that he hit anything—Fido was no pushover, and it took Damian quite the effort to put a dent in the mutant monster. He blocked and dodged more than he struck, clearly distracted, but all he needed to do was throw Fido off long enough to make it to Sage. He cut off one of Fido's legs at last, and it took him fifteen minutes to accomplish that feat. It would have been less had his comrades intervened, but no one moved. Not even Agathe's soldiers. This was Damian's fight, and he made it to Sage just as she arrived at the snowmobile.

"Sage, wait!" Damian panted. "Please, allow me to explain."

"Explain what, Damian?" Sage snapped. "The fact you let Agathe hump you like a dog? You really want to torture me, don't you?"

Damian got to his knees. Fido came lumbering behind him, but she didn't attack. She looked to Sage, who grew increasingly irritated at having to deal with this drama in the middle of Squid-infested territory.

"Get up, Damian," Sage spat. "Get up and go back to Diamond City."

"Forgive me, Sage."

"Leave, Damian."

"Please. I have never asked for anything in my life, but I'm asking you to find it in your heart to forgive me."

"I've never asked for anything, either," Sage said. "All I wanted was you that night. But it's obvious where your loyalties lie and I suppose I understand when your true love is standing over there—"

"She's not my true love," Damian said roughly, still facing the ground. "She's not, Sage, so get that out of your head. I don't know where you got that from, but this isn't a game—I'm not manipulating you into *anything*."

"Yes, you are. You're here to take our children away, you sick fuck." Sage raised her Squid laser gun. It was the only weapon she had left, and it'd more than do the trick to get rid of Damian. Sage could never kill him, but she could wound him enough to send him packing to Diamond City.

"Get the fuck out of my sight, Damian."

"Those are my children as much as yours."

Sage fired the gun and blasted Damian's left hand off. He didn't have any rings on his fingers, so at least he hadn't lost any jewelry.

Damian didn't twitch on the ground, but his rebels came forward. Gertrude was crying at the top of her lungs now.

Sage stuck out the middle finger at her. "Fuck you."

Sage turned to the rest of the rebels. "And fuck all of you. All you motherfuckers, who looked at me as if I was some kind of monster, cleaning up your fucking mess and helping you get back into the city. Why don't you all teach Agathe how to have proper sex so she doesn't embarrass herself when it's one-on-one time with Damian?"

She turned to Agathe, who was smirking so wide there wasn't enough room on her face for her lips. "He loves blowjobs. He loves when you take him all in and then work your way to the base. You might gag a bit, but it's so worth it. He cums in just ten seconds."

Damian curled into himself. He clutched his bleeding stump to his chest. He sobbed.

"Come on." Sage waved at Fido, who withdrew her second head and ran into the snowmobile. Sage was about to follow when she heard the draw of a sword and felt the presence of a blade at her back.

She turned to see Damian in position, brows drawn in determination. Then he threw her another sword—*her* original sword—and gripped the one she had returned to him.

"We fight," Damian said. "If I win, I see our children. If I lose, I'll pack up and leave you alone."

"I'm not fighting you," Sage said flatly. "You're injured and I'm exhausted."

"That doesn't matter, Sage. This is for our children. At least allow me to redeem that much."

One hand? Damian didn't stand a chance. Then again, Damian was powerful and Sage never underestimated him.

She readied her sword, too. Samson's sword. She hadn't wielded it in so long. She missed the weight and thickness of Damian's sword, but this was the way it had to be. This was the way it should have always been. At Mousafeld, Sage's sole mission had been to aid the Warlord. Nothing else. No kisses, no sex, and no promises of grandeur.

Damian's eyes were full of tears. He was fighting so hard to stay focused, to not let his grip slip despite the blood gushing out of his left stump, but he had to do this just as much as Sage did.

It was he who attacked first. He flew forward so fast that Sage almost didn't block the vicious stab of a blade that had just helped her kill six Squids. Her sword wasn't big enough for that kind of defense, and the Slainium rebounded with a force that made her step back. Damian lunged again with every intent to disarm, and if Sage hadn't jumped, she would have been stabbed.

Sage froze as his left hand regenerated before her eyes. She hadn't expected it to happen so quickly—if at all—because even Enhanced couldn't regrow limbs. Her Cells must have been hard at work in his body, even if Damian had probably destroyed a bunch of them after his drinking spree. It made Sage angry, so that's what she used to fuel her movements.

She and Damian sparred like they always did, like they had that time in the training grounds in front of Louis, but this time each blow meant something.

If Damian won, he'd be tagging around her like a lost poppy. Sage couldn't let him anywhere near their children with that bitch Agathe in the background—no way—Sage hissed—God, she hated everyone and everything—all those assholes standing back there, watching them—Gertrude pretending to cry and Mega Woman looking like she was about to shit herself.

Damian ducked another swipe and elbowed her right in the chest. Sage staggered, but she didn't let his blade touch her. Her uppercut sent Damian sprawling. She followed up with a strike she hoped would end this scuffle, but he caught it.

With his left hand that was now a claw. Five sharp talons closed around the blade and yanked her forward.

What the hell? Damian could shape-shift, too? Because of her Cells?

Sage let go and stepped back. She had had no idea her blood was that potent, but it was the least of her worries now.

Another searing cramp attacked her side, and she lost consciousness in the moment Damian should have claimed his victory. The ringing in her ears was deafening. The darkness in her vision was drowning. For a few seconds, Sage had no idea what was going on. When she came around, she was on her knees.

Damian was standing before her, both blades in his hands. His left arm was bare, but the sleeve on his right was rolled up, and Sage could see that dreaded tattoo: sage leaves twining up and around his forearm. It'd be there forever, a memory of what they used to have, and it hurt. It hurt him, too.

He stood there in a show of triumph, but he didn't celebrate this victory in any way. He watched her closely, fully aware that her cries for him that night had not been fake. Maybe that's what he was thinking of as he fought with every fiber of his being not to hold her. Instead, his eyes filled with more tears because he couldn't offer her comfort.

Sage didn't want it. She didn't want the swords, either.

"You broke my heart, Damian." Sage sobbed. Tears trailed down her cheeks. "And I can't forgive you for that. I gave you all of me . . . the girls . . . my restaurant . . . my life . . . and you never really cared. You played me like a fool."

"I was weak," Damian croaked, a soft wind carrying his hair from his face. His beautiful sharp face with those plump lips of his. Sage couldn't stand to look at them. "And I admit that much. I was a weak *fool* and I deserve every blow you delivered to me tonight. Every one of them. But I *never* played you. I never tricked you or used you like you think I did because those are the ideas someone else planted in your head. From the moment we met, jealous bastards have done nothing but try to tear us apart. In response, I should have ensured I'd never jeopardize the small amount of trust we did establish between us. I fucked up and I accept it. But to claim that I worked with Agathe because I wanted to use you to rear children and become the Allseer? I was ready to give up everything to be with you, Sage."

"And what is everything?" Sage winced because of her damn abdomen. God, it felt like two worms were kicking and hissing in there. "Your plan with Agathe?"

Damian stepped away. He turned around and trudged back across the snow, toward his waiting audience. Gertrude and Mega Woman, who were closest to him, stepped aside and let him pass. They all watched him with bated breath, wondering where he was going, because he didn't board the ship. He stepped over to Agathe, who was as smug-looking as ever. Her soldiers stood by, eyes on Sage, but they should have been paying closer attention to Damian.

Maybe they thought he was about to give her a kiss. Congratulations were in order after all—he had just felled the great Sage, brought her to her knees. Pregnant or not, Sage wasn't easy to beat.

It looked like Agathe was about to say something, but her final words got stuck in her throat. That's because Damian plunged a sword right through it.

Sage's eyes widened. Some of the rebels jumped while others froze like statues. It took almost an entire minute for Agathe's lackeys to register her gargles as sounds of death, and even longer for them to aim their weapons at Damian. By then, his rebels sprung to action and took them out. It was easy enough when they caught them off guard. Perhaps the soldiers got a few shots in, but warriors like Turtle, Eye Candy, and Rockstar were too battle-hardened to be dented. The whole scene reminded Sage of a colony of ants overthrowing and eating their queen. Agathe didn't just choke to death—she lost her head while she was at it.

It was some time before Sage got to her feet. She competed with Preacher, who didn't have the valor or the energy to offer any blessings. Maybe he was still wondering if Damian's actions were warranted or not. Did a sexual dalliance with the Allseer mean it was necessary to kill her? Did Damian want to snuff out some of the guilt on his conscious, or was he indirectly admitting that he had, indeed, had devious plans with Agathe? They were no more now, of course . . . and that's what he was trying to show her . . . but Sage was horrified.

Terrified.

Damian was capable of anything behind the guise that he loved her. What other strings was he pulling behind her back? Sure,

Agathe was dead, and Louis would be after his head forever, and Damian would probably be banned from Diamond City as punishment again, but that didn't erase the past.

"Holy shit..." Sage croaked.

She had fallen in love with a monster. She had had sex with a monster. And she was carrying his children, ones she had to defend at all costs.

CHAPTER 12

What Matters Most

Sage had been betrayed many times in her life. Not necessarily by her lovers, but by the people she cared for. Her lovers like August had never plotted behind her back—he had just left to join Damian's rebellion against the Allseer. Gregory had tried to use her to rear children, too, but the sex wasn't good, and Sage was more interested in her pizza shop than politics. Looking back at it now, Sage appreciated Gregory's efforts to let her live her life, the one she wanted. The biggest and ugliest betrayal was Bram. First, he had exposed her to the royal family and then sold his daughters to the council. That was unforgivable.

But this . . . why did this feel ten times worse? Maybe because Sage had put her heart and soul into a relationship with Damian. In her head, she had pictured her fairy-tale future of getting married in the Color District, working the pizzeria, and raising children. She had finally gotten everything she ever wanted and then . . . poof . . . gone. There was an ugly reality in its wake instead, one she desperately wanted to escape from.

Agathe was dead. Damian was a wanted man. His rebels were in deep shit. They didn't deserve this at all. They had been fighting for so long, constantly putting their lives on the line, and now, because their Warlord couldn't keep his penis in his pants, they were back to square one.

Fido nudged Sage's arm with her nose. She was panting slightly, aggravated, but fully aware that there were half-frozen women who needed help. And then there was Sage herself who wasn't feeling too hot. If more Squids showed up, she'd be fucked.

So Sage stood up from the ground. She felt so goddamn heavy. She trudged past the half-frozen women in the cage and manned the snowmobile. Fido licked her face and bumped her neck.

I should have never let that wolf have sex with me, either, she seemed to say with her eyes. *But he was leader of the pack and his coat was shiny. I fell for it.*

Sage laughed. Wow.

Surprisingly, the snowmobile still worked. It turned on and drove them out of there, pulling all the weight at its rear across the snow. There was a navigational system on the screen, so Sage knew what direction she was traveling in. Herman and Tyrus were supposed to be by the Winterfeld cemetery, and that was miles north from here. Two hours, according to this thing.

Sage didn't bother to look behind her. Of course, Damian was following in his aircraft, now with six occupants less. Live ones, anyway, because he probably hadn't left the bodies in the Outskirts to freeze. The less evidence he left lying around, the more creative the story he could invent. Not that Louis would ever believe a word that came out of Damian's mouth. Sage surely didn't.

"Fuck." Sage rested her head against the chair. She rubbed her abdomen and held back her cries. God, it was so painful . . . When she pressed on her skin, she felt the shell of something hard, like cocoons. Based on the corpses they had found in Smallfeld, why did Sage get the impression this wouldn't be a vaginal birth?

Because it wouldn't be. The Squids obviously knew that any human or humanoid carrying one of their own would have to have the cocoons extracted. Sage couldn't believe she was about to do this, but there was no fucking way she was holding out for two more hours. Her heart was racing and sweat was starting to trickle down from everywhere. The little lives inside the cocoons were thrashing, and Sage already knew what she had to do if she wanted to live.

She had to live. She had to be there for her babies, or Damian would take them from her. This was the worst imaginable scenario, but Sage should have seen this coming from months ago, when she had witnessed Reina's gruesome death at the hands of her own offspring. Subliminally, Sage had. But now she had to deal with it.

Sage got out of her seat. Fido looked up, fully alert. Sage staggered to the back of the snowmobile in desperate search of something that could be anywhere, if there was one here to begin with. A scalpel? A knife? Behind the seats for the crew was a med kit. It was strange that Squids would actually have one. Their array of medications was foreign to Sage, but she did recognize the tools. She found the scalpel she was looking for, didn't bother trying to decipher which one was the anesthesia, and crumbled to the floor. She scooted back until she hit the wall that would serve as her support. Nearly wheezing, she pulled up her shirt.

"God," Sage croaked, looking up to the skies. The lights in the ceiling were awfully dim. "Please help me. Please help my babies live. Please don't turn them into monsters."

Fido started barking. She got a bit crazy, as if she could sense Sage was about to commit suicide. Sage wasn't really paying attention, but Fido jumped around the controls, stopped the vehicle somehow, and rushed out through the passenger door. Were there more Squids outside?

God, Sage hoped not. Cutting herself open was so fucking hard, and her hand didn't stop shaking around the scalpel. She pressed that blade to her slightly round belly, swollen now from the growing cocoons, and sliced.

Sage screamed. She screamed until her throat burst. Until the muscles in her neck ruptured. Until the blood in her incision just swelled up and flowed all over her body, dripping to the floor. She dropped the scalpel as she went in, hands gripping each side of her belly, and pulled herself apart.

Sage screamed again. Adrenaline skyrocketed like mercury in a thermometer, so she didn't feel too much pain after that. She got to see the cocoons for the first time in her life. They looked like small brains tucked in her uterus, connected to the lining with what looked like cobwebs.

"Yes, yes, yes..." Sage cried to herself, unsure of what the hell she was saying. Her bloody hands shook as one took the scalpel and the other held the cocoon on the left side. Very gently, she sawed through the cobwebs. Really, that was the only thing keeping those wrinkly bundles of life in place. There was no umbilical cord, so Sage was able to pluck the left cocoon right out of her. Just as she made for the second one, unconsciousness seeped in. She dropped her head, fighting the darkness, then heard Damian's voice.

"SAGE!"

She saw his blurry silhouette as he rushed into the snowmobile. Sage cried as he tripped over himself, hit the ground with his knees, and crawled to her side. His arms immediately held her, cradling her as his eyes assessed the mess. Sage's hands were still shaking, going for the second cocoon, but Damian stopped her.

"I've got it, darling," Damian croaked. He sat her up against his chest and reached in with his own hands. For someone who claimed he had passed out when Ileana gave birth, he was surprisingly precise when it came to sawing through the cobwebs then plucking his own child from their mother's womb. He placed the cocoon alongside the first, then focused on closing Sage's incision. He pulled the flaps together, holding her belly in place. There were stitches in the med kit, but he didn't need them because Sage regenerated pretty quickly. It was the blood that didn't stop flowing for some time. Damian kept his hands on it for pressure. He looked over his shoulder at the cocoons beside him, side by side, in a puddle of Sage's blood.

And they were pulsing?

Damian didn't notice it. He was too busy crying at the sight of them. "A-are those my babies?" he croaked. He clearly wanted to touch them, but Sage was more important right now. The cocoons seemed to be fine. If anything, they were much more pinkish after absorbing Sage's blood. Was it because of her Cells?

Gertrude and Mega Woman were inside the snowmobile, too, but they didn't come any closer. Fido kept a close eye on any visitors, ready to tear out throats if anyone dreamed of taking those babies. She stood between them and the door, and Sage couldn't have been any more appreciative. Except, right now, she rejoiced at the cocoons Damian finally handed to her and cried.

"Oh, God . . ." Sage croaked, holding them to her chest like a pair of pillows. She kissed each of them, heard and felt the life within. "T-they're alive . . ."

Damian kept a protective arm around her shoulder at all times. He drew her into his chest, and Sage rested her head on it. She cradled her babies, smiling into their shells.

"A-are they seriously in there?" Damian asked softly. He ran a finger over each of the cocoons, feeling the grooves. Surely, he felt the life within, too. He grew silent as he listened to the steady thumping. If Sage could see his face, she imagined it would look quite wondrous.

"Sage?" Gertrude called from the front of the snowmobile. She couldn't get any closer thanks to Fido. "Are you . . . all right?"

"She's fine," Damian answered. "She's fine. S-she's just given birth . . . to two beautiful boys . . ."

Sage furrowed her brows. She looked up at Damian. "How can you tell they're boys?"

Damian sighed peacefully. He continued stroking the cocoons. "I can feel it."

Sage exhaled. She let her head drop back onto Damian's chest and closed her eyes. Perhaps she fell asleep for a little bit. Damian didn't move, but he did have his rebels return with food. There were sandwiches and water bottles they had packed from Diamond City. Sage's backpack was still in Smallfeld somewhere.

"Here, darling." Damian opened a water bottle for her. He helped her drink. He fed her the sandwich, too, because Sage didn't want to let go of the cocoons. She was dirty and bloody, but moving would be impossible for her right now. Damian knew that, but he had to stand eventually.

Night had fallen, and parked out in the middle of nowhere wasn't very safe. He kept her steady, body against his, as he reclined one of the seats and tucked her in there. He put a pillow behind her head and kissed her forehead. "You are the bravest woman I know, my Star," he whispered to her. "And you did fabulously."

Sage met his eyes. She probably looked like hell, but she managed a smile. "Thank you..."

"Sir." Rockstar called him from the driver's seat door. "When you have a chance, can you come out here and take a look at this?"

At first, Sage thought Fido had given birth outside. But no, the beast was still sitting next to her, sniffing the cocoons. Sage looked out the window and found Rockstar by the cage of women.

Sage's heart dropped. She had completely forgotten about them! She couldn't believe—

"Congratulations!"

Sage jumped and whipped around. Sonia was in her face, beaming at her. She was leaning over the seat in front of Sage, bundled up in a leather jacket that belonged to Damian. He must have given it to her when he found her. "I can't believe you actually gave birth to cocoons! That's so rad! L's going to be *so* jealous!"

"Jealous?" Sage said. "Why would she be jealous?"

"I think pushing those out of your vagina is much cooler than a nine-month-old baby, don't you?"

Sage blinked at her cocoons. She looked back up. "I didn't push these out of my vagina."

Sonia's jaw dropped. "Wait—so you performed a cesarian?"

"I'm not human, Sonia. My injuries heal quickly and the pain is much less."

"Would these have never come out of your vagina?"

Sage shook her head. "Don't know."

Sonia looked wondrous. "So... how on earth did you know to cut them out?" Her eyes widened. "Is it because of Smallfeld? And what the Squids had done to the women there?"

Sage held her cocoons closer to her chest. "Yes."

"Oh." Sonia gaped at her. "Then you're definitely the strongest fucking woman I've ever met. If the Warlord wasn't so defensive of you, I would definitely ask you to marry me."

Sage chuckled. "Then L would really be jealous, wouldn't she?"

"Yeah." Sonia beamed. "For sure. But that's the point. She's probably going crazy right now wondering where I am."

"Will you go back to her?"

Sonia hesitated. "I suppose ... eventually, I will. But not for right now. I'm worried about you and what's going to happen to these rebels. I actually kind of like them. That chick over there," she nodded at Gertrude, "taught me a thing or two on self defense! Want to see?"

Sage smiled. "Sure."

Sonia jumped to the aisle and assumed an offensive stance. Then she ducked, pretended to grab a wrist, and turned her invisible opponent on their back.

Sage nodded. "Nice."

Sonia wasn't the only one who came to congratulate her—all of Damian's rebels came by at some point. Sage read so much from their facial expressions. Like, Gertrude and Mega Woman, who had seen some of the procedure, were relieved. Turtle, Rockstar, and Eye Candy were traumatized, as if they couldn't begin to imagine what it'd be like to have little brats growing in their bodies. That would be worse than death. Clara, Butcher, and Sailor were more quiet and appropriate, sitting by her and keeping their thoughts to themselves. They seemed more tired than sympathetic. Preacher, of course, just had to bless the newborns and recite a good-luck prayer. There was no greater honor than having a bunch of dead Squids looking after you.

While that was nice and all, relations between Sage and the rebels remained strained. Just hours ago, Sage had yelled at all of them to fuck off. Now, it looked like they'd be traveling together. Sage was too exhausted and too entertained by her babies to drive this snowmobile.

For that reason, they stayed put for the night. Sage wondered how the women were doing, and if they'd survive any more time in the freezing cold. She was sure Damian had taken care of them. She asked him about them when he finally returned to the snowmobile with some more food and a fresh change of clothes for her.

Damian didn't answer her question right away. He placed the cocoons on the seat next to her so he could take off her coat and bloody shirt. He did her pants and boots, too.

"Damian," Sage said tightly.

After dressing her, Damian handed over a sandwich and some water. Sage ate by herself this time, but she kept a protective arm around her cocoons. She knew they needed to feed soon. Maybe when she was done eating. In the meanwhile, she waited for Damian to answer her.

"The women are dead," Damian finally said.

Sage gasped, nearly choking on her water. "What?"

Damian held up a hand. "It's not because of you. They've been dead for a while."

"Are you for real?"

"Sage," Damian said steadily. "It's not your fault. But there is something I wanted to ask."

Sage stared. She was an expert at reading Damian's facial expressions, but this one was as blank as a clean slate. "What is it?"

"You found these women when you ran into the Squids, right?"

"Yes. I was hoping to take them to Herman and Tyrus."

"And your intentions were good. But ... I ... don't think those women are human." Damian pursed his lips. "Sage, they look like you."

Sage got to her feet right away. She secured her babies then stepped out of the snowmobile. She passed the small bonfire Sonia had started and approached the cage where Mega Woman and Turtle were gathered. Sage didn't look at them—she focused on the frozen corpses. The faces she could only half see. But now that Damian had mentioned it, Sage caught on to the resemblance immediately.

"What the hell's the meaning of this?" Sage croaked. God, there was no mistaking her long nose, freckles, and angular chin. There was no hair on these women, but Sage would recognize her own face anywhere. "What the fuck is this?" She raised her voice.

But it wasn't fair of her to demand such information from the rebels. How the hell could they possibly know what these corpses were? The ones who did were dead in the snow some miles back. All that Damian's rebels could do was carry the women out of there and lay them down on the ground side by side.

Sage looked to Damian, who was standing next to her. He remained stoic as he took a moment to study the faces that he knew so well. When he turned his head to meet her eyes, Sage whispered, "Are they … me?"

"I don't know," Damian said softly.

"How can they be you?" Turtle said. "I say the women look like Sage, but they're definitely not her."

Where had the Squids gotten them from? Sage burned with a horrible curiosity that would never be appeased. Unless Herman and Tyrus knew …

While Turtle's words did appease Sage's distress somewhat, because he was right—they couldn't be her—Sage got another horrible feeling. When she took a seat in front of the fire, clutching her cocoons, she started to doubt *everything.*

Everything.

That included her mother, father, sister, and even half-sister, Aurora. But Aurora couldn't have played any part in this, since she was born many years after Sage. Those were memories that Sage carried in her head, so they had to be real. What she didn't remember, however, were the years before Aurora's birth. Nothing at all. No recollection of her mother, father, and real sister. Maybe she remembered snippets … and maybe her Squid father was in there somewhere, but sometimes Sage confused him with Samson. She swore that her father had told her to run and hide, but now she doubted that, too. That could have been her mother warning her whenever they got to close to officers. The Pugnator, as her father was called, had never shown his face again. He had left his family to rot in the Cut District with no real plan to free them. He hadn't even come back to find out about Wren being sold to a bunch of human scientists. No, Sage's first true memory was of Aurora's birth, when her mother had gone to the hospital and popped out a small, delicate baby.

"Sage," Damian called her. He took a seat next to her on the snow. "What are you thinking?"

Nothing that Sage wanted to share right now.

"Why don't you go inside the ship and lay down for a bit?" he suggested. "You can use my bed."

That aircraft he was traveling in had a few private rooms in the back. It was one of Agathe's very own. It was called the *Mistress*. A perfect name, in Sage's bitter opinion. As equipped and prepared as Damian was in Mousafeld, he had never had the luxury of driving an aircraft this big. Sage thought about Justice, and she wondered if Damian had seen the grave. She didn't ask. She didn't argue with Damian's suggestion about using his bed, either, because she was that tired. And so long as she had her babies, she felt like she'd be fine.

Damian followed her onboard. They passed the rows of seats for the crew and reached his room. Had Damian truly slept here? Probably not. His bed, for starters, was pristine and untouched. He didn't have a single piece of clothing anywhere. Not that he would have had time to pack his bags and settle in. The shirt and pants folded on the chair belonged to Sonia, so she must have used this space to change or splash water on her face. She probably hadn't been able to sleep, either.

Sage sat down on the edge of the bed. The way she sunk into the mattress indicated that this was going to be a terrible sleep... but it was better than the floor. She and her babies needed what they could get. She clutched them tighter to her body, knowing they had to feed. Without teeth or weapons, she opened a cut in her thumb. Damian had never seen her do something like that, so he stiffened. He watched quietly as Sage let her blood flow onto one cocoon and then the other. Life pulsed within.

"How do you know they need that?" Damian asked softly.

"I didn't," Sage said. "Until I saw them absorb my blood when I . . . gave birth to them." She supposed that's what she had done, even if the whole thing wasn't very traditional. Technically, the babies had yet to take a breath of fresh air.

"Right," Damian said as Sage placed the cocoons on the bed and took off her jacket, pants, and boots. He eyed her abdomen, which showed no traces of that morning's surgery. He watched her get into bed and hold the cocoons like pillows. He pulled up a chair and sat in it because he didn't detect any hostility from her. Sage allowed him to do that much. There was no way he could steal her babies without her knowing it now.

"Sage . . . I wanted to ask."

"About what's next?" Sage finished for him. "What we do now that you've killed an Allseer and we're in the middle of fucking nowhere?"

"Precisely," Damian said. "Our children are still so very vulnerable. Do you really want to wave them around in the face of Squids? This Herman and Tyrus that you're so deadset on finding—can you really trust them?"

"No," Sage said honestly.

Damian exhaled. He looked like he had been braced for a fight or argument against that idea. So now that Herman and Tyrus were no longer an option, his previous question still stood.

"We go to Centerfeld," Sage said. "Have you ever been there?"

"Yes," Damian said quietly. "They were the very first town I visited when I started building my rebel forces in Mousafeld. Let's just say that Franco wanted more than just an alliance."

Sage arched a brow. "Why am I not surprised? One of your previous allies, whom you got kicked out of Diamond City, wanted to take advantage of you by having sex with you and making you his lover?"

Damian frowned. "I didn't get him 'kicked out.' He had a choice when we rebelled against the Allseer, and he knew the risks. You cannot blame that shit-show on me."

"Well? Did you have sex with him?"

"Of course not, Sage. I was seeing Ileana at the time. That's why Centerfeld rejected me."

Sage shrugged. "Here's your chance, Damian. You're free to pursue your relationship now. Hell, maybe you can get Franco to help you get back into Diamond City."

Damian's face fell slowly. When his eyes were that dark and his cheeks were that hollow, Sage knew he was mad. Not that Damian could do anything about it. He didn't have any outlet in this small space. He had yet to lash out at her physically, but perhaps he would do so verbally. Sage was up for the challenge.

"Do you think that low of me?" Damian asked calmly.

"I do now. I, for one, no longer trust you."

"I made a mistake."

"And it cost you dearly," Sage said. "That's if you ever really cared for me. I still say you and Agathe had planned something more for me and the both of you played me like a goddamn fiddle."

"I never played you."

"What was going through your head when you picked up that drink, Damian?" Sage sat up a bit more. That way, she was eye level with him. "What the fuck were you thinking? After all the shit we went through in Mousafeld trying to get you sober, you decide to throw it all away? What's wrong with you?"

"I thought I could handle it," he said quietly.

"Why were you drinking in her presence?"

"Why not? Was she an enemy I didn't know about?"

Sage didn't believe that Damian had been completely oblivious to Agathe's advances. Contrary to the earnest look on his face. "Of course she was," Sage said. "You're telling me you never noticed how much she wanted you? And you purposefully put yourself in a vulnerable position? Damn it, Damian, you're not an idiot, are you? You couldn't tell that Agathe wanted to suck your dick?"

Damian rubbed his face. "I know I didn't do myself any favors that night, but you weren't very honest with me, either. You kept the pregnancy a secret all this time—"

"I wonder why," Sage said. "I didn't trust you. I was afraid of what you were plotting behind my back, and I'm glad I was. Admit it, Damian: you never really loved me. You wanted to dominate me, impregnate me, then capture me. That's what you and Agathe had planned. You never married her, but you were working with her. Do you deny it?"

"I love you, Sage," Damian whispered. "That's why I never went along with anything that Agathe wanted."

"So you killed her instead? In this last desperate attempt to win me over?"

"I killed her because she was a threat to our children."

"So you were working with her?"

"I DIDN'T WORK WITH HER!" Damian yelled. "Damn it, Sage, are you that paranoid that you can't even believe that? I fucked up—I should have never met her that night—but I wasn't working with her! Is it because of all the ideas everyone else has planted in your head?"

Sage handed him his ring. That shut Damian up instantly. As the seconds passed and no words were spoken between them, his eyes got big and shiny. His brain processed what Sage was telling him with her actions. The Diamond City insignia inside the gemstone shined in the darkness of the room. That ruby had never looked more like blood than now.

"You're a liar," Sage said. She forced the ring into the hand on his lap. She settled back on the bed, still glaring at him. "Fuck you."

Damian got up. He didn't wipe his eyes, so Sage wasn't sure if he was crying or not. He stepped out of the room quietly, without slamming the door. He simply left her in peace, and Sage was glad. As soon as he was out of the space, she could breathe.

And she went right to sleep.

Sage expected Damian to run away, but he was hanging out by the aircraft the next morning, talking to Mega Woman and Gertrude. He and the rest of the rebels had buried the dead women in the snow. They had also laid Agathe and her six bodyguards to rest. Sage saw the extra graves, a good distance away from the poor women. While she felt bad for those six bodyguards and their shitty sacrifice, she contemplated a nice, big spit on Agathe.

She decided it wasn't worth the energy.

The rebels were ready to head out to their next destination. Damian had been waiting for Sage. The bastard even had the gull to look at her and smile.

"Good morning, Sage," he said cordially. "And good morning to my beautiful babes." He pushed his mug of coffee to Mega Woman and swept the two cocoons out of Sage's arms. He held them in each of his, planting a kiss to their rough exterior. Gertrude served Sage some coffee with a smile of her own, but Sage didn't smile back. Gertrude's eyes fell to Sage's left hand, the now naked finger.

"Candice and Olivia," Sage said. While Gertrude grieved another broken relationship, Sage wondered what had become of her nieces when their assigned guardian was here and not in Diamond City. "I told them to stick to you."

"They're fine," Gertrude replied. "I left them at the capital. With Louis. He knows we left in search of you. He—"

"I don't want to hear it," Sage spat. "Not one more word about another fucking Allseer. How's Geoffrey?"

"F-fine. I mean, I haven't heard anything more, so I assume he's still at the facility."

Sage snatched her mug and stepped away. She had Sonia in her peripheral, the only person who could direct them to Centerfeld, but she didn't want to talk to anyone. She figured Damian had already gone over today's itinerary. She decided to spend some time with Fido, who was busy prowling the grounds some miles away, muzzle to snow.

Rubbing her arms, Sage approached Fido. It took her some time to reach the beast that had laid down on the ground, in sleeping position.

"Hey," Sage said. "What are you up to, girl—"

She stopped. Six pups had torn out of Fido's belly. Not just her womb, either—the cocoons, too. They had hatched. And now, they weren't looking for milk—they were actually eating her, tearing at her already open flesh and spilt guts.

A true mother's sacrifice. Her pups were what mattered most to her.

Sage screamed. "STOP!" She ran over, yanking the pups back, but they whined and protested. Their small muzzles were smeared with their mother's blood, without a single care in the world. Perhaps this was natural to them. Sage wasn't having any of it, and she screamed again.

Sonia and Gertrude were the ones who reached her first. Damian stayed back with the cocoons in case there were Squids on the horizon, but no Squids here. Only a mother giving birth and sacrificing her life for her pups.

They're what mattered most.

CHAPTER 13
Centerfeld

The Fido incident traumatized Sage to no end. After Sonia and Gertrude steered her away from the corpse and took care of the pups, Sage went back to the snowmobile to be alone. She closed the doors and sat behind the controls, just looking out at the plains of the Outskirts. Tears burned her eyes. The pain in her chest hurt so much. She couldn't stop thinking of the dead Fido or the look on Damian's face when she had shoved the ring into his hand. She cried because she wanted Damian to hold her—there was no one else to comfort her. No Samson to wave his big hands in the air, or the girls to distract her with their dramas and future shopping sprees. Even Geoffrey had started to grow on her with his dazzling smile and optimistic attitude.

Sage must have fallen asleep at some point. The next time she opened her eyes, the sky was dark. Damian entered the snowmobile with the cocoons in what looked like a baby sling. With that contraption, he must have been holding them against his chest all day. It looked silly, especially when Sage pictured him barking orders with two mounds hanging from his neck and shoulder, but it worked. He placed the sling with the cocoons on one of the seats as Sage reached out and embraced him.

"Sage," Damian said softly, wrapping his arms around her.

He still smelled like teakwood and lavender. That scent reminded her of the time they had met at Mousafeld, become allies, promised each other to fight until the very end, and dreamed of a future together. Sage's head would be on his chest or in his pillow, inhaling what she had come to associate with comfort. Hope. Even love. But now the smell of teakwood and lavender was all false, shattered by the image of Agathe on his lap.

Sage had to take a step back. Her breaths were shaky.

"Damian," Sage said, looking at the cocoons in order to avoid his eyes. "Where did you get that sling?"

"Bed sheets," he chuckled. "You have to be resourceful."

"How are they?"

"Castor and Pollux?"

Sage furrowed her brows. She looked at him. "Who?"

Damian nodded at the cocoons. "Castor and Pollux." He gave her a sincere look, like a kid asking for ice cream, in hopes she wouldn't refute the names he had decided for their children. Sage was more than intrigued to know why them.

"Castor and Pollux are twins immortalized in the constellation gemini," Damian explained. "Back in the Clarity District, I learned that an ancient civilization called the Greeks viewed them as the patron gods of seafarers, or people who were lost." He shrugged. "I feel like we're pretty lost now."

"Your name is of Greek origin, too," Sage said.

"Indeed." Damian beamed. "So the names fit."

Leave it to Damian to come up with the names. Sage wasn't about to burst his bubble. She crossed her arms, this time asking about the pups.

"The crew's taken them in." Damian pursed his lips. He grimaced, as if someone had forced him to swallow olive oil.

Sage arched a brow. "What's with that look?"

"I hate animals."

"What? Really?"

"I don't understand their behaviors, therefore I'd rather not deal with them."

"Right," Sage said. "You'd rather deal with people you can manipulate and seduce."

"Yes," Damian admitted.

Sage laughed. She didn't know why she found that funny, but she did. The more she thought about it, the more it made sense: Damian was clean, coordinated, and orderly. Animals were, for the most part, unpredictable. Messy. But so much fun to be around. Sage longed for attention and that sense of adventure. She had been living by the books for far too long. At least she had six newborns to look after now.

"Come." Damian picked up his sling with the cocoons. "Let's get some rest. I think tomorrow we'll head out to Centerfeld. We've wasted enough time on this barren wasteland. I really do need a change in wardrobe."

Sage studied him from head to foot and noted that he was in different clothes than this morning. Right now, he sported a jumpsuit with a long black leather jacket. So he did have something else to change into.

Damian frowned. "I need more than just five sets of clothes, Sage."

Sage snorted.

"What?"

Sage shook her head. Damian was trying to start conversation, but she was ready to retire for the day. It was her turn with the makeshift sling, and she carried it all the way back to the *Mistress*. There, she showered and got into bed without talking to anyone.

It was unanimous among the group that going to Centerfeld was a necessity. Sonia was more than happy to take them there, more than excited for some reason. She had seen Damian execute Agathe in cold blood, but maybe she deemed that a positive thing. What town in the Outskirts wouldn't pine for strong warriors to defend them? Franco surely would.

Sonia was sure of it. And while it seemed like a grand plus for any town in need of defense, Sage couldn't take a single step into Centerfeld. She couldn't put herself, her babies, or the pups in danger. She kept all those thoughts to herself, though, until she was ready to tell Damian that it'd be better for her to lay low. She didn't want to crush the semi-hopeful energy that Damian's closest Enhanced had managed to gather. They were traveling as a team again, having left the snowmobile behind, and they were on a mission just like they used to be.

Sort of.

The Warlord's crew had no idea what the future had in store for them. They were just good sports about it and didn't complain, but their access to Diamond City was non-existent. The very thing they had worked so hard to achieve had been ripped out from their hands the moment Damian plunged a sword through Agathe's neck. They seemed to be carrying around a false sense of security, as if Sage and Damian really had all this under control. That was the kind of confidence that Sage didn't want to destroy with her negativity, so she let Sonia take the lead when they finally arrived at the prestigious Centerfeld.

As Sonia and a few other rebels bumbled off the aircraft, Damian looked like he had a fever. He was pale and sweaty. Perhaps it was another bout of withdrawals, but he wasn't rushing for the toilet. The way he massaged his temples said he was nervous and uncertain about something. Fingers opening and closing into fists said he was agitated. Did he have some sort of bad memories here? Other than getting kicked out after denying Franco a night of sex, what else could have possibly gone wrong? Damian didn't say anything, and neither did Gertrude, the queen of gossip.

For Sage, it became yet another issue she had to talk to him about. She waited until everyone was off the ship before pulling him aside. No one asked questions—they respected privacy between her and their notorious Warlord. Sonia knew how to talk to Franco, so the rest of them just had to stay quiet and play their cards right.

"Damian." Sage looked him in the eye. "I'm not going."

"What do you mean?" Damian said. His makeup wasn't as pronounced as it usually was, as if he didn't have the strength in his hands to apply eyeshadow or eyeliner correctly.

"Castor and Pollux aren't safe. Everyone sees me holding cocoons, and you don't think people are going to ask questions? They could be terrified of us—*me*—so I'd rather keep a low profile."

"I understand," Damian said softly. "And so I will stay out here with you. Let me just go to town to get supplies for you, the babies, and..." He eyed the corner of the aircraft, where the six pups were sleeping in their crates. "Them."

Sage nodded. "All right. I'll be out here."

Damian breathed out. He ran a hand through his hair before turning around and walking away. Sage couldn't help it.

"Are you all right?"

Damian stopped. He looked at her and said, "I'd rather not deal with Franco if I don't have to. We didn't exactly part on...good terms."

"Why? Did you fight him when you said no to sex?"

"Yes," Damian said honestly. "I was a married man. I wasn't into orgies...at the time. But he had so many ideas for a night well spent that he was offended when I denied him. Extremely offended."

Right. Yet he had said yes to Agathe. Sage would rather not drill it in, so she got ready to retreat, but he beat her to it.

"Please believe me," Damian said.

Sage said nothing. Her silence was enough to prompt Damian to leave, since there were no further words to exchange between them. She withdrew into the ship for some much needed silence and peace. She held her cocoons as she watched over the six sleeping pups. With a picture of Agathe grinding against Damian, she eventually went to sleep, too.

I t was dark the next time Sage woke up. She hadn't turned on the lights inside the aircraft, so it was pitch-black minus the glow of the moon. The pups were whining because they were hungry. Sage had some raw meat for them in the refrigerator. Her back and knees cracked when she got up, from lack of proper rest and exercise. Perhaps she'd give the cocoons to Damian so she could take a run outside—

And then Sage remembered.

Damian wasn't here.

Again, her mind wanted to say, but Sage didn't let it. Agathe and Arian were dead. Franco, however, was not. Damian was probably still in Centerfeld with everyone else ... He had promised to return, and it was already eight o' clock.

That same dreadful feeling from the Color Dome shivered through Sage's limbs, making goosebumps erupt across her skin. Sage held and rubbed her arms.

She stood by the window near the cockpit and looked out at the expanse of snow. She saw lights in the distance. That was Centerfeld. It was a bustling town, drawing too much attention for Sage's taste. Then again, Centerfeld seemed to be doing just fine against the Squids if they were still standing and warding them off. She couldn't criticize them nor deny them their fun ...

The pups were gnawing at the beef. They made whiny noises, but Sage didn't move from the window. She saw Centerfeld, but she also saw an army coming across the field right to the *Mistress.*

Something was horribly wrong.

Sage didn't hesitate: she secured the cocoons in a chair then grabbed her sword. She stepped outside to confront the dozen or so soldiers running right at her with their weapons drawn.

They were in skin-tight jumpsuits that left very little to the imagination. Silver and thin, as if someone had dabbed live human bodies in paint. Sage didn't underestimate the potency, though, knowing that her blade might not be able to cut through whatever material that was. She aimed at the head instead, also coated in silver, but with protective goggles that allowed the wearer to scan their surroundings and see through turbulent weather.

Sage was quick enough to get the first strike on the soldier closest to her. She slammed the hilt of her blade into each eye then smashed the soldier's chest, a woman. She winded her and knocked her back, but the *ping* also told Sage that this metal wasn't going to break with a sword's blade. She had to rely on her agility and hilt to knock these bastards off one by one, and between the ground and trees, she was able to dance around them fairly well.

The soldiers didn't speak or shout orders—perhaps there was some internal communicator they used for that—and fell silently at her feet. Sage didn't know if the blows had been hard enough to kill them, but she didn't stick around to find out.

She raced back inside, strapped the cocoons to her chest, hid the crate with the pups inside the closet, then jumped out onto the sea of bodies. She ran past them and headed straight for Centerfeld. This was a bit crazy on her part, doing this with two babies on her chest, but she didn't trust any other way. There was no chance in hell she was leaving the cocoons by themselves on the ship. Even if she was exposing them to danger, she was confident enough in her abilities to shield them in a clutch situation. Besides, she couldn't fight unless she knew her children were safe.

She barreled through the snow until she finally reached the entrance to the largest town she had ever seen in the Outskirts. The walls around it towered over ten feet, although the tallest skyscrapers stood way beyond that. They weren't straight and sleek—they were geometric, as if the engineers and architects had tried their hand at something new to alleviate boredom. It might have been an interesting feature to admire if Sage wasn't in rescue mode and she didn't smell trouble like someone smoking fine tobacco.

There was another unit of soldiers waiting for the first one's return. Sage didn't engage them—she jumped right over them. She stabbed her blade into Centerfeld's wall, and, using it as an anchor, leapt over to the other side.

She landed in some kind of checkpoint station with supply rooms, aircrafts, and barracks. Anyone who came and went was accounted for, processed in the system, and tracked with a chip. Smart and secure.

"Hey!" cried the first soldier to notice her. "Who are you?!"

Sage dashed past them and into the street. She weaved around all kinds of storefronts, vendors, churches, offices, and even an amusement park with the biggest merry-go-round she had ever seen. The blinking lights were a blur as she sped by, her body taking her right to the heart of Centerfeld, where a massive crowd was gathered around a makeshift stage.

Perhaps, on a normal night, bands played here. Magicians went live, or aspiring artists tried their hands at entertainment. There were screens and speakers to reach crowds from all corners of the town. A nearby billboard said that someone by the name of "Sword Devil" was going to put on the craziest show of their lives. They even had mega fastball players perform on hanging platforms and single strings, all without breaking the volley. Insane. If this town weren't so hostile and bloodthirsty, Sage would have loved to see the show and pick up a few tricks herself. Tonight, the guy up there with a microphone was no artist.

Franco.

Sage knew her fair share of Enhanced from her time in the Unification War, and this wasn't one of them. She took a good look at his face—from the butterflies drawn on the side of his temples to the ultra red lipstick he sported—and then his bare chest, pierced nipples, and black-out tattoos. Sage never questioned anyone's artistic expressions, but this was one guy that terrified the living daylights out of her.

Unpredictable was Sage's first thought. Damian was flirty and energetic, but Sage could read him like a book. That guy on stage was crazy as hell, prancing in front of Damian's rebels like a psycho about to execute punishment for fun. Even Sonia, a very resident of this town, was up there, with L clawing faces and arms to get to her.

Sage planned on joining her in that endeavor—she was going to make this quick.

"Sage!"

Before Sage jumped, she whipped around and found Damian shoving his way through the crowd. His face looked so bare with old washed-out makeup, and his clothes were a bit ruffled, as if he had been running and fighting all day, but it was the fear he exuded that made Sage truly stop.

"Stars, Sage!" Damian croaked, eyes finding the cocoons strapped around her chest. "What are you doing here?"

"Looking for you." Sage didn't ask questions—she unstrapped the babies and gave them to him. "Hold them."

"You're going up there?"

"Shall you or shall I?"

Damian must have been planning to crash Franco's fun. Somehow, he had escaped arrest and slithered through the streets of Centerfeld until an opportune moment for attack like this one had presented itself.

But it was clear that Franco was putting on that display up there on purpose, actively torturing Rockstar with a laced whip and eating someone's torn-off fingers as if they were chicken wings. From the power of Turtle's howls, the fingers must have been his. Turtle wasn't one to go down without a fight or curse, and he must have said something truly abhorrent to warrant that kind of treatment. Sage could almost hear him in her head: *Why don't you rip off your ugly-ass nipple rings if you're so bored, asshole? Do you have dick rings, too?*

"Are these the kind of people you attract?" Sage said.

"Not all." Damian beamed, although it was wry. "I attracted you, didn't I?"

Sage was in no mood to engage him. She trusted him to take care of the babies, then got to work. She jumped onto the stage, flying over many heads and making people gasp.

By now, all the rebels who were chained and drugged up were looking at her. Their eyes were completely glazed over, some with blown-up pupils and bloodshot sclera. Blood dripped from the wounds that they probably couldn't even feel, and that was a mercy judging by how gruesome this scene was. Their hands and feet were chained with spikes that cut their skin like barbed wire. Most of them were naked, flogged and skinned like animals in a butchery, and unconscious on the stage floor. Even rebels that Sage hated, like Rockstar and Eye Candy, didn't deserve this torture in front of a mesmerized crowd. Sage must have caught the show halfway through because Clara and Butcher were still in one piece, albeit squirming and crying at their grisly fate at the hands of this maniac. Preacher was nowhere to be found—maybe he was hiding in the chapel amidst his brethren.

"Lex?" Franco chortled. He had a nasally voice. "Is that you?"

Sage had no idea who this "Lex" was, but Franco was also very high. On what, Sage could only guess. It wasn't enough to soak in or drink blood—whatever was in his system cast him into space and beyond. Or maybe he was just that senseless and cruel, making him the biggest psychopath Sage had ever met. The closer she looked at him, the more she realized that this behavior wasn't normal and she figured out why.

It wasn't the drugs—he had more Cells than the average Enhanced. It showed in the size of his veins and the definition of his muscles. His fingers were longer than usual, more like talons ready to shred opponents to pieces.

Sage wasn't deterred, because she had faced monsters like Taz before, but a certain doubt took root in her core. It didn't faze her, but it did make her wonder something very important.

Taz had gotten his Cells from Wren. Where the hell had Franco gotten his from?

Sage clutched her sword. The crowd held its breath. She could read their thoughts: *This little bitch isn't going to be a match for him.* But she was. Five strikes—that's all it took—and Franco was facedown on the stage, wheezing.

"WHAT ARE YOU DOING?!" he shrieked, veins in his throat. "YOU'RE NOT MY LEX! LEX! LEX!"

Sage plunged her sword through Franco's head, pinning him to the floor. L finally made it onto the stage amidst the stunned crowd and scurried over to her lover in her own pool of blood. It looked like Franco had torn off a piece of her scalp.

"S-Sage . . ." Sonia whispered. "Behind . . ."

Sage turned, and Damian was there to fend her from an incoming attack. Babies against his chest, he used his sword to block the strikes from someone Sage couldn't see. The movements were too quick and Damian's head was in the way—his body, too, shielding her despite the clear tension across his shoulders. He seemed frightened by his opponent, but Sage didn't have time to investigate who it was. She freed her allies then aimed to make her escape from this wretched town.

That wasn't going to happen, though—weapons continued to clash, Damian couldn't cut down whoever he was fighting, gunfire went off, and Damian had to jump back to save the babies from being hit.

Sage whipped around to confront . . . herself?

Her eyes made immediate contact with the identical dark ones in front of her. For an instant, her mind screamed *Wren?!*, but after a quick assessment, she realized this wasn't Wren.

No.

Wren didn't have short, ruffled hair. Wren didn't have that seriousness in her gaze, the death glare that could make anyone melt from the inside. Wren also didn't like to get her hands dirty, and so she wouldn't have had her own pair of long ugly talons full of blood to cut down her enemies. Damian was having a hard time keeping his composure, and perhaps Sage was, too, because she started shaking and her heart started racing out of control.

What the actual *fuck?*

Sage's eyes were burning. This wasn't usual behavior in the face of any opponent, but something was so very horrible and wrong that Sage wanted to do nothing but sob. She wanted to crumble right there on the stage, amidst the bodies of her contained comrades, and just cry because she didn't have a fucking clue what was going on—how this was possible—how there could be another one of her—did she have more sisters?—had her mother lied to her about her siblings?—then what about those clones from the Outskirts?—what were the Squids doing?—were they actually clones?—What was she?—HOW COULD THIS BE POSSIBLE?!

"Sage!" Damian snapped.

Sage composed herself. She didn't shake her head or make any sudden moves, but she did turn to meet Damian's eyes for a brief second. It felt more like hours. So many words poured out of Damian's gaze. They rushed into her brain all at once.

Focus, darling. Don't think about what you're seeing—this changes nothing. This doesn't alter the fact we have two beautiful boys waiting to hatch and that you have a life to live. This is just another mystery that we have to figure out, but you're still you. You're still our Star.

"Stand down," Sage said assertively to her opponent.

Lex.

Lex was in a tank-top with a cleavage that was too low to be decent and booty-tight shorts that showed off all the muscles in her legs. This girl looked more like a dressed-up doll that served one sick man's fantasy than a warrior. Still, Sage didn't underestimate her. If Franco had been calling out for Lex, this was a fighter who knew how to pile up heads.

"LEX!" Franco dislodged the blade from his head and sat up. Miraculously, he was still alive. The Slainium was going to take a while to take its course, and he still had a few things to say before he kicked the can. "KILL HER! KILL HER!"

Franco didn't have the slightest bit of curiosity to appease here—he was desperate to secure his town from all these intruders. Lex followed his command and launched the first strike—also not asking questions about her doppelgänger—and flashed forward so fast that Sage nearly got hit by those sharp-as-hell claws.

There was only one reason Sage would win in a scuffle against Lex, who was by far the strongest fighter she had ever faced. Taz was more of a mindless monster just swinging arms, and the Squids had been too frazzled to put up any kind of challenge, even as a group. Lex, however, knew what she was doing. She used her focus to time every one of her movements, going for spots like the neck, belly, and thighs, to cut major arteries and then tear out organs to put her enemy on the ground. Sage, though, saw all that coming because she had Samson's Cells. She was that much faster, intuitive, and powerful.

And so, after a series of dodges on stage for all to see, Sage rammed her elbow into Lex's chest. A resounding *crack* said many bones had broken. The force of it made Lex stagger, and that's all Sage needed to complete the killing blow.

No mercy. Not for monsters. Not for sick psychopaths like Wren and for sons-of-a-bitches like Franco, who had a circle of decapitated corpses on display around the stage for everyone to see. Sage would have compared the gore to what Damian used to have in his compound with the heads, but there were small bodies between the large ones. Some had breasts that hadn't fully developed.

Children. Teenagers.

Damian threw her his sword. Sage caught it and ran it through Lex's belly. Then she sliced up, cutting her in half, and ended her with a swift decapitation.

Killing hybrids was no easy feat. Sage had a feeling that Lex would somehow be able to pull herself back together. She got ready to do something she had never done, but if that's what it took to silence Lex, then so be it. If consumption was the only way—

"Sage." Damian held her arm. He didn't force her to look at him, though. All Sage had to do was listen. "She'll die."

"She won't."

"Sage—"

A blast from nowhere made Sage jump back. It had come from L, who was panting and holding a massive laser gun in her hands, one she had confiscated from a nearby guard. She was standing aside her torn-up lover with a wild look in her eyes. L's beautiful black hair was in a nest of waves around her face, streaks of blood showcasing the struggles she had endured to make it up here. Lex's body was a pile of ashes, but they weren't out of the woods yet.

Guards were on standby for commands from their wailing leader, who screamed, "DON'T SHOOT! DON'T SHOOT!"

L had already decimated his bitch. That gnarly bitch who had defended the town but also terrorized it.

The townsfolk were so shocked that they didn't move or run. They stood there, watching, waiting to see what was going to happen next. Was L about to finish Franco, too? Was Franco about to die? And who was the Lex-lookalike, someone who clearly didn't take orders from Franco and who didn't appear crazy enough to go on a slaughter frenzy?

Sage stepped forward. She held out a hand to L, stopping her from shooting Franco.

"Wait," she said. "I need to talk to him."

"Fuck that!" L shrieked. "This asshole's tortured us long enough! He deserves death for all the shit he does to us and all the 'favors' he demands!"

"I understand that," Sage said calmly. "But you also have to understand that we are still an open target to the Squids. If we're going to keep this town secure, there are a few questions I'd like to ask him."

"WHO ARE YOU?!" Franco wailed.

Head wound and everything, he didn't shut up. Sage grabbed him by the waistband of his pants and hauled him up. She grabbed her sword and cleaned it on the floor. The smell of his coppery blood was in her nose and it was making her dizzy. She pushed him off the stage—he stumbled right into a ring of his own guards, who didn't move a muscle to help him. Sage didn't want to know what the dynamics were, but based on how Damian had reacted when they arrived here, she had a feeling the contempt was mutual.

"Move." Sage made him walk.

Franco stumbled like a drunk. When he tripped over himself, all his guards stood back. They kept their weapons up in a show of peace. This made kicking this idiot into a room easy.

There was a bar right across the street, and the owner didn't have any qualms about allowing Sage to use it as needed. The customers cleared out. Sage would have apologized for disturbing them, but they weren't protesting. They were glaring at Franco, who had very limited time to talk.

His Cells were dying, and so was he: age was ever so slowly creeping into his face, wrinkling his skin, and sucking away his vitality. He'd die a horrible death soon.

"D-damn…" Franco croaked, looking up at her with huge bloodshot eyes. He was trembling in his chair, not even glancing at the old bar owner, who was casually drying glasses while waiting for the revenge of a lifetime. "Y-you look just like my Lex…so pretty—"

Sage punched him in the face. Then she kicked his chest and knocked him over on the floor. Franco started convulsing. Sage grabbed his hair and hauled him forward. Damian barged inside just as Sage asked, "Where did you find her?"

Franco coughed up blood. Sage asked again.

"Where did Lex come from?"

"Give me your Cells," he rasped, "and I'll tell you."

"Sage—" Damian stepped forward, but Sage stopped him. He looked a bit ridiculous carrying the babies around his torso, but there was something subdued about him. Motherly and protective. Franco noticed and widened his eyes.

"D-Damianos," Franco breathed, looking him up and down. "My love…you are as handsome as ever…Rearing more children, I see? But these are not human."

Sage slapped Franco's face. "Focus on me. Tell me where Lex came from."

"GIVE ME A BREAK!" he roared, chest heaving. "YOU FUCKING KNOW! YOU'RE ONE, TOO!"

"I'm a what?" Sage pressed angrily. "A what?"

"One of their weird fucking clones!"

"How do you know there's more of us? You said 'you're one, too,' implying that there are more."

"Well." Franco wheezed, blood still dribbling from his lips. "I'm looking at you, aren't I? And do you want to know a secret?"

Sage waited, but Franco wasn't going to give her more. All he did was laugh, and the next word out of that humongous mouth would have been "Cells" had Damian not gotten to him first.

Two gunshots. They rattled the entire bar, making the liquor shake in their display cases. A small exhale from the counter said the owner was relieved. He would have started cheering, but Sage blew a gasket.

Sage whipped around to Damian. She gritted her teeth, nostrils flared, and yelled, "ARE YOU KIDDING ME?! You shot him?!"

"He's better off dead, Sage," Damian said stoically. He didn't look her in the eye. "You have done this town a great favor. Good fucking riddance."

But Sage couldn't say the same. Not when she had so many questions on her tongue, ones that slid to the back of her throat then choked the living hell out of her. Rage consumed her, but before she could take it out on anyone, she turned and stalked off.

"Sage, wait—"

Sage hit Damian's hand away. So not fair—so not fair—she shouldn't have been taking out her anger on Damian—but she couldn't help it. Sage was so thankful L found her the next second because she would have said something she'd deeply regret.

"Fuck me," L breathed, gazing at Franco's still-twitching corpse on the floor. "He's dead."

Sage kept walking. She had had enough.

"Where are you going?"

"Away from here."

Sage burst through the doors, but L didn't let her get far.

"Wait!" she exclaimed, with the balls to grab Sage's arm and yank her back. "Wait just one fucking moment, bitch—"

Sage punched her, too. L fell back on her ass, blood gushing from both nostrils. Sage wasn't here to play games or accept abuse.

"Don't call me 'bitch'," Sage spat. "I am not your 'bitch'. I am not fucking Sonia bending over to get a pat on the head or ass from you. You have that poor girl wrapped around your finger because you enjoy giving the orders and calling the shots, like some sick role-play or something. Is the sex good afterward?"

L blinked. Franco's guards, who had before made way for Sage, were taking care of the victims on stage and mounting them into ambulances for medical care. Sonia was one of the ones strapped to a gurney, being reeled away. She had heard every one of Sage's words, though. Tears filled her eyes.

"I hope Sonia breaks up with you." Sage spat on the ground, at L's feet. "She deserves so much better."

And with that, she finally walked away. This time, no one stopped her. Everyone else was too frightened to make any moves. They were all looking at her and wondering if she was their new leader and what sort of sick plans she had for them. Would she make them do "favors"? Or would she put on shows for entertainment?

Sage couldn't take much more of this. The emotional trauma was growing again, and she had to get out before the last straw broke. She didn't even ask Damian for their kids because she didn't want to see his face and she knew they'd be safe.

Right now, she wanted to be alone.

CHAPTER 14

Faith

The people of Centerfeld were in disarray after the deaths of their leader and protector, as demented and hated as the two had been. Perhaps it wouldn't take the people long to elect a fitful and fairer ruler. They probably already had someone in mind, or someone on standby, who had been salivating to execute those two and take power for themselves.

Sage had to cut through a lot of the town to return to the *Mistress*, so she got to see the confusion firsthand. She also got to see people make way for her and point at her, whispering and asking if she was Lex's sister, wondering if she was just as vicious.

"She doesn't look it," someone said out loud.

"Still . . . let's not approach her."

When Sage finally got out, bypassing a busy checkpoint by jumping over all the heads, she could breathe. Her lungs grew, filled up with oxygen, and relaxed the rest of her body. Sort of. When she arrived at the aircraft, the reality of what she had done, seen, and heard came crashing over her. So much so, that she fell to her knees, touched the ground with her face, ignored the whining of the locked-up pups in the closet, and cried.

She screamed.

Sage screamed so loud that the pups started screaming, too. She screamed so loud that her throat turned raw and she started coughing. She got mad at herself, wanted to hurt herself, and as she balled her fists to do just that, a pair of hands encompassed them.

Sage stared at those hands. The fingers didn't have their usual rings. She had memorized each one of them.

Typically, on the left hand, from thumb to pinky, was a stackable band, mood ring, signet ring (the Diamond City one Damian had given her), mother's ring for the birth of Phoebe, and a birthstone ring. On the right hand, from thumb to pinky, was a snake ring, cocktail ring, claddagh ring with the heart facing in (because he had already found love), class ring from his time in school, and nothing on the pinky. He switched them out on occasion.

Today, he only had the claddagh on his ring finger.

Sage looked up. She found her babies nestled inside Damian's open jacket, and then she gazed into the dark eyes above. No makeup. Just exhaustion.

"Sage," Damian said softly.

His hair was a bit messy. There were flakes of snow in his strands. His skin was pale from the cold, blue around his eyes and lips. He did sort of look like a vampire.

Sage got up. She rubbed her eyes. "Can you put the babies to bed and let the pups out, please? I'm going to take a shower."

Damian said nothing as Sage retreated to the bathroom. It was a rather tight one, making it easy to contain the steam and the warmth she needed to feel comfortable. Sage stripped of all her bloody clothes and stepped into the stall. She let the water pound into her sweaty hair and body. She touched her shoulders, her small breasts, her belly, and then her legs. As she scrubbed off the soap, she found little bruises on her skin. Those must have been from the fight. Pretty soon, they'd dissipate until there was nothing at all.

Sage sat down in the corner, knees up, because she no longer had the strength to stand. For some reason, despite the steam in the room, she felt so . . . cold.

For a second, she pictured Damian entering the stall and drawing her into his arms, into his warm chest. Despite all the blood and sweat, he'd still smell like teakwood and lavender. He'd still remind her of comfort.

They had a future together, after all. They'd be getting married in the winter, moving into their own home, running the pizza restaurant, seeing the girls off to school, and raising their own two boys. It'd be a dream come true.

Sage's very own fairy tale. And, ironically, that's exactly what it was. A *fairy tale*. All that it was ever supposed to be.

Sage stood up, stopped the shower, and stepped out of the stall. She found Damian ushering the pups back into their crate after their potty break outside. He had moved them from the closet to the front of the ship again.

"Why do they slobber so much?" he muttered to himself. When he saw Sage, he smiled, but took a step back when he noticed the tightness in her shoulders and the clenching of her fists.

Sage slapped him. Hard. Damian hit the floor and scurried away from her. Sage grabbed him by the jacket and shoved him against the wall.

"WHY DID YOU CHEAT ON ME?!"

Sage slapped him again.

"Why, Damian?! I thought you loved me! I-I thought you wanted to spend the rest of your life with me!"

Damian lowered his head. His shoulders shook.

"How the fuck am I supposed to keep looking you in the face?" Sage croaked, trembling like a leaf. She hadn't even shook this hard in front of Franco and Lex. She was completely petrified now. "Fighting by your side, pretending that you're going to be a role model to our children? How, Damian?"

"I . . ." Damian took a deep breath. "I never intended to cheat on you. I never desired Agathe. I told you that from the very beginning."

"But you plotted with her behind my back?"

"No," he said. "I never plotted anything. She was the one with the ideas and I just played the game. It's what I had to do if we were going to survive, Sage."

"Is this because you wanted to be Allseer?" Sage seethed. "You wanted her favor?"

"I never had her favor. She wanted sex, and I didn't."

"But you gave it to her."

Damian sighed. "She took advantage of me when I was drunk."

"So she raped you."

"I don't know what I said when I was drunk!" Damian snapped at her. "And that was my fault. I deserve all the punches and slaps you wish to dish out—I'm sorry I didn't come to you that night—I wanted to surprise you with our wedding. I didn't intend to do any-thing with Agathe—I was an idiot, Sage—and I'm sorry."

The pups were listening intently. Their large amber eyes—just like their mother's—oscillated back and forth between the two, as if they could sense the tension between them. Perhaps, one day in the future, they'd be in a shitty relationship, too.

"I loved you," Sage croaked. She sounded like a big fat toad, but those three words were more painful than a blade to the gut. Espe-cially the second one. The past tense. She couldn't say it again. It'd imply that she no longer loved Damian.

"Do you not still love me?" Damian asked quietly. His voice was steadier than hers, but the pain in his eyes was raw. It ran down his face like hot wax, scorching and burning everything in its wake.

Sage held her face. Damian touched her shoulder.

"I made a mistake," he croaked. "I killed Agathe. There is no more plan. Chances are I will be executed if I step foot in Diamond City. But I'd rather spend my time with you."

"You can shower," Sage said quietly, still not looking at him. "I'm going to bed."

Sage turned and walked away. In her room—*his* room—were the cocoons tucked into a makeshift crib. They were wrapped in a thick blanket with frills. There were two large bows on top. Where

Damian got such things, Sage had no idea. But the sight of them made her cry.

Sage was looking at the family she'd never have. At the family she had to let go of because she couldn't look Damian in the face. She couldn't stay with him. She couldn't stop thinking of Agathe no matter how hard her heart was pounding or how horribly empty she was inside.

Sage didn't want sex. Well, maybe she did, but no dick—no matter how big and thick—could fill the void in her chest. Regardless of the sex, she'd still feel soulless. She'd still feel like someone had draped a heavy blanket over her shoulders and tied it tightly at the neck. She knew this because it wasn't her vagina that was hurting—it was her chest.

It was so strange because she had never felt this way with anyone else before. Even after breaking up with August and divorcing Gregory, she had never plunged into such a forlorn abyss. She had never felt so trapped within her own mind. Perhaps she had had Samson there to scold her or her family to remind her that there was still so much good in the world. But would they have made a difference now? Could they convince Sage there was still hope after everything she had been through since Louis' 114th birthday party?

She had found Damian—someone she loved, someone she trusted, and someone she had given her heart to—all to lose him to some sniveling bitch Allseer? Sage didn't want to play that game anymore.

Tears burning her eyes, Sage laid on the bed and brought her knees up to her chest. She cried silently. She felt so empty inside. Like a hollowed-out shell that had been thrown on the beach, discarded because it didn't have anything of value.

Damian eventually came into the room. Sage kept her eyes closed, but she heard him. He caressed each of the cocoons and kissed them. Then he stepped over to Sage and kissed her temple.

He smelled incredible. It was that strong herbal essences shampoo from the bathroom. Sage had used the same one, but she couldn't smell it on herself.

"I will always love you," Damian said softly against her head.

Before he turned around to leave, Sage grabbed his hand. She looked at him over her shoulder.

"Stay with me," she whispered.

As badly as she wanted to have sex, this was more for holding. To feel his warmth. To have his body spooned behind hers so she wouldn't do anything crazy tonight. Sage's emotions were a wreck. Her anxiety got worse when thoughts of Lex and those dead women from the cage entered her mind.

"Don't think," Damian said to her. "We'll figure it out in the morning."

Maybe. So Sage closed her eyes and sighed, seeking reprieve for just a few hours. She held Damian's hand on her belly then fell asleep.

Sage woke up when her body was completely rested. She didn't need any more sleep, so she was fully alert in seconds. For a few minutes, she stared at the window. The blinds blocked out any sunlight from outside. Only seven in the morning, according to her clock. Then she looked over her shoulder and spotted her babies all cozy in their blankets and crib. She smiled.

Damian was snoring lightly behind her. His hand was still on her belly and it had never ventured farther than that. He never took advantage of anyone, especially when he wasn't wanted. That was one of many qualities Sage appreciated. She only wished she could get over Agathe.

Sage turned onto her back. She kept her eyes on his face, which was as relaxed as it had ever been. Perhaps it had been days since he'd had a good sleep like this one. Sage didn't want to disturb him, but there was no way to get out of this bed without making noise. She didn't mind lying there for a while longer, just watching.

"...Do I still look beautiful...?" Damian mumbled.

Was that in his sleep? Or was he truly asking her?

"Yes," Sage said.

Damian opened his eyes slightly. He gave a lazy smile then nudged her nose with his. Sage did the same. This was the part where they would kiss, but they didn't. Damian was waiting for her to make the first move, and Sage decided she still wasn't ready. Didn't want to. Couldn't trust him again. Had to distance herself as much as possible. But was that really what she wanted? Maybe she did want to kiss him. That didn't really mean anything, did it? A kiss?

"I will always love you."

Maybe it did. Sage knew it was complicated and that her emotions were all fucked up. God knew what her hormone levels were after "giving birth," but she felt particularly aggressive and possessive. Maybe it wasn't such a good idea to engage in any kind of sexual activity because she wasn't sure if it was her mind or body or both telling her that it was fine, that this was just a kiss, but she did it anyway.

It wasn't even a kiss. It was a press of lips, one that lasted a long-ass time. Sage didn't think about Agathe. She didn't think about anything at all. She breathed through her nose and gazed into his eyes.

Damian touched her face with his hand. He held her, prepared her for a more assertive kiss. The pressure between their mouths increased. Sage closed her eyes as he sucked on her upper lip. Sage decided to do his lower. So plump and soft just like she remembered. His gloss was her favorite, but there was none to savor so early in the morning. Then they alternated and did it again.

At long last, Sage caved. Now she was kissing him and he was kissing her. Their lips got tangled with one another's, and Sage had an opportunity to slip her tongue inside but something kept holding her back. In one of her more daring moments, she brushed his teeth by accident. She went to withdraw, but Damian caught her before she did. Now their tongues were twining around the other, and that made fire explode in Sage's groin.

Sage couldn't focus on the kiss anymore. She had to stop and breathe. She also had to acknowledge that she was about to have sex with a man she no longer claimed to love. This wasn't going to fix anything.

So why did her body yearn for it? Why did Sage bring Damian onto her, right in between her legs, and hold him like she used to? Because the feel of his genitals was so good and promised so much pleasure. The thought of what that mouth could do to the rest of her body made her go insane. There was nothing like Damian devouring her whole and making her climax hard and fast. Perhaps that's what Sage wanted, but she wasn't going to get it. Not today.

Damian didn't move from above her. It was as if he sensed her hesitation, knew he no longer held her heart and soul like he used to. The love, trust, and promise between them was gone. The spark was missing.

Damian bowed his head in shame. He didn't get off her. He gave her what he could. A little nuzzle in the neck was the equivalent of a dog licking his master's wounds after hurting him.

Sage stared at the ceiling. She wasn't sure how much time she laid there with Damian's body on top of hers, but it felt endless. His lips were on her skin, suckling her here and there, but she felt nothing.

Eventually, Damian stopped. He kissed her forehead and did something Sage would have never dream he'd do: he got off her. No seduction. No sex. He sat on the edge of the bed, like a child that had been scolded.

Damian didn't move for a long time. Sage couldn't see his face from her angle. She did see him wipe his eyes, though.

"I have made many mistakes in my life," Damian said softly. "Some small, small big. But this one, with Agathe, is devastating. And the scary part is I'm not sure there's anything I can do to erase it. To get you back. But then I realize it's not you I have to win . . . it's myself."

Someone sounded the intercom from the front of the ship. A visitor, it seemed, although Damian wasn't in any hurry to answer it. He stood up slowly. He didn't bother putting on a shirt—he stayed in his spandex with a crotch that was more show than tell So not appropriate. Sage would have laughed, but she couldn't even move from the bed.

Damian stopped by the crib. He caressed each of the cocoons His shoulders were down, relaxed, and his feet were together when they were usually apart. Damian was always ready to fight. He was ready to be a father, too. He had lesson number one for Pollux and Castor.

"You were just about to see how you were made," he said loud enough for Sage to hear. "There are a plethora of positions that work. The key is that I ejaculate—"

Sage threw a pillow at him and she got him right in the ass. Damian rubbed it on the way out, way too slowly to relieve any pain.

He went to get the door. Sage sat on the bed for another moment, wondering if this was how her future was going to be. She and Damian, an estranged couple, keeping up fronts for their children. Divorced parents.

Thankfully, Sage's family had never seen many of them. Maybe one, but the separation had been civil. For the most part, all her nieces and nephews had sustained healthy relationships. Bram was the only nephew who had lost his wife early on. Sage, of course, always pitched in as a parent and filled in the gaps. She had just never thought she'd be the one dealing with the drama.

It was hard as hell to get out of bed. Sage had to feed the cocoons, though. She opened a cut on her palm and let her blood dribble right onto one before moving on to the other. As she stood there, watching drops of her life seep into that of her children's, she listened to whom Damian was talking to up front.

"Darling," he called to her. "Someone by the name of 'L' is here to see you."

"My God," Sage breathed. She had been hoping for Gertrude, but of course it had to be the person she wanted to see the least. L brought with her that black cloud of hatred and negativity as well as all the terrible memories from last night. All the questions about where the hell Lex had come from burned in Sage's chest, and she'd rather not deal with it right now. In fact, all she wanted to do was stay by her children until they hatched.

Sage sighed. She left them in the safety of their crib with a grunt and thought about what she was going to say to make L go away and never come back. Damian would help her, and L wouldn't dare say anything against him, the notorious Warlord.

"What the fuck are you doing?" L sputtered as soon as Sage met her at the door. L looked as if she had never seen anyone in a shirt and shorts before. That wasn't why she was cussing, though. "I thought you had broken up with him!"

"You've got to be kidding me," Sage spat. "That's why you're here? To criticize me and my relationship? Why don't you take care of yours and I'll take care of mine?"

"Fine." L held up her hands. She had a beanie on her head, but most of her hair was loose and whipping around in the wind. Sage hadn't invited her onto the ship yet, and the chances of that happening were diminishing by the second. "I admit I can be an ungrateful bitch. I admit I've manipulated Sonia into doing a lot of things, like becoming Lex Warriors, partaking in orgies with Franco, and even eating grass-flavored ice cream—"

"What?" Sage breathed. From "Lex Warriors" to "orgies" to "grass-flavored ice cream", her mind was spinning.

L took a deep breath. "I'm a shitty person. But even Sonia will tell you we did it for survival. Hell, even *he*"—and she pointed at Damian—"will tell you why we did. When he and his rebels came knocking on our door for help all those years ago, he cut and run when he knew what he was dealing with. Franco is a crazy psychopath and Lex was his pet. We all had to follow orders or we'd be dead. At the same time, we had to sacrifice what we had to become stronger and stay alive. That's why we became Enhanced. Or Lex Warriors."

"Right." Sage cleared her throat.

"That's me, though." L's eyes returned to Damian. "But you said that bastard manipulated you. Sonia told me what he did to the All-seer in an attempt to win you back. You don't seriously trust him, do you—?"

"You mean am I sleeping with him?" Sage drawled. "That's none of your business."

"He's using you!"

Damian brushed past Sage and stomped down the ramp. Shirtless in zero-degree weather, he whipped out a gun and pointed it at L's face. Like a werewolf the pups would be proud of, he snarled, "Are you fucking kidding me right now? Is this why you're here? To berate Sage for her decision to stay with me when you don't know the first things about our relationship? I don't know who the fuck you are, but you better turn the hell around and march right back to Centerfeld where you belong.

"You want to talk about being manipulative? How long did it take you to crown yourself ruler of the town once Sage killed Franco, bitch?"

Most women would have put their hands up and walked away. Others might have apologized and just turned around. But no, not L, who took out her own gun and aimed it at Damian.

Sage wasn't going to take this. God, she hadn't even had breakfast and these two were fighting, about to kill each other. So she stalked right over to them, right in the line of fire, got to L, and pried the gun out of her hand.

"Hey—"

Sage threw it across the field.

"Get out," Sage spat in L's face. "I don't want to see you ever again."

L threw a punch. Sage caught it, grabbed her by the arm, and drove her into the snow. She was seconds away from cracking it, but this was L's dominant arm. Then again, L was an Enhanced, so this would regenerate in no time and L would think twice about bothering her—

"SAGE!" L roared. "S-STOP! PLEASE! I-I'm not here to fight you!

On the contrary, I'm worried! Not just about Centerfeld, but about you! I saw the way Franco treated Lex and I don't want that asshole over there doing the same to you!"

"BREAK HER FUCKING ARM!" Damian barked.

"I can take care of myself," Sage hissed into L's ear. "Got it? Now if you're ready to talk like a civilized person, I'm going to let you go. You're here to talk to me about Centerfeld and not who I'm giving blowjobs to at night."

L's heavy breathing was the only answer. Sage slowly got off her.

L got to her feet. She rubbed her right shoulder. She took deep breaths to calm herself, as if wondering if Sage really was giving blowjobs to the asshole, before she was ready to face Sage.

"Can I come in?" she asked quietly.

Sage didn't say yes or no. She retreated to Damian's side and led him up the ramp to the ship. She pulled a shirt over his head and asked him to start breakfast. It went without saying that they weren't going to be showing off the cocoons to someone who was crazy. In fact, once L was in the kitchen, Sage blocked the only exit.

"I really wanted to talk with you," L started, eyeing Damian, who was cracking some eggs over a pan. She eyed his ass, still in tight shorts, before looking back at Sage, who was obviously hiding something from her. L didn't question it, though. Perhaps Sonia had already told her about the babies. "About last night. Franco and . . . Lex's deaths."

"What about them?"

L scowled. "It's a big deal." She sat down in a chair, still in her coat and beanie with a ton of snow. "They were our leaders. Now we have to figure out who's going to be in charge, and someone by the name of Gertrude said you'd be perfect for the job."

Sage would be perfect for the job. Not Damian. But the latter didn't take any offense—he was scrambling eggs now. He added more salt and pepper.

"I don't want to be leader," Sage said. "I want to stay out here.

Isolated. Don't you see that? I want fucking peace—is that too much to ask?"

"Fine, and I get that. Sonia's recovering from her injuries, but we're Franco's stand-ins. No one has to know anything—they don't even have to see you—we'll just do as you say." L gave her an earnest look. "We have a town to run and defend. We'll bring you everything you need to know—status reports every day—so you can guide us in the right direction. How does that sound to you, Sage?"

"Where did Lex come from?"

L blinked. She already had her mouth open, ready to argue if Sage had said no to her proposition, but she had to close it and recalibrate her response. Sage's question was a bit from left field, but fair and warranted. Even L couldn't have mistaken the striking resemblance between the two.

"I don't know," L said sincerely. She relaxed her face so Sage could see that she was telling the truth. "After the Warlord's Rebellion thirty years ago, we lost all contact with Diamond City. The Allseer didn't want anything to do with the Outskirts anymore, so we were up shit creek without a paddle. Franco came to us as an Enhanced offering protection because he needed shelter and we needed a warrior, as futile as it was against potential attacks from Squids."

"And did you ever run into any?"

"No," L said.

"Well, I did." Sage took a seat, glaring at L. Damian came over with their breakfast. After so much practice, he was an expert at eggs, toast, and orange juice by now. "I fought six of them."

L gasped. "And you beat them?"

"That's not the point. They were lugging around bodies." Sage scowled. "*Me*. People that looked like me. Care to offer any reasonable explanations?"

"That's not fair, Sage. How the hell am I supposed to know? I mean, I don't know why you guys look alike or anything like that—all I know is that Lex came from Emerald City."

Sage and Damian glanced at each other. Their eyes reflected the same exact questions, too fast for Sage to register, but understanding all the same. With her temperature rising and her heart rate increasing, Sage quickly forgot about the delicious breakfast on her place mat and said,

"Emerald City?"

"That's what she said when she happened upon our town," L said. "She came as an ambassador, and she wanted an alliance. And now that we've—uh—killed her, we're in deep shit. Which is why we need you, understand?"

"I've heard of Emerald City," Sage said, thinking of her date with Louis. Caviar tasted like shit. "But I've never been there."

"A lot of us haven't. We've never ventured very far because of the dangers out there. Lex kept Centerfeld a respectable distance away from Emerald City politics, too, because she had a job to fulfill: turn us all into warriors. Like the Warlord"—L's eyes made a pass to Damian—"we were getting ready to venture around the Outskirts to recruit more warriors. Eventually, we'd have wanted a truce with Diamond City. Not sure how that's going to work out now."

L took one look at her food, then asked, "This isn't poisoned, is it?"

"Taste it and find out," Damian sneered.

L stuck out the middle finger.

Sage was amused. "You two would make an amazing couple. I'm not sure you'd make it through a whole day in one piece, though."

Both Damian and L snarled at each other like animals. Sage supposed she could appreciate the entertainment.

"So Emerald City sent Lex to become friends with Centerfeld?" Sage said.

"Yes," L replied.

"And what about the other clones? Did they play a role in this as well?"

"Lex never mentioned anyone else," L said.

"For someone who was so powerful, you sure don't seem very mournful that she's gone."

L snorted. "Because I'm not. No one is. It was hell here, Sage, and

I'm not sure it was a life worth living. Yes, we're all Enhanced, most of us stronger than the average fighters thanks to her, but you don't have any idea of the *shit* we had to do to get there. Lex and Francc liked to put on shows. They liked to experiment, too."

L had pictures of a room inside one of the lab facilities. There in incubators, waiting for the day they'd hatch, were tons and tons of cocoons.

"W-what is that?" Sage croaked, her composure crumbling.

"Eggs?" L shook her head. "Like fuck I know. We just got intc the facility last night now that Franco and Lex aren't guarding it with their lives. Our scientists claimed that there were babies inside, but they're all dead—"

Sage got up and ran to the bathroom. She heaved violently. Damian was right behind her, holding her hair and body as she vomited, and then after, when she cried.

"Don't cry," he whispered against her temple. "It's fine. Those aren't ours—ours are safe."

"Why are they all dead?" Sage croaked, clutching Damian's shirt. The tiles felt so cold against her bare legs. "W-why are the babies dead?"

"I don't know, darling, but they're not ours."

"Sage?" L approached the bathroom, but Damian snapped at her.

"Can you leave us the fuck alone? Haven't you delivered enough bad news?"

"I'm sorry!" L croaked. "I didn't mean to upset you—I just thought you wanted me tc be honest—"

"It's fine." Sage got to her feet—Damian helped her. "I did."

"I know you have children of your own, and if there's anything we can do to help—"

"Do you think I'm going to ask your scientists for help when they couldn't even help those two demons?" Sage snarled. She didn't mean to sound condescending or snappy, but she was as riled up as ever. She was itching to take her cocoons and the pups out on a walk. Perhaps she'd do just that as soon as she sent L on her way.

L raised her hands. "Understandable. Just know that we're here for you."

"Thanks." Sage turned on the faucet. Damian splashed water on her face. When she was a bit more cleaned up, she said to L, "I want you to throw a party."

Both L and Damian arched their brows.

"It's what the rebels do when there's something to celebrate," Sage said. "And I'd say there's plenty of celebrating to do. Those two tyrants are dead. Maybe now we stand a chance of unity. What do you say?"

"Um." L didn't know how to refute that, clearly. So she didn't. "Sure," she concurred. "I'll tell everyone to relax for an evening."

"Send me everything you know about Centerfeld, and I'll review it. We'll take it a step at a time."

Which was the hardest part about all this. Sage had so many questions that she was going to explode if she didn't go on that walk. She wrapped her cocoons up in that make-shift sling Damian had made, released the pups from their crate, then left the ship to wander around the snowy grounds. She watched the pups jump and nibble each other when they weren't peeing or pooping. Damian stayed by her side, cozied up in his jacket.

"Can you tell me what's on your mind?" Sage asked quietly.

"The party," he said truthfully.

Sage laughed. It just burst out of her. "Of course. What you're going to wear."

"You're throwing a party, but you are coming, right?"

"No." Sage rubbed her cocoons. "I just want peace and quiet."

"Darling." Damian grasped her chin. "It's just one night."

"I'm not leaving the children."

"You don't have to. We'll make them a part of our attire."

"Don't be ridiculous."

Damian chuckled. "I'm not."

"Are they really all dead?" Sage said. "Those babies in Centerfeld? W-what if our babies are dead, too?"

"They're not." Damian touched them with his hand. He held

it there for a moment, feeling for life. There was movement from within. Past that was a steady thumping. "Feel them."

"When are they going to hatch? When are they going to wake up?"

"When they're ready. And when they do, we'll be there, Sage. I don't say this often, but … have a little bit of faith. Not in Squids," he said quickly when Sage glared at him. "But in a higher, better power. One that's good and cares for us."

"Do you really believe that?" Sage said. The pups were tumbling in the snow now.

"I do," Damian said. "He brought me you, didn't he? Why can't he bring me my children, too?"

Sage smiled. Perhaps without being aware of it, Damian leaned down for a kiss. This time, Sage met him halfway.

CHAPTER 15

Love Forever

The party was the best thing Sage could have asked for. It didn't happen right away because there was so much to tend to in Centerfeld and so much to prepare to make any celebration worthwhile, but it was the anticipation of it that brightened everyone's mood. Damian's happiness was in designing costumes for hours in the meeting room and shopping at Centerfeld's biggest fashion stores. His rebels had plenty of time to recover from Franco's show, and the rest of the town accepted that better days were ahead under a new leadership. The transition was amazingly painless, and it still surprised Sage, who had expected tons more resistance and doubt from the people. No one was putting up any fights. That's what Gertrude and the other rebels, who came out to visit Sage on a daily basis, confirmed. L had not made an appearance since.

"Things are definitely looking up," Gertrude said. She, Mega Woman, Turtle, Rockstar, Eye Candy, Butcher, Sailor, and Clara were sitting at the table waiting for breakfast. Sage was making pancakes today. It was nice to see that Turtle had all his fingers back and that the rest of the rebels were in one piece.

According to them, the doctors in Centerfeld were extraordinary. They could mend any wound, reattach limbs, regenerate nerve cells, and bring anyone back from the brink of death. They even had stasis pods with actual people inside, a chosen few who'd be waking up many years in the future. Sage didn't know much of the details, but Franco and Lex had coordinated all of this. In addition to putting on shows, they had chosen who lives, dies, and sees the future.

Sage wasn't surprised. She supposed they were a lot like Allseer Marchello. The only difference was this was a relatively small town where word spread like wildfire. In Diamond City, news never left the capital unless the Allseer willed it, and he had the eyes and ears to ensure there were no slip-ups.

All this political talk made Sage grateful she wasn't a part of it. So long as the right people were in charge, the rebels were happy. Preacher was sucked up in some sermon despite how scarce piety was nowadays, doing what he loved. Apparently, there were plenty of people in Centerfeld who wanted to listen to him. Damian was still sketching away with the cocoons in his own little world, hidden from anybody that came to visit the *Mistress*. It was crazy to think he wasn't more involved in Centerfeld's leadership. Perhaps he didn't care for politics much, either, so long as everything was running smoothly.

"L and Sonia have become the new leaders," Turtle remarked. He sipped some coffee. "Although Sword Devil looks like a pretty tough chick."

Rockstar chuckled and patted his buddy on the back. Everyone knew that Turtle had screwed up with Gertrude, and this was his chance to make amends.

"I'm appreciating her skills!" Turtle snapped. "Goddamn, can't make a comment here."

"We all know you're salivating after this chick," Eye Candy said. "So why not take advantage and ask her out? Show everyone you can be a decent person."

Gertrude said nothing. Sage was more interested in perfecting the color of her pancakes.

Mega Woman snorted at Turtle. "It'd definitely be a nice change Maybe people will respect you better."

"Fuck off! People *do* respect me, and, unlike you, I actually have friends. Who do you have, bitch?"

Mega Woman's silence said she didn't have anyone. Butcher Sailor, and Clara kept a low profile in case they were bullied and insulted later.

"Come now," Turtle continued because he wasn't scared of Mega Woman. "What was it that you said on stage? That you'd be a better person if you lived?"

Sage turned around at this. She arched a brow. "What?"

"Yeah," Turtle said loudly. "Mega Woman was crying when Franco stabbed her five times. She prayed to the Squids and said she was sorry for all her transgressions. From then on out, she promised to be the best person she could be."

"Well, you can start with your attitude," Rockstar said to Mega Woman. "You don't have to look like you're taking a hard shit all the time."

"Am I really supposed to sit here and take this?" Mega Woman said out loud.

"Yes," they all responded.

Sage figured after a show like Franco's anyone would be willing to change their ways forever in exchange for a chance at life. She was glad she had woken up in time to investigate what had been taking the rebels so long in Centerfeld. Either way, Damian would have done something to save them.

"So there's Sword Devil," Turtle went on, "and then there's this extreme fastball player called Tai. I think he's of Asian descent or something, but he's supposed to be incredible on the court. You know that Centerfeld has their own teams? They play against each other."

Sage was really paying attention now. Now that Turtle had mentioned it, she didn't remember seeing any team flags from Centerfeld in the Mousafeld stadium. That meant these people were cultivated, and if they had each other for competition, then they had to be crazy good.

The pancake was burning, and Sage cursed. She got to it right away. No one noticed because they all started arguing about the incredible people in Centerfeld.

"They're like robots," Clara agreed. "And they scare me. Like they're not really people."

"They have to be, though." Sailor patted her hand. "They had appearances to keep around Franco and Lex."

"But it's like they're all good at something, even the commoners. It's as if they each have a mission, a purpose. Centerfeld is like one well-oiled machine."

Under Franco and Lex's leadership, perhaps the town was in tip-top shape. It was what Mousafeld had aspired to be in its heyday. Now the rebels were scattered all over the Outskirts, with some still in Mousafeld, some working for the Diamond City military, and a dozen others following their hopeless Warlord around. Eight of them were at this table, and they grew quiet when they wondered what would become of them next.

Gertrude gave them hope. Of course they were joining forces with Centerfeld. L and Sonia had welcomed them with open arms, so this was their chance to climb back up the ladder after killing Agathe and committing treason. Sage said nothing. She felt bad for them, knowing that Damian's actions weren't their fault. She tried not to think about Justice and Little Man.

After breakfast, the rebels left. Gertrude was the only one who lingered. She looked like a lost child who didn't know how to walk straight. She kept fiddling with her fingers and twiddling her thumbs. "Sage?" she asked softly.

"Yes, Gertrude?" Sage cleaned the dishes at the sink.

"Are you doing all right? The babies and such?"

"Just fine."

"So . . . this party. Want to go shopping with me?"

"No," Sage said.

"Just thought I should ask." Gertrude looked down at her feet. "I know you need your time alone . . . but I'd like to hang out with you some time. I found a Portable Projector the other day and I thought about you. They're pretty rare, so I bought it." She shrugged. She put it on the counter because she must have been afraid Sage would toss it in the garbage.

Sage didn't even look at it. She had completely forgotten about her own until now. It was always hanging around her neck.

And it always made her think of Damian.

"We can see the stores, talk to the locals, and maybe meet up with those fastball players," Gertrude went on. "I know you want to."

Sage slammed the plates non-too gently on the drying rack. "Why?"

"I thought we were friends."

"So did I." Sage finally turned around. She glared at Gertrude, who was even worse than Damian in the face of her fury. Gertrude backed away like a child who didn't want to be scolded. "I thought we were friends, too. But then you gave me all these fucking death glares after Little Man died, as if it was my fault. Explain to me how that's fair when all I tried to do was save the two of you—I TOLD YOU TO RUN!"

"I-I know and I'm sorry! But Sage—I never blamed you for one moment!"

"Yes, you did," Sage hissed. "You're a liar. You threw a hissy-fit without thinking how it would affect me. We were *all* mourning his loss, but you blamed me anyway, and that's not fair. I just don't have the energy for that. I don't take death lightly, and I miss Little Man..." She stopped. She took a deep breath and composed herself, or else she'd start crying. The wounds were still too raw, and a mere thought could send her spiraling. She had stayed away from fastball in Diamond City for a reason, and she'd stay away from it here, too. "I miss him so much. I-I can't stop thinking about him or Justice or even Mohawk and Blondie because I can't ever get over when loved ones die. It's like I hold them in my chest, and they become like a knife until I can't breathe at night. I have serious emotional issues and I can't deal with people who see me as an enemy."

"I never saw you as an enemy—"

"Get out."

Gertrude blinked her large eyes. Sage kept her expression blank.

"Please leave, Gertrude. They need you at Centerfeld."

Sage brushed past her. The pups were fast asleep in their crate, bellies full from today's breakfast. Jealously pricked Sage, who wished she could escape in a dream. She supposed she had Damian, and she was going to pick a fight for the hell of it, but she stopped when she glimpsed him coloring some designs on the table. The cocoons were in their crib by his side. His breakfast plate was clean, so he must have shoved food in his mouth amidst coloring.

"Darling." Damian looked up with a smile. When he saw her face, his fell instantly. "What's wrong?"

So many things that Sage was too exhausted to recite out loud. She plopped down on a chair next to him. She looked at all the designs scattered on the table. He was pumping these out like toys in a factory. There was every which way imaginable to wear green and silver here, from big fluffy dresses to low neckline gowns. They had all been ripped out of his sketchbook and they were probably the ones he had discarded and wasn't going to use. Right now, he was sketching her and the twins.

"Want to see?" Damian asked, showing her his work in progress.

Wow. This looked exactly like Sage. It was scary. And to think he had pulled this off with a pencil and a few crayons.

Sage's hair was long and without frizz. The sweat and the cold kept it damp and plastered to her face. Her freckles were as pronounced as ever. She had lost a great deal of mass on her frame, but she was still muscular. In the drawing, she was in a side-swept gown, all green, with silver accents on her hips. Her gloves were fingerless and silver belts wrapped around her forearms. She held her cocoons in each arm, and they were dressed up, too, some ridiculous onesie with buttons and clips.

"They haven't even hatched yet," Sage said.

"So?" Damian countered. "They are part of the party, too. Trust me—they'll remember this."

Sage doubted it. She didn't think the twins could feel anything in their cocoons and she preferred it that way. She didn't destroy Damian's spirits, though. It kept him busy and away from trouble, and perhaps he liked the solitude of his sessions, too. It let him concentrate on his fashion, while Sage had nothing to do.

No pizza. No fastball. But then . . .

Sage touched the Portable Projector around her neck. Her eyes welled with tears as memories of when she had fallen in love with Damian rushed back to her all at once. No longer able to breathe, she took the cocoons and the pups out for a walk. And while she had composed herself some when she returned to the *Mistress*, she was a bomb ready to go off at the slightest nudge.

Damian read her like a book. He didn't ask, he just watched her. He had boxes of fabrics everywhere now. He must have purchased all this from Centerfeld, including that expensive-looking sewing machine he was fiddling around with. It was as easy as uploading designs and inputting measurements. God, Sage really didn't want to ruin this, but—

"I hate you."

Damian blinked. He looked so horribly guilty that Sage wanted to cry.

"I hate you, damn it!" Sage exclaimed. "Fuck you!"

Sage went to flee, but Damian caught her in the hallway. She cried out, slammed her elbow into his gut, and made to run, but Damian caught her again. They tumbled to the floor where Sage got a few good hits in: she punched his face, broke a few bones in his chest, and bruised his ribs. Damian didn't stay idle—he struck her in the shoulder and pushed her onto her back.

Sage squeezed him. She meant to cut off his air and kill him, but then all her energy dissipated. It leaked out of her like air out of a punctured balloon. Limp and useless, Sage cried instead. Loud, heart-wrenching sobs. She scratched his back and kneed his groin, but Damian never got off her. He pressed her to the floor until she stilled. It didn't take long.

"We were supposed to get married," Sage croaked, eyes puffy

and full of tears. "We were supposed to be together..."

"We are together, darling," Damian said, lips against her temple. "We will always be together. Even if you don't wish to be with me, I will always be by your side. I will defend you and everything you stand for no matter what happens between us."

"HOW CAN YOU SAY THAT?!" Sage screamed. "AFTER YOU BE-TRAYED ME!"

"I didn't mean to, darling." Damian nuzzled her face. He did it to hide his eyes. "I didn't mean to."

"You wouldn't be with anyone else? Just to be by my side?"

"Yes."

"Oh, God." Sage sobbed. She didn't know why this hurt so much. She couldn't stop thinking of Agathe and the devious plot Damian had planned behind her back. How on earth could she trust him now?

"What else is left for me, Sage?" Damian asked her quietly. "Agathe is gone. Louis will be after my head. I have no home, no place unless it is by your side. The rebels respect you so much more than they do me. Tell me what I can possibly be plotting now?"

"Are you only doing this because you got caught?"

"No, darling. I was a fool and I made a mistake. Had I never lost my head drinking like a drunk, I would have had to deal with Agathe another way."

"Can you get off me?"

Damian did. He got to his feet despite the fractures in his torso. He meant to help her up, but Sage scooted back from him.

"I want you to leave me alone," Sage said. Her body shook viciously, as if in protest to her words. But she forced them out anyway. "Take your things and go to Centerfeld. You can visit the twins in the morning while I take the pups out on a walk. I don't want to see you."

"I understand." Damian bowed his head. Then he turned around and withdrew to his room to pick up all his designs and fabrics.

Sage pulled her knees in. She clutched them hard. She drew blood from her own skin. Her chest hurt so badly that she thought she was having a heart attack. Words wrestled their way up her throat and into her mouth, but they never came out.

Damian didn't speak or prod her for a reaction. He understood that she needed her space, so he walked right by her and left.

Sage couldn't remember a darker moment in her life. Everything that happened from then on out was a blur. That's because she never got out of bed. She wasted away on that mattress because she didn't have the strength to do anything other than lay there. She often screamed when no one was listening. Faces flashed in her mind's eye, ones of Samson, Bram, the girls, Damian, her twins, and the rebels. They played in succession, mesmerizing her for hours, days, and maybe even weeks. She didn't hear when Damian came to visit the twins because he never bothered her. Despite her severe depression, Damian respected her wishes and stayed away.

It wasn't easy for him, either. One night, Sage overheard him yelling in the hallway. She sat up, startled, wondering if they were under attack, when she realized it was just him and . . . Gertrude. Perhaps Turtle, Rockstar, and Eye Candy were there, too, and maybe Preacher, who was the quietest he had ever been in his life.

"I can't see her like this!" Damian sobbed. He sounded muffled, so maybe he had his head in Gertrude's chest. "I can't! I-I can't—I can't go on like this—why am I such a fucking failure, Gertrude?! Why do I always fuck everything up?!"

"You don't, sir," Gertrude croaked. "You don't—we all make mistakes."

"I can't live this way—I'd rather die than see her like that!"

"Think this through, sir—if you die, then you won't ever see your children."

Damian howled in pain. Sage had never heard sounds like that leave his throat. They didn't sound natural. They were guttural, as if someone were torturing him. And then she smelled blood.

"Sir," Rockstar croaked. "Please . . . stop . . ."

What was Damian doing? Whatever it was, Gertrude grabbed his wrists. The scratching noises stopped.

"Help me…" Damian continued to sob. "Take this pain away…"

"Sir, please control yourself," Preacher said gently. "The lady will recuperate her will. She just needs time to process the events of the past. You will see improvement soon, just have faith."

"I CAN'T CHANGE WHAT I DID!"

"We all know that. And that is why you must better yourself and show everyone that you have learned from your mistakes. Life is a journey with many trials and temptations, and we are not expected to pass every one. Some of us might fail multiple times. If anyone knows that, the lady does. She is just so very hurt by your actions at the moment, but she will learn to accept them and forgive you."

It was strange to hear Preacher talk like that. No mention of Squids? Sage sat up a bit. Her stomach was searing because she hadn't eaten in a while, but she had to listen to this.

"You vowed to stay by her side no matter what," Preacher went on. "Allow yourself some time to mourn her state, but then compose yourself, sir. There are many dangerous battles ahead."

"I-I want to hold her—"

"You must not. You must honor her wishes."

No. Sage wanted Damian, but when she got up to see him, he was already gone.

Sage hit the floor with her knees. She touched the Portable Projector around her neck. With a horribly sad smile on her face, and thoughts of Aurora in her head, she pressed the play button.

Over a hundred years ago, they'd lay on the living room floor and watch a ton of episodes. They'd dream about the future, about a united Diamond City. Aurora would get married in the Clarity District because she was dying to wear one of those quirky masks the preachers wore for respect. Sage would get married in the Color District because she marveled at the fashion and colors. What would it be like to be on stage? She hated attention, but no one would recognize her as the Optimum. She'd be a star for a different reason.

"That means your husband would have to be a fashion designer," Aurora said thoughtfully. She had a pen to her lips, feet swinging back and forth on the bed. "Because you suck."

"Hey!" Sage threw a crayon at her. She was on the floor. "I don't suck!"

"Sage, you always wear T-shirts and cargo shorts. You need help."

Sage sighed. She looked down at her attire. Aurora was right.

"All right." Aurora got back to her notebook. "What would he look like? Your dream husband?"

"Handsome, of course," Sage said, looking up at the ceiling full of Star Raider stickers. "Fine features. Not too manly because machos are like brutes. I want someone gentle . . . funny . . . but strong. Oh—strong! He has to have a lot of muscles."

"Ooo," Aurora mused, sketching away. "What else?"

"Long hair. I love long hair on guys."

"So why do you hang around that August guy? He's so ugly."

Sage glared at her. "He's not that bad."

"Come on, Sage—he's got a big mole on his cheek!"

"So?"

"Whatever." Aurora kept sketching. "Fine, long hair. What else?"

"Dark eyes. Sharp nose. Beautiful lips full of gloss. And then he'd be dressed in this incredible suit, silver and green. He'd have confetti in his hair and makeup on his face. He'd look like a sexy fairy warrior that no one can beat. He might be flamboyant, but he's dark and mysterious."

"You love bad boys!" Aurora giggled. "That's dangerous. They'll break your heart."

Sage shrugged. "That's part of the thrill, right? To make me feel?"

"If you say so. But if he does break your heart, you have to be strong."

"And love him anyway?"

"Only if he really loves you," Aurora said. "And he doesn't fuck up again, of course. He has to be willing to earn your trust. To learn and grow. You, too, though—you'll mess up, too. But like him, you'll become a better person."

"All right," Sage said. "I think I can handle that."

"Don't be afraid, Sage. Making mistakes is a part of life. Reach for the good, just like we've done growing up with Mom. There is no fairy tale without hiccups. You're going to have to fight for it, even if it means accepting the bad."

"There will always be bad, won't there?"

"Always. Now close your eyes and picture this: it's dark outside. There're fairy lights hanging from the trees. The moon is shining. The snow is thick. Everyone's dressed up for the party, and they're waiting for you, Sage. The entire town is there."

Indeed, the entire town was out there. When Sage came out of the *Mistress*, she was shocked not only to see Damian and the rebels, but the *entire* town.

They had taken the party to her.

It truly was a wonderful night.

"Everyone is in green and silver," Aurora said from atop the bed. "And they're all just living life the best way they know how. Maybe there are a few competitions here and there, like who can drink the most Cupid's Arrow without getting drunk or keep the longest fastball volley."

"There's no court, though."

"You can just bounce the ball between you and someone else."

True. And, surprisingly, there were quite the number of people doing it that way. Tai, the extreme fastball player that entertained crowds for hours with his insane volleys, was out there now. He and Turtle's love interest, Sword Devil, were going at it. That ball never hit the floor. It was like an all-air tennis match. The speed was what captured and held everyone's attention for almost an hour. Sage stood among the crowd, impressed as hell. Candice and Olivia would have loved to see this. She wondered if Geoffrey liked to play, too. Winterfeld used to have a fastball team.

"But you're not there to think about fastball," Aurora said, waving a hand in her face. "Keep walking. Look at all the pretty hues between the trees. Listen to the music in the distance. Feel the warmth of the bodies around you. These are people who care about you. They've come all the way out here for you. Even people who once hated you at Mousafeld are happy to see you dressed up."

"What am I wearing?"

Aurora sighed. "Silly. You know what."

It was that dress Damian had drawn. It was one of the more modest ones he had created, perfect for a casual night like this one. It had long sleeves, a belt at the hips, and an ankle-length gown. It was easy to move around in and wasn't overly showy. Sage didn't like the spotlight, no matter how much Damian thrived in it.

It was clear how much he enjoyed it. He moved as gracefully as a deer through those trees. He was the star of whatever was going on around him, wherever he went. Sage was just along for the ride.

"When he holds you, you just forget everything," Aurora said.

That was so true. Damian extended his hand like Blackburn had done at Louis' birthday party. Here, though, there were no bright lights in Sage's face or royal couples to bump into. The crowd was either small or had withdrawn to leave the two alone. Or maybe it was Sage who got lost in Damian's eyes and forgot about everything else.

Green eyeliner, silver glitter. Perfect foundation on his face and gloss on his lips. Long black hair framed his face, touched his chest. That had grown a lot over the months. Silky, like a waterfall. Sage touched the strands gingerly. Then she rested her hands on his bare shoulders, the low cut of his top. He was incredibly beautiful. That sexy fairy man wandering through the woods . . .

And warm. Damian brought her up against him. Sage melted. This wasn't good for her.

"You can always walk away," Aurora said. "You have the strength to choose. But you know you love him. And he loves you, too."

"I will love you and cherish you forever," Damian whispered against Sage's temple. "And I will always be by your side to protect you. I will get stronger so that you won't have to fight, my Star."

"Damian," Sage said softly. "You don't have to fight my battles for me."

"I do. I absolutely do."

Sage reached into her pocket. Gertrude had bought her this

Portable Projector, but Sage didn't need two. *Defenders Unite!* was enough for her. Damian, on the other hand, loved *The Rainbow in Me.*

They had only seen the first three episodes at Heart before the craziness started. The main character, Doug, had started to contemplate his true feelings for the cameraman who was always following him around. But then, at the end of the third episode, he had caught the eye of the dancer on stage. Sage wasn't sure what happened after that, but she had the whole season here.

Sage thought it was the perfect gift. She didn't remember downloading this, but this was an ideal dream, so she had.

And Damian was floored.

"For me, darling?" he croaked. He gazed at that little projector as if he had never seen one before. It was small like a gold sphere. It looked like jewelry from afar. "Oh, I will definitely be finishing the season now. Who do you think Doug chooses?"

"Whoever his heart chooses," Sage said. "Sometimes we can't help how we feel."

Damian smiled. "That is true."

Sage lowered her head. "I told you to leave, but I don't want you to."

"I would never leave you," Damian said to her. "I will be here for you as a lover or a friend. However you will have me, darling. I promise."

"I do, too," Sage said.

Sage shook her head at Aurora. "Too good to be true."

"Why?" Aurora held her cheeks with her palms, feet still swinging back and forth. The lazy smile on her face said she was lost in thought. "It's not, Sage. Don't be such a hard-ass. Just go with it, right?"

Sure. Preacher hovered nearby to bless them, conveniently. There was clapping in the distance. Some hooting. Maybe Sage drank some wine and a few shots of Cupid's Arrow because she got drunk without meaning to. Her defenses were low and her stomach was empty.

"Don't forget the sex!" Aurora giggled.

"Not if I'm drunk," Sage snapped. "Or I won't feel anything! And besides . . . I kind of don't want to wake up. It was such a good night."

The only thing Sage remembered after all the booze was making out with Damian on his lap. Maybe it got a bit spicy for being in front of people, but there were plenty of perverts who wanted to see their Warlord in action. No one denied Damian was the best kisser among them, a title he had proven to more than half his crew at some point. It wasn't just his lips and tongue—it was the way he used his hands. How he convinced his lover that they and only they were his world. Sage was completely under his spell at this point.

He inspired other couples to do the same. Gertrude was holding someone's hand, but Sage couldn't see whose. Rockstar and Eye Candy had come a long way since being shown up by Sage at Mousafeld, and they had learned their lesson in humility well. So much so, there was a spark in their eyes that hadn't been there before, toward each other. Clara, Butcher, and Sailor were off somewhere in the distance with a bunch of Centerfeld folk, learning the art of precision and mind over matter. Tai and Sword Devil could tolerate pain like no one else, and they demonstrated just how much by doing freaky things like lighting their hands on fire or puncturing their own eyeballs with needles. There were a lot of "Whoas" coming from their group, but Sage wasn't interested at the moment. The closest to Sage was L and Sonia, who were on their own chair cocooned in each other's arms, mouths engaged in a furious battle.

"I don't want the night to end," Sage mumbled to someone— Damian?—Aurora?—but it did.

And when Sage woke up, she was in her pajamas. She was in the same spot she had fallen asleep in on her bed. Her gown from last night was nowhere to be seen. The sun was shining through the window. The crib was empty. Damian must have taken the babies.

Sage cried. She clutched her body and curled into herself. God and here she thought last night had been real . . . that she and Damian had held each other, danced, kissed, and gotten lost in a moment of peace. One of the few they had ever had.

"Damian . . ." Sage sobbed. "Damian . . ."

She called for him, but could he hear her? Was he outside? Sage should get up. She threw the covers off her then froze when she found her dress hanging from the closet door.

Wait.

Sage blinked at it. She analyzed it closely and noticed the hem of the gown was a bit dirty. Used.

Wait . . . so she had worn it?

Sage clutched her head. It was pounding. She was going to throw up, so she rushed to the bathroom. God, was this some bad hangover?

After washing up, Sage rushed out of the ship. She didn't have to go very far to find Damian some distance away, the cocoons in an official sling (he had done shopping at Centerfeld) and the pups bumbling around in the snow. She heard him talking.

"No, Castor," Damian said to the cocoon on his right. "That's not Greer—that's Red. And that's Yellow over there, see?" A few seconds later, he leaned toward the cocoon on his left and said, "Good, Pollux. Indeed, that's Orange over there, nibbling on the root. And you already know that Violet loves the snow. Blue doesn't, but she wants to impress Violet everywhere she goes."

Sage looked at the pups jumping around. Had Damian named them?

"Do you want to pet her?" Damian asked Castor. "You, too, Pollux? All right. Blue." He whistled. "Here, my lady."

Like a sonar, Blue perked up. Called by Damian, she bumbled over to him wagging her tail. She rolled around on the snow at his feet, then stood on her hind legs to sniff the cocoons. The other pups stared, clearly jealous that their sister was getting all the attention. Then Damian called them one by one, and, responding to their names, they did.

What the hell?

When Sage got closer, Damian finally turned to look at her. His hair was loose and his makeup was plain, so he must have gotten up recently, too. He had his jacket and the cocoons beneath it.

"Good morning, darling," he said happily. "You look awful. And you're in zero-degree weather without proper wear—are you trying to catch a cold?"

"I'm not cold."

Damian raised his arm. From this angle, the cocoons tucked against his chest made it look like he had boobs. "Come, darling. There is room for you here, too. Castor says he's willing to share my nipple."

"Damian," Sage hissed, coming closer. "Why do you look so happy?"

Damian arched a brow. "Why wouldn't I be?"

Sage was confused. She had thought Damian was going through a rough depression, too, but he seemed more composed than she was. Was there a reason for that? But then she found the Portable Projector around his neck. It was tucked into his shirt.

The one she had given him last night?

"I had the best kiss of my life yesterday," Damian purred. "And mind you, I've kissed a lot of people. But I swear that if your tongue were a penis, you'd have destroyed the hell out of my throat—"

"What?" Sage choked, not because she was thinking of her tongue transforming into a penis, but because last night had been *real?*

"Indeed." Damian beamed. "You seemed very motivated to get it out of your system, darling. But we were in front of people and you were a bit drunk, I think, so we didn't go any further than lips." He kissed her hand. "What do you say we go to town today and just relax? I really think you should try out that fastball court they have. Maybe Tai can give you a few pointers."

"Damian ..." Sage held her head. "I-I don't feel well ..."

"You're hungover."

"Last night was real?"

"Wasn't it magical?"

Yes, it had been magical. The most wondrous time of Sage's life. That's why it still felt like she was floating on top of a cloud. Or was that the hangover?

"I can make it better," Damian said sultrily.

A kiss from Damian would be like taking a shot of Cupid's Arrow. Sage's head couldn't handle it right now, so she was going to have to pass until she was better.

"Where is everyone?" Sage asked, eyeing all the lights still hanging from the branches. No litter, but she did spot globs of paint here and there. People had done all sorts of crazy things last night, like strip of all their clothes and soak in silver and green buckets. Then they had rolled on the snow or rubbed up against each other, creating what they called "artistic masterpieces." Damian had pictures on his phone, making Sage gasp. Cupid's Arrow was so dangerous. At least no one had died or become intoxicated. And Sage was happy she hadn't moved from Damian's lap and done anything indecent like that because he would have *never* let her live it down. Just what had she been thinking getting drunk like that last night?

But she didn't remember drinking...

"Did they all go back to Centerfeld?" Sage asked.

"Indeed," Damian replied. "Shortly after we retired, they all left, too."

"Damian, I think there's something wrong with me. I-I thought it was a dream..." Sage screwed up her face. She didn't want to cry, but she also didn't want to wake up. "Oh, God, what if it was a dream?"

"If it was a dream, what are the chances an entire town would be able to attest to it?"

"So why does it feel like a dream?"

"Is that a bad thing?" Damian asked. "Isn't our wonderful life together like living a dream? The world is far from perfect, but we can't let it affect how we feel toward each other."

"World" reminded Sage of Diamond City. She gazed at Damian and whispered a very dreaded question. "What are we supposed to do? You killed Agathe. Louis will most certainly be looking for us."

Damian sighed. Sage didn't like the sound of that.

"I know," he said quietly. "And I don't know the answer at the moment. I suppose we'll figure it out after Castor and Pollux are born."

"What if we don't have that long?"

There was no way they did. It had been two months since they left Diamond City. By now, Louis had to be close. A nest of worries that Sage hadn't paid much attention to before flourished now, when she wondered what would become of her life if she couldn't go back home . . .

Her pizza restaurant.

"I had set out to find Tyrus and Herman," Sage said softly. "I thought they'd be able to help me with the pregnancy . . . or at the very least I'd run into Samson."

"You don't exactly need them anymore, do you?" Damian said.

"Louis would decimate us. You know that. And if Lex is gone, Emerald City has a reason to send out reinforcements." Sage looked at him. "I don't think it's a good idea to stay here long. I'm not sure it'd even be a good idea to wait for the twins."

"Where do you propose we go, darling? But before you think of leaving, why don't we try to do this amicably? You're thinking the worst of Louis and the ambassadors from Emerald City."

"I have to be ready for the worst," Sage said.

"Let's sit tight," Damian suggested. "Build Centerfeld's defenses. The 'Lex Warriors' seem capable. I've been watching them train, and these are people who are exceptionally paranoid of a Squid invasion. Why don't you take a trip to town and see for yourself?"

Sage didn't have a choice, actually. She knew she hated when Damian's phone went off because it was never good news. On the other end was Gertrude, who said, "We need her."

Sage heard it loud and clear.

Emerald City was here.

CHAPTER 16

Protector

Damian had to stay with the cocoons—there were no questions asked. The last thing Sage wanted was a bunch of foreigners finding out she was another Lex who had birthed children somewhat successfully. Sage didn't want to think about the lifeless carcasses in that research facility in Centerfeld.

She threw on her coat, pulled up her pants, and tied her boots. She didn't have any more Slainium bracelets, but she had her gun, dagger, and sword, although she hoped she wouldn't have to use them. According to Gertrude, their visitors weren't Squids. They were Emerald City officials, one from the council and two soldiers for defense. They were huddled at the capital of Centerfeld, a small building across from the infamous stage, which had been cleaned up. It was a relief to see a plain floor with a normal screen and speakers—no bodies or blood for show and scare tactics.

Sage's fingers grazed the hilt of her sword more than once, subconsciously. The rebels had already formed a circle around her, escorting her across the town to the meeting place. Gertrude was waiting by the double doors. Preacher was hanging by the church, looking out in worry. A lot of people had their heads turned toward her.

"They're inside." Gertrude gestured at the room down the hall. Sage found what she had been expecting.

Three Emerald City officials. They had thick cuffs around their arms much like Diamond City officials would wear. Their insignia was an emerald with a crown on top. That looked a bit gaudy in Sage's opinion.

The three were sitting down in a show of submission and respect, but got to their feet as soon as they saw her. The councilman, who held a similar ranking as Gregory had in Diamond City, wasn't in robes or overzealous wear—just a long coat with weapons at the waist. The two on either side were in dark green uniform with gold buttons and chains. Sage sensed an unnaturally high number of Cells in their bodies, like she used to in Taz.

"Alexandra?" one of the soldiers whispered. Josiah Walsh. His name was on his chest pocket. The other one was Jarka Miloslav. Sage had never met anyone with a name like that.

"Not 'Alexandra'," Gertrude said, entering the room, too. "This is Sage. She fights for Diamond City. United the districts a hundred years ago."

All three visitors bowed their heads in acknowledgement and respect. Sage remained stoic, watching each of their moves closely. Nothing but reverence shined from their forms, like Preacher bowing before the might of a Squid. Josiah even broke into tears.

"It's been so long," breathed the councilman, Takuya Ito, wondrously. "S-so long since we've last seen you . . . Sage."

"What the fuck are you talking about?" Sage asked quietly.

The three braced themselves. Sage didn't like the twisted looks on their faces at all. She especially didn't like what they said next.

"We created you over a hundred years ago," Takuya offered. Since he, apparently, was the doctor, he was the only one who had the right to explain. "You and your 'sisters' are our experiments. You and your sisters were created to liberate the districts in Diamond City."

Sage clenched and unclenched her fists. Three times. She was drowning in her own head. A lot of her surroundings got blurry and disappeared. At first, she didn't even hear when someone else barged into the room. Her eyes actually made contact with that of Damian's above her, and that's when her stomach plummeted.

No, no, no, no—her babies! Sage didn't want them anywhere near these three crazy fucks who were claiming she had come from a laboratory! She searched for them in Damian's jacket, but his chest was flat. Where the hell were her babies?

"Darling?" Damian sure knew how to draw attention. He reeled Sage to his side like a protective octopus in the face of these three foreigners. Sage hadn't realized how much she needed his presence until now, when she was leaning against him, shaking uncontrollably with the words these three were spewing at her like a broken geyser.

Laboratory? *Laboratory?*

"W-wait," Gertrude spoke up first. By now, all the rebels were in the room. Sonia and L were here, too, as quiet as ghosts in the background. "How can you say Sage is from a laboratory? She's from Diamond City—was born there—had parents—a human and a Squid—this doesn't make sense—"

"She might have had parents," Takuya said, fixing his glasses on his nose. He looked like the Japanese version of Dr. X. "But those weren't her birth parents. Like her sisters, she was created to fight."

But . . . how? Sage remembered her father. She remembered the Pugnator. And if she had been created for the sole purpose of freeing Diamond City from the Squids, why had one delivered her to Diamond City himself?

"We never fought the Lolligo," Takuya answered her thoughts. "We were fighting the humans. They're the ones who took over the districts and established Overseers. Tell me: did you ever fight a single Lolligo in the Unification War?"

"They were the ones controlling the Overseers!" Gertrude argued.

Takuya glanced at the two on either side of him. It looked like this was the first time he had ever heard of such a thing. Perhaps he was wondering who had started such rumors. All Sage could think about at that moment was Preacher, who always defended the Squids as great . . . but victims. He had asked her the very same thing at the chapel in Mousafeld: Had she ever fought a Squid in Diamond City?

"I was the one who delivered you to Arram," Takuya said. At the confused look on Sage's face, he added, "Arram is the Lolligo you refer to as 'Pugnator'. Arram was his birth name. I gave you and Wren to him and his lover, who I assume is who you mistook as your mother."

"So then what happened to him?" Sage asked. "What happened to the Squids in Diamond City?"

Takuya cringed and the soldiers hissed at her insult. They shook it off, though, and Takuya answered her question. "They were killed. Martyrized. You don't think everything written in the Clarity District is false, do you?"

"But Samson—"

"Was saved by you. He and you were the Lolligo's only hope of survival in Diamond City."

"Don't pretend that the Lolligo are totally innocent!" L spoke up at last. Everyone turned to look at her as she stepped forward to get her two cents in. She hadn't forgotten the massacre at Smallfeld that easily. "They've been running around the Outskirts kidnapping women! T-they've been terrorizing us!"

"Are they the ones who have been terrorizing you?" Takuya asked casually. "Or is it the humans that have been terrorizing each other? The Lolligo are an endangered breed. They don't need humans to reproduce—they've been persecuted by the humans in the Outskirts for decades."

"SMALLFELD!" L blew up. "We buried *all* the fucking women there! All of them! You mean to tell me those weren't because of those ugly Squids?"

"I don't know Smallfeld," Takuya said patiently. "And I can't speak for every Lolligo out there. But I do know that many of the towns who housed one of Sage's kind have been dabbling in reproductive experiments. Was Lex not doing the same here?"

L and Sonia knew better than anyone that was very much the case. What Sage didn't understand was the *who*. If it wasn't the Squids abusing all those women, then someone else was behind it. Someone else was trying to create more hybrids.

Damian pulled Sage a bit closer to his body. "What do you want?" he asked the three steadily.

Takuya fixed his glasses, looking at Sage again. "Sage, of course."

The whole room flinched, as if Takuya had slapped them. Damian pulled out his gun. That was a very rash decision against people whose threat levels Sage had yet to assess, but he was as defensive as ever. "You're not taking her. Not for one damn second. I still don't believe that you created her in a laboratory—you filthy humans will say anything to gain the upper hand. And even if she was your experiment, what the fuck do you want with her?"

Takuya raised his hands. Josiah and Jarka on either side of him had their weapons pointed and ready, too. Sage grew nervous only because Damian was in the line of fire and God knew what those weapons were capable of.

"We want peace with Diamond City," Takuya said calmly. "We want to put this bitter fighting behind us. Emerald City is far too isolated to make it on its own. If it's true the Diamond City Overseers are dead, we should be able to build roads between our cities and aid the also-vulnerable towns out here. Is that not what you want as well?"

Damian fired his gun. Sage was stunned for the brief moment the bullet struck Takuya's knee, injuring him and not killing him. Regardless, the two soldiers on either side of Takuya came to life, using not only their weapons to shoot them all, but an energy that overwhelmed Sage's senses.

Sage reacted before any of her allies were decimated—she used her mind to still the blasts in their places, then threw them right back at the soldiers.

Takuya saw all this with blood spurting out of his knee. His injury mattered so very little when he was an Enhanced himself and he was witnessing what one of his experiments could do.

Sage didn't like this. At all. God, she wanted to cry again, but she had Damian there to hold her tightly. He told her without looks or words that they were going to get out of this mess together. His rebels stepped forward to quell the tension, and L took over the talking like the leader she was.

"We don't want to fight," she established. "We don't want any more fighting because we've been doing it all our goddamned lives. You're *not* here for Sage. You want unity? We're willing to work something out. It's just Diamond City isn't in the best of positions right now. They've just established two new Allseers and one . . . well . . ." she didn't look at Damian as she said, "is dead."

Sonia glanced at Sage. Her clear blue eyes shined with all the fear in the room multiplied by two.

Louis. Where was Louis?

"Where are the Squids?" Sage asked the trio. "Are there some in Emerald City?"

"No," Takuya said quietly. He clutched his wound, which had already stopped bleeding. The bullet popped out and landed on the floor with a clink. That was Slainium in his blood, but that was an easy fix at the clinic. "We don't know where the Squids are. Since we created the hybrids, they haven't made contact since. Perhaps they're afraid of being betrayed."

They had every reason to be afraid, Sage wanted to say. So many people—Diamond City officials included—wanted to kill them or portrayed them as enemies. On the other hand, Sage sensed a malicious intent behind the Squids' actions, too, especially after her fight with that troupe a couple of months ago. They hadn't been carrying around those hybrids in their snowmobile for nothing.

Sage was a hybrid . . . but not a natural one. She hadn't been conceived through normal means. No Squid had had sex with a human, who had then given birth to her. It was Takuya who had done a miraculous job of fusing Squid and human cells together.

Sage tried not to think about it too much or she'd be sick. In fact, she wasn't sure she wanted to be in this room anymore. Damian sensed that, so he pulled her toward the door. Takuya moved, as if making for them, but the rest of the occupants stood together to create a barrier. Damian took Sage outside.

A few hover cars zoomed overhead, transporting people or goods from one end of the town to the other. Franco and Lex might have been crazy, but they had kept this town alive somehow, as traumatized as everyone seemed to be. Sage didn't look anyone in the eye, but she felt their gazes and heard their whispers.

"Are you sure that's not Lex?"

"Stars, it looks just like her."

"Let's stay away from her. She's probably just as fucked up in the head."

Sage clenched her fists tightly. Before she did anything crazy like scream or break down, Damian bought her a cherry soda. There was a bendy straw in it. It had red-and-gold stripes. Diamond City colors.

"Does it change anything?" Damian asked her quietly.

"It doesn't," Sage concurred. She sipped on her drink quietly.

"Does it matter if you came out of a test tube or someone's vagina?"

Sage dribbled on herself. She choked with laughter. "Seriously, Damian?"

"Yes or no?"

"It doesn't—I know."

"Then you don't have to feel bad about it." Damian took her hand. "Not for one moment, Sage. Don't let those assholes fuck with your happiness. That doesn't change the life you've lived or the one you're going to live in the future. Understand?"

Sage gazed at him wondrously. Since when had Damian become her counselor? She suspected he wanted to get on her good side, but Damian was looking out into the distance. A couple of Lex Warriors were standing at the end of the street. They were holding hands, but their conversation was low.

"I don't trust that Takuya guy or Emerald City," Damian

declared. He continued walking. "Did you see the way they looked at you?"

"What do we do?" Sage asked quietly.

"Absolutely nothing. We are not anyone's ambassadors, nor are we here to forge alliances between anyone. Do you really think Emerald City is in such dire straits? If that loser scientist truly has the capacity to create something like you, why would he need Diamond City?"

Sage gazed at Damian, who gazed right back. It looked like they were searching for the answers in each other's eyes. Slowly, Sage came to a certain realization. Damian voiced it first.

"Emerald City defeated the Overseers because of you," he said. "The four Squids Claritians pray to were killed and martyred, according to Takuya. Who's to say they didn't do the same to the Squids in Emerald City? Regardless of who's pulling the strings, the Squids and the humans are still at war with each other. And something tells me that Emerald City doesn't need much help in the strength department. They just want to make sure they're the biggest bullies in the playground."

Sage had gleamed that much. And now that Emerald City's intentions were clear, she asked the most obvious question of all.

"Damian, where are the babies?"

Damian nodded at the church. He had been taking her right to it. As soon as they stepped inside, Sage understood.

"And so the powerful Lolligo have designated me to look after the offspring of their greatest warrior! They have offered their incredible genetics to science to create the esteemed hybrids, one of which brought justice and unity to Diamond City! And it is her incredible offspring, in turn, that rest in my arms! Oh, dear, Forefathers, look at how beautiful they are!"

Preacher puffed up his chest. To Sage's amusement, the sling was strapped on to his torso so it looked like he had boobs, which he was flashing at those Squids above the altar.

Sage laughed a little. Then she gazed at the four portraits honored in every Claritian church. Each one represented the four districts of Diamond City. Sage was a bit surprised to find them way out here, too, but it looked like a lot of these people were exiles who had brought their traditions and beliefs with them.

There was Pugnator for Cut, Luminator for Clarity, Clandestine for Carat, and Laetus for Color. All four of those Squids had had their portraits painted with utmost detail. Their amber eyes bore right into anyone who locked at them. Right now, they were gazing at Sage's unborn children.

Sage took a seat in one of the benches. Damian remained on his feet, arms crossed, watching Preacher bumble around the altar.

There was no better babysitter, that was for sure. After he was done jumping and blessing the cocoons, he sat by one of the steps and told them a story. This one was called The Ultimate Sacrifice.

"There was once a young man who loved a young woman very much," Preacher said to the cocoons against each of his pecs. "So much that he bought her a rose every day. He swore to always be by her side no matter what happened. For you see, their parents didn't want them to marry. The young man had a farm to look after and the young woman was set to marry the crown prince. Typical, you might say, yes, but there is a lesson to be learned here, children. While many of us don't believe in destiny, sometimes certain events are made to happen for a reason. The young man and woman happened to meet and fall in love. And, one day, when they were at a carnival, a group of thugs came to terrorize the people. The young man hid the young woman with the sheep and went out to distract the thugs from searching the pen. And there—"

"The young man met his untimely end." Damian leaned against one of the benches, arms still crossed. "But the young woman lived and went on to marry the crown prince. And that's all that mattered to him: her life. Her happiness. He had made the ultimate sacrifice."

"Very good, sir," said Preacher. "You know all the scriptures by heart."

"Of course. I heard them nearly every day."

"So that's it?" Sage said. "The young man couldn't make a deal with the thugs or something? To spare his own life?"

"No, my lady," Preacher said. "That would defeat the purpose of the sacrifice."

"Sacrifice doesn't mean you have to die. He could have worked something out with the thugs, offered to aid them in one of their missions, in hopes that he'd see her again."

Damian looked impressed. Preacher grew frustrated.

"My lady, we cannot corrupt our hearts and souls just because of our desires."

"We get this one life to live," Sage said. "And if there's something I want, you better believe I'll do anything to get it. Depends on what it is, of course, but I think the young man could have explored other options."

"Unfortunately, there was no other way out for him."

"You don't know that."

"The Lolligo have proclaimed it!"

"But even they don't know everything," Sage said. "Or else, they would still be alive."

Preacher gasped. "My lady! Do not insult the Forefathers! They gave their lives for justice!"

"I'm not saying they didn't. But I think they could have played their cards smarter as well."

Maybe Sage was talking shit here. Who knew what sort of plans the Squids had had, or what their intentions with the hybrids had been. Maybe they had performed the ultimate sacrifice by keeping quiet about the hybrids and allowing the hybrids to run their own natural courses. Wren, by creating Enhanced . . . and Sage, by fighting the Overseers.

"We will truly never know." Damian walked over to Preacher and took back the babies. He patted a grumbling Preacher on the back. "But why don't we open our minds and consider Sage's suggestion? Let's be smarter about our sacrifices."

Preacher opened his mouth to argue, but a faraway cry made him jump.

Sage got to her feet and Damian whipped around.

"The Lolligo have heard us!" Preacher declared. "And are devastated by how we have undermined their sacrifices!"

"We are not undermining anything!" Sage snapped, but this was not the time to argue.

More cries in the distance. Seconds later, the town's warning alarms went off with a shrill wail that had everyone moving like programmed soldiers. It seemed everyone knew what to do but Sage, Damian, and Preacher, who ran out of the church, still glancing hopelessly at one another, and rejoiced when familiar faces found them at last.

"Sage!" Gertrude cried, rushing over to her. Mega Woman, Turtle, Rockstar, Eye Candy, Clara, Sailor, and Butcher were on her heels. All of them were holding weapons. "We've just received word! Centerfeld is under attack!"

"W-what?" Sage croaked.

"Our drones sighted an incoming force ten thousand strong!" Mega Woman panted. "We've got our defenses assembling as we speak, but you and Damian need to get the hell out of here! Hell— *we* need to get the hell out of here!"

There were so many things wrong with that statement, but Sage's brain was too jumbled to make sense of what was ethical and what wasn't. Leaving all these people behind, for instance, was extremely unethical. She still had that stupid hangover, but even alcohol couldn't cloud reflexes when danger was front and center. She had her sword at her belt, and that was all she needed—

Damian grabbed her arm. He hissed, "*Are you fucking insane? Are you thinking exactly what I think you're thinking?*"

Lex Warriors were rushing to defend the town, and all Damian cared about was Sage? What about these people? There were innocents here that were about to become Emerald City's prisoners!

"Sage!" Gertrude choked. Her eyes were huge. She didn't know what to do. Neither did the other rebels, who looked ready to cry. They weren't prepared for this. Not at all. They were a measly group of twelve, a sliver of what their numbers had been in Mousafeld. Plus, they didn't know how to fight alongside Centerfeld forces. Twenty thousand strong, yes, but half of those numbers were commoners who were depending on their warriors to defend them.

"Take the ship," Sage said to the rebels. "Go back to Diamond City. Tell Louis what happened and how we've run into trouble."

"Yes, that includes you, too," Damian said. "You're coming with us."

"And let these people get slaughtered? I'm not going anywhere, Damian. Emerald City is here for me. They knew that something was wrong in Centerfeld when they didn't hear back from Lex. They either suspected it was Squids or Diamond City, and they're here to find out. You're right: they're on a mission to dominate everyone and eradicate anyone who poses a threat, including me—"

"YOU'RE NOT FIGHTING THEM!"

Unfortunately, Damian didn't have much of a say here. Sage would die before she let any town become a pawn in another city's schemes. Centerfeld, clearly, was ready to defend itself: they had their warriors on the north side of town, all in formation like a trained army and all in that sleek silver armor with weapons on their shoulders. There was no Lex or Franco to bark orders, but they had Sonia and L.

Sage hadn't seen a more organized unit since her days in the Unification War. Ten thousand warriors, all privileged enough to receive Cells from Lex, were ready to fight to the death. Sage hadn't drawn her sword, but she trudged through the snow to reach Sonia and L. They spotted her instantly.

"Are Takuya and the other two still in the meeting room?" Sage asked them, wind whipping her face. The town alarms continued to blare across the field.

"Yes," L said carefully. She had that hard look in her eyes. She had her armor down from her face, to better see Sage, and there was something wondrous about her expression. Subtle, but there. She was looking at the legendary Optimum, who'd be sure to lead them in battle and prove why she was the greatest warrior of their time. Sonia wasn't that honored.

"Wait—Sage—where are you going?"

To negotiate. Sage hadn't a clue if this was a good idea or not, but it was her last ditch effort to save them all from a bloodbath. She shook just a little bit inside, the pounding in her head coming back with a vengeance to remind her that she wasn't fit for the battlefield right now. She thought she could hear Damian crying from somewhere, and it turned out he was right behind her.

"SAGE!" Damian grabbed her arm, hauling her from the group of warriors.

"Are you kidding me?!" Sage hissed, yanking her arm right back. "SAVE THE BABIES! GET THE FUCK OUT OF HERE, DAMIAN!"

"NOT WITHOUT YOU! We are a family and we're not going anywhere unless it's together!"

Damian was mad. He had to be losing it. His rebels were chasing him now, bypassing Centerfeld's very disgruntled warriors. The cherry on top of the cake was Preacher with his robes billowing every which way, a stupid mask on his face as he called upon the Squids to aid them in these perilous times.

"We are sorry for insulting you earlier!" he called to the skies. "The lady didn't mean to insult you! We all honor the sacrifices you've made!"

"We are in the middle of a battle, you idiot!" Sage hissed at Damian. "Don't you understand that?! TAKE THE CHILDREN!"

"Do you trust Gertrude?"

"What?"

"Do you trust Gertrude?" Damian asked patiently. "Do you trust her skills in battle, too?"

"Of course I do—"

Damian threw off his jacket, took off the sling, and gave the two cocoons to Gertrude now. Gertrude took them immediately, looking confused and a bit exasperated by the responsibility that could get her killed if she screwed it up. But Damian wasn't here to play games—he drew his sword, too, planting himself by Sage's side.

Sage punched him. She got him in the face, breaking his nose with a satisfying crunch. She would have gone for more, but then Damian punched her, too—he got her in the gut, making her double over.

"S-sir!" Turtle croaked; Rockstar and Eye Candy held their breaths. The rebels stiffened. Sonia and L were looking over, wondering what the hell was going on.

"Goddamn it, Damian!" Sage cried. "Get the hell out of here!"

"We do this together, Sage," Damian said, sword up. Sage's sword, of course, since it was his preferred weapon. "You're not throwing me aside as if I'm a liability."

Sage would have given *anything* to have his ass back on the palanquin right now. Where was the lazy Damian who loved to give orders and bark commands? That must have been what his rebels were wondering, too.

Sage moved out of pure anger—there was no way she was letting this bastard stomp all over her. Damian shared her conviction because he didn't step aside, either—he actually fought back. Their swords clashed, sparks flying, as they gave it their all to win.

And that's when Sage realized something very important. As she met each of Damian's blows, the clang of metal on metal rattled her bones and stirred the dormant nausea in her stomach. Pain flared up in her limbs as days and days of not eating and depression took their toll. Her movements slowed considerably. Before she could fully retaliate, Damian actually ran her through with his sword.

All the rebels gasped. Sonia and L were watching in horror.

"I vowed to you," Damian said to Sage, who stumbled back, losing her grip on her sword and falling to the snow. Sage rolled away from him, grabbing a dagger. She wasn't going to back down from this bastard. "I vowed I'd protect you."

Not by himself. Not like this. Not *now*.

Sage launched at Damian, but since when had he gotten so damn fast? Since when could he move like that, as if he could read her thoughts, or was it just Sage who was incredibly slow? Was she that weak that she couldn't land a single hit every time she slashed at him with her blade? She couldn't even block him—she got stabbed again. This time, Damian kept her pinned to the ground with his sword.

Sage glowered at him. Blood dribbled from her lip, but it was the least of her embarrassments right now.

He was making a fool of her. A goddamned fool, bested in front of fucking everyone. In the distance, about a mile away, was the force Mega Woman had warned them about. And just like the Lex Warriors, they were witnesses to this blatant display of weakness on her part, too. They were all in the same military uniform as Josiah and Jarka because they didn't need armor like Centerfeld did. God only knew what sort of Cells Takuya had given them, what sort of experiments they'd undergone to wield the most amount of power possible. They readied their weapons when they noticed the scuffle on the snow.

Damian was done with Sage, though. He was straddling her now, leaning over her, so he wouldn't have to see the hate in her eyes as he said, "Protect the children."

"You said you'd always give me a choice!" Sage cried angrily.

A long time ago, that's what Damian had claimed to give Commander, his best fighter, when visiting Winterfeld for the first time. He had let Commander participate in the campaign because of honor. Where was Sage's honor now?

"I vowed to you," Damian whispered against her cheek, "as your faithful protector . . . to do what it takes to ensure your and the children's safety. Well, this is what it takes."

Sage screamed. With a final burst of energy, she pushed Damian off her. She dislodged the blade from her gut, but before she could do anything with it, Damian shot her.

In the head.

With that annoying pistol he carried everywhere, the one he slept with under his pillow. Sage had never asked him about it because she did the same with her dagger, but maybe it did hold some significance to him. Who on earth carried that old rickety thing from the Old World? No one unless it meant something.

Well, Sage couldn't ask now. And it definitely wasn't the pistol that held her attention as unconsciousness struck.

Damian.

It was Damian who captured her attention.

Not because he was impressive standing in the snow like that, hair whipping about his face and coat flapping behind him. But because he wasn't human.

Sage realized it now.

Not human.

Not Enhanced, either.

CHAPTER 17

An Occupying Force

It didn't take long for Sage to wake up again. Gertrude and the rebels had already carried her and the cocoons all the way back to the ship. Her makeshift home was about to be used for its true purpose—to get them the hell out of Centerfeld—and it saddened Sage considerably.

Despite her many weeks of hardship and depression, she remembered nothing but triumph. She remembered coming to peace with herself and Damian's actions. She remembered the little life, the little love, she had celebrated deep in these woods just last night. Now that they were about to leave, Sage felt like it was all about to burst. It was slipping away like the colors on a washed-out canvas, messy and dribbling like big fat tears. The worst part was Sage could do nothing about it.

She was weak. Tired. Drained. All she could do was stare out the window as Mega Woman manned the controls and took off into the sky. Hijacking the ship and forcing it to fly toward the battlefield would be suicide on Sage's part. Sage would get herself, her babies, and the entire crew killed just because she was hotheaded enough to fling right back into a battle she couldn't win.

There were explosions in the distance. Sage wasn't sure if it was the ship's engines, so cold after so many weeks of idleness, or the battle between Emerald City and Centerfeld forces.

What Sage didn't understand was . . . why.

Why?

Why had Damian stayed behind? Why hadn't he come with her? Why had he traded places with her, when she was the one they wanted? What would he achieve, other than death, by staying behind?

"Sage." Gertrude took a seat next to her. She had the babies tucked beneath her arms, in that sling Damian had bought them. Her large eyes bored into Sage's, gauging the life she found there. By now, Gertrude was an expert at reading Sage's moods and facial expressions. They had been friends for only a year, yet they knew practically everything about each other. Right now, Gertrude was dealing with a Sage she wasn't familiar with.

A defeated one.

Sage extended her arms. Gertrude gave over the cocoons. Like a mother hawk, Sage cradled them against her own chest now. She brought them to her bosom as she laid her head on the glass of the window. Her eyes saw nothing, but her heart felt all.

The look on Damian's face as he pointed the gun at her. The coldness in his eyes as he shot her. If he hadn't, Sage would have continued to fight. That's what she was programmed to do. She fought for the people she loved—she fought for justice.

Soria and L. How were they going to pull out of this?

"We can't seriously go back to Diamond City, can we?" Turtle was saying from the front. Gertrude looked up. Rockstar and Eye Candy backed up his concerns. Clara, Sailor, and Butcher were quiet. Mega Woman had her orders.

"We're going to Winterfeld," she said.

Good. Yes. That was a safe place. Sage could hatch her children there comfortably. She wouldn't have to worry about crazy scientists trying to take them away from her. She couldn't go back to

Diamond City, as much as she wanted to see her nieces. God, how were they doing?

"What is he, Gertrude?"

Gertrude had already been looking at Sage, but her eyes refocused when she had to answer a question. She didn't understand.

"What is he?" Sage repeated.

This time, the entire ship was looking at her. Mega Woman was still at the controls, but she was listening. Preacher had a large book of Squid scriptures on his lap, reciting prayers to ease the mood and tension so very prevalent among them. "The Lolligo never relented!" and "Remember, they fought on!" rang throughout the cabin.

Suddenly, as Sage let those words sink in, it made so much sense to her. Why hadn't Sage ever considered that the Squids were victims just like the people of Diamond City had been? Perhaps because Sage had been brainwashed, too. It seemed everyone was asking the same question. Turtle, Rockstar, and Eye Candy, who always insulted the hell out of Preacher, were quiet this time. Butcher, Sailor, and Clara stood there like statues. They had learned so much about Diamond City today, but there was one extra detail they had to acknowledge.

"He's a hybrid like me," Sage said quietly. "And don't pretend like you never noticed."

"Sage," Gertrude said patiently. "We sincerely have no idea what you're talking about."

"He's a hybrid," Sage said again. "An experiment, or whatever the fuck you want to call it."

"Think about what you're saying, girl," Turtle growled. "The Warlord? A hybrid? Are you for real—?"

Sage chucked a dagger at Turtle's face. She got him in the forehead, incapacitating him. She didn't make any further moves, so no one scrambled for cover. They did brace themselves, though. Sage looked like she was ready to blow up, but she didn't. She was too tired, or maybe she realized that yelling at a bunch of Enhanced wasn't going to change a thing.

"Phoebe wasn't his real daughter, was she?" Sage said. "He couldn't have children of his own. Either Ileana was already pregnant or she had had sex with someone else. Nonetheless, he raised Phoebe as his own. Maybe he even believed she was his."

"What the fuck?" Rockstar rasped. "For real?"

"S-Sage," Gertrude croaked, as if Sage had just spoken blasphemy, "how can you possibly know this? That the Warlord's a hybrid, I mean?"

"I sensed it," Sage said. "From the moment I laid eyes on him during the Allseer's Challenge. I knew he was much more powerful than he let on. When I was with him face-to-face for the first time, something told me not to cross him or underestimate him. My instincts are never wrong. I just never dreamed he would be a hybrid like me."

"W-wait." Eye Candy laughed robustly. "So does this mean that he comes from a laboratory, too?"

"Cushion is his mother!" Mega Woman exclaimed. She had been to his compound enough times to know that much. And while not too many people were aware that the cute little old lady was indeed his parent—seemingly, as a few of the rebels arched a brow—there was no *proof* that Cushion was his blood mother. Just like Sage had no proof that she had a blood mother, too. Just a very nice woman who had taken her in and raised her like a daughter, alongside a sibling, even.

"This can't be," Gertrude said. She wasn't done refuting Sage just yet. "He said he was from the Clarity District!"

"And I'm from Cut," Sage said. "It doesn't change where I truly came from, does it?"

"F-fine—what about Blackburn? His older brother—"

"So?" Sage interrupted. "What makes you think Takuya didn't birth more than one hybrid using the same eggs and sperm cells? Wren was my twin, but Lex wasn't. And neither were those women the Squids hunted down in the Outskirts. We were all just sisters, siblings with similar genetic makeup." She held her cocoons. "Nothing more."

"So the Warlord has more siblings, too?" Butcher said, but what he really meant was, *There's more of him?*

Sage would have laughed. But right now, she didn't think it was funny at all. Damian had known she was a hybrid and hadn't said a thing about himself. While the Phoebe situation was understandable, there was no way he had been oblivious to his own physique.

"So that means Blackburn is a hybrid, too?" Clara said. "But if he's a hybrid, then why wasn't he able to beat Sage? I mean—why is Sage the Optimum and not them? Wait a second—didn't the Warlord become an Enhanced at the age of eighteen? Hadn't they given him Wren's Cells?"

Sage didn't know. A lot of humans had become Enhanced on the streets. Some even in makeshift labs. August had gotten his dose of Cells behind a dumpster after an illegal transaction under Overseer Callus' nose. Early transformations hadn't been monitored by any government officials, nor had the scientists who had developed the Cells paid much attention to the soldiers receiving the shots. So long as they were paid, they'd inject a cat. Perhaps, after the Unification War, they had been more choosy because of Allseer Marchello . . . but not before. Damian could have received the Cells and become an "Enhanced", what he'd say to fool them all into believing he was just a measly human like everyone else. Sage had spewed the same story to survive in Diamond City.

"What happens when a hybrid takes the Cells of another hybrid?" Clara asked.

Sage had given Damian her Cells before. She supposed nothing. Perhaps it was like receiving a blood transfusion.

"The Kilstrongs never knew, did they?" Rockstar said. Turtle had stopped screaming. He was rubbing his eye. "Never knew that the Blackburns were hybrids right under their noses."

"I'm sorry!" Turtle threw the dagger on the floor. He spit at Sage. "But I don't believe this fucking bullshit. It just doesn't make any sense—these people from Emerald City delivered a bunch of hybrids to Diamond City to defeat *humans*? Couldn't they use weapons instead?"

"My sister was sold to science," Sage said quietly. "And scientists used her blood to create Enhanced. In a way, Enhanced are a sort of weapon. They were able to unite and fight off the Overseers. I, on the other hand, became the Optimum, their leader. As for Damian . . ." She closed her eyes and sighed. "I never asked him about his father. I only knew about his mother. But something tells me that his father was a Squid like mine."

"What about the other two districts?" Clara said. "Would they have received a pair of hybrids, too?"

Sage hadn't a clue. But the more she thought about it, the more sense it all made. Growing up, Damian and Blackburn had been trained to fight for Diamond City. They had become Squid worshippers, the fate of every Claritian. But then Damian hadn't cared for clerical studies—he had wanted fashion, shaming his family. As a result, he had tried to end his life . . . and then come back to it when he met Sage. He had joined in the war and taken down the Overseers. But clearly, he and Blackburn hadn't seen eye to eye on a lot of things. They always accused each other of wanting to steal the Optimum. Had they suspected the Optimum was a hybrid? Was that, perhaps, the only way they could reproduce? Blackburn had never had a family . . .

"So there can be more hybrids out there," Rockstar said. "But why is Emerald City so interested in Sage if they can just make more?"

"Because the Squid that gave me his genetics is dead," Sage said quietly. "I might be lab-made, but they needed someone's DNA to make me. The other three Squids are dead, too. That's why Emerald City was so vested in Lex."

"But what about the Warlord?" Clara sputtered. "If he's truly a hybrid, can he beat them? O-or is he going to be captured—"

"TURN THIS SHIP AROUND!" Eye Candy exclaimed, making Mega Woman jump. "RIGHT NOW!"

"We can't!" Gertrude spoke up at once. "He told us to take Sage to safety!"

"Don't you see what he's done—he's sacrificed himself so that

Emerald City can spare the rest of us! But we need to get to Emerald City right away or they'll turn him into a lab rat!"

"And what if they exterminated Centerfeld?" Sailor said.

"EXACTLY! We need to go—"

"WE CAN'T DO ANYTHING!" Gertrude exclaimed this time. She got to her feet as if she was getting ready to fight. For someone so small and reserved, she was impressively adamant. Just a year ago, she had covered in the face of these raucous rebels. Now, she was taking charge like a true leader. "Sage is weak! She can't fight— she couldn't even defeat the Warlord."

Eye Candy snorted loudly. "Since when do I give a shit as to whether Sage is up to par or not? This isn't about Sage—this is about us, his followers, who have to defend him! We'll leave her in Winterfeld, and then go after him ourselves! Right, Rockstar?"

But even his faithful partner was quiet. No one seemed very inclined to agree to that. Surprisingly, even Mega Woman, who was always on Damian's side, kept driving quietly. Butcher opened his mouth to speak.

"With all due respect, what chance do we have without Sage? We don't even have an army. Do you truly expect to infiltrate Emerald City like this? With just the twelve of us?"

Not realistic. And their chances of success plummeted when they reached Winterfeld and found that they had a welcome crew. Diamond City airships were docked all around the town, waiting for any news from the missing Allseer or Sage. Damian had cleared out this town months ago, but the military was here in hopes they'd intercept someone of interest. They knew so little about the Outskirts and what dangers lurked out there that it was better to lay low than cause trouble. A typical Kilstrong move.

Sage couldn't believe it, though. Had the military been waiting here for a whole two months? Had Damian known they were here all along? Perhaps he thought she'd be safe with Louis, but Sage was still shook and so were his rebels.

"I-I don't like this," Turtle croaked. "Where the fuck did so many of them come from?"

"It's not just the numbers," Rockstar said. "We can deal with the numbers, because those are our allies down there. But what I don't like is fucking Blackburn—why is he here? He's supposed to be in custody!"

"Maybe Louis is desperate," Eye Candy said. "That little shit can't do anything unless he has a powerhouse at his side, and there he is!"

Sage jumped out of her seat before they even touched down and grabbed for the controls. She was about to get them the hell out of there when every foot soldier below pointed their weapons at them and cried, "FREEZE!"

"Sage!" Mega Woman exclaimed.

This might have been the first and only time that Mega Woman showed true fear, but Sage's mind was racing too chaotically to acknowledge it. This was one of those do-or-die moments because if she turned this ship around, they'd be blasted to smithereens. But, if they landed, they'd all be surrounded, arrested, and interrogated for Agathe's death. While that was fine and all—Sage had plenty of stories up her sleeve to spare these rebels around her—what truly struck sheer terror into her very core was Blackburn.

He wasn't here for fair. He'd twist any story to have Damian's head on a platter, and if he saw the babies, then Sage was fucked.

"Sage, look." Gertrude pointed. Not at Blackburn pulling his army into formation, but at Candice and Olivia, who came sprinting out into the open.

Both of them looked up at her, eyes wide, tear stains on their cheeks. Olivia's eyes were bloodshot from all the crying. Although they had access to plenty of maids, no one could do their braids like Damian could. Even their clothes weren't quite as royal-looking as usual, a bit disheveled and wrinkled from so much traveling. The two weren't alone, either—a cured Geoffrey was standing right by their side, gazing longingly at the ship that held his esteemed Optimum. Sage could almost read his mind.

She'll save us. She'll know what to do.

If only he knew what the inside of Sage's head looked like right now.

"Sage," Gertrude said again. Imploringly. This was one mess they couldn't abandon. They had to touch down.

Sage pulled out her sword. She tightened the straps on her babies, threw on a coat, zipped it up, and got ready for the fight of her life. Before any battle, Sage assessed her surroundings, her opponent, her chances of winning, and any potential strategies that could save her life in a clutch situation. Right now, she went in blind. She went in without thinking at all, jumping a hundred feet from the *Mistress'* door to land in front of what now looked like Diamond City's entire military. Thousands of soldiers skittered out from behind airships or vehicles like roaches. Either Louis had freed everyone in custody or he had used Blackburn to create more Enhanced. It was possible.

"Well." Blackburn stepped forward. He had the girls and Geoffrey a fair distance away. Without Gertrude, the trio were under the care of a designated babysitter. This one was tall, dark, and bald. She looked aggressive, too, like a hyena. Her name was Shenzi, and it meant vicious in Swahili. Sage knew because Candice and Olivia's mother had taught her a few words in that language, one passed down in the family from the Old World.

No fear. Never any fear. Sage couldn't back down in the face of these soldiers, whom she wasn't quite sure were enemies or friends. She supposed Damian's enemies were now her own, because she had Agathe's death to answer to all the same. No one had reported it, but Louis wasn't stupid.

Surprisingly, he came forward next. He was in his royal garbs, the traditional white suit with gold cuffs, a shining star among this sea of white and black. He had a cape over his right shoulder and a few shiny pins on his jacket, but he was as conservative as an Allseer could get. He had changed a hell of a lot the past few months: his hair was longer and smoother thanks to appropriate conditioner and care. He had makeup on, too, which Samson would have chastised him for—*true leaders speak with their actions, not appearances*—and he had a pair of swords at his hip. Had he been training with the military also?

"Stand down," he commanded of Blackburn immediately. When he ran through the snow, he didn't tumble or fall. His quads were powerful enough to propel him through the inches of slush without fail. Louis was no foolish boy—he had grown into his father's glorious position well, and he knew how to use that and his charm to confront Sage and avoid unnecessary bloodshed. Without his intervention, that's exactly what would have happened.

"Sage." Finally, Louis focused on her. He got closer to her, and he didn't seem to care there was a sword in his face. By himself, he stood no chance. Sage could cut him and kill him as easily as Commander had done Kenna. That was a fight none of them would ever forget. "You're here. You're … alive. We've been looking for you."

"I know you have," Sage said quietly. "That's why I had to run away from my own city. *Again.* Your sister and …" She gritted her teeth. She knew that plan was trivial at this point, but it still hurt to think about it. "Your sister and the Warlord had plans for me, Louis. I suppose you're right and I shouldn't have trusted him."

"Please." Louis raised his hands. He was panting—the cold was piercing. It cut his lungs with every breath he took. Sage could tell from how curt his breaths were. "Let's not fight. We can do this without killing each other. Sage, where is she?" He looked for his sister among the rebels. He looked for Damian, too. The clear blue eyes returned to Sage. "Where are they?"

Sage laughed. "Did you think I was traveling with them? Are you for real? That I'd ever step foot in a vessel with Agathe after she humped the fuck out of my fiancé in front of my eyes?"

Louis closed his eyes and took another ragged breath. That, he must have heard all about from Color District officials. There were always some nosy assholes raring to get on the Allseer's good side.

"Agathe is dead," Sage said.

It was only her, the rebels, and the Diamond City military out here, but it felt like the whole world had heard her statement. No string of mountains was high enough to block the gossip from reaching every pair of ears out there. Even the trees had heard her. Perhaps the dead in the cemetery, too.

Sage wasn't here to keep secrets, though. She was done pretending to care what other people thought or believed. She was done hiding like she had been for a hundred years. She raised her sword higher.

"I killed her."

It shocked the hell out of everyone else, but Louis didn't flinch. It almost looked like he didn't believe a word that was coming out of her mouth. Perhaps he had already anticipated his sister's death. It had been so many weeks since he had last communicated with her. But he probably hadn't thought it was Sage who had dealt the killing blow. Neither had Blackburn.

"Liar!" Blackburn hissed. He sounded like a giant anaconda defending his mound of dead rats. "She lies, my lord! Do you think my brother played no part in this? The female Allseer was under *his* care. If he truly wanted to spare her, why did he allow the Optimum to get close enough to kill her? None of us were there when it happened, but I know Damianos like the back of my hand—that sniveling bastard is salivating to dominate Sage, and after his slip-up with the female Allseer in the Color District, he lost all her trust. The only way to get it back was to execute the female Allseer, and he did. Or else, Sage would never believe that he loves her. Do you see how she defends him?"

No, Sage couldn't move yet. She had to hold still. She had to keep her composure. She couldn't kill Blackburn in her condition. She couldn't lunge at him and put her nieces in danger. They were standing too close to that soldier with the fierce look on her face. They were also right behind Blackburn, who could turn and shoot them in the blink of an eye. Additionally, Sage had her babies right up against her chest—she'd be exposing them.

"Is it true?" Louis asked Sage quietly. The wind carried his words into nothingness. Sage couldn't tell if it was night or day out here. She felt like she was standing in an endless void, and the more time she wasted, the more danger Damian was in. What the hell had become of Centerfeld?

"She's dead," Sage repeated. "She and her lackeys, Louis."

"Where's the Warlord?"

"I don't know. We had to run from Centerfeld because Emerald City is on the hunt for us. They want their experiments back." Sage nodded at Blackburn. "Blackburn included."

No one in the military flinched. All those fuckers knew—they knew that Blackburn was a hybrid, too. Perhaps Louis already did as well because no look of surprise flashed across his perfect face.

"I'm going to make this very simple," Sage said. "And I want you to use your pretty-boy brain to make the right choice. I am the strongest hybrid you will ever meet." She glanced at Blackburn again. "Even more than your toy soldier over there. Do you want to know why? My roommate, Samson, gave me his blood. I am a hybrid enhanced with Squid cells that will tear you and all those sniveling fucks behind you to pieces. I'm an 'Enhanced,' too, get it?"

Louis raised his hands. He shook his head. "I don't understand why you are speaking so aggressively—"

"MAYBE BECAUSE YOU HAVE YOUR ENTIRE MILITARY POINTING THEIR GUNS AT *ME*!" Sage roared. Her voice echoed through the plains. It might have reached Smallfeld some miles away. Tears burned in her eyes. "From the very moment I put Diamond City together—gave my life to defend justice and chase away the Overseers—I have been nothing but persecuted by you and your family. I-I have to run from my own city . . . my own fucking pizzeria . . . my own goddamned nieces that you turned against me!"

"AUNT SAGE!" Olivia cried, making to run toward her, but Shenzi held her back. Candice was crying silently, shaking her head, as if to deny she had ever seen Sage as an enemy. Geoffrey gave Sage an earnest look, indicating this was one big misunderstanding.

And maybe it was. Everyone was confused. No one knew whom to trust.

"Maybe you did have to run," Louis said to Sage calmly. "But that was under the old Allseer. My father. As for your nieces, you know they love you, Sage. They're here with me now because they snuck out on their own to try and find you. Even Geoffrey tagged along so he could thank you for looking after him when he was sick."

Sage wiped her eyes. "I have done nothing but sacrifice myself for others. I'm done, Louis. Just leave me the hell alone. Let me walk away . . . and you'll never see me again. You have Blackburn to defend you now. He's the hero here, isn't he? He tortures his own brother and he gets all the shiny medals."

"Sage—"

"Leave me alone."

"SAGE!" Louis roared. Veins popped out of his forehead and throat. "I'm trying to talk to you, damn it, and you're not listening! I am not here to kill you or arrest anyone—we have to figure this out civilly first, get it?"

"Agathe is dead," Sage whispered. "And you're going to let that go?"

"We'll figure it out."

"My lord." Blackburn stepped forward. His way of trudging through the snow was like that of a wolf's. Always the taller, righteous one, but this guy was no idiot. Sage didn't like the gleam in his eye. "Are you seriously going to let her get away? There are a thousand of us and twelve of her—what's left of my brother's rebel gang."

Sage noticed there were hardly any rebels or Outskirts allies in the sea of white and black. Of course the military had left them behind in Diamond City on purpose. These soldiers were faithful cocksuckers only. And not even to Louis—to Blackburn, who broke protocol as well as formalities when he was standing that close to Louis in a show of clear defiance.

"Arrest her, Allseer," Blackburn said.

"Shit . . ." Turtle croaked, cowering just a bit. Like the rest of the rebels, he sensed the power shift. The one who was really calling the shots here.

Louis was having none of it.

"And why would I do that?" he said casually, without ever turning his back on Sage. "Didn't you hear her, Commander? She is stronger than all of us. Stronger than *you*, even, unless you're friends with some Lolligo I don't know about."

"She is *outnumbered*, Louis."

"Did that ever stop her in the past?"

"Step aside, Louis."

Sage had only milliseconds to act, but one way or another, something bad was going to happen. Either she was going to yell at the rebels to run or move Louis out of the way, but she couldn't do both. Time wasn't on her side, and neither was her health. She just wasn't fast enough to throw out a tentacle from her back, grab Louis' ankle, and haul him out of the line of fire without getting his head blown off.

Gertrude screamed. It echoed all throughout the field, shattering Sage's concentration. It caused her allies to rally in fright, to back away like scared sheep and get the hell out of there before they were arrested and tortured, too. Turtle actually grabbed Gertrude by the collar and hauled her away.

"SAGE! SAGE! SAGE!"

Sage had nothing but a headless Louis in her grasp. *Cells, Cells, Cells* were the only words pounding in her brain, but she was worthless in the face of an army that was amazingly loyal to Blackburn. Without comrades of her own, who didn't like her anywhere near enough to stick out their necks and risk another round of torture from the cruel Blackburn, they ran. After everything Blackburn had done to Damian, Sage didn't fault them one bit.

"Oh, my ..." Blackburn laughed. He found the escaping aircraft a sight for the ages. Of course his own went chasing after it, and all Sage could hope for was Mega Woman's skills behind the controls. Maybe she was a star pilot and no one knew it. "Look at that. Are they what you call comrades, my sweet Sage?"

"I don't need comrades," Sage spat. "I never did."

"Oh? So you plan to take me on your own? And with your own children tucked beneath your breasts?"

"I can be popping babies out of my vagina and still defeat you."

"I suspected you'd never be able to carry Louis' children," Blackburn said casually, as if Louis' neck wasn't spurting out torrents of blood. "Because I already knew that hybrids couldn't mate with humans or Enhanced. That's why you were always really meant for me."

"And who came up with that decision?" Sage said, still holding her ground. "You or Kilstrong?"

"Kilstrong, yes." Blackburn laughed. "What I loved about Marchello was his ability to follow orders. I knew that his brother, Francis, had been hiding something from us. Had we known Wren had become his pet, I would have tried mating with her. But, alas, Francis had other plans, and those two set out on their own to do their fair share of conquering. Sending you to meet my brother, though . . . Well." He cleared his throat. "I tried to warn you. As soon as he whiffed you were the Optimum, he was going to do what it took to worm his way into your bed. Those are his beautiful children, I gather? My nephews?"

Sage took a step back. Her tentacle remained wrapped around Louis' torso. Inch by inch, she pulled him closer to her. Both hands remained on her blade.

"I don't understand what you could possibly accomplish with two children," Sage said.

"Not just two," Blackburn said. "But an entire army, my dear. If we were able to conquer an entire city with just one, what do you think a hundred or even a thousand hybrid children will be able to do?'

"Is that all you can think about?" Sage snarled. "Power and expansion? Isn't what you have good enough already?!"

"Was it not good enough for *you*, Sage? You were the first one to chase after Louis when you got bored of your little life. You blame Bram for selling you out, but he did the very thing he needed to do to get you that stardom you always wanted."

"I didn't want to be treated like a commodity, asshole!"

"Sometimes the end truly does justify the means," Blackburn said casually. "But why are we arguing about the past? One way or another, we all have to fulfill our destiny. We are hybrids, born and raised to conquer. Genetically, we are human and Lolligo. Abloudor—this whole planet—is ours. No one can take it away, can they?"

"THIS DOESN'T JUST BELONG TO US!" Sage exclaimed. "OTHER PEOPLE LIVE HERE, TOO!"

"And that is fine. But we are the strongest here, Sage, so we must be the leaders. Even my brother has acknowledged that much. Although we will never see eye to eye because of his insistence on civil liberties, I have to commend his ability to pull together a ragtag militia of losers with no cause. They are loyal to a fault. Where did they take off to, I wonder?" Blackburn cocked his head to the side. "Back to his side because they don't feel comfortable by yours?"

Sage didn't care. If they did go back to Centerfeld, then that was good—that's exactly what she wanted them to do. Only, she didn't know if they were going to make it there with all those Diamond City ships on their asses.

"Damianos created Enhanced just like I did," Blackburn admitted. "But he doesn't understand there should be limits to the kind of power we give people. Why do you think Diamond City has flourished in the last hundred years? We ousted all the rebels and anyone with foolhardy ideas. We run a tight ship, Sage."

Sage made sure to puncture Louis' body with her tentacle and blow him up with her Cells. Blackburn couldn't see a thing from that angle, so that was good. Just more time. More stalling. She grew weaker by the moment, but so long as Louis lived, there was hope—

Blackburn lunged for her. Sage blocked him with her blade, ignoring that terrible rattle in her bones. It was the same one from before, when Damian had struck her, but now she was fighting for her life. Now, she had to rise up to this asshole and push him back.

"Surrender, Sage," Blackburn said from in between their crossed swords. His eyes were like two huge pools of space, just sucking her in. Whereas Damian's promised a mystical stroll through the dark woods, there was nothing but blackness in Blackburn's. "You're finished, darling."

Sage unleashed another tentacle that pierced Blackburn's chest and shot him into the air. Blackburn had agility and strength, but he didn't have the shape-shifting capabilities that Sage had. If she ever saw Samson again, she'd be sure to thank him for all the training and blood he had given her. That's the only reason she survived now, and the only reason Louis' body started convulsing, twisting and turning as it shifted into a non-human.

The Diamond City military was already rushing forward to aid their commander. No one asked about Blackburn's decision to take out Louis because they didn't care about the pretty Allseer. Besides, Louis' actions would have allowed someone like Sage to get away. It was all eyes locked on her.

The distraction, perhaps, was enough for Candice and Olivia to run. While Shenzi should have been moral enough to steer two innocent girls from the chaos, it was Geoffrey who took the initiative and pushed them out of there. Sage saw the top of his small afro as he wove through the crowd of soldiers and toward the safety of Winterfeld. Eventually, he disappeared.

In the clear at last, Sage flung Blackburn at the sea of incoming soldiers. Then she jumped into the air as Louis came flying to her rescue.

She had ridden a monster like this before. Wren had shown her that this kind of transformation was possible with the right amount of Cells. Sage was losing vitality fast, but Louis flew them the hell out of there because his life depended on it. He swerved around blasts and bullets that came at them from every angle and headed straight for the Roaring Mountains in the distance. Just when Sage thought they were safe, someone shot him and clipped a wing. Louis nose-dived fast.

"L-Louis!" Sage cried, choking the hell out of his throat as she hung on. She scrambled for what to do—how to pull his body up—but there was no way—they were going to crash hard.

Sage jumped to time the landing—to protect her babies at all costs—and she paid the price when her skull and shoulder hit the ground.

Sage blacked out. The ringing in her ears never stopped. The explosions in the distance rattled her head. She heard voices at some point, and she could make out some words even if they were a bunch of garble . . .

"Attack them—hurry!"

"Fast!"

Wait . . .

Sage cracked her eyes open. There was a wetness beneath her head. Blood pooled and spread like crazy, staining the snow, but that's not what caught her attention.

Were the voices speaking Lolligo?

Sage gasped. She shuffled back, eventually bumping into Louis' comatose form. Her heart came to life at a crazy rate, forcing her body back into complete attention. She was in pure, unbridled shock because there were two enormous Squids standing in front of her, shooting lasers at the Diamond City military and activating what seemed to be a forcefield of sorts to keep Sage and her winged friend safe.

To this day, Sage still startled at the sight of them. She might have fought off six of them not that long ago, but she was in a terribly vulnerable position now with her cocoons stuck to her breasts. She couldn't do now what she had done then, and if these Squids were out to kill her, she was fucked.

Sage grabbed Louis by the clipped wing—he yelped like a banshee. This made the Squids turn around, their faces nearly identical to Samson's, and focus on her. Although they were so very unfamiliar to her, Sage thought she knew exactly who these Squids were.

In seconds, she assessed they were defending her—not killing her. Or else they would have shred her and Louis to pieces and taken off with her babies, if birthing children had truly been their intent. Of course, there was always the mystery behind what the hell had happened in Smallfeld, but Sage was starting to believe it wasn't the Squids. Someone had gone around impregnating women and using them as experiments, and it must have been a male hybrid, either from a nearby town or Diamond City itself. Isn't that what Takuya had said?

"But I do know that many of the towns who housed one of Sage's kind have been dabbling in reproductive experiments. Was Lex not doing the same here?"

"Herman and Tyrus," Sage whispered with blood still running down the back of her head. She cleared her throat and spoke in Lolligo. "Those are your names."

"Yes," spoke the one on the right. He had his overly-large coat zipped all the way up to his chin, amber eyes flashing. His teeth clicked together when he spoke. "Samson told us about the one called Sage. He said you'd be able to speak in our language."

"W-where is he?" Sage croaked. God, this was not the time—the Diamond City military was right on their asses—but certain questions couldn't be contained any longer. "Where is Samson?"

"Samson's at home," Herman said. "He is our Prime."

CHAPTER 18

A Safe Haven

Sage stared. It was the only response she had. If it wasn't for those two Squids who stomped their way over to her, picked her up, and dragged the howling Louis out of there, she would have been captured and killed by Blackburn and his goons. Her babies would have been taken, used for whatever purpose Blackburn had in mind. Perhaps they'd be proof that two hybrids could mate and reproduce, or maybe the two babies were enough of a force to conquer other cities like he wanted. Whatever the case, Blackburn wouldn't be getting his way today.

Herman and Tyrus moved quickly. The first grabbed Sage and the second threw a squirming Louis over his shoulder like a lightweight potato sack. Sage didn't fight the arms that held her, nor did she look over her shoulder to see if they were being followed. She hoped she'd see Candice and Olivia making their way toward her but it was a good thing they weren't. That'd mean they'd be smack in the middle of the battlefield, and Sage was pretty sure her heart would give out if anything happened to her nieces.

Please be fine, Sage said to herself, squeezing her eyes shut. *Please . . .*

As Samson had written in the note, the two Squids took them past the Winterfeld cemetery and into the woods beyond. If they were truly that close, then it made sense that a group of them had found their way to Sage a few months ago. They had been holding Reina, but why did Sage get the feeling that they weren't the ones who had impregnated her? Perhaps Reina had come from Smallfeld...

The Squids arrived at a clearing, and there was nothing there. Trees and snow, but no signs of a camp. That's because there was a forcefield hiding it from view. Herman and Tyrus walked through it like stepping through a veil.

Suddenly, Sage could see three buildings planted in the ground, the biggest one in the middle. They were portable, just like the ones the rebels carried with them on their campaigns.

Surveyor was the word that came to Sage's head. Not scientist... doctor... or anything else. Just a quiet, brooding traveler taking note of everything they saw. There was a moroseness that Sage couldn't quite describe, one that often accompanied hopelessness. Tyrus and Herman had seen a lot in the Outskirts, and their reports weren't very good. Humans were populating the Outskirts and Enhanced were building technology and biochemical weapons that could rival that of any Squid's. It seemed the Squids were at a growing disadvantage, unless they could find a means of retaliation before it was too late for their race.

Inside, Tyrus lowered Sage into a chair. Herman threw the twitching Louis on a table. The papers and pens that fluttered down must have been of no importance.

"Cell surplus," Herman said in Lolligo.

In other words, there wasn't much they could do for Louis in this state. They had intravenous fluids they could administer, but it'd only be a matter of time before Louis' body gave out. The strain would kill him. He'd never be able to function as a human being again.

Wren had never intended for Taz to live that long, either. She had merely seen him as a weapon to be discarded. With so many humans around, it was easy to replace him.

Herman took a scalpel and slit Louis' throat. Blood poured out of that wound like a waterfall. The thick redness of it mesmerized Sage for a moment. She was so exhausted that her body felt like it weighed a thousand pounds. She had to really think and focus in order to find the strength to get up and save Louis' life.

She had seen Wren do this to Little Man, so this couldn't have been that difficult. All Sage had to do was touch Louis' blood and call the Cells right back into her body … or something like that. She held her fingers close to the gaping gash, warm blood coating her whole hand and wrist. The coppery smell hit Sage hard, making her wince as images of dead bodies sprang up in her mind. She held fast, though, concentrating to take the monstrosity back into her veins as Louis twitched on the table.

If only it were that easy. Sage wasn't too sure what she was feeling for. The blood kept running and splashing, and perhaps a part of her was there, but she had a hard time pinpointing what she needed to extract and how.

"It's natural," Herman said from somewhere behind her, in Lolligo. "Take back what you gave."

But Sage couldn't. She didn't know what the hell was wrong with her. She got showered in blood and she still hadn't withdrawn a single Cell. The thickness soaked into her jacket and clothes, possibly into the cocoons, too. Sage didn't know. Her eyes were burning with tears. Her entire body started shaking out of nowhere. Was she doing this wrong? Why couldn't she concentrate?

Thanks to her, blood flooded the table and floor. Herman plucked her from Louis while Tyrus prepared a gigantic needle. It wasn't a syringe, though—it looked like the one August had used on himself—the Extractor.

"Human is coming back," said Tyrus.

Sage stepped back. Herman and Tyrus were studying Louis, whose body started to shrink. She bumped into the counter where she intended to wash her hands, but she wound up staring at Louis instead. Watching. Adding this to a list of things she never wanted to see again in her life. Creatures like that shouldn't exist.

"Come." Tyrus directed her to another room. A bathroom. It had a stall, a toilet, and a sink big enough for people that measured over seven feet tall. "Clean up," were his instructions.

Sage stripped. She took off her clothes, baby sling, weapons, and boots. She started the shower, turned the water as hot as possible, picked up the cocoons, and curled up in the corner of the stall.

And then Sage slept. Thoughts of Damian entered her mind. She knew it was a dream, but it was still nice to see him. She was standing behind the counter at her pizzeria, watching him attract customers. He kissed the hands of everyone who crossed the threshold, helped the elderly to tables, and entertained some of the kids by showing them how to do the maze on the kids menu. He could run this whole place by himself. He could even work the kitchen. He had become an outstanding cook in such a short amount of time.

"Two Hippos, please," said the next customer to Sage. "And the Minefield."

Right. The new pizza Damian had come up with. Sage smiled.

"Coming right up," Pollux squeaked from next to Sage. He bumped into Candice and Olivia on his way to grab the pie. His brother, Castor, was more serious, prepping the pizzas in the back with a fierce concentration. He murmured a "thank you" to Geoffrey, who delivered another container of mozzarella cheese.

A scream made Sage whip around. She saw Damian draw two blades from his arms. He was a clean shape-shifter. A powerful one, who'd defend Sage and her children from the other hybrids wandering Diamond City. Takuya had confirmed there were more, after all.

The hybrid that barreled into her restaurant was from Carat. Sage wasn't sure how she knew that, but she did. There was something gaudy about the way that hybrid was dressed, with flashy jewelry that was a bit over the top, that told stories of greed. That hybrid was here to kill and take, and she sent Damian flying across the restaurant.

"Sage!"

Sage sprang awake. Through the shower door, she saw a figure smash into the bathroom. A blond head revealed it was Louis, who was panting as if he had a run a marathon and sported blood-stains around his throat and chest from his earlier wound. That had mended some time ago. Just how long had Sage been in the bathroom?

"Sage?" Louis opened the stall. Sage was still on the floor with the two cocoons cradled in her arms. Louis didn't ask any questions—he just cried. Not the sobbing, whiny Louis that Sage was used to, either. The poor man was under great stress, and Sage surmised why.

The entire military had turned its back on him. Blackburn had completely undermined his authority. His life was in danger, and his life in Diamond City was destroyed. But then Sage realized that wasn't why he was sobbing at all, or why his hands were white and trembling as he helped her to her feet—wet, naked, and everything—something else was going on.

Something serious.

"What's happening?" Louis croaked. "Oh, God...what's happening?"

Sage's stomach sank. Actually, it plummeted. The dread spread through her veins like ice. She didn't quite understand what the current situation was, so she lost control of her emotions. Her heart started racing and her vision got a bit blurry. She tripped as she reached for a towel and more or less covered her chest and hips. She stumbled out of the bathroom after Louis, who grabbed her arm and led her past the messy table in the middle of the room.

Sage froze.

Tyrus and Herman were dead.

Their huge bodies were on the floor, upright against the counter, side-by-side like college kids waiting for their chemistry professor to arrive. Their heads were thrown back, exposing thick, stretched-out necks that Sage found a bit disturbing. It looked like an armadillo might have crawled out of there, forcing its way out of the Squids' esophagi. Both Tyrus and Herman had dislocated jaws, mouths gaping open with blood and saliva still dribbling down their chins. That's when Sage noticed two round eggs on the floor.

Eggs. Sage instantly thought of Samson and when she had found him in the Clarity District. He had hatched months later, long after the Unification War had ended. He had been as tiny as a tadpole.

"W-what's going on?" Louis croaked.

Clutching her cocoons, Sage got closer to the two Squids. She smelled rot. Old vomit. It made her dizzy. "They gave birth," she said.

"They gave birth? T-to what?"

"The eggs, Louis."

"No!" he exclaimed. "I mean, why are they *dead?*"

Sage hadn't a clue. She didn't have a damn clue why. Samson had only ever admitted they were asexual, not that they died after giving birth. Honestly, all this time she had believed the Squids were abducting women and using them as incubators. It seemed Sage was wrong.

Sage stepped back. She turned to Louis and quietly asked, "Can you get the eggs?"

Louis didn't seem very inclined to retrieve them, but he didn't whine or complain. Sage grabbed a coat from the closet. She couldn't stand to be in this room much longer, so she stepped out into the freezing air.

The snow was thicker than before. Her ankles got lost in the slush. She went for one of the smaller houses alongside the trees that must have belonged to either Tyrus or Herman.

A curious Sage would have reveled in the opportunity to snoop through Squid-anything. A present Sage didn't have the mental focus to do it, even if there were piles of books on a table, folded clothes on a chair, and photographs of everything in the Outskirts galore. In the corner of her eye, she glimpsed a map with Emerald City as one of the dots. But really ... what was she supposed to do with that now? Against the Diamond City military prowling the forest in search of her? Against the forces of Emerald City that had probably kidnapped Damian and sent him to a lab for experiments?

Sage slid to the floor. She looked out at the room in a daze. With the life of her cocoons throbbing in her arms, she looked down and made a cut in her finger. She let her blood dribble over them, watching as it disappeared into the hard shells, absorbed like liquid in a paper towel.

Damian.

There was something wrong with Sage. Hopelessness blanketed her once more, like it had those weeks in the *Mistress*. It wrapped its arms around her body and squeezed the life out of her, casting her into a deep sleep. She only realized it when Louis came into the room, looking for her.

"Sage?" he said. That shirt was grossly oversized because it was a Squid's. After waking up cold on the table, there hadn't been anything else to wear. He padded over to her, gently took the cocoons so they wouldn't fall when he lifted her, and helped her into bed.

Meticulousness seemed to be a Squid trait. Like hell Sage knew how anyone could make a bed this perfectly, but she didn't feel gross laying in sheets that were foreign to her. They smelled fresh, like lavender. Louis tucked her in, then placed the cocoons on either side of her.

"Rest now," he might have said. "I'll take care of things here."

Louis? Taking charge? Sage wanted to snort. She had seen *The Royal Court* too many times, had the whiny, snotty, spoiled Louis of old in her brain. This new behavior startled her, but nowhere near enough to wake her up. Right back to sleep again, because that's all she seemed to be doing lately.

Or maybe she was dying. Fido had died after pup birth. Tyrus and Herman were dead after spitting out eggs. Maybe Sage was supposed to die, too.

"**L**ook, look, Star!" Twinkle Fairy exclaimed in her high-pitched voice. Sage's least favorite character, for sure, but at least Twinkle Fairy was loyal . . . and a guy who was head over heels for Star Raider. "He's coming—he's coming! You see? I told you it was the Shadow King!"

The Shadow King: Star Raider's love interest, forever a villain. The most memorable moment of the show was when Star Raider's most trusted partner had turned out to be the mastermind behind the attacks in the city. Terrible.

Sage remembered crying. She and Aurora hadn't been able to sleep that night.

"I'm sure there has to be a reason," Aurora said as they laid in their beds, staring at the ceiling above them. "The Shadow King can't be evil for nothing. He cares for her too much."

"Does it really matter?" Sage said. "If it's him, that means he killed all those people in the Energy Explosions. What justification would there be for that?"

Aurora shrugged. "Maybe he was being forced. We don't know what was driving him, Sage. Give people a chance."

"I can't, Aurora. Maybe the Shadow King—if he's truly being manipulated, like you say—should have stuck up for what's right."

"Maybe there was more at stake than just those people affected in the Energy Explosions. What if he had had to choose between those people . . . and the City of Starlight itself? What if this was the lesser of two evils?"

Sage had scoffed. That didn't make it right. No chance. And so she and Aurora had discussed all kinds of possible motives behind the Shadow King's betrayal. One night they had even forgotten to do their algebra homework, because all they could do was talk about the show and wait for the next episode that weekend. It had become an obsession—their bulletin board was swamped with Star Raider and Shadow King pictures. Sage shipped them hard, but then Aurora thought of another possibility.

"What if Twinkle Fairy and Star Raider are meant to be together?" she asked.

No way. Sage would never go for that.

"You like the bad boys," Aurora giggled. "That's what you like. I know you already. Sage likes the bad boys! Ooo!"

"Yup," came Louis' happy voice out of nowhere.

Sage turned her head. Louis was curled up on the couch, the cocoons in his arms.

"Your mom's favorite show. What did you guys think?"

Was Louis talking to a pair of cocoons? Yes. Damian had done it, too. Sage was sure the babies couldn't hear a thing in there, and if she were them, she wouldn't want to be disturbed from her slumber. Not that Sage was going to scold Louis for that, though. There was simply no one else to talk to in this isolated nook next to the Roaring Mountains.

"Look," Louis cooed to them. He beamed brightly. "She's awake now."

Sage didn't make any moves to get up. The next *Defenders Unite!* episode started, but that's not what she was looking at, either. Sunlight was coming in through the window. The silence outside was daunting. Blackburn and the Diamond City military even more so. What the hell was going to happen next?

"Hey." Louis sensed her distress. He got up to sit on the bed next to her. His hair was damp from an earlier shower. The blue eyes were darker than usual, as if someone had doused them in a bit of misery. The gauntness of his face said he had gone a few days—maybe weeks—living a non-palace life. Out here, there were no servants to tend to him. In fact, they had to fend for themselves because Tyrus and Herman were dead. Louis confirmed that without saying it. He took a deep long breath that made Sage anxious as hell. She clenched the sheets as she gazed at him.

"They're out there," Louis said quietly. "I heard them. But they can't see us . . . because of the shield. At least, that's what I think it is. I looked through some of the research that the Lolligo left behind. The problem is I can't read a word of it. I found pictures, though— diagrams—and that's how I can guess the kinds of weapons and technology they're employing. They also have a picture of what looks like different defense mechanisms. I imagine the one that looks like an energy dome is the one we're in. It was in one of their journal entries."

"Samson," Sage said quietly.

Louis sighed. He placed the cocoons side by side on the bed, gently. "I can't read what they've written."

Sage sat up a bit. Why did her body hurt so much?

"Take it easy," Louis said. "You've been asleep for a few days."

Sage stared at him. Then she glanced at the door. She found one of the weapons Louis had mentioned, a huge shotgun that fired highly concentrated lasers that disintegrated opponents or anything standing in its way. Whole Outskirts towns, too. Louis must have have been patrolling for incomers. Based on his lack of wounds and rips, he hadn't engaged anyone. Thank God. But how long was that going to last?

Louis gave her a look. *Not very long*, he seemed to say with his eyes.

"Candice and Olivia," Sage said quietly. It would be dumb of her to ask Louis where they were. She supposed she was indirectly asking what the chances of their safety were.

"Blackburn has them," Louis said. "And their friend. He wouldn't dream to hurt them if it means leverage over you. Not that I trust him, though … obviously." He snorted. He pushed his hair back. Not in a charming way, but in an act of frustration. He let his arms rest on his lap in an exhausted sort of manner. He, too, felt the hopelessness of ever recuperating what he had lost. "He's out there. I saw three of his soldiers make an awfully close pass to our perimeter. I was ready with the gun, to do whatever it took to defend us, but …" He laughed wryly. Nervously. He hugged his body, clearly still traumatized over how close he had been to fighting for his life and losing it. In a scuffle like that, there was no way he would have been able to escape with Sage, the cocoons, and the two eggs. The Diamond City military would have overwhelmed them in seconds. It would have been all over. "Sage … we can't stay here."

In other words: *I need you to get better so you can find us a way out of here.*

Sage wasn't annoyed by it. She understood that if Louis got caught out here, it was over for him. She pulled the covers off her, shaking slightly as she got out of bed.

"Sage," Louis said softly.

Weak. Skinny. God, why did it look like Sage hadn't eaten in days? Well, maybe because she hadn't. And maybe because all this turmoil was getting to her. Losing Centerfeld, Damian, the rebels, her nieces, and nearly losing her babies was shredding her to pieces. The room spun viciously when she planted her feet on the floor and stood up for the first time in days. Louis got up to steady her. Sage noticed the two eggs in a carry-bin with hay, as if Louis was a farmer caring for his favorite hen's newly-laid eggs.

"Sage."

Sage stepped forward. Barefoot and all, in an equally large shirt that looked more like a dress, she picked up the gun and staggered outside.

"Sage!"

The cold sliced right through her. Goosebumps erupted across her skin as her body fought to regulate its warmth. Sage had to wait a moment for that to happen.

She stood amidst their small camp, their safe haven for now. Louis was right: perhaps the regular human couldn't hear it, but Sage did listen closely and she did detect the sound of voices. Miles away, though.

"Sage, you can't go out there now!" Louis caught up to her, panting like crazy. He wasn't zero-degree temperature ready by any means. His breath was a thick mist as he spoke to her. "If they catch you, we're fucked."

Sage looked at him. She had to admit she was surprised to hear Louis using expletives. Since when?

"Please listen!" he implored her. "Please! Can you just rest and recuperate for now? I know you're worried about your nieces, but we're safe here for right now and we need to come up with some kind of strategy. It'd also be amazing if you could read through what the Lolligo left behind so maybe we can communicate with them." He held her wrist. He forced her to look him in the eye. "Can you listen to me, please?"

"Shh." Sage kept an ear out for the voices that quickly became yells. Louis had heard that, too, because he stiffened instantly. Brows drawn, Sage edged closer to the edge of their bubble. She could see everything on the other side, even if the alert squirrels on the branches couldn't see her. They, too, were looking at something in the distance. Just what the hell was going on?

A roar made Sage gasp. As if someone had punched her in the chest, she whipped around to Louis with large eyes.

"What?" Louis pressed.

"Did the Kilstrongs ever experiment with animals?"

"What do you mean?"

"Cells," Sage said impatiently. She did not have the energy to be so articulate right now, but Louis' brain was going a hundred miles per hour. She had to understand that. "Did the Kilstrongs ever inject Cells into animals as bioweapons?"

"N-no—I mean, yes, but animals are out of control. Why do you ask?"

Fido. Sage had been wondering if Fido had belonged to the Squids, was some sort of sick experiment on a wolf, but it seemed Fido had dabbled in some Cells by accident. Possibly from the corpse of an Enhanced or something else with Cells.

Louis was right—the animals were untamable—because the yells in the distance were from overwhelmed military soldiers. Something was attacking them. It sounded big judging by the vivacity of its roar. Holy shit, what was that? A bear?

"Louis." Sage turned to him. "Can you get the other weapons and watch the . . . er . . . children?"

Two Squids and two babies in cocoons. The most unique family ever.

"Fine," Louis hissed, lowering his voice as the roars got closer. The ground trembled. The squirrels ran for cover. "But what about you?"

"I'm staying here at the border. Do as I say, please."

Unlike Damian, Louis retreated. It was the wrong time to be thinking of him, but Sage was once again mesmerized by the look he had given her when he shot her in the head.

Not Enhanced. Never Enhanced.

The thumps got closer. Trees rustled and dust blew everywhere. Bits of snow sprayed Sage's face.

No bear. Not anymore. Maybe not in a long time. At over ten feet tall, with monstrous shoulders and quads, any characteristics of the kind of animal it used to be had vanished. It was all red and pink like Fido had been, skin smooth but splotchy with blood, blisters, and scabs. It was rancid like a rotting corpse, saliva dribbling like thick cement from a truck. Its claws carried old pieces of fur and flesh, caked on from years of trudging through innocent camps and tearing apart lost adventurers and hikers. Its chest was massive, but its belly was round and protruding. Something squirmed in there. Sage pictured worms.

Cells did this. Cells had done this. Create monsters.

Like Damian?

Like ... Sage? She was a monster, too. A hybrid. She, Lex, Damian, Blackburn, and any other hybrids out there were all monsters with powerful blood that could create more monsters, and birth more monsters if they mated with each other.

And only with each other. As all the women in Smallfeld had proven. Who had done that? Who had impregnated all those women? Which hybrids? All for nothing because neither humans nor Enhanced could carry hybrid babies.

Sage held the shotgun in her right hand, but didn't aim it. Any kind of movement would attract this creature's attention. Already it was sniffing around the perimeter, perhaps sensing the energy field encompassing what would be its lunch.

Kill it, was her instinct. *It's not going to leave you alone.*

Sage raised the shotgun now. She rested the butt against the sweet spot between her chest and shoulder. She kept her hands steady, eyes on her target. One blast, and maybe she'd give herself away. But that one blast would silence this monster for good. It had clearly done a number on the military, so maybe Blackburn had moved on to elsewhere. But could Sage really worry about the military when this monster was about to sniff her out? It already had. Its roar was so powerful that it destroyed her eardrums. None of that fazed her when it was life or death.

One shot, and half of the creature blew away. Tentacles snapped out as regeneration kicked in, but Sage shot it again. In blowing its belly, tiny worms plopped to the ground and started slithering all over the place. She couldn't let those infiltrate the camp, so she blasted them, too.

And then the gun needed to recharge.

The creature wasn't dead yet, and not all the worms were dead. As they wiggled their way toward camp, Louis popped out of the office with another gun and didn't hesitate to shoot. Only now Sage was defenseless without a weapon and that creature was regenerating at the speed of light.

"Sage!" Louis threw her her sword.

Sage unsheathed it, trying hard not to think of Damian, and leapt forward.

Free from the confines of the bubble, she felt so exposed. It was so much colder out here, despite the fact her safety came from invisibility and nothing else. She avoided snapping jaws as she perched herself on the creature's broken shoulder, swung around to its back, and stabbed it in the back of the neck.

The creature howled. The blade went right through, cutting its trachea. It was up to Louis to finish the job, and he hesitated to shoot because Sage was still dangling from the creature's back. The Slainium was working—Sage could feel the creature sagging—but she couldn't dislodge the damn sword!

"DAMN IT!" Sage cried out. She perched her feet on the creature's lower back, pulling at the sword with all her might, but nothing.

"SAGE!" Louis hollered. "MOVE!"

Damian's sword! Sage couldn't let it go! She cried.

"SAGE!"

Sage let go. She hit the ground, and then there was a flash of light.

"The Warlord regrets that he cannot return your sword," Fahrenheit said in Sage's ear. *"But he offers another weapon in her place."*

The sword was gone. Decimated. The one Damian used to hold, the one he had deemed worthy enough to be his. Sage had never asked him for its origins. Actually, Damian had told her once the sword was neither male nor female, so *their* was the correct pronoun. Sage didn't have a clue how Damian could sniff out people's (and inanimate object's) genders so quickly, but she'd never get to see him do it again.

Damian was gone. Somewhere in Emerald City. How was Sage supposed to get him back now, especially without the sword?

Blood showered Sage, who quivered in the snow. Pieces of gunk hit her everywhere. The smell made her vomit.

Louis trudged through the snow to get to her. He picked her crying form off the ground. He didn't ask her if she was all right after nearly getting blasted—he ran with her back to their camp. That thing's carcass out there was a dead giveaway there were hiding persons nearby, but Louis was obviously more concerned over her. He took her inside, to where the children were tucked into bed, and sat her on the floor. He checked her for any missing body parts. All he saw were tears.

"His sword's gone," Sage croaked.

Louis held her face. He got to his knees. He was fighting to keep his panting under control—Sage could hear it.

"But his children aren't," he said, even more softly than her. "And that's what matters . . . right?"

When Sage looked into the eyes above, she noticed the darker hue was gone. They were crystal clear now, readable like a book. They bore into hers, telling her everything that he felt deep within his heart. Words, perhaps, that he had not been able to tell her in the past. Whether because of fear . . . or hesitation . . . or inappropriateness . . . Sage guessed all the above.

"Do you love him?" Louis asked her quietly.

This was the rawest Sage had ever seen Louis. It felt wrong when there was a sizzling carcass just feet away from their camp and Sage was covered in blood, but that question was more of an emergency than their need to secure their safety right now.

"I do," Sage said. Whether she wanted to or not. And God knows she had tried to let him go. She had asked him to leave. She had asked him to leave her alone. But the moment he had, she withered away. Depressed. Pitiful. Sheer agony those days on that ship without him. Without his stupid remarks or tons of designs. His beautiful face and makeup, long silky hair, and powerful body with so much muscle that drove her crazy. She missed their banter, his endless need to impress her, the way he treated Candice and Olivia, and how he brought them all together as a family. He always made her laugh. And Sage hadn't laughed in such a long time . . .

"I do love him." Sage touched the Portable Projector around her neck. Was he still wearing his? Or had Takuya ripped it from his neck? "I love him a lot."

Louis closed his eyes. He took a deep breath. Either to steady himself or his emotions. He couldn't lose his head over something he couldn't control, no matter how badly it hurt him. It clearly did.

"But that doesn't mean we're getting married," Sage said. "Or that we're even a couple."

Louis snapped his head up. He looked like someone had slapped him.

Sage looked away. "Not anymore."

"Wait—is this because of what happened with my sister?"

"Partially. But I've also realized that I . . ." Sage hesitated. But she said it anyway. "That I can't be 'clingy.' I can't give myself to a person so wholly like I did with Damian. So I've distanced myself and settled for being partners. Nothing more."

Louis gazed at her seriously. He looked like he was examining a specimen under a microscope. "Does he know this?"

"I'm not sure."

"Sage, loving someone or being with someone doesn't mean that you're 'clingy.'"

"Apparently, it does," Sage said. "My own niece noticed it. Damian snapped at me for it when I called him on the phone and told him not to go to that meeting with your sister."

Louis shook his head. "I don't know what happened there, but it sounds like you're still upset. You have every reason to be, of course, but I don't see that as clingy at all."

Sage snorted. "And you expect me to care what you think? I've already made up my mind. I've had enough heartache for a lifetime. I just want peace."

"Give yourself some time. Once this is all over, maybe you'll feel differently. Loving someone wholly is a beautiful thing."

"Do you say that because you care about me?" Sage asked him "Or because you want your shot with me?"

"Both," Louis admitted.

Sage shook her head. "I don't know what to say. I don't want to play these love games anymore."

"So you're willing to ignore a chance at a relationship just because it didn't work out with Damian?"

Sage narrowed her eyes at him. "Fuck off, Louis."

Louis chuckled wryly. "I'm sorry. I told you this before, but I'll tell you again: I knew he had you wrapped around his finger, just like you did him, but I thought it was more of a political game than love. I didn't think you *truly* loved him. I thought you'd have children and that'd be the end of it."

"I didn't have sex with him just to have children," Sage spat. "I don't understand you or Blackburn—why is this all about reproducing? Why can't anyone just dream of being in love and living a decent life?"

"I understand. But do you think that's what he wants?"

"Does it matter? We're not together anymore."

"That's fine, but you shouldn't let that destroy your chances for a future relationship with someone else. Sage, of course you were hurt. He and my sister had plotted to use you. He killed her because you found out. It wasn't you—I know you were covering for him— but did you know he killed Bram, too?"

"Fuck me!" Sage exclaimed angrily. "You, too—?"

"Suicide, he told you?" Louis said quietly, as if he didn't want the children to hear him. "That was no suicide, Sage. He executed Bram as soon as he woke up from his transplant surgery. His own rebels in Mousafeld told me everything."

"He said suicide."

"That's a lie."

"And what proof do you have?" Sage spat. "Word of mouth? Hearsay? Is there footage of him doing it?"

"Does there need to be?" Louis said. "Why would his own rebels lie about it?"

"BECAUSE THEY'RE ALWAYS TRYING TO DESTROY OUR HAPPINESS!" Sage yelled. Louis raised his hands. "*MY* HAPPINESS, DAMN IT! Just what the fuck do you think you're doing, Louis, admitting to me that you love me? You don't even know me!"

"I know all about you," Louis said calmly. He kept a straight face despite how fast Sage was breathing. His composure was impressive. Had Samson taught him that? "I know how you love your sister, Aurora, and how *Defenders Unite!* is everything to you. I know how pizza is in your blood, and you're like a dough doctor or something because you know how to make the perfect dough. I know that you'd give anything for the happiness of your nieces, but most of all, I know that you love Diamond City with all your heart. You want a family that loves you, but you also want to feel valuable, like you're making a difference, without the fighting. You want unity and you want people to get along.

"Does Damian know that about you, too? Probably. But does he know that your lip quirks to the right when you draw your brows? Or that you clench your fists three times when you're getting ready to fight, like a runner on the count of three? Does he know that when you braid your hair you do an under-and-over maneuver, not the standard way?"

Sage gasped. It felt like someone had punched her in the gut. She even clutched her abdomen and curled into herself as she remembered Damian that night in Winterfeld . . .

"Sage?" Louis pressed.

Sage stood up. Her knees wobbled. They almost gave out, but Sage held strong. She had to as she realized something very important.

Louis got up, too. "I do love you. I have for a while now. And I'm not just saying that because I want babies. I obviously can't have them with you, but I swear to always defend you and Castor and Pollux. Right now, I'm pretty much title-less, but I'll get it back eventually. There's no way you're going to let Blackburn win."

Sage walked away. She refused to engage in this conversation any further. She needed to take a shower, because the rot was driving her crazy, so she went straight into the bathroom. Her movements were methodical and with purpose—fast, because they didn't have a lot of time. Blackburn was probably still out there prowling the grounds, and it wouldn't be long before he came across that monster's body. Sage dried up and tied a towel around her body.

When she came out, Louis wasn't in the room. She glanced at the children, who were quiet and still in bed. She threw on another oversized shirt, found a pair of trousers that she had to tie at the waist, knees, and ankles, and these slip-on boots made of a slick steel that conformed to any shape. She looked a bit ridiculous, but it'd do for now.

She had to find Louis and figure out what the hell they were going to do to get out of here. Unwilling to leave the children alone, she grabbed hers and secured them in the sling while tucking the eggs into their bin. She trudged toward the office where she found Louis looking through a ton of files. Rather, he was throwing them all into a backpack.

"We can't stay here," he declared. "So we'll take what we can."

"And where do you propose we go, exactly?" Sage asked him. "You seem rather sure of yourself."

"I don't know, but I think anywhere is better than here. I tried looking for the mechanism that's creating the forcefield, but I can't find it. Either way, I think we should head to Smallfeld since it's close to here—"

"We're not going there," Sage said. "I'm not going there."

Louis looked over his shoulder at her. "Sage, we can't stay!"

"I think we should." Sage sat down at the table. "If Blackburn doesn't find us, why not? It'll give me time to look through all this Squid stuff. Hell—we might be able to communicate with Samson."

"But what if Blackburn does find us?"

"Then we can get the hell out. But for right now, I think we have enough provisions to last us a while. Even if it's all canned meat."

There was a small microwave in the corner with neatly stacked cans right next to it. There was probably more in the drawer.

"What did you do with the bodies?" Sage asked quietly.

"Buried them," Louis said. He stopped his task of packing. He went over to sit next to her at the table. "It's only the right thing to do. I just can't believe Samson never mentioned this about Lolligo. They're asexual, sure, but they spit up their own eggs and die?"

"Seemingly."

"Is that what happened to Samson, too?"

"I only found the egg," Sage said. "Not his body."

Someone must have left the egg on purpose. Samson's objective to spy on Sage made sense, too. Even though he had never met a single Squid in his life, he probably carried memories from his past life. As fascinating as it was, and as many questions as Sage had regarding what the newborn Squids would remember and do, something else took centerstage in her mind.

"Tyrus and Herman said he was their Prime," Sage said. "Do you think Samson knows we're here?"

"Did they tell him?" Louis asked, surprised to hear that tidbit of Samson he had been unconscious for.

There was no way to know unless Sage could decode all the information in this room. Perhaps, somewhere in these tidy piles of research and blinking electronics, there was a whole conversation between Tyrus, Herman, and Samson. Of course, she wasn't going to know until she started reading.

And that was going to take a long time.

CHAPTER 19

The Rebel Gang

Three months. That's how long it took Sage to analyze every bit of information the Squids had stored in their camp. They were in the month of Strength now, but she couldn't tell because it was always cold out here. It was hard to believe, but only two months away from a new year. This marked Sage's first anniversary with Damian. It was crazy to think of everything that had happened since meeting the beautiful Warlord, but Sage didn't have a lot of opportunity to when she was viciously searching for signs of Samson.

It had been so difficult to find anything. The gazillion emails these Squids had been sending to and from their camps across the Outskirts were by the thousands. Sage's Lolligo wasn't perfect, but it had definitely improved now that she was reading through all these messages. There were months and months of logs that described every detail of seemingly everything the Squids had done. It was a bit scary how meticulous it all was, as if the Squid's only purpose was to observe humans and the terrain they lived on.

Tyrus and Herman had been here since Damian's successful campaign in Winterfeld. That meant it wasn't the Squids who had been kidnapping all those women, as Nova believed, because someone else had been doing it long before their arrival. While the two Squids never revealed where they had come from, they did note there was plenty of disarray in Winterfeld.

In their words, the technology in these parts was impressive for a band of humans so far out from Diamond City. The Squids didn't understand the use of androids because they did everything themselves. The weapons, however, fascinated them. The two that Sage and Louis used had been discarded by a Winterfeld guard and enhanced by Tyrus and Herman.

And that's how the rest of the entries were. Kind of boring, unless Sage was interested in random deer and bunny doodles. Tyrus had drawn what looked like a penis with a bunch of question marks everywhere. He had seen a human take a leak. He said that penises were the ugliest parts of a human being.

Sage couldn't help a laugh. What would Damian say about that?

Later entries described Herman and Tyrus' longing for home. Although they didn't have parents, the Squids lived in a city where everyone worked toward survival. They feared the humans greatly and watched them from afar to keep their distance. Herman described the Enhanced as "barbaric" and questioned just how much they could trust hybrids. Sure, hybrids had liberated Diamond City from rogue humans and shared most of their DNA, but did the Squids really want them in their cities? Tainting their cities?

Sage supposed she understood the discrimination. If she were a Squid, she wouldn't trust a hybrid so readily, either. It made her appreciate Samson that much more, how he had truly cared for her and gone out of his way to train her. Prepare her.

What was he doing now?

It wasn't until the last week of the month of Strength that Sage finally found a message from Samson.

Sage had the Squid equivalent of a phone in her hand. It was a thick, bulky communicator that transmitted messages thousands of miles away and over the longest mountain chain in Abloudor, even without signal. It was a handy laser, too, blasting holes in the steel floor, and a scanner.

Sage scanned Louis with it and she could see his innards, as if she were peering at the anatomy of a human in a biology book. He didn't feel a thing, but Sage could see his beating heart, the acid in his stomach, and even his crotch, which she quickly looked away from.

Sage turned to her cocoons in the corner. She pointed the scanner at them, and her heart dropped at what she saw.

Two sleeping babies. Boys, from the genitals, as Damian had said. They were curled up in fetal position, large heads tucked into their knees. The cocoons had grown significantly the past three months thanks to all the blood Sage fed them. She had always wondered what was inside them . . . wouldn't trust anyone else to tell her . . . but now she knew. She wished she could keep this picture in her mind forever. Possibly tattoo it on her ribs or something.

For right now, she'd have to settle for saving it in the camera roll, right alongside the other pictures of humans, animals, and nature. She got back to the messages and found what she was looking for.

"Louis," Sage said.

Louis was at the stove, cooking noodles and frozen pork bits. Just like Samson had done in the Circular Forest when they left Diamond City for the first time. Louis wiped his hands and came over right away.

"Look at this."

Louis couldn't read it, so Sage translated it. There wasn't a whole lot of correspondence back and forth, but there was a conversation.

" 'We think we ran into her and the man,'" Sage read out loud. "I think 'man' is supposed to be Damian. 'As you said . . . she's staying at Winterfeld. We passed on Reina. Orders?'"

The response to that from Samson was, " 'Stay put until she shows up. She'll come back to Diamond City and find my message.'"

" 'The end of our lives is near.'"

" 'Let's hope she makes it quickly.'"

And that was it. Sage looked at Louis, who was hyperventilating.

"Message him!" he said instantly. "Go!"

Not a moment to waste—Sage did just that. Her thumbs shook as she typed in Lolligo. Just when she thought she was an expert after all the reading she had done, she realized she sucked at writing this hell of a language. She had never used a keyboard with all those slithery symbols and never put them together on paper, either. But she did know enough to form basic sentences, so she wrote,

Samson, it's Sage. Are you there?

"Damn!" Louis breathed. "Do you think he'll get our message?"

They had to wait and see. Sage had a good feeling about this. Hell, what if Samson was on his way now? Surely after not hearing from Tyrus and Herman for so long he'd be concerned enough to send reinforcements. Or perhaps he had ... and run into Blackburn instead.

A loud bark made Sage and Louis jump. They glanced at each other and moved accordingly: Sage picked up her shotgun, and Louis had the blaster. Sage rushed out of the building, then slowed her pace when she got outside and looked for the source of the noise.

It was strange to hear barking. Most of the time, it was either rustling or growling. Animals rarely ventured into camp. Thankfully, ever since Sage and Louis had defeated that monstrous bear creature, there hadn't been anymore. That didn't mean Blackburn had evacuated the premises, though—his soldiers passed by occasionally, and Sage and Louis had been lucky enough to watch them walk on without a single glance their way. It amazed Sage that Blackburn was so persistent, willing to spend months in search of her while duties piled up in Heart. He must have suspected she was hiding here somewhere.

But this time, it wasn't Blackburn. It was another strange creature the size of a fox, with fleshy smooth skin that was pink and red in all the wrong places.

Fido?

It looked like her, but it wasn't. This was one of the pups—Sage remembered because the last time she had seen her, Blue was rolling around in the snow, kissing up to Damian like anyone with genitals would. Three months later, she was twice the size with keen enough senses to sniff for her person. Right after her mother's death, Blue had stuck her nose in Sage's chest enough times to recognize her anywhere. But what the hell was she doing out here?

Louis whipped out his gun, but Sage held out her arm.

"No, Louis," Sage whispered. "I think I know her..."

"'Her'?" Louis whispered back. "How? Sage, that's a wild animal trying to kill us!"

No. Blue looked worlds different now, but it was still her. Like anyone with Cells, she aged slowly, but she was big enough and trained enough to cause heavy damage. The longer Sage studied her, the more confident she became in that. She tested out her theory by whistling like Damian used to and calling, "Here, Blue."

Instantly, Blue perked up. She didn't understand what she had heard because she couldn't see where it had come from. Her eyes were so much smaller now, but much more focused and vigilant. They were amber, vibrant and brilliant, and they locked onto Sage's, even if they couldn't see her.

Blue barked. She whined and jumped in place. Then she paced back and forth, confused. Perhaps she could sense the barrier, and she took caution not to run into a field that could decimate her, but Sage assured her it was all right.

"Blue! Here, girl!"

It was her person's voice, and Blue trusted her, so she ran forward. When she crossed the barrier and saw Sage, she yelped, jumped five feet into the air, chased her thin skeletal tail, and then raced into Sage's arms.

Blue knocked her over. Paws on Sage's shoulders, she gave her face the licking of a lifetime. Louis thought this was an attack, so he had his gun up, but Sage's laughs assured him she was in no danger. Louis was just confused by how Blue had found them and where the hell she had come from. Sage wondered the same thing.

"Blue." Sage gripped the animal's face, pulling back her lips to see all her very sharp teeth. Drool dripped all over her. "It's so nice to see you."

Blue jumped back, whining now. She stomped her front legs. Perhaps she wanted Sage to follow her. But she was way too hyper, and that was no way to communicate with humans. She seemed to remember Damian's training, and she sat down and kept her excitement under control. She opted for grunting instead. It sounded like she was sneezing.

"How did you find me?" Sage breathed. The answer to that was too painful to bear. It meant a slew of different scenarios. One of them was that the rebels had released the pups somewhere in the Outskirts, possibly abandoning them, and taken off to find Damian. Another was that the rebels had come back for her and were using the pups to sniff her out. Could that be it?

As smart as Blue was, she couldn't talk. She did lock eyes with Sage, and communicated quite a bit with her intense gaze. There were subtle booms in the background. Explosions from far away. Was that from Winterfeld?

"That's suicide," Louis said immediately. "We can't go there, Sage."

Obviously not. But who was attacking who? And what if her nieces were in danger?

"Sage." Louis grabbed her arm, forcing her to look at him. "We can't put ourselves in the line of fire. If it's true the rebels are here, attacking Blackburn, then this is our chance to get back to Diamond City."

"How?" Sage said. "We don't have any ships—just a damn hover scooter." What was it with Squids and mopeds? "Do you honestly think that's going to get us back into the city? With all the shit we have to carry?"

"This is a fight for survival!" Louis barked. "How can you even begin to think we're taking any of this stuff with us?" He glanced at the phone in her hand. He nodded. "That's as good as it gets."

"What about the children? They'll be exposed! If there are aircrafts flying overhead, attacking from up above, what are we going to do if we're sighted? We'll be open targets."

Louis pursed his lips. It wrinkled his mouth and eyes, making him look like an old man. He was worlds different from The-Royal-Court Louis, and Sage had to admit she was a little impressed. He also used his brain and realized that she was right.

"Fine," he said. "So what do you propose?"

More rustling from afar. Sage knew it was Violet and Orange, who were always on the lookout for their clumsy sister. They couldn't see her, so they started howling in worry. Blue bumbled out to meet them, then led them into the barrier so they could see Sage.

More happy introductions and grumblings from Louis. "More of them?" he grunted under his breath as Violet and Orange attacked Sage next. Not for long, though—there was no time to waste—and the two stepped back and made lunges toward the woods. The whining said they were desperate for Sage to follow.

The rebels had to be out there, and Sage was going to have to take a risk. She yearned for Damian's sword, but the guns would have to do. She went back to the main building for the children only, and that's when she froze.

Sage covered her mouth.

"I'll get the eggs!" Louis ran in after her, and nearly rammed into her back. He stopped, too.

His eyes widened. He looked like he was watching a woman give birth. It would have been hilarious had Sage not been looking into the beautiful, chubby faces of her gurgling children.

Sage sunk to the floor, on her knees. Louis started a nervous laughter.

"W-whoa..."

Blue, Violet, and Orange entered the room. They glanced at the eggs inside the bin, then sniffed around the broken cocoons in their cradle. The pups were calm, but alert, recognizing who Castor and Pollux were instantly.

Like lizards, the two babies had torn through the cocoons with their heads and hands. They were working on their feet. Slowly and lazily, as if they had all the time in the world to be born. Their large eyes gazed up at the ceiling, little fists clenching and unclenching.

"Sage!" Louis called nervously, bending over to look at them. "L-look!"

How the hell was Sage going to get up off the floor? God, she was so tired all of a sudden. It was the pups that helped her stand, biting her sleeves and leading her to her own children. When the two babies saw her, they giggled loudly.

"M-my God . . ." Sage croaked. She picked up the cocoons and held them to her chest. She dug her nose into each head, sniffing then kissing. Castor and Pollux reached for her with their hands, knowing very well whose arms they were in.

"That's insane!" Louis bumbled. "T-they actually hatched! I-I mean, I know some animals and birds do that, but I never thought I'd see a human do it!"

"They're beautiful." Sage beamed.

"Yeah, and they look like you. Look at their brows—totally you."

But they had Damian's nose. His sensual lips. Those were characteristics Louis didn't want to acknowledge when they were about to run for their lives. The three pups reminded them that while this was a tender touching moment, there was a fight going on outside. It was time to get the sling.

"Does that mean they still need your . . . blood?" Louis asked as Sage accommodated them against her chest, cocoons and all. "Or . . . milk?"

"I don't think breast-feeding them right now is a good idea," Sage snapped. "Unless you're suggesting that so you can see my tits."

"N-no!" Louis turned a horrible red. "I was just curious, is all."

"I don't know what sort of nutrition they need right now, but it's something we'll have to figure out later."

"Sage." Louis grabbed her arm again. It was the only way to stop her and get her to look at him. "Are you sure this is a good idea?"

"No," Sage said quietly. "I'm not sure of anything right now."

"Say that the rebels are out there . . . will they kill me?"

"I won't let them," Sage promised. Either way, Louis wasn't the bad guy here, and the rebels had to know that. It sounded like the showdown was between them and Diamond City.

Sage grabbed the scooter on the way out. She trembled with excitement because her newborn babies were in her arms at last, and she was finally leaving this secluded camp. If the pups were here, then the rebels had to be close by, and Sage had to take this opportunity to find them if she was going to rescue Damian. She revved the engine and the scooter floated up into the air. Louis was sitting right behind her, egg bin in between their bodies.

The pups led the way. Like snow dogs, they charged out of the clearing and into the trees. Sage followed, maneuvering the scooter around trunks and branches. She thought of Rick in moments like these. Speedstar Rick was an expert driver—it didn't matter the kind of vehicle he was on. His tattoo was on Sage's left wrist, covered beneath her gloves. She wondered what he would say if he saw her now, weaving through the densest forest she had ever been in. She cut her turns close too many times to count. The three pups in front of her never let up. The snow was getting in her eyes and they were starting to sting. The booms and yells were getting louder. There really was a fight at Winterfeld, which was where the pups were taking her.

They broke into the cemetery. Why did Sage always find herself here when she was fighting for her life in some way? If not against monsters, then the Diamond City military. As she listened for nearby movement, the dreary silence hovering over these graves swallowed her completely. There wasn't any activity here, but Sage got a horrible feeling in her bones. The three pups stopped because they knew it, too. Getting any closer to Winterfeld meant she'd be in danger.

"Sage!" Louis croaked as Sage got off the scooter. "Seriously?"

Sage trudged across the cemetery. Her boots sunk into the thick snow, a satisfying crunch to her ears. It allowed her to remove herself from the fighting going on up ahead and focus on the headstone of Phoebe Damaris.

A young girl Damian had taken in as his own daughter. Not that they had ever been blood related . . .

Castor and Pollux gurgled from inside Sage's coat. She peeked at each of them to make sure they were all right. Their big eyes blinking at her confirmed that they were. For a pair of newborns, they surely didn't cry a whole lot. Sage couldn't say she was complaining. Perhaps they sensed mother was here, so there was nothing to be afraid of. Until, of course, Sage got closer to the town. The two started squirming and crying out.

"Sage!" Louis hissed. "This is insane! You have no idea what's going on out there."

Very true. The blasts and shakes didn't stop. There was no way to know who was winning. When that much was clear, so was Sage's next course of action. She unstrapped the sling and gave the babies over to Louis.

"W-what—?"

"Take care of them," Sage said, adjusting the straps across his chest and waist. "Their lives for yours. Got it?"

Louis was too flabbergasted to speak.

"Stay with him, please," Sage said to Blue, Violet, and Orange. While she wouldn't have minded taking them with her for protection, Louis needed them far more than she did. The pups understood.

Eventually, Louis backed up toward the forest for cover. He kept eye contact until he disappeared behind the trees. The pups continued to circle around him, and then they were gone, too.

Sage, in the meanwhile, had a mission to accomplish. She clutched the Squids' enhanced shotgun like her life depended on it, knowing she'd use it as soon as she detected any hostile movement. As she got closer to Winterfeld, she kept it at the ready. She saw the first line of houses up ahead. Nova's wasn't too far away.

That's where Sage was headed. She wasn't sure why, but she had a feeling that her nieces were there. Not only was it a place they'd feel comfortable staying at, but the enemy suspected it'd be Sage's first stop, too. Where else would she look with the entire town under watch? It was one big, fat trap, but Sage was going to have to take her chances. Better the house than the middle of an open battlefield. She crept up on Nova's backyard slowly, one foot after the other, with her eyes scanning all the windows for movement.

All was still. Good—

A scream and gunfire. Sage heard it, and then saw a flash from within.

Like a runner at the ready, she took off. She had never pranced through snow faster in her life, or smashed through glass with her heart stuck in her throat. It made breathing exceptionally difficult, and when oxygen wasn't making it to her brain, her ability to rationalize decreased. She became a liability, an open target, and completely useless in the face of whatever threat was making her nieces scream like that.

Yes, her nieces. Her fucking nieces were under attack, and Sage was panicking. Instead of surveying her surroundings and identifying the threat, she rushed right past the kitchen and barged into the living room where the commotion was.

"AUNT SAGE!" Olivia squealed from behind the couch.

Sage had the shotgun up and pointed at that bitch, Shenzi, who was wrestling Geoffrey off her back. From the gun on the floor, it looked like Shenzi had been about to shoot Candice, who was scurrying backward, when Geoffrey intervened. Reckless, of course, because while he had knocked the gun out of her hand, Shenzi was too skilled a warrior to be beaten by a hormonal teenager. She flipped him onto the floor like an acrobat and held a knife to his throat. To make matters worse, Shenzi wasn't the only one playing babysitter here—she had comrades who stormed into the room with their own weapons up and pointed.

"Lower it," Shenzi hissed at Sage like a hyena. Her white sharp teeth would make the biggest of monsters cower.

Sage didn't have to. Candice did the smart thing and curled up behind the armchair, hands over her ears. Olivia held her position behind the couch, clearing the way for Sage to shoot Shenzi right off of Geoffrey.

The blast was loud and blinding. Sage was already anticipating retaliation from the four soldiers, so she jumped before any bullets hit her and grabbed onto Nova's precious chandelier. No one had seen her move, meaning she had the element of surprise on her side. As the dust cleared, Sage unleashed her daggers on the soldiers, one for each of them. She prepared one for Shenzi, but there was nothing left of the vicious female warrior. Blood and guts lay in a pile of burnt white-and-black strips of fabric. Smoke hissed from the remains, filling the room with the smell of decay. Sage nearly gagged.

"GEOFFREY!" Candice shrieked.

Sage looked down, and her heart stopped for the second time that day. There were no babies to celebrate, only a dying Geoffrey to stare at.

Sage couldn't quite process what was happening. Blood was spurting out of Geoffrey's neck in torrents. His throat was wide open, the inside of it perfectly visible from where Sage hung. She could see all the muscle inside, the throbbing aorta, and the well of blood that continued to gush out of his body with every beat of his heart.

"GEOFFREY!" Candice was screaming now. Olivia joined in, rattling Sage's brain.

Survival mode threw Sage from the chandelier to the floor. Justice was dead because this hadn't worked, but Sage wasn't going to stand by idly while this precious young man lost his life. She slit her arm with a dagger, gathered as much blood as she could into her mouth, and dribbled it right over Geoffrey's wound. She might have been kissing another pair of lips, one of the grossest things she had ever done to a dying person, but she was desperate. Candice and Olivia were sobbing as if they were being lashed. Sage couldn't stop delivering blood until she was sure it was in Geoffrey's body, and it was—she could feel it—but she didn't stop.

"Please work," she croaked, taking more blood into her mouth and pouring it directly into Geoffrey's gash. "Please work!"

Geoffrey coughed up blood. His eyes were losing focus and his body stopped twitching.

"Geoffrey." Sage grabbed his face with a bloody hand. She looked directly into his eyes. "Look at me. Look at me, damn it."

Geoffrey was looking at her. His beautiful hazel eyes bored into hers. Blood was still seeping from the gash in his throat, but his chest was still moving, too.

"Control yourself," Sage said. "Control your breathing."

Geoffrey closed his eyes. More blood spurted out from between his lips, but he swallowed and controlled his breaths. Veins were popping out of his forehead. They were everywhere now, actually, big and thick. His head was moving back and forth on the floor, like a kid playing in the snow.

"A-Aunt Sage?" Candice croaked, coming closer. Olivia had stopped screaming, too. She had tear stains on her cheeks. "W-what's happening?"

Geoffrey was groaning now. His hands were clenching into fists and his feet were stomping the ground. He squirmed as if something were coming to life inside him. There were audible cracks coming from his very skeleton, making Candice and Olivia flinch. When Geoffrey opened his eyes, they were amber.

"It's fine." Sage laid a hand on his forehead. She kept an eye on his wound, which had stopped bleeding all together. There was a massive scar there now. "It's going to be fine."

The front door burst open, and the girls screamed. Sage grabbed her shotgun, but she recognized the all-silver battle suits from Centerfeld. She didn't loosen her grip until one of them called out to her, "Don't shoot!" Another actually fired at the regenerating Shenzi behind Candice and Olivia.

What the hell? Shenzi had been raw and bloody, but still fully functional? Sage had totally missed that. She could only wonder if Blackburn had given her an extra dose of Cells back in Diamond City.

"Sage!" L lowered her mask. She had led the charge with Sonia and two others that Sage recognized as Sword Devil and Tai. They all lowered their masks to show her they were friendlies.

"Oh, God!" Sonia cried, running forward. "Sage!"

"Hold it!" L grabbed her partner and reeled her back. She gaped at the twitching Geoffrey on the floor. "Fuck me—what's happening to him?"

"He was about to die." Sage got to her feet. Her knees were quaking terribly. "I-I couldn't let him. So I . . . um . . ."

"Gave him your blood?" Tai finished.

Extreme fastball player. This was the wrong time to think about games, but that's what Sage saw when she looked at this man. His body was solid muscle like Little Man's, but much trimmer and slimmer. Powerful, but as swift as a ballerina. His slanted eyes promised much pain to whoever crossed him, and his hair was in a Damian bun so it wouldn't get in the way.

Sword Devil, on the other hand, didn't need guns. She had two swords in her hands, and the sky was the limit. What would fighting her be like? She, like the rest of the Lex Warriors, knew exactly what Sage had done.

"He needs a medic." L got to her knees and checked Geoffrey's pulse. "We need to get him back to the ship."

"Take them," Sage said to them. "Take the girls, please."

"No!" Olivia cried. She threw her arms around Sage's waist. "We want to stay with you! Please don't leave us again!"

"You're in good hands, I promise," Sage said to her. "But I have to find Damian."

Damian. Oh, God. Where was he now? Was he even alive?

With horror twisting in her chest, Sage looked up at the Lex Warriors. She still didn't understand what the hell was going on. They had come back for her? Why now?

"He's here," L said steadily.

Sage blinked. "What?"

"Yes," Sonia said, with an encouraging smile. "Damian came back to Centerfeld with Emerald City reinforcements! That's why we set out to find you. The rebels told us that Diamond City had their entire military stationed here. We didn't know where you were, but we figured you'd survive."

"Did you?" Sage said icily. She couldn't be mad at them, though. Even Centerfeld would have struggled to attack Diamond City on its own. But with Emerald City reinforcements? They actually had a chance of winning. Sage's next question became, "How? How did Damian get all those reinforcements?"

"We don't know," L said quickly. "But we can't linger here. I think we have a handle on these bitches, and we need to run."

"Where's Damian?"

"He's fighting Blackburn," Tai said. "He sent us and the dogs to search for you."

"Stay with them," Sage commanded of the girls, who didn't protest this time. They looked worried, but Sage wasn't sure it was for Damian. Or maybe it was now that they had dealt with people far worse.

The Lex Warriors didn't stop Sage from rushing out. If anything, they knew she'd turn the tides in their favor. They focused on securing Geoffrey, the girls, and the rest of the perimeter as they closed in on Diamond City.

Sage had run through Winterfeld like this before. Gertrude had just taken her to Nova's house for the antidote to Thickener, one of Gavin's poisons. It would have killed the rebels had it not been for the young scientist. That was the day Commander had lost his life in the ballroom. The poor man had already been weakened by Slainium, only to digest another poison on top of that. It had made him easy pickings for Gavin's androids.

Sage would rather not remember that day, but she couldn't help it when she was rushing through these streets. She identified a few Emerald City soldiers in their dark green uniforms and gold chains in combat with Diamond City soldiers. There were blades, bullets, and lasers flying in all directions. It was crazy to think that Sage wasn't fighting on Diamond City's behalf, but she would never support Blackburn. Both sides called out to her when they saw her—"Hey, stop!"; "STOP HER!"; "Don't let her get away!"—and she did slow down at times to search for Damian.

He wasn't here, though.

Sage passed Capital Square. It was strange to see the plaza so dark. The buildings were lined with lights, but they were all off today. Bodies littered the ground, facedown in the snow. It was hard to tell which city's casualties they were, so Sage stopped.

Maybe she shouldn't have. This horror show was all too familiar to her, and it stroked the dormant memories of her past. The Unification War had procured many deaths. Sage had crossed a street full of dead bodies in the Cut District once. The first push against Overseer Callus hadn't been easy. So many had underestimated the power of his military. Even some Enhanced had fallen before the might of those laser guns.

August had been there to support her, no matter how hopeless the war might have seemed. Right now, there was no one.

"Damian?" Sage called. She didn't know why. If Damian was one of those bodies, he wouldn't respond.

Sage held her arms. She grew uncertain of what to do. If someone was dead, there was no bringing them back, right?

A clash and a roar made her jump. Sage whipped around toward the noise and realized it was coming from the front of the town. At the slightest chance it was Damian, Sage took off.

It didn't take her much longer to reach Winterfeld's double doors, the ones leading right into the Outskirts. They were already ajar, and one was cracked. Sage pictured Emerald City barging in, but not too many had made it through, seemingly.

Everyone was still outside. Swords were at work, smashing against the other, with the occasional grunt that sounded like Blackburn. Sage wasn't going to draw attention, so she scaled the wall and took cover behind the parapet. She looked out at the expanse below and located the heart of the confrontation.

Actually, it was more like a duel. On one side, blocking entry into Winterfeld, was the Diamond City military. On the other was an incoming army that was just as big but had much more to lose.

Damian always had much more to lose.

That's why he fought the hardest. That's why he was so focused, sword at the ready, with no signs of slowing down. Rips and tears in his Emerald City uniform showed he had slipped up a few times in the face of his brother, who was potentially stronger than he was. The sleeve on his right arm was torn—or had it been blown off?—and Sage could see the sage leaves on his skin. That didn't faze Damian, though. He wanted this win too badly. He was in the presence of his soldiers and he had a reputation to uphold.

Sage blinked. Her brain was taking forever to process what her eyes were seeing. Damian was here with more than just his rebel group and a few reinforcements—he was here with a whole *army*. And Sage didn't have the capacity or the capability at the moment to figure out how he had managed it.

Like everyone else on the field, Sage watched Damian and Blackburn square off amidst corpses, blood, and discarded weapons. Green, Red, and Yellow were right behind him, but they didn't intervene. No one did.

"You've got quite some fucking nerve, Damianos," Blackburn spat. "Going home, whining to Mother for help, then coming back here to attack me with your new toy soldiers?"

Damian didn't speak. Sage held her breath.

Going home . . . whining to Mother?

Cushion? From Mousafeld?

"How did she allow this, I wonder?" Blackburn said. But then, ever so slowly, horror crept into his face. "What have you done, Damianos?!"

Damian flashed forward. His strength and accuracy were scary, throwing off Blackburn, who hardly evaded Damian's blade with his own. The two met each other's blows repeatedly, but what made Damian such a fierce warrior was his inability to fall. He didn't let any hits or slashes deter his drive, and that's what had Blackburn stumbling back.

"ANSWER ME!" Blackburn exclaimed. "Why would she grant you this much power? Does she truly intend to take over Diamond City as well?"

That seemed to make Blackburn nervous. Perhaps he had been hoping his mother—who was clearly in charge of Emerald

City—would stay out of Diamond City affairs, and that he wouldn't have to confront the possibility of another invasion. The Squids were scary enough. Internal conflicts had weakened Diamond City significantly. Diamond City had also spent a considerable amount of funds holding out in Winterfeld, too.

That all made sense to Sage. What she still didn't understand was the *how*. How had Damian achieved an army? She had no fucking clue what sort of dynamics Damian had with what seemed to be his true birth mother, but according to Blackburn, they weren't good.

"Haven't enough people died under your command?" Blackburn spat. His breaths were fast and uneven now. His hair was plastered to his face, sweat coming down despite how cold it was out here. Even so, there was no way in hell he was putting down his sword in the face of his brother.

Damian attacked again. The way he swiped, dodged, and jumped was like a well-oiled machine. It was mesmerizing to watch, part of the reason why no one moved. Emerald City and Diamond City didn't have to fight if their fates depended on the outcome of this battle. It seemed Diamond City soldiers became less inclined to follow Blackburn's orders when he might not have been the strongest warrior, after all. Many were probably wondering what would become of them if Damian actually won. It was only a matter of time before he got a hit, and then it happened: Damian pierced Blackburn through the shoulder, pinning him to the ground.

"Wasn't it you that said we had a mission to accomplish?" Damian said, hair curtaining his face. "Well, that's exactly what I'm doing. And now that you're on the losing end, you don't like it very much."

Blackburn laughed raggedly. "Me? On the losing end?" He kicked Damian in the chest. He removed the sword—Sage's sword, of course—that Damian quickly reclaimed, not with a swipe of a tentacle or some other shape-shifting spectacle, but a bullet. Blackburn shook his hand, cursing.

Sage couldn't stop staring. She had known Damian was powerful, but holy shit … He had never moved like *that* in their sparring sessions. She wondered if he had pumped himself up with more Cells, but there weren't any signs that he had. His eyes were black as night and the veins sticking out of his body were natural. Impressive, but the vascularity was all from adrenaline.

"Do you think your love-struck bitch is going to allow you to claim Diamond City for yourself?!" Blackburn exclaimed. "That she's going to allow you to take the throne?!"

"I'm not here to claim anything," Damian said steadily. "That was never my intention, nor will it be. I don't care what Mother wanted and how she meant to achieve it. There are ways of forming alliances civilly, if that's what Diamond City wants."

"You? Civilly?" Blackburn sneered. "Please, Damianos. There is nothing civil about you. The moment that Diamond City shuts her doors in your face, do you honestly believe you'd turn around and walk away without a fight?"

"First of all, Diamond City will not shun me," Damian said. "All-seer Louis is open to Outskirts negotiations, and Emerald City is one of many prospects. Don't tell me otherwise—I was his general before he pulled you out of prison, and we had extensive conversations about our next moves. I agreed to them, because Diamond City needs help. She needs allies, which she will have."

"In exchange for what? More taxes? Human sacrifices for the sake of science and expanding Emerald City's army?"

"That's what Mother wanted, yes. But I've taken care of that."

Blackburn stiffened. So did Sage behind the parapet. She had never been so tense in her life, straining her ears to hear every word coming out of Damian's mouth.

"Y-you what?" Blackburn croaked.

"You should be thanking me," Damian said stoically. "I killed her. Isn't that what you wanted? So you could take over Diamond City without orders from her?"

Maybe that's what Blackburn had wanted … or maybe he had wanted her alive to prove that he was the better son. It was always a game of competition between brothers. Sage recognized that, and a few other revelations as well.

"Mother" was the Emerald City Allseer. And, somehow, Damian had killed her.

"I had to." Damian stood up straight. There was an emptiness in his eyes that Sage wasn't familiar with. The gauntness in his face wasn't a result of drug addiction or withdrawals—it was one of fatigue. Maybe even fear. He kept looking around, as if hoping to see Sage or any signs of his children. He still hadn't gotten any confirmation they were in one piece. He had to focus on his brother, though, and so he announced for all to hear:

"When I turned myself in to Emerald City, I saw firsthand the absolute hell my mother had unleashed on the people there. How do you think hybrids were born? *Her* idea. She used her eggs and Squid DNA to create me and my brother, and she didn't stop there— she funded other experiments, too, to create even more hybrids. When the Squids left to create Diamond City, she started other experiments. That's what Emerald City was to her—a playground— but oh." He sneered. "Sounds familiar, doesn't it? The Kilstrongs did the exact same damn things with their citizens, eliminating Enhanced, targeting the Optimum for reproduction, and completely isolating Diamond City from everybody else. That's what you always wanted, wasn't it, Dawson? To compete with her? To show her you had done it—you had climbed the ranks, taken out the Allseers, and crowned yourself king? You came so close, too."

"Aren't you the righteous one," Blackburn spat. "You, the mistake of the family, always prancing around in dresses and drawing rainbows every fucking where when your head should have been in our mission. But no—you wanted to suck and play with dicks at night. It wasn't enough that father kicked you out, was it? You just had to come back and ruin everything, worming your way into soldiers' beds at night for the sake of getting close to the Allseer. You planned to execute Marchello for your own selfish desires— the very thing you are accusing me of doing—but your own lover turned you over." Blackburn laughed. His voice echoed across the expanse. He loved bringing up David's betrayal every chance he got, because it was one of the worst moments of Damian's life. Every soldier circled around them was so stiff they looked like corpses.

"I tried to kill you," Blackburn went on with a chortle. "I really did. But like a roach, you never seem to die. You fled Diamond City, and how I prayed for your death and that you'd disappear off the face of this goddamn planet. But here you are, always in my face, always hanging on by the skin of your teeth. Do you really think that Emerald City is loyal to you?"

"I'm their Allseer," Damian said. "They don't have a choice."

"YOU ARE NO ALLSEER!" Blackburn roared. Spit sprayed from his mouth. "You are a failure, Damianos—everything about you! You will never be a great leader! You are going to destroy Emerald City and then Diamond City, and then what? Going to throw your best fighters against the Lolligo? Or is that why you birthed children with the Optimum?"

"I would never throw my children into battle," Damian said quietly.

"No. Everything will just fall to pieces like it always does under your command. Let's say you are man enough to be a father—do you think you're man enough to handle the Lolligo?"

"Would you rather Diamond City conform to the Squids like you and your lot have been doing the past hundred years?" Damian spit on the ground. "The Squids are no friends to humanity. We stand our ground and create our boundary, but we never give in to their imperialist ideals. They created hybrids to bring down the Overseers, and ever since they did, their Prime's been biding his time, looking for ways to defeat them in turn. Sage and Wren were two big experiments, and God knows what other research they've been conducting on our kind."

Was that why Samson had taken Wren? To find an easier, quicker way to defeat hybrids?

That's why he spied on you, said a voice in Sage's head, reminding her that Samson had been her roommate for more than just helping her with the rent and feeding her boiled eggs. Sage thought of the eggs in Louis' bin.

"I have warned every Allseer and every official about you," Blackburn said. "And you must be eliminated no matter what it takes." He let his shoulders drop. He looked like a boxer ready to hang up his gloves. Perhaps, in a way, he was. Maybe he couldn't defeat Damian in this form.

So he pulled out a syringe.

Sage couldn't see what was in it from this angle. She had a full view of Blackburn's back. His hair whipped in the wind. His left hand clutched his sword tightly. He wouldn't be needing it anymore, though.

"Your little scientist from Winterfeld is very resourceful," Blackburn said. "She took the bodies of those dead hybrid babies and extracted all their wonderful Cells. I'm not sure what she did, but she claimed to be working on a 'booster' of sorts for the Diamond City military. Without the Optimum," he chuckled, "we're sitting ducks, aren't we? It's not finished yet, of course, but I took it just in case. Something told me you'd be showing your face here, Damianos."

Emerald City soldiers tensed. Sage glanced at the sea of them. Her heart jumped when she found Turtle, whose eyes met hers. Unlike Lex Warriors, none of the soldiers were in fancy armor with headpieces. Sage could see each of their eyes and when they widened in recognition. Turtle turned to Gertrude, who was clutching her gun, and then Gertrude found her, too.

"*Sage!*" she mouthed, but she could do no more than that.

"You are worthless!" Blackburn went on to Damian. "And you are not fit to be the Allseer of *any* city, much less Diamond City, where so many people have sacrificed their lives! Where the Optimum fought off the Overseers in a way that neither you, me, nor any other warrior in our time will ever match. An eighteen-year-old girl who was much more level-headed and powerful than you and me, and this is how you want to squander her memory?"

"I am not squandering anything," Damian said calmly. How could he just stand there and watch his brother fiddle around with that syringe? "I worship the very ground she stands on, and I will let nothing tarnish her. Not you, not politics, and not some demented Squids."

Damian seemed to be pretty confident with his words. So much so, that he flashed forward again to strike the syringe out of Blackburn's hand, but it was too late.

Blackburn had already stuck it into his neck.

CHAPTER 20

Big Brother

Neither Diamond City nor Emerald City moved. It was kind of crazy, but the soldiers didn't fight one another. They all pointed their weapons at Blackburn, who roared into the falling darkness like a monster.

Sage clutched the top of the parapet as she witnessed the craziest transformation she had seen yet. Whereas Taz had grown into his monster form over the course of many months, Nova's ultra-concentrated concoction turned Blackburn into a crazy shape-shifting behemoth in just seconds.

First, Blackburn's uniform ripped. His body swelled to three times its size, muscles bulging everywhere as if someone was pumping meat into them. Thick veins burst out of his skin, engorged with whatever was flowing in his bloodstream. His hair fell out as his snout grew, long and wrinkled like a bat's. His teeth sharpened like a piranha's, spit flying everywhere.

Just what the hell had Nova created? It must have been a prototype. There was no way this was intended on a regular soldier—there was no rhyme or reason to Blackburn's twitching and screeching. This wasn't something that could be used in large regiments or close spaces.

The transformation didn't stop there, either. Long, ugly talons grew from Blackburn's arms and spine. A membrane formed between his wrist and hip, perfect for flying. Just a flap had soldiers on both side shielding their faces and holding their ground.

Sage didn't want to imagine the sort of damage Blackburn could cause now. Neither did Damian, who was close enough to strike Blackburn through the heart with his sword. Unfortunately, the attack was a bit too late, and it did nothing to Blackburn, who swiped his brother with those sharp claws.

Damian hit the ground hard. He caught the tentacles that flew out of Blackburn's belly, about to pierce his chest. He yanked on them, pulling Blackburn forward, and whipped out his trusty pistol.

He fired two bullets—one into each of Blackburn's eyes. Blackburn screeched and let go, allowing Damian to jump back on his feet. He didn't have any more weapons on his body, so he had to grab his sword if he was going to stand a chance. He did so with one of Sage's maneuvers, elongating his arm to snatch the blade right back.

This was suicide. The fight was too uneven, but neither side attacked. Now, all the rebels were staring at Sage, who didn't intervene. Not yet. She was looking for signs that Damian couldn't win on his own. He was a hybrid like her, but he had spent the better part of the day engaged with Blackburn, who was no pushover. He had to be tired, worried, and desperate to find his children. There was no way he'd be lasting much longer out here.

Blackburn recovered from his temporary blindness and swept a large wing across Emerald City's forces. Everyone jumped in time, including Damian, who landed on the creature's shoulder and thrust his sword into Blackburn's neck. That should have cut a few veins, but Blackburn's regeneration was too quick to allow for any effects. He grabbed and threw Damian into the sky, then sent a series of talons after him. Damian blocked a few, but one got him through the shoulder.

Sage watched as Damian crashed into the ground miles away, a claw embedded in his body. That left soldiers on both sides open to Blackburn's rampage, and they weren't stupid: they opened fire. Both bullets and lasers hit their targets, but Blackburn didn't let any of that slow him down—he took off into the air with his mega bat wings.

Damian. Blackburn was going for Damian, who had no weapons.

Sage wasn't sure if her decisions in battle had ever been reckless or greatly calculated, but she felt she was doing a bit of both this time. She climbed onto the parapet, and without much of a running start, she jumped amidst gunfire to land on Blackburn's back. She clung onto one of the talons there and grabbed the hilt of Damian's sword with the other.

Soldiers gasped from below and halted all fire. Blackburn screeched, disgruntled at the nuisance on his back, but bumbled toward Damian all the same. Little tentacles sprouted out of his spine to dislodge her, but Sage didn't plan on staying long.

She yanked Damian's blade from Blackburn's neck and sent it flying right at him. Not at his chest—at his left hand. There was a syringe between his fingers, similar to Blackburn's, possibly with different contents, but Sage didn't care.

Not Damian. Never Damian. Never a monster.

Damian whipped around. He found her on Blackburn's back and his eyes widened. Perhaps he wanted to shout—he opened his mouth—but he must have quickly realized there was nothing to say. His right arm was fucked up, but he had his left and the sword. Yes, a massive disadvantage, but Sage could even out the playing field for him.

Sage dodged Blackburn's tentacles and rolled off his body. She free-fell for a good twenty seconds, but she used that time to ready the gun on her back. It was locked and loaded, so as soon as she hit the ground, she aimed and blasted half of Blackburn's body to smithereens.

Damian didn't waste any time getting to his feet. He had a monster to finish.

Sage took a step back. She had every intention of watching this fight to the end, but then she heard her name.

Her heart dropped.

"SAGE!" Louis called. He was riding that ridiculous scooter with the bin of Squid eggs and the babies to his chest. Blue, Violet, and Orange were still tagging behind him. "We have to go! W-we can't stay here!"

"ARE YOU CRAZY?!" Sage screeched. "I TOLD YOU TO FUCK-ING HIDE!"

"THERE ARE CRAZY SOLDIERS AFTER ME!"

The blood on Blue, Violet, and Orange's muzzles proved that they had run into some trouble. Blackburn probably had soldiers prowling around everywhere, including the forest where Louis was supposed to be hiding.

It was time to go. Damian was battling what was left of Black-burn, jumping around like a ballerina and slicing limbs that attacked him, but he craned his head to see Sage, Louis, and his newborn babies. He must have seen their bald heads against Louis' chest, because he gasped. His eyes visibly widened and his stance stiffened in the middle of the fight. Unfortunately, he couldn't take a step toward them without being skewered by one of Blackburn's flailing limbs. Damian did make an effort to find Sage's eyes again, and with his own he communicated a ton of anxiety. Why were their babies in Louis' custody in the middle of freezing temperatures?

They're fine, Sage tried to say, but she wasn't convincing anyone right now. The babies were wailing uncontrollably without the security of their true parents. Either that, or Louis smelled badly from all the running and sweating.

"Give them to me!" Sage yelled at Louis. "Now!"

Louis undid the straps quickly and handed the babies to her. Sage pulled them against her body as she jumped onto the scooter behind him. Castor and Pollux stopped crying immediately. Their eyes were full of tears, but they gave little smiles and hiccups when they recognized her. It was the cutest fucking thing ever, but Blackburn was wailing like a dying beast and Damian was still jumping around with that sword. Plus, soldiers were skittering all over the fields like grasshoppers, and Sage didn't want to confront any of them with two babies under her tits.

"GO!" Sage hit Louis' shoulder. "GO, DAMN IT!"

Louis took off across the Outskirts. This thing flew now that they didn't have trees to dodge. Louis glanced at Blackburn.

"What the hell is that?"

"Just drive!" Sage exclaimed.

"Look," Louis went on, "I don't know what Damaris' intentions are, and I'm not sure you do, either. At this point, I'll take him over Blackburn, who was salivating for the throne. He hounded us for three fucking months in that forest and he would have killed us—we both know that. I'm willing to listen to whatever the Warlord proposes, but please be careful, Sage. He's in charge of the entire Emerald City army—"

"I know that! Can you please just get to safety?"

Another roar from Blackburn, but Sage couldn't see what was going on. She kept her hands on the shotgun, thighs squeezing the seat of the scooter as they raced through the open fields. The three pups trailed behind them. They didn't yelp or wonder why Sage and Louis were running away from their allies—they knew it wasn't safe for them out there.

Sage wondered where Candice and Olivia were now. How was Geoffrey doing after becoming an Enhanced? Where they still with Sonia and L?

"Are we seriously making it all the way back to Diamond City on this thing?" Sage asked.

"We've got nothing else," Louis said. "Now hang on—I think this thing has a turbo feature."

Now that they were in the clear with the fighting at Winterfeld far behind them, that's what Louis activated. He must have studied the hell out of the manual that Tyrus and Herman had left behind because he navigated them right through the Outskirts and toward Diamond City. It wasn't even visible in the distance yet.

"We've got a lot of miles to cover," Louis said. "But we should make it soon."

"Does your new council know?" Sage asked quietly. "About Blackburn's betrayal? Again? He had some syringe from Nova that turned him into a monster. Did you allow him to obtain that under your nose?"

Louis said nothing, but his silence answered her question.

"That desperate, were you?"

"And what would you have done, Sage? Both you and the Warlord—my strongest fighters—were gone. I didn't hear back from my sister. I had to depend on someone to get me answers, didn't I?"

Sage supposed that was true.

"Well," she said coldly, "if you and your sister hadn't planned to backstab me—"

"I never backstabbed you," Louis spat. "That was your fiancé who did that. My sister, too, but don't throw me in that mix."

"Fine," Sage concurred. "But she was the Allseer and you should have known what she was up to. Just like you should have been able to stop the Red Fever—"

"We did," Louis said. "We did stop it, thanks to Nova. But *I* never created that. In fact, Nova told me it seemed to be biologically engineered—it's not even a natural contagion from the wild—"

Sage grabbed the controls and swerved them sharply to the right, barely avoiding a laser that had come out of nowhere. The blast blew them off balance and sent the scooter into a tumble. Sage held fast to her babies and landed hard on her back. Louis had the eggs, although he rolled in the snow.

Blue, Violet, and Orange roared. Their snouts grew as their teeth elongated. Tentacles burst out of their backs as they went on the offensive.

"Take care of them, darling."

This wasn't Damian. This was a voice from the other side of the smoke and snow. Sage couldn't see a damn thing, but she did roar to the three pups.

"MOVE! NOW!"

And because they listened, they dodged a blade that would have sliced them to pieces.

"BACK!" Sage screamed, climbing to her feet as Castor and Pollux wailed at the top of their lungs now. "BACK!"

The three pups, hissing and spitting, did take a step back. All pairs of amber eyes locked onto the ones above them.

The ones that belonged to a tall slender woman, who was much too pretty to be a warrior, but waved her sword with a skill only Damian or the Sword Devil might possess. The movements were so clean and precise that she could have cut the air into cubes.

But wait—that was no woman. Her features shifted in one quick shimmer, reverting to that of a man's. Her eyebrows thickened, her nose hooked, and her tongue lengthened and curled like a snake's. If Sage didn't know better, she'd say he was getting a better taste of his surroundings, but this was purely a scare tactic.

Dread dropped like a bomb in Sage's stomach. She stepped back as the man grew two extra pairs of arms from his sides. He grabbed all the swords sheathed at his hips, like some sort of ninja or something. Sage was absolutely terrified of ninjas. They always wore black, lurked in the shadows, and struck you from behind—never in your face. Sage feared any opponent she couldn't see or calculate.

Not only was this ninja skilled with a blade, but those arms were thick and powerful, each with finely defined muscles that wouldn't budge or waver in the face of any force. Guns weren't going to do any good here. This guy ate Enhanced for a living, filled with Cells from other hybrids, too. This was just another day in the Outskirts for him—who knew what he'd run into next.

"Ooo, wait! What do we have here?"

Sage didn't want to lose sight of ninja-person for one moment, but she did glimpse the other body standing a few feet away. This must have been ninja-person's partner, and it scared her to think that they were related in any way. Seemingly, they were.

"She's a hybrid!" gasped Big Brother, who was carrying some sort of pouch across his chest. "Look, look, X@me—a hybrid! You can have babies with her! Although . . ." He frowned. He rubbed the pouch. Why did Sage get the horrible feeling there were cocoons in there, too? "Looks like she already has a pair."

God, Sage didn't have her sword. She was a sitting duck here without it. The gun in her clutches wasn't going to do her any good against X@me. *Ch-at-me*? It sounded like an email address from an illegal website. Sage didn't know what it was about the Outskirts that inspired people to adopt such strange names, but that was so irrelevant right now.

Neither Sage nor Louis were getting out of this alive unless she could defeat these two in battle. Or, rather, X@me, because Big Brother didn't seem like a warrior, just the one who barked orders and babysat a couple of cocoons.

"Louis," Sage croaked. She cleared her throat, trying her damned hardest not to sound like she was dying. Perhaps her bravery was. She was about to battle another hybrid, and this was no Blackburn. X@me looked like he went to bed swinging those blades for fun. "Please . . . take the babies."

Sage kept the shotgun clutched in her hands as Louis made his way over to her. By some miracle, the eggs inside the bin were unscathed. Either Squid eggs were made of steel or Louis had done a damn good job of keeping them safe. Sage trusted him to do the same for Castor and Pollux when they were in a life-or-death situation. As if he was walking on land mines, Louis edged closer to her and finally took them. Sage never lost eye contact with X@me.

X@me was so fast that Sage only knew he moved because she felt the wind. She threw up her massive shotgun to block all six blades, and the force pushed her back across the field. Sage didn't hesitate to fire a few shots, but of course X@me flew right past them and was right back in her face. This time, he landed all six blades against her body.

"SAGE!" Louis screamed.

Cuts were nothing—they healed quickly. It was Sage's fear and lack of composure that took away her focus. That's because she knew she was outmatched. Just a few hits, and it was obvious her opponent was far stronger than she was. Faster, too.

Sage didn't fire at X@me—she fired at the ground in front of his feet. He didn't even move—didn't flinch—and was ready to retaliate with the six blades again. One cut her aorta.

The three pups snarled, but like Green, Red, and Yellow at Damian's side, they knew not to interfere. If anything, they ran right back to their master for help.

Sage didn't have a clue if Damian had defeated Blackburn, but she couldn't think about that right now. She had to focus. She took a step back as her wounds healed again, but in the stoic face of her enemy, she wavered quite a bit.

This was not what Samson had taught her. Why was she acting like such a little bitch right now? Why did she want to cry? She kept looking at her babies in Louis' arms, but goddamn it—that should have motivated her to fight, not make her knees quake. Those were her children she had to defend right now. No one was coming to her rescue, so their lives rested on her shoulders.

Sage was done being a clingy bitch.

Sage grew a blade from each of her arms. It sprung from her skin as natural as any limb on her body, thick and powerful beneath the darkness of the sky. She was sorely out of practice after so much bedrest, but she didn't have a choice right now.

Big Brother started a vicious clapping. "Bravo! Do you see that, X@me? She can shape-shift!"

Sage wasn't here to show off. Without her sword, she was at a sore disadvantage, and this was the only way to level the playing field. Her blades looked thick and bulky, but she utilized them well enough to stand a chance.

This wasn't about rushing at the enemy and getting a lethal blow in. If Sage did that, she'd lose her head. This was about striking with purpose and finding a weak spot, an opening that would grant her victory. It was a way to read her opponent, too, which she was able to do now that she wasn't blocking and dodging.

Sage and X@me clashed repeatedly. Six blades versus two, but Sage didn't need any more than the ones on her arms, especially when she could shift them into whatever limb she needed—a shield for parrying, a tentacle for tying, or an extra thin blade to get the hit, which, frustratingly, didn't happen.

Damn.

X@me swung around with three blades—Sage ducked and shuffled back, winded and panting. Why did the snow feel like sand?

"Whoa!" Big Brother hooted. "Little lady over there can fight! Imagine what she'll be like in bed, X@me!"

Sage swore that if she wasn't up against this fucking monster that she'd cut that guy's penis and balls off. It was another distraction that she had to ignore, but it was so hard when she kept glimpsing that smug-as-hell look on that asshole's face.

All right, all right—she could do this. More or less, she knew how X@me moved, which way he dodged, which side he favored, and how much time it took to complete a swing. Sage was severely fatigued now, but all she needed was a successful bout to gain some much-needed momentum.

She took a deep breath and then she attacked again. Always for the right side since X@me favored his left, but then he did something completely unprecedented: he attacked with his right. He dodged down instead of to the side, and took a half a second less to complete his counter.

X@me had switched up on purpose. Of course, Sage knew there was always the possibility of that happening. That's why she was already prepared to adjust her strikes, set herself up for the blow that would count, and pull the shotgun right off her back.

One second: that was all she had to squeeze the trigger as X@me readied his blades for another round. He made contact with her arm, but didn't cut it off because he needed that time to dodge. Unfortunately for him, it was too late either way.

Sage got the hit.

The boom and then the pushback was the most satisfying kick

Sage had ever felt in her life. The blood that rained on her face and clothes fueled her frenzy. Not enough to make her reckless, but enough to go again if she needed to. She was so focused on her opponent that she didn't even glance at Big Brother, who was uncharacteristically quiet. Louis' breathing was tight. Both waited for the aftermath.

Sage held her ground as the snow and dust cleared to reveal a torso-less body. Without Slainium, regeneration was imminent. Sage blasted her gun again, but X@me jumped back and grew another torso, complete with head and arms. His boobs weren't big enough to be a woman's, but his muscles were defined all the same. Eyes popped out of random spots on his face as his skin bubbled and his bone structure shifted this way and that. It was like booting up a computer, and while it would have been fascinating to watch, all Sage could stare at was death.

X@me wouldn't be making the same mistake twice. Now he knew she was going to use that gun. All he had to do to win was exhaust her until she fatigued and finish her. Sage would have to change her approach, but she was running out of options. Her eyes took a quick glance at the field: the scooter in the distance, Louis clutching the babes with Squid eggs at his feet, and a truck even farther away.

Wait, did that truck belong to X@me and Big Brother? Probably. Maybe there were weapons, but acquiring them wasn't an option for Sage. As far as she could see, these were her choices: use Louis or the scooter. She couldn't put Louis in danger, so maybe she could use the scooter?

X@me rushed her. Fast. No blades this time—just six arms with his own flesh-made blades attached to them. He didn't need to shift them into anything else to win because Sage had a hard time deflecting them with her own.

Focus! her mind screamed at her. *Block!*

She had to block—had to keep blocking—if she was going to find a way to get that damn scooter. She had to study every strike that X@me delivered and identify any patterns in his movements, so she could safely lasso a tentacle around the vehicle that had a chance of giving her the upper hand.

But wait—Sage didn't need her arms to do that. All she had to do was grow a tentacle out of her lower back. She was so out of shape, and every single damn muscle was on fire, but this was life or death, life or death, life or death—

Sage did it! She kept X@me engaged with her blades as the tentacle from her back shot out and grabbed the scooter. It reeled it right in, close enough to jump, and that's what Sage did. She hit the energy pedal and took off, in a semicircle around the confused X@me—who probably hadn't seen that coming—and knew this was her chance. Her eyes quickly made contact with Louis', who was already way ahead of her.

Babes and all, Louis fired his gun. It was never meant to hit X@me—it was just the distraction. Sage pulled out her own gun, braced herself on the scooter, and fired.

Another satisfying hit—she blew X@me's torso right off again—and if she had her sword, she'd finish this son of a bitch that much quicker. Sage got aggressive, jumping off the scooter and readying another blast, but X@me was already regenerating and another hit was only going to delay the inevitable—

"Darling."

A sword was coming. Sage shot out her left hand and grabbed the flying blade by the hilt. She felt its warmth from Damian's grip and its power forged by Samson over a year ago. This was her sword, but not really—not anymore. It was too small and light for her now, but it'd do the job here.

Sage skewered X@me through the groin. She wasn't sure if there was a penis there, but the point was the blade made contact with his blood. She watched up close as the tentacles whipping out of his hips slowly stopped. Despite the number of Cells in his blood, he only had half a body left. He had already regenerated so many times, and fatigue had to be setting in. Plus, Sage made sure to cut him up into tiny pieces.

"Darling."

Sage didn't stop. She had to make sure this monster was dead.

"Darling."

A pair of warm hands touched her shoulders. The gloves were ripped, fingers raw and bloody from fighting. Long and slender, tender when they needed to be, but fierce now when Sage wasn't herself. When she wasn't thinking clearly. She glimpsed no rings on any of his hands. Perhaps jewelry hadn't been a priority that morning. Or the past three months. The only thing that mattered to Damian right now was her and those two babies on the other side of the field.

Damian wrapped a secure arm around Sage's waist. He brought her body up against his chest. He was breathing just as raggedly as she was. Not because he was exhausted from his battle against Blackburn or because there were wounds that hadn't healed yet, but because—after three months—he finally had her in his arms. He could press his nose into her neck and inhale her scent.

Sage did the same to him. She had her face in his temple with some of his hair in her eyes. The teakwood and lavender was so very faint, masked by the coppery stench of blood. He still had Blackburn's claw marks on his cheek, but those seemed to be fading. Sage used her hand to feel his right shoulder, the wound that Blackburn had left behind, and found clean skin. Sensitive, because Damian grunted, but at least it was mended. Sage used her eyes to evaluate the rest of him, and other than a ripped and dirty uniform, he was in one piece.

No monster. Never a monster.

"You did beautifully." Damian checked her wounds now. Sage still had those six cuts from that blade, but nothing life threatening. "Sword Devil and Tai have never seen the great Optimum in combat. Look at their faces."

Sage spotted the two Lex Warriors a fair distance away. Sonia, L, and some of the rebels were there, too. They looked like they were on standby, ordered not to interfere unless there was an emergency.

When the fighting was up to Sage, there didn't seem to be a need for anyone else's assistance. Sage wondered if the rest of the armies were still at Winterfeld.

Damian looked across the field to Louis. Sage couldn't see his face, but his grip tightened on her body. She read his energy expertly: how dare Louis touch his boys. Despite what a great job Louis had done keeping them safe during the battle, Damian was far from comfortable. He looked ready to fly over there, but Big Brother was still a threat. Any sudden moves would put them at risk.

"Oh," Big Brother said, studying Damian. "You're a hybrid, too. From the way you're holding her, would you happen to be the boys' father? They are rather beautiful children. Any that X@me and I tried to conceive with ordinary humans or Enhanced died."

Sage's breaths tightened. The image of all those dead women used like lab rats in Smallfeld had never quite faded from her mind. There were pictures from the Unification War that would never go away; there were scars that Sage carried forever, treated only with time, good experiences, laughter, and family. But even then . . . in the darkest moments at night . . . Sage was haunted by them.

They had all been wrong. It had never been the Squids.

"You killed him," Big Brother said emotionlessly. "My brother."

Damian spat on the ground. "Then good riddance. What was it that you said? 'Imagine what she'll be like in bed?' Fuck you."

"You're only saying that because you've successfully mated with her. Not all hybrids have had that luxury. Maybe I was fortunate enough, but I really wanted a future for X@me."

"I'm sorry, but I don't go around raping every single woman in towns to see which one is going to bear me a child. I am not that desperate."

Big Brother nodded. Something felt horribly wrong here. He cracked his fingers, shaking the ground with some explosive power, but not charging forward to kill them. He could fight them—Sage sensed there was more to this guy than met the eye—but he took a step back.

Actually, he turned around and walked away.

Both Sage and Damian held their ground until it was clear. They stared right at their babies—forget Big Brother and who he had mated with to rear his own. Castor and Pollux came first. Plus, Sage was about to collapse. She was so tired that she sagged against Damian's body, wondering if there was truly something wrong with her.

"I've got you, darling," Damian said, holding her tightly.

He always did.

CHAPTER 21

A Hybrid's Mission

Everything that happened from that moment on was a blur. Sage was so weak that she couldn't really stand on her own. Damian held her, but he also took his children from Louis when it was safe enough to cross the field. X@me wasn't regenerating. His remains were beneath snow now.

"Oh my goodness," Damian chortled as he brought Castor and Pollux into his chest. "Look at how adorable they are!"

Castor and Pollux were still crying, afraid, but they giggled when they saw Damian. Sage supposed anyone would, especially with all the really dumb cooing he was doing.

"Who are the most beautiful boys on the planet? Who? Oh, I know—you are!" Damian nuzzled each of their heads. "Who's got the most handsome father known to mankind? Oh, I know—you do! Yes, you do—yes, you do—and you're both going to grow up to look like me!"

The babies shrieked with laughter when Damian blew fart noises into their necks. He made gnarling noises as if he was a bear, then rubbed each of their noses with his own. When the show was over, he frowned.

"Have they been fed?" Damian asked.

"Right," Sage drawled. "Because I totally had the time to give them my tits while I was fighting."

Damian laughed. "That would have been epic."

"What is it with men and breastfeeding?"

"It's fascinating how milk comes out of there. After Castor and Pollux, do you mind if I—?"

Sage had a shotgun and she aimed it at Damian's head. "I'm not a cow."

Damian raised a hand. Castor and Pollux gurgled.

"Forgive me." Damian fought the stupid grin on his face. "You don't have to breastfeed if you don't want to. We have plenty of nutritious blends that they can drink on the ship."

The *Mistress.* Sage looked out in the distance and found the same aircraft that had abandoned her against Blackburn parked on the snow. She had seen that ship fly away in a time of great need. The same crew stood there, too, waiting, with two very valuable additions.

Candice and Olivia.

Sage took off. If she had been about to tip over before, the adrenaline brought her right back up to speed. The girls ran, too. They met halfway and embraced.

Sage squeezed the life out of her girls. Candice and Olivia sobbed. They smelled like eucalyptus and chamomile, as if they had soaked in a tub before heading out to find her. Their hair was braided royally and tightly, so Damian must have gotten a hold of them on the way here. He had probably seen the blood and debris from the scuffle at Nova's house.

"You're in one piece," Sage whispered. "Thank God." She gazed into the horizon through her blurry vision. Tears welled up fast.

After that horrible fight with Shenzi, it was a sheer miracle. If it hadn't been for Geoffrey, Candice would have been shot. Dead. Her lifeless body on the living room floor. What the fuck would Sage have done then?

"Where's Geoffrey?" Sage asked, trying hard not to think of the alternatives.

"He's inside the ship," Sonia replied, her cheeks round and pink. "He's resting. Sometimes, it takes a little while for the transformation to run its course. I also imagine your Cells are a bit more potent than Wren's."

Right.

Sage stood up. Candice and Olivia hugged her waist. Sage held them tightly to her sides. She rubbed their backs, assuring them in the best way she could that they'd be all right. It seemed all the fighting was over ... for now.

The girls didn't have much to say. They left the talking up to Gertrude and the rebels who circled around her. The six pups were sitting at attention on the snow, waiting for orders. Scarily enough, they were in a perfect line. Had Damian taught them that?

"Hey, Sage." Gertrude gave a light smile.

Sage wiped her eyes. She smiled back. Somewhat. She was too tired to hold any grudges, no matter how awkward it was to look at them in the face after they had run away and left her alone. Mega Woman, Turtle, Rockstar, Eye Candy, Sailor, Butcher, Clara, and Preacher. Then again, could Sage really have faulted them for leaving? Had they stayed ... they probably would have died.

"The Optimum has defeated her enemies once again!" Preacher announced. "Let us praise her and her efforts!"

"You're incredible!" Sonia said, hopping over to Sage. Her big blue eyes shined with respect. Her lip with all the rings trembled. "I mean, I've seen you fight before, but ..."

"Damn."

Everyone turned to the source of the voice. Even Tai looked to his silent comrade.

Sword Devil didn't speak. She didn't have to. Those blades at her hips could write books on all the trials they'd experienced. Just a single word from her lips was a huge compliment, no matter what it was.

Tai cleared his throat. Both hands behind his back, he said, "We've all heard of the great Optimum, of course. Even in Center-feld, where she was mostly just a rumor. A lot of us weren't alive during the Unification War, so we heard stories of a young girl who was a god on the battlefield—"

"I'm not a god," Sage said quietly. She squeezed her girls again. "I just fight for what I love."

Tai bowed his head. "Commendable, my lady. But regardless of what you fight for, it is obvious you have a gift. The way you can intuit your enemies and their moves. I saw how you studied your opponent's patterns, counted in your head the seconds it took for him to complete a move, and adjusted your own to gain the upper hand. Truly incredible."

Sage bowed her head. "Thank you."

"I don't ask this often," Tai said. "But will you play a game of fastball with me?"

Sage blushed instantly. Candice and Olivia gasped.

"She'd love to!" Olivia squeaked. "Although she sucks at it!"

"Hey!" Sage exclaimed, the red in her cheeks turning darker. "I don't! I mean, I'm a decent player, but probably not like you."

"It matters not," Tai said happily. "It will be for fun."

Sword Devil stepped forward. Like L, she had long dark hair that she liked to hide behind. Only one amber eye was visible and it poured right into Sage's soul. "Can you spar with me? To the death?"

"Careful," L grumbled to Sword Devil. "If you kill her, you'll have big-bad-brute over there on your ass."

Damian was twirling around in the snow with the babies in each of his arms. Pollux and Castor were laughing their heads off. They were hanging on in their cocoons, having the time of their lives.

Sage smiled. She wasn't sure what it was, but the air felt . . . light. Like she could breathe. She had defeated X@me, but what about the situation in Winterfeld? Was Blackburn dead?

It felt like it. Sage sensed it in the air like she'd hear someone singing. The rebels wouldn't have been looking so relieved if that wasn't the case. Knowing Damian, he had probably shipped the head back to Mousafeld already. Gertrude amended those thoughts.

"Yes," she said. "Blackburn is dead. But no—the Warlord didn't take the head." She cleared her throat. "Like he usually does. He said he was done looking at heads. I can't say I blame him." Gertrude chuckled wryly. "We're shipping Blackburn's body back to Diamond City where they'll analyze him and what the hell was in that syringe that turned him into a monster. Since being a hybrid seems to be the in thing, it's important to learn as much as we can about them, right?"

Sage thought Wren had already been the sacrificial lamb for that. She said nothing, though. She glanced at Damian, who was hopping up and down like a bunny rabbit now. Castor and Pollux didn't stop laughing. They were egging him on, and that was dangerous. Sage hoped they knew what they were getting into. Then she glanced at Louis, who looked as stiff as a totem pole, Squid eggs in the bin next to his feet.

"Mind if I go inside?" Sage asked quietly. "I would like to get some rest."

Damian didn't hound her about the breastfeeding anymore. He took over Castor and Pollux's first true meal while Sage took a shower. They were about a day away from Diamond City, and she was raring for some sleep at last. There were a lot of people waiting for her, hoping to get a word in, but they closed their mouths when they saw the dark circles under her eyes.

"Sage?" Sonia said carefully. "Are you all right?"

Sage didn't know. She supposed it was all the stress and fighting. There was so much she wanted to ask, such as where the Diamond and Emerald City military were now, what had happened at Centerfeld the past three months, and what Damian had done in the city he hailed from, but that was only going to add to her exhaustion, so she didn't even speak. Everyone acknowledged her fatigue.

When Sage got into bed, she thought of all the dreary things she had suffered in this very room. She would have never imagined, especially not in that horribly dark abyss she had lurked in for so long, that her life would have ever been this happy again. Damian came in to see her, rocking Castor and Pollux like they were on a swing. The babies were still laughing. They must have had lungs of steel.

"Mama looks tired, doesn't she?" Damian said to the babies. He took a seat next to the bed.

The babies were out of their cocoons. Sage sat up for a better look, a grin spreading on her face now. She took them into her arms, reveling in their wiggling arms and legs, and saw them in full for the first time since their birth.

"They're bathed and fed," Damian said proudly.

"And you actually have diapers on board?"

"I brought them just in case. Back when I left Diamond City, actually, when you told me you were pregnant." Damian frowned. "Wasn't my best moment... but I'm happy it's behind me. *Us*," he amended.

Sage didn't reply to that. She kept her boys close to her chest and kissed the tops of their heads. They smelled like baby shampoo, and their skin was so soft. They had small patches of fuzz for hair. So cute.

And then, so very quickly, and without taking a closer look at Damian and the frilly getup he had changed into, Sage fell asleep.

Again.

"Then Dada didn't know what to do..."

A gasp.

"But then he figured it out! And he said to Mama, 'Will you be with me forever?' And she said yes! What do you think, Pollux?"

Pollux clapped. Castor gurgled, concerned.

"You think I came across too strongly?" Damian asked Castor. "Maybe you're right. You have to be subtle and thoughtful with Mama. Growing up, I was always so direct with what I wanted. Like this boy that I really liked in school—I told him straight out that I liked him."

Castor and Pollux hiccuped.

"He ran away from me at first, but then he came back, eventually. All my relationships were like that: direct. I tried to be like that with Mama, but the risk with her was sky high because she'd stab or hit me. Not fun."

They giggled.

"So I have to be very subtle and gently. I think I've gotten the hang of it. Don't worry—I'll teach you how to get what you want from her."

Sage opened her eyes and found the trio in the corner of the room. It was nighttime because it was dark and Damian had the lamp on. The boys were in blue onesies with matching bear hats to cover their bald heads. Where the hell had Damian gotten that from?

"Why are you making me look like the bad guy?" Sage mumbled to him. "Did you tell them how obnoxious you are?"

Damian chuckled. "They love it. And you know you do, too."

"Maybe a little."

Candice and Olivia entered the room then. They were here to show a very rejuvenated Geoffrey where their aunt and baby cousins were. The intention was not to make any noise, but then they saw that Sage was awake.

"Aunt Sage!" Candice exclaimed.

It was the most energetic Candice that Sage had seen yet. The fifteen-year-old clambered onto Sage's bed without a care in the world, as happy as a bee. She threw herself on Sage and then it was Olivia's turn.

"My God," Sage rasped. "Since when did the two of you get so heavy?"

"Come on, Geoffrey!" Olivia waved him over. "You can join in, too!"

Geoffrey chuckled. He rubbed his still-wet hair as he stepped further into the room. "I wouldn't want to suffocate her."

Sage craned her head for a good look at him. She was relieved to see that Geoffrey looked normal. Minus the nasty scar on his neck, of course, which he didn't seem to have a problem leaving out in the open. His shirt wasn't buttoned all the way on purpose. Maybe he was proud of his heroism. Or maybe he was thankful that Sage had saved his life.

"I know it looks gross," he said shyly. "I'm putting on a cream that should remove it soon."

"How are you feeling?" Sage asked.

"Um." Geoffrey cleared his throat. "Different. Sonia and L told me what you did. How you saved me … turned me into an Enhanced. It's … well … I'm honored."

"Of course, dumbass. I wasn't going to let you die."

"Don't worry," Damian said to Geoffrey. "She calls me the same thing."

Geoffrey laughed. "I know that the Optimum is tough." He touched his chest with a smile. The Optimum tattoo. "And I know I have to be, too. I mean … Is this what you feel, Sage?"

Sage arched a brow. Candice and Olivia had gotten off her, so she could breathe.

"I feel so light," Geoffrey said. He flexed his hands. "I'm stronger than before. I nearly broke the mouthwash bottle when I tried to open it. I know it sounds dumb, but I was a little surprised. My surroundings aren't the same, either. I feel like I can see and hear things I couldn't before. People's breathing, heartbeats, clicking nails, humming—everything." He made a face. "It's as if my perception of the world around me has totally changed."

"I've never been human," Sage said softly. "But I imagine that everything would be different. And I know it's going to take some time getting used to."

"Sonia and L told me a bit about their experiences. You know— when they first changed."

There'd be no one better suited. Geoffrey got a bit dizzy just standing for too long, so he had to take a seat. Sage had never thought about what it was like for a human to change. August had never complained about it. Then again, Sage had never really asked.

"You have really cute babies," Geoffrey admitted.

Sage chuckled. "Thanks. I definitely did most of the work."

Damian looked at her. He arched a brow. "Excuse me? But I seem to remember doing most of the thrusting, darling."

They all laughed.

When they finally arrived in Diamond City that morning, Sage had a sleeping Castor and Pollux on her body. They still fit perfectly in their slings. The six pups trailed closely behind her, so well behaved. If Damian had been in Emerald City all this time, then someone else must have trained them.

Gertrude shook her head. "No," she said. "They respect Damian. The six were total nutcases with us in Centerfeld. They became so aggressive that we had to lock them up. Mega Woman said they were too dangerous to have in public. We all figured they were worried about you. When Damian came back, it's as if someone had turned off a switch."

Sage snorted. "Wow."

"I know. But it's the same with people, don't you see?"

True. Damian's rebels and the handful of Lex Warriors who had tagged along with them in the *Mistress* kept their respectable distances and followed orders to the t. No one questioned who was in charge in Damian's presence, even if Sonia and L were Centerfeld's official leaders.

Louis led the line to the palace. There was a strong sense of déjà vu here. Sage was in the exact same training field as before, when she had traveled from Winterfeld to Heart for the first time earlier this year. Now, in the month of Strength, the leaves were actually red and brown. The drizzle didn't stop, but the seasons were beautiful. She couldn't wait to show Castor and Pollux the city.

Louis met up with a few of his guards and told them about Blackburn. It sounded like the Diamond City military had quickly surrendered to Emerald City in Winterfeld to avoid unnecessary deaths. Without Blackburn leading them, the soldiers had had no one to turn to. Louis had been too busy riding a Squid scooter to give orders at the time. Now, the fighting was over and the two sides were at a standstill.

It was up to Louis... and the Emerald City Allseer to decide what came next.

Sage looked at Damian.

Tall, dark, and handsome. He wore the leather attire he kept on the *Mistress*, a bit ordinary in Sage's opinion. His hair was loose, fluttering in the wind, when it was usually tied in some intricate pattern. He had done the girls' braids, but nothing to his own. He had very little makeup on, too. His skin was still smooth and beautiful, but Sage could hardly see any eyeliner. His gaze was stoic, devoid of emotion.

It was very unlike him. The Damian from months ago had a sparkle in his irises and a crude smirk on his lips. This Damian looked serious and a bit worn out. This Damian, strangely enough, was not flaunting his new position of power. Sage would have expected bursts of green with the Emerald City insignia on his chest for all to see. He probably would have had some of his rebels waving around flags or throwing fluttery fabrics into the air. Today, Damian was no Allseer. He was just an ordinary citizen walking the streets.

There was so much Sage had to talk to him about. When she thought of what their future would be now that he had a city to run, she grew anxious and afraid. If he demanded their children, Sage would have to go to Emerald City with him. But then what would become of Candice and Olivia? There was no way they'd go with her...

Sage took a breath. Now wasn't the time to ask him such things. She had to be patient.

Louis was still leading the way. Damian made sure to remind everyone that Sage wanted the complexes across the palace, but Sage shook her head.

"It's fine," she said softly.

Damian arched a brow. Last time they neared the palace, Sage had thrown up. So it was a bit strange that she was so detached now, as if she had gotten over her trauma. Sage assured him all was well. Truthfully, she had worked on herself a bit the past three months in that Squid camp. She couldn't be afraid of the past. That's what Aurora's husband had taught her, when Sage had struggled so much to cope with her post-traumatic stress.

Sage thought long and hard about those days, so she got even more quiet. Damian wrapped a protective arm around her waist. He took her from the training field to the palace Sage had dreamed of for so long. This time, Sage didn't rush for the bathroom.

Candice, Olivia, and Geoffrey never strayed far. Leave it up to Olivia to ogle at the beautiful interior of the palace, high arches and pillars casting anyone who looked up into another world. Sage had come down those magnificent steps when Wren and Taz had attacked. She had seen blood, bodies, and Little Man's death in this very foyer. But the sleeping Castor and Pollux kept her grounded. The confident Louis caucusing with his advisors told Sage that she couldn't think of the harsh times. She was at the palace now, exactly what she had wanted. This had been her dream . . .

"We'll call the council in right away," said Louis' most trusted advisor, Darius. An Enhanced, of course, with a trimmed beard but a rather alert disposition. He was older, too, so he must have turned in his fifties if he had all that grey in his hair and sideburns. Someone like that was good for Louis, who was learning how to be a true leader. "In the meanwhile, our servants will accommodate your guests on the top floor."

Not the same suite as before, but close to it. The size of a single family home, so Candice and Olivia had their own rooms. They screamed in delight because they'd get to customize it however they wanted. Geoffrey was there to help, but only for a short while. His grandmother was still at the capital, and she was probably worried sick about him.

Their excitement energized the pups, who started racing up and down the hallway. The six of them resembled race hounds, and their joy made Sage laugh.

Damian helped Sage into the biggest bedroom in the suite.

They had a beautiful balcony to enjoy the training field below. There were aircrafts coming in and out, transporting goods and soldiers from Winterfeld, mostly. Sage thought of the first time she had seen Damian in the palanquin, challenging the Allseer on that very ground.

"I was glorious, wasn't I?" Damian breathed thickly in her ear.

"Lazy-ass," Sage grumbled under her breath. "Couldn't fight yourself, could you?"

"Actually, I had been rather incapacitated then," Damian admitted. "High as hell on Stars. I couldn't see straight. To this day, the whole challenge feels like a dream. Did I really look like a fool on that palanquin?"

"Yes."

"But I still looked beautiful?"

"The most beautiful I've ever seen," Sage admitted.

Damian smirked. He nipped her nose. "What are you wearing for tonight's dinner?"

Sage hadn't even looked inside the closet. There were servants galore in the suite to direct her, but Sage wasn't sure she was up for going anywhere. She kissed her sleeping babies on the head, knowing she'd have to feed and bathe them soon.

Damian had brought over their formula from the ship. He had put it together himself based on what he called "common sense," tips from Sonia and L, who had raised a few babies in their lifetime, and online videos. It had a lot of milk and cereal for calories, but who knew if it was enough to satisfy them. Sage supposed they'd have to see based on how the boys reacted to it, because like hell she was taking them to any disgusting doctor.

Sage had some experimenting to do. She intended to spend the rest of the afternoon and evening with her boys until Olivia burst into the room.

"Aunt Sage, can I have Castor and Pollux, please?" Olivia asked. "Candice wants to practice for when she has babies with Geoffrey. She says she wants to get pregnant one day."

Sage gasped. She stood there, a bit stupefied, as Olivia collected the boys from her and skipped out of the room with them. "All right, Candice, I got them!"

"They'll be entertained for some time," Damian offered with a chuckle. "In fact, I'm sure they'll babysit if we ask them to. That way, you can relax."

Sage was still thinking about a pregnant Candice. She'd murder Geoffrey for sure. "Yeah."

Damian touched her shoulder. Sage's body was shaking. "Darling," he said gently. "Are you all right?"

Sage shook her head.

"Don't worry. Candice isn't ready to have sex yet, but when she is, I have already spoken to Geoffrey about protection—"

"It's not that." Sage crossed her arms. She sighed. "Well, it is that, because I *don't* want them having sex, but it's also Geoffrey. He's alive . . . and Justice—Humberto—isn't."

Maybe it sounded wrong, saying it like that. Sage had in no way intended to imply that she'd choose Humberto over Geoffrey. She just wondered why she hadn't been able to save him.

"I saw his grave," Damian said softly. "We were all very devastated that he had passed."

"Why couldn't I save him?" Sage said. "Why couldn't my blood save him like it did Geoffrey?"

"You were pregnant at the time, darling. It's obvious that your body was going through a lot of changes, and perhaps your Cells weren't as potent. Knowing Justice, he was grateful for all your efforts to save him. He loved you, and you know that."

Sage nodded.

Damian drew her into his chest. He breathed out raggedly as he said, "Remember there are things we cannot control. That was one of them. While I miss Justice—"

"His name was Humberto. He wanted to be remembered by his real name."

"Forgive me," Damian said. "When we were exiled from Diamond City, we all chose other, non-conventional names. It was a way to hide our past lives. Humberto will forever be remembered and honored by Diamond City. I had his body exhumed and moved here."

Sage looked at him. "You did?"

"Of course."

"I'm sorry. I didn't mean to bring up such dark topics, but I think about him a lot. And then Geoffrey. I'm glad I saved him . . . I only wonder what will become of him now that he's an Enhanced. Is he still doing nuclear engineering? Or will he be like . . ."

Me, she wanted to add. *A warrior. A fighter.*

"Geoffrey will do as he wishes," Damian said. He rested his chin on her head. "Life is very different for him, yes. He might be more inclined to fight. But that will be up to him. Just like Candice and Olivia will choose their careers."

"Candice and Olivia were out in Winterfeld for three months," Sage said. "They missed the beginning of the school year at Royal Academy. What are they supposed to do?"

"We'll enroll them," Damian said. "And they'll get right back into their studies. I'm sure they'll catch up fast."

"I don't want any of them in the military."

"Remember what we talked about," he replied gently. "The girls just went through another shit show. Give them time to figure it out and don't impose on their decisions."

Sage nodded. The true question here was Damian's future in Emerald City, but she was too overwhelmed to speak about it without breaking down.

Sage picked a beige dress without really looking at it and went to change in the bathroom. As she took off her clothes, uncertainty started churning in her stomach like ice cream. She was plagued with that familiar horrible feeling all of a sudden. This time, it was around Damian and the babies. There was no hiding from those two ugly questions.

Would he take them away from her? Would he force her to move to Emerald City with him?

When Sage came out, Damian was sitting in front of the mirror. He was applying red eye shadow. He was already dressed and groomed. With hair that silky, it didn't take long to fix it. He probably had a monthly fashion schedule. Sage had yet to figure out what it was. She hadn't been around him long enough to pinpoint any patterns.

"Goodness," Damian breathed when he saw her. "You look gorgeous."

"I don't," Sage said flatly. Her hair was a mess. Her skin looked too plain. She had lost a considerable amount of muscle mass (again). If anything, she was the definition of sickly.

Damian stood up. He waved to the seat. "Come."

Barefooted, Sage stepped over. She sat down, but refused to look at herself in the mirror. She looked at the counter instead, at the array of makeup that Damian carried everywhere. This must have been his personal stash from the ship.

"Your hair has grown quite a bit," Damian said as he brushed her strands. He smoothed them all the way down her back. "And it has grown softer as well."

Sage didn't think so. Half of the time it was either sweaty, wet, or frozen.

"I don't want you to cut it, though. There are so many styles we can try."

Not for the wedding, though. Not anymore.

"Whatever you say," Sage said softly. "As long as you don't cut yours, either. You know how much I love your hair."

And his had grown a lot, too. It was pinned in certain places, but the back locks nearly touched his hips. How on earth did it grow so perfectly?

"I know," Damian purred. "But you love other parts of me more."

Sage rolled her eyes. "Please. Now you're making assumptions."

"They're not assumptions when I know they're true."

"You can't prove it."

"Do I need to?"

Sage sighed. "I guess not. What difference would it make, right? I love everything about you."

"Details, darling."

"I'm too exhausted. But since you know me so well, I'm sure you can fill in the blanks."

"I most certainly can." Damian smirked. "One starts with a 'p' and another starts with an 'a.' Am I right?"

Sage arched a brow at him through the mirror. "Penis and ass?"

Damian roared with laughter. "And you call me inappropriate! I was thinking pecs and arms since you're always feeling me so much, but I suppose the other two make sense as well—"

Sage swiped at his balls, but Damian jumped back and hit the wall. He nearly choked on his own dribble, the idiot.

"Asshole," Sage hissed. "You set me up!"

"I don't know what you're talking about, darling."

Damian knew damn well what she was talking about. And he accomplished his mission because that heavy weight that had been sitting on Sage's chest lifted. Sage smiled and lowered her head so he wouldn't see her amusement. She played with her fingers on her lap as Damian continued brushing her hair.

"So." He cleared his throat, tone turning more serious. "Where were you these past three months?"

"Hiding with Louis in the woods," Sage replied. "We found Tyrus and Herman's camp. But I think the question you're trying to ask is: did I do anything with him? Did we bond in that one-on-one time we had together?"

Damian stopped for a moment. Whether that was his question or not, Sage didn't know, but she spoke her mind.

"I didn't. But even if I had . . ."

We're not a couple anymore, Damian. We're not together.

"I want to know why it's acceptable for you to dally with Agathe but not acceptable if I did it with Louis," Sage finished uncomfortably. "Is it because you're a man and it's fine, and I'm a woman so I have to behave?"

"That's not it at all," Damian said softly. "First of all, I never intended to do anything with Agathe. Secondly, you weren't drunk when you were around Louis those three months, so, unless he raped you, it would have been a willing act on your part. Thirdly, I don't believe in cheating or having nonconsensual sex, no matter the gender. I am loyal to those I say I am loyal to, whether I am in a relationship with one person or many people. Understand?"

That was an outstanding answer. Damian owed her a few more, but Sage had to prompt him for them. Slowly.

"Isn't there a a bit of explaining you have to do?"

"Yes," Damian said. He kept brushing her hair.

Sage braced herself. "Why didn't you ever tell me?"

"What difference would it have made?" Damian said. "Whether I was human, Enhanced, or hybrid? Does it really matter?"

"It doesn't," Sage admitted. "I don't care what you are. But I think it makes a difference in figuring out what our purpose is. What a hybrid's true mission is. We were created for a reason—all of us. Four Squids founded the Diamond City districts with fighting machines and warriors under their belts. My father left me with my mother, and I'm sure the same happened to you. Foster parents raised you. Cushion isn't your real mother. Obviously. Did you ever meet your Squid father?"

"Luminator," Damian murmured. "That was his name. He was the Clarity District patron. In my religious indoctrination, I was taught all about him and his ideals. We were supposed to enlighten people, get them to trust in the Squids. I hated that bullshit. I didn't care about politics or brainwashing anyone. I just wanted fashion and shows. When I couldn't do that, I tried to end my life. I figured if I bled out enough, I would die." He stopped brushing so he could sigh. "I never got to find out because of you. Then, after I left the hospital, I became obsessed with power. I took in more Cells and joined the coalition against the Overseer."

"Is that why you and your brother were at ends? He believed he was fulfilling his duty as an Emerald City 'representative' while you were just playing games with power?"

"Precisely." Damian started doing something to her hair. Possibly more braids, or some fancy do. Sage just stared at the wall, wondering how long ago the paint had been applied. After Wren and Taz, Heart had remodeled the entire palace. "At the same time, my brother didn't care about the overall picture."

"And what was that? He accused you of wanting to take over Diamond City and force us into a war against the Squids. Isn't that what he was doing as well?"

"Yes and no. Dawson wanted power, but he wanted it for himself. Not Emerald City. And if he could, he'd keep us out of a war, even if it meant bending to the Squids' wishes. I'm all for peace, but not slavery or bullying."

"So what's your plan?" Sage said. "To create an alliance between Emerald and Diamond City?'

"Yes," Damian replied. "That can't hurt, can it?"

"Depends on who we're making friends with and what their goals are. I don't know anything about Emerald City. Clearly, you do." Sage turned in her seat to look at him. "Your true mother is the Emerald City Allseer?"

"*Was*," Damian said softly. "Her name was Yasmine Ott."

"Did you know who she was?"

"I had never met her in my life. Only heard about her through my foster parents."

"Wow," Sage said, wondering what it was like to meet a blood parent. She knew her father, but who was her real mother? "What was that like?"

Damian chuckled wryly. He was still twisting and turning strands of her hair. "Terrible."

"You killed her."

"I had to kill her. If I didn't, she would have stuck me in a test tube for the rest of my life. She didn't trust me, especially when I told her I would never conquer in her name. She had been hopeful that the hybrids would have cleared out and taken over Diamond City by now. She wanted to worm her way in, and I told her no."

"Just like that?" Sage said.

"I wasn't there to beat around the bush," Damian said curtly. "I wanted to make it very fucking clear that I was not anyone's pawn.

You have no idea, Sage—this woman had *slaves*. Fucking slaves. They were at her every beck and call. She treated them worse than wounded animals, chained up and yanking on them every which way. This is a woman who thoroughly enjoyed power. Takuya was her personal lapdog, her preferred scientist who gave her everything she wanted. Jarka and Josiah were one of many biologically-engineered soldiers. We're not even talking Enhanced or hybrids anymore—these people are a different species." He finished her hair. He dropped his hands. "They're not ..."

"Human?" Sage offered.

"It's not fair to call them non-humans," Damian said. He was looking down now. "They have feelings and personalities like all of us do, and the way they were born is not their fault. We are all experiments, I suppose. Emerald City, like Centerfeld under Franco and Lex, was hell."

"So then Marchello did do the right thing," Sage said. "In isolating Diamond City from that."

"I suppose he did."

And if Damian was admitting that much, then Emerald City must have truly been hell. He had definitely seen quite a bit, maybe more than he let on. His eyes welled with tears.

Sage's stomach twisted into knots.

"Damian?"

"Sorry." Damian turned around.

Sage stood. "Damian."

"I-I'm sorry."

"Damian, you're scaring me. What happened?"

"I really don't want to talk about this now," Damian said tightly, still facing the wall. "Tonight is supposed to be fun and carefree—"

"We're going to talk about it right now, damn it!" Sage snapped angrily. "It's been three whole months! How much longer am I supposed to wait to hear what happened to you? I don't care what it is—tell me. *Now.* Or I swear I'm going to blow a gasket and start fucking up people, because I'm starting to believe that that bitch did something to you."

"She cuffed me with these binds that nullified my strength," Damian said. "They had teeth that cut into my skin. I found out later they were laced with Slainium." He wiped at his face, still not looking at her. "Then she threw me into a dungeon, and personally lashed me—"

Sage grabbed a handful of Damian's shirt and shoved it right up his back. He moved to throw her off, but Sage slammed him into the wall and restrained him.

"Why do you have to look at that?!" he yelled, fighting her. "Damn it, Sage, let go!"

Sage started shaking. She stared at a nest of horrific scars, poorly healed thanks to the Slainium binds. That's probably what it was—she was sure there was a way to fix this—

"Darling," Damian said, frustrated. "That's enough—"

"I can look at whatever the fuck I want." Sage let go of his shirt. She took a step back. "You don't hide anything from me, damn it. If you had to see blood pouring out of my vagina, then I have to see what that bitch did to you."

Damian turned around at last. He looked her in the eye. "That's different," he said quietly.

"How?" Sage demanded. "How is it different?"

"What you went through was your body's reaction to the pregnancy. What I went through . . . was at the hands of an external force that wielded power over me. I was *weak*, Sage, and that's what these scars are: a symbol of my weakness."

"You're a fucking idiot, Damian. I told you to let me fight—I TOLD YOU I WOULD TAKE CARE OF IT!"

Damian held her face. He was so gentle, he might have been carrying rose petals. He shook his head. "No, darling. Fighting Emerald City would not have been worth it. You would have been arrested and forced to go through the hell I went through. Centerfeld would have been decimated. You don't understand the kind of soldiers they have—"

"What else did she do?" Sage said. Tears were burning her eyes and she prayed to God they wouldn't come running down her cheeks. She didn't want Damian to see them.

"She took my Portable Projector," Damian said. "She crushed it in front of my very eyes."

"I don't care about a damn gadget. What else did she do to *you*?"

"She turned me over to a torturer." Damian's lip trembled. "Who … t-took an interest. H-he took an interest, but he didn't tell her. He told me the last time he wanted a prisoner, Yasmine had him cut to pieces. So he kept his interest in me a secret. He didn't want to torture me, because he wanted to have me clean. He actually mended my lashes from earlier. I-I was horrified, but I had to exploit him. T-that was my chance … or else …" Damian touched his neck. It looked like he was feeling for his Portable Projector. "Or else I'd never see you and our babies again. I had to make the Ultimate Sacrifice."

"You had sex with him because of some fucking story?!"

"No, darling. In the scripture that Preacher recited to our children, the young man dies. Like you said, he should have struck a deal with the thugs. He should have lived so he could see his true love once more."

Sage gaped at him. "Damian—"

"I didn't want to die!" Damian yelled at her. "So I had to do it, damn it! I had to lead him on, persuade him to get me out of that dungeon! He was a lonely, desperate creature, so it didn't take a whole lot of convincing on my part for it to happen. If he wanted good sex, he had to cut my binds. I promised him the fondling of a lifetime, and he fell for it."

"And this was in a cell?"

"Yes," Damian said through grit teeth. "He couldn't take me anywhere else. So, in the darkness, we kissed. I let him touch me so I could reach for a weapon. They don't know that you gave me your Cells, so they didn't know I could shape-shift like you. And so, with that maneuver, I ended his life. I cut off his finger and used it to free the other prisoners. I was able to rally a few of them. We had plenty of weapons at our disposal, and I had made sure to pay attention to the palace when I was being led to the dungeons. Together, we killed the Allseer. But as for the Portable Projector, I . . ." Damian palmed his eyes. He took a deep breath. "I-I couldn't salvage it—"

"It's a damn gadget!"

"It's *your* gadget!" Damian cried. "A-and I don't know if Doug hooked up with the dancer or not!"

"Damian, that show is everywhere. We can watch it together or get you another Portable Projector—"

"You don't understand! Portable Projectors have been discontinued! I've looked for one everywhere—I even called up people at Mousafeld—and there's no more!"

"Damian." Sage didn't know whether to laugh or cry. "It's a *gadget*. A material object. One that you grew attached to because of me, right?"

Damian's eyes were puffy from crying. It was a miracle that his makeup hadn't started running yet. "Y-yes," he admitted miserably. "It was your one and only gift to me and I lost it. I-I'm sorry."

"There's nothing to forgive, Damian. I'm just glad that you're here and that you made it out of Emerald City in one piece."

"Right." Damian cleared his throat. "It was a miracle. As soon as I could, I set out for Centerfeld to find you. That's where the Lex Warriors told me about what had happened in Winterfeld."

"You're the Emerald City Allseer now," Sage said quietly, still processing everything that Damian had just told her. "Does that mean we're allies?"

"Yes." Then Damian hesitated. "But I am not the Allseer. Not for long, anyway."

Sage stared. "What do you mean?"

"In a week's time, once the Emerald City council arrives, I will renounce my title."

Sage's eyes widened. "What? Why?"

"I cannot leave you and the babies alone," Damian said resolutely. He caressed her face with the pads of his fingers. They felt like feathers. He must have been cleaning her cheeks. "And I cannot ask you to leave Diamond City to come with me."

"Wait—no—we can talk about this." Sage had been thinking of her future, but she didn't know Damian had already made his decision. She didn't know he had been thinking of ditching his title to be with her. Or rather, their children.

"There is nothing to talk about, Sage," Damian said. "If I am Allseer, I cannot be with my children."

"I-I'll come with you—"

"And the girls? Geoffrey? Your pizzeria?"

"We can all move together!" Sage exclaimed. "We can make it work! Whatever the case, Damian, you have to be Allseer!"

Damian blinked. "Why?"

"Because I don't trust anyone else! The council? How do you know they won't turn their backs on us? Look at how shitty the Diamond City council was after Marchello died."

"Let me finish your makeup, darling."

"Forget my makeup! Can you please answer my concerns?"

"I'm not leaving our children," Damian said strictly. "That is not negotiable."

Sage couldn't say anything. That's because, if she were him, she'd do the very same thing. Like hell she would leave her children behind to rule some city she wasn't even loyal to. But then she couldn't just abandon the people there, either, right? Unless there was a way to bring her children along as well . . .

And that call was up to Sage.

Sage took note of Damian's silence. Perhaps it was too soon to talk about the future of Emerald City. Maybe Damian had a lot of thinking to do, too, despite his decision. Regardless, there was no point in arguing any further, so Sage sat back down on the bench.

Damian did what he was so good at. Sage could see every eyelash, every light wrinkle, and every piece of glitter on his face, but all she could think of was Emerald City.

What the council would do without a righteous leader.

Damian? Righteous? Sage nearly died of laughter.

But no. Wait. This Damian was different.

I trust him, Sage thought, losing herself in his eyes. *I do. I trust him.*

"I love you, darling," Damian said to her. "You and our beautiful boys. Alongside Candice, Olivia, and Geoffrey, we're going to run the pizza shop. We are finally going to be a family."

"The Emerald City council," Sage said at once—she just couldn't hold it in. "I don't trust them."

"Can you give them a chance?" Damian asked sincerely. "When they come, you can meet them. You can see them for yourself. We can talk this out diplomatically."

"I want to stay with you," Sage said. "Whatever happens, Damian, I can't leave you alone. So either you stay with me . . . or I go with you."

Damian arched a brow.

"I want to be with you," Sage said again. "Y-you're really good-looking."

Damian laughed. "Is that how you describe me?" he teased. He just had to finish her mascara. Sage hated it, but she held still. "How about beautiful, gorgeous, and irresistible?"

"Don't push your luck. You're lucky you're being complimented at all."

"Do you want to know what I think of you?" Damian said.

Sage smiled. "Yes."

"You're the only goddess whose altar I would worship."

Sage blushed a little. "I'm not that attractive."

"Yes, you are," Damian said a bit breathily. "And when you're cutting off another guy's penis? Even more so."

"He deserved it. He . . ." Sage hesitated. "Raped a lot of women."

"Indeed." Damian finally finished. There was a sultriness in his eyes that called to her, made her heart race just a little bit faster. "You ended him at last. And although his brother is still out there, we will worry about that later. Right now, I just want to tell you that I am madly in love with you. Regardless of where we stand in our relationship, I would do crazy things just to make sure I can be with you. That's why I want to stay."

"I know," Sage said quietly.

"I want to kiss you. Actually . . . I want you to kiss me like you did that night in Centerfeld."

"You mean when I was drunk?"

"Yes," Damian said. "I had to masturbate twice that night because I went to bed thinking about it. I woke up with the biggest goddamn erection I've ever had."

Sage rolled her eyes. "It can't possibly be any bigger than all your other erections."

"It swelled up a lot."

"You're so explicit."

"And you like it."

Sage stood up. "Sit down, then."

"Did you at least look at yourself in the mirror?" Damian said.

"I don't want to look at myself. I want to look at you."

The night she had had the biggest make-out session with Damian was a blur, so she didn't know what she had done or how. She had lost herself in the moment, propagated by the drunkenness, so it was going to be impossible to replicate now.

Or maybe it wasn't. Sage was about to straddle the lap of the most beautiful man she had ever seen. His long dark hair was like an endless waterfall from the abyss, so silky that she could bathe in it. His eyes were outlined expertly, the shadows on his lids like a butterfly's intricate wings. His long straight nose gave way to those sensuous lips that she was about to suck the life out of. The lapels with the silver chains were for playing as she rocked against his body, took control of the kiss and the tempo of their mouths.

Sage was on fire. If she had ever wondered what it was like to burn, she was feeling it now. Almost as if she had swallowed coals and took one more into her body every time she tasted Damian's lips.

God, and then there was his smell. The teakwood and lavender that was more subtle now, replaced with an airer, breezier scent, as if Damian had just elevated himself to elf king in that fairy world Sage swore he had come from. It made her want to devour him, and she did.

One time, she had her tongue so far down his throat that he gagged. Sage didn't let up, especially when those lonely nights she had longed for him resurfaced in her mind. Those feelings of old powered the ones coursing through her veins now, egging her on and intoxicating her completely. She was drunk now, as if she had downed Cupid's Arrow for the tenth time in a row.

There was the possibility that she hadn't really been drunk in that last make-out session—maybe it was just Damian. His glittery skin as if he was a piece of diamond, the smoothness of it as Sage ran her hands inside his shirt. A few of the buttons were loose.

"Touch my nipples," he said breathily against her lips.

They were hard and pointy just like the bulge in his pants. Damian leaned back against the dresser so that Sage could eat from his body. She could run her tongue down his chest then devour one of those pink buds like candy. When she bit him, Damian yelled.

He didn't curse, though. He groaned in pain, arched his back, and squirmed like a worm beneath her. He clutched the table, opened his legs some more, and rolled his head back and forth all over the strewn brushes and open makeup kits.

Sage ripped open his shirt some more, descending now on those glorious abs of his. He was thin but lean, ribs visible and flexing with every breath he took. She ate out his bellybutton, proof that he had been attached to an umbilical cord at some point in his life—possibly in a test tube—and used her tongue to thrust into him. She went as deeply as she could, then pulled back when she felt him cum in his pants.

"Stars," Damian panted crazily, a hand on his forehead. "What did you do to me, darling?"

Sage got off him. She nearly fell thanks to wobbly legs, but she laughed at the dark spot in the crotch of his pants. "Wow. I'll give you a hundred Diamonds if you show up to dinner like that."

" 'Dinner'?" Damian panted, looking at her. "You think I'm going to dinner?"

"You wanted a kiss, didn't you?"

Damian wanted so much more than that. His eyes were huge

and wild, chest still heaving, legs still spread wide open with a semi-hard penis that would be ready to go again in a minute. He clambered off the dresser and ripped off the rest of his shirt like a beast. With the smudged makeup around his eyes and lips, he looked like a man possessed. Like a true and powerful god, he seemed to glow beneath the waning sun outside their window.

But Damian didn't attack her. He stood there, and so did she. They had the stare-off of a lifetime, perhaps twice as intense as that kiss, if that were possible. Sage had a hard time breathing. Her belly was pounding. Her legs wouldn't support her any longer. But still, she didn't lose eye contact.

Not even as Damian got closer to her, wrapping an arm around her waist. There was no way in hell he was articulate enough to loosen all the laces in her dress right now. He didn't really have to take it off, though. Sage had everything she needed when she yanked down his pants and underwear. All Damian had to do was her underwear, and that wasn't too difficult for him once she laid back on the bed.

Sage grabbed his bare shoulders with her hands. His skin was so soft, muscles well defined from training and battles. She ran her hands down his back, clutched his ass, and brought him right up against her hips. She closed her eyes and arched her back. Just feeling him there cast her into an abyss of pleasure. Pictures of Agathe crept up in her mind, of how she had humped him and given him her nipple, but Damian's mouth was near her ear to soothe her.

"Please forgive me," he whispered.

Sage supposed she had forgiven him. At some point . . . maybe the night of the vows? The one she had thought was a dream? She didn't say it. Didn't speak. She gave him a serious look. It wasn't because she was angry—she just wanted to gaze into his eyes.

The room was huge and yet it felt so small, trapping the heat of their bodies. She was sweating beneath her gown. Her heart was beating so fast, and her belly was pounding and near exploding with anticipation.

Damian thrust all the way inside, crying out like a madman. He was shivering and huffing and puffing. But no foul cursing. No sex talk. He held himself there for a bit, shaking like a leaf, then hid his face in her shoulder. He used a hand to free her left breast, knead it like dough, then clutch it as if it were a handle.

Sage grabbed a fistful of his hair. She held him as he started thrusting. She didn't move because she wanted to feel him. She basked in how thick he was inside her, how he quivered from pleasure, tensing whenever she decided to give him a squeeze.

Despite his grunting, Damian went faster. He chased that release relentlessly, no matter how painful it became for him, and finally found it. His hot seed swelled inside her like water in a balloon, and it's how Sage reached her pinnacle as well. Damian never stopped, squirting like crazy and thrusting his hips as if he was still working toward a climax.

"Damian," Sage breathed. She threw her head back, exposing her neck. Damian nuzzled her, bit her, and even drew blood. Sage didn't know what the hell he was doing, but it felt damn good. The pounding in her groin started up again. "I thought vampires were disgusting."

"They can be sexy, darling."

"Drinking someone's blood is sexy?"

"Isn't it? The taste of yours is turning me on right now."

"You're just horny."

"No, there's something wrong with me," Damian whispered against her skin. He licked her wound some more. "I can't think straight."

Sage couldn't, either. It was a miracle Damian finally had the composure to unlace her dress. He snaked his hands to her back and undid all the knots like a pro. Sage wasn't sure how, but maybe it was easy because she was arching. Or maybe it was her breasts he wanted to play with so bad, and the more he fumbled, the more he'd have to delay.

As Damian did that, Sage finished pulling off his pants and underwear. She tossed his boots.

When they were finally naked, Sage brought him back against

her body. She tied her legs around his waist. He was already so hard inside her, but he didn't start thrusting. He embraced her, too. He clutched her to his chest, as if he'd never see her again. When his shoulders started shaking, Sage knew he was crying.

But Sage still said nothing. It was sad to hear his sobs. Her eyes burned, too. She had just experienced what she had nearly lost. Damian was in the same boat. He, above everyone else, knew how close he had been to losing Sage forever. He had lost so much in his life already, but this was what he treasured the most—the tattoo on his right arm said it all.

Eventually, Sage rolled him onto his back. She straddled his hips, but she didn't stay looking at him. She bent over, face on his shoulder like he had done to her, and rode him slowly. Really slowly. It was more like a rubbing than a grinding. It all had to do with relishing in the moment. If she went too fast, it'd be over in minutes. For Damian, perhaps that would be the case either way.

"Stars," Damian rasped beneath her. He dug the back of his head into the pillow, his Adam's apple bobbing up and down as he swallowed. He groaned because it was the hardest sexual moment of his life. "Stars, Sage!" He clutched the sheets, but he didn't dare make her go faster. This was a challenge he didn't mind accepting. It was entertaining as hell to watch him.

Actually, it was Sage who caved first. There was only so much moving she could do with a huge penis inside her before she found her end. As she rode out those wonderful bursts of pleasure, Damian finally climaxed. He squirmed even more on the bed—pounding the mattress, making noises, bending his knees, and curling his toes—like a kid throwing a tantrum for a toy he couldn't have.

"Why do you torture me like that?!" Damian yelled at her.

Sage laughed.

It was revenge time. Damian grabbed her body and pinned her down on the bed.

Then, as he laid there in between her legs, thrusting, tongue swirling lazily in her mouth like an eel, Sage thought of something.

It just happened. It popped into her mind just like that. With the way Damian was moving inside her, gentle but determined, and the way he clutched her torso to his chest, holding her like he would his own heart and soul, she realized her dream had come true.

It had, hadn't it? She was in the palace. She had found true love. Candice and Olivia were safe. Her boys were so beautiful.

Sage was living the fairy-tale dream now. Each thrust from Damian served as a reminder. As a revelation. That this was what she had spent her entire life fighting for. She thought she had found it that time in Winterfeld, after seeing her girls off to the festival. She had wondered then how long it would last.

Despite the love aflame in her chest, and the love Damian so clearly portrayed to her as he kissed her and sucked her soul into his body, she wondered the same now.

CHAPTER 22

The Royal Amusement Park

When Sage woke up, she was curled against Damian's side. He had an arm around her, holding her like he would a pillow. His cheek was on her head. He was snoring lightly despite the soft giggles coming from the kitchen.

"You can't feed them like that, Olive!" declared Candice in her motherly tone. "You have to hold him at an angle or it'll spill all over the place."

"Wow, this is hard."

An echo of barks. It sounded like Red and Green agreed with Olivia.

Sage sat up. She looked down at Damian, who had all his makeup on from last night. The eye shadow was beautiful. She had no idea how he had detailed them so perfectly, complete reflections of each other.

"How gorgeous do I look right now?" he asked her with his eyes still closed.

Sage crawled over him, body flush with his. She held herself on her elbows so she was face-to-face with him below. "Pretty damn gorgeous," she said. "Like a diamond on display."

Damian purred. "Not on display, darling. That implies I can't be touched."

"I'm the only one with a key."

"Then that changes things."

Kissing Damian took a lot of energy. It was like trying to conquer a bear in hand-to-hand combat. By the end of it, Sage was completely drained, as wobbly as jello. Damian was huffing and puffing, equally weak beneath her. But it was a lot of fun, so Sage kissed him again. She could barely hear Candice and Olivia now. The dogs were trotting up and down the hallway. That was probably Blue, Violet, and Orange. Unfortunately for them, Sage wasn't getting out of this bed any time soon.

Damian wanted free rein over her, and Sage let him. He rolled her onto her back and took her hard and fast before they got interrupted. Not that the girls would bother them—they respected their privacy—but perhaps Louis would come by to wonder why they hadn't been at dinner. The answer to that was clear.

When Damian got out of bed, he took Sage with him. They bumbled into the shower together, still kissing, touching, and having sex like animals in heat. That's how it was with Damian. That's why Sage was so addicted to him and this. It was like a drug, and now that Sage had tasted it again after so long, she didn't want it to stop. She loved the way Damian felt in between her legs, how he pinned her to the wall and rolled his hips up, or how she pinned him to the wall, threw a leg over his hip, and did the same. There was something about that angle that made him come hard and fast. Sage was completely overwhelmed. After they were done, Damian slid to the shower floor in a daze.

"Darling," he rasped with his eyes lidded. "You little vixen."

"Please don't compare me to a fox," Sage said. "I'm not a fox."

"You're right. You're more like a black widow."

"A spider, Damian?"

"You're killing me," he said simply.

"Stop complaining." Sage got him up from the floor. She had to be quick if she was going to escape from another round of sex, so she turned off the water, dried herself, threw on some clothes, then debated on what to do with her hair. Damian offered to do a French braid. His long fingers cut through her strands so easily, without pulling or pain. Sage sat there, eyes semi-closed, not thinking about anything in particular.

"You look a bit tired, darling," Damian noted.

"My vagina hurts."

Damian chuckled. "That's a good thing. It means you've been pleasured thoroughly."

"I have been," she admitted.

"You deserve it. After all the trials and fights we've been through." Damian cleared his throat. Perhaps he was thinking about their battle before Agathe's death, a day Sage was desperately trying to forget, but his mind was on the birth of their boys. "How did you know to do that?"

"I think they would have killed me," Sage said. "Had they stayed in there. I don't know ... maybe they wouldn't have. It's just I saw the bodies in Smallfeld, and I was trying to copy what the ..." She couldn't say Squids. Big Brother and X@me. Damian knew. "Perhaps it worked."

"You were awfully brave, darling," he said softly. "I wish I had been there when you made that decision."

"You were there. You took out one of the cocoons. I'm surprised you didn't faint."

"I actually preferred that than something coming out of your vagina," Damian said. "It just creeps me out that a person can come out of there."

Sage laughed. "Me, too."

Damian leaned down and kissed her. He was already dressed and ready for the day. He wasn't in anything too extravagant, because, according to him, he had a lot to discuss with Louis concerning Emerald City. This was a casual meeting with the Diamond City Allseer and council. To think Damian had been their general just months ago. Now, he was their equal in every way. Sage wondered who'd take charge of the military now that Damian had graduated.

"Why don't you just relax today?" Damian said, holding the bedroom door open for her. It was time to join the girls and pups for breakfast. "And give politics a break? We'll talk tonight."

Sage silently agreed to that. She watched Damian speed-walk into the kitchen as if he couldn't get to the boys fast enough. Both of them were in their carriers, guarded by Green, Red, and Yellow, who were looking out at Candice and Olivia preparing the food. Pollux looked confused whereas Castor looked serious. They both giggled when they saw Damian, the clown.

"How are my two little munchkins today?" Damian sang, picking each of them up. They were bundled tightly in their blankets so they looked like two little beans in his arms. "The most beautiful creatures I've ever seen. Wouldn't you agree, Mama?"

"Please don't call me that," Sage grumbled. "It just sounds weird."

"That's what you are."

"Fine, but that doesn't mean I'm going to call you 'Dada'."

"Maybe you should try it," Damian purred. "I'll be your Dada any time."

Olivia laughed. Candice had a smile on her face, although it was reserved. The four of them might have been reunited again after many months, but Sage hadn't forgotten that horrid morning she found Damian at the Color Dome. *Clingy bitch.* Is that what Sage still was now?

It was hard to tell. While Candice kept that smile on her lips, allowed Damian to braid her hair, and even embraced him when he left for the day, there was a flash in her hazel irises that indicated there was something she desperately needed to tell Sage. It was nap time for the twins now that they had been fed (Damian wanted to get a rubber nipple and Sage had said no), so Olivia put them to bed. Candice and Sage were alone at last, hanging out in the living room, one in the armchair and the other on the couch. Sage didn't plan to lounge around all day, but a bit of downtime wouldn't hurt after all her crazy fights in the Outskirts. Damian had taken the pups for company (would he sic them on Louis?), so the room was pretty quiet.

"I'm sorry, Aunt Sage."

Candice spoke first. Sage stared at her bare toes on the carpet. She wasn't one for pedicures, but damn her nails looked horrible. Damian had sucked on her big toe last night, embarrassingly, but he didn't seem to care about cracked nail beds as long as he was giving Sage the pleasure of her life.

"I didn't mean to disrespect you," Candice croaked. More emotion flooded her tone. "*Ever.* I love you so goddamn much. You are my role model—you are the person I strive to be. I didn't mean to insult you or question your judgment."

"I was a clingy bitch," Sage admitted. "I still am. I'm nearly a 120 years old, and sometimes I feel like a child. It's like I want something so badly that I don't see anything else. I feel like I'm missing an important detail because of it. I feel completely blinded by him and all the promises he whispers in my ear."

"Aunt Sage." Candice got on her knees. She was in house shorts, so walking on them like she did probably burned like hell. It didn't matter. She got in front of Sage and held her hands. From this angle, Sage could see her face fully. Beautiful. Candice and Olivia were spitting images of their late mother. The fine features were the envy of every woman who saw them. Sometimes, even Sage herself. "He loves you. There's no doubt about it. But I was wrong."

"What?"

"He didn't kill Poppa. It was Louis who gave the order."

"*What?*"

Candice dabbed at her eyes. "Gertrude told me shortly after you fled from Diamond City. The rumor was that Damian had done it, but in actuality, Louis had given the order. Apparently, he had made friends in Mousafeld, people who wanted his favor just in case he became the Allseer. There was a high chance that was going to happen, and it did. When Poppa was jailed, and right before Damian woke up from his surgery, Louis didn't waste any time."

"How the hell do you know this?" Sage croaked. "Who the hell would tell Gertrude all this if it was true?"

"She's friends with everyone at Mousafeld," Candice said. "And she knows who to talk to, whether they're long time friends or recent acquaintances. All the Warlord's rebels stick to him like glue, but not every exile in the Outskirts is his friend. Some hate him with a passion. Apparently, Louis knows how to talk to people very well and he managed to convince a couple to execute Poppa on his behalf."

"Then blame it on Damian?" Sage said.

"Aunt Sage, think about it: Louis and Agathe *both* hate him. Damian killed their father. They both distrust him greatly, whether he's genuinely interested in defending Diamond City or not. On top of that, their goal was to drive you and Damian apart as much as possible. Agathe might have set Damian up in the Color Dome, but Louis was doing the same with Poppa's death. He executed the Private Guard, too, since he didn't trust them to keep secrets about the Allseers."

So only a handful of people in Mousafeld knew the truth. Obviously, there was a huge coverup in place. That meant Louis had plenty of control, more than Sage believed.

"I don't know what to make of it," Candice admitted, still on her knees. She was kneading Sage's hands nervously. "I know that Poppa was no saint. I know that he hated the pizzeria because he talked shit about it all the time. I know his goal was to climb the ladder, and he used you and..." She hesitated. Her lip quivered. "A-and us. Me, Olive—he used us. He wanted to get you to come back to Diamond City, to ambush you, and he did. He just didn't dream that Louis, the Allseer, would be the one to deal the killing blow. And perhaps..." She sobbed, as if it pained her to say this. "Perhaps it was for the best..."

"Candice." Sage got on her knees, too. She brought Candice into her chest, embracing her. The skinny body shook in her arms. She wanted to say that Bram didn't deserve to die, but it was so hard when Sage thought of the alternative. It was incredibly difficult to picture Candice and Olivia in the hands of Squids—

Wait. Not Squids. They weren't the bad guys. Candice and Olivia would have been safe, but Sage hadn't known that at the time. The council clearly hadn't given two fucks if the Squids would rape them or not and that was unforgivable. But despite all that, would it have been acceptable to kill Bram?

Not without a fair trial, Sage said in her mind. *Not without questioning him first.*

But Candice wasn't done yet. She composed herself because she had already cried about it and that was the end of that. It was done and in the past. There was more she needed to tell Sage, so much more from her six months in isolation at her great great great grandmother's house in the Cut District. Aurora's house. It was a safe haven for them if the need arose. But apparently, Bram had used it for more than just hiding—it had been a meeting place, too.

"Poppa was talking to a lot of shady people," Candice admitted. She and Sage were face-to-face now, in the middle of the living room floor. All was quiet in Olivia's room. It sounded like the twins were in bed, and Olivia was taking her chances on the eavesdropping. Little shit—Sage had told her not to do that, but she wouldn't scold her about it, because she'd be doing the same. Besides, these were topics that Candice wouldn't have brought up in front of her.

"You already know that the Private Guard was distributing Stars across the Outskirts," Candice said. "And you probably know it came from the Carat District. If anyone's in on the substances coming in out of the city, it's them. Do you remember the Red Fever scare from a few years ago? And its resurgence last summer? Well, it was the Carat District and some crazy, wacky experiments they were performing. The Allseer covered it up and said it was from the Outskirts, but it was the Carat District behind the scenes."

Candice took a deep breath and let it out. She shook her head. "I'm sorry. I'm saying Carat District, but it's not all their fault. It's this woman named Venus."

Sage stared. "Venus?"

"I saw her a couple of times." Candice broke out crying again. Olivia was as still as a board in her hiding spot in the hallway. Perhaps she was crying, too, because the tension spiked like mercury in a thermometer. Sage was breathing incredibly hard. "O-one time I caught her . . . o-on . . ."

Sage held Candice again. Her own eyes were wide, picturing the shit that Bram had gotten himself in to all because he wanted to glorify his image in the Allseer's eyes.

"Poppa knew I had been listening," Candice hiccuped, "but he told me it was necessary. That sometimes we did things for business. And he said Venus was necessary for business, that she was doing what he and the PG asked of her."

"What does she look like—?"

"Horrible!" Candice exclaimed. She was so agitated by the memory of this Venus that she jumped to her feet and nearly tripped over the ottoman. "She's a weird, mutant freak! She looks like a freaky human plant walking on two legs! But it's not even that, Sage—you know how much I like the Zootopia show in the Color District and respect people who do that because it's their calling—but Venus isn't any of that!"

Candice clenched her fists. Tears in her eyes, she croaked, "She's a monster. And she uses her image to get what she wants."

"And what does she want?" Sage asked quietly.

"Chaos. She lives to feed off of people's fears. Disease, drug addiction, death, rape—all of it. I really don't understand why Poppa would choose to deal with her, but I guess I sort of do if finding his way to the Allseer's lap was his thing. That's why I think he's even more despicable than her and perhaps he did deserve to die."

"Don't say that, Candice."

"I just can't take it anymore, Aunt Sage!" she yelled. "Why can't we just live in peace? I was afraid to say anything when we got back from the Outskirts, because I didn't want to ruin your wedding with Damian! I blamed you for not telling me about Poppa, but I understand why you did it. I understand you're trying so hard to move on, but you keep getting sucked into battles. I-I didn't say anything then, but I'm saying it now because I'm afraid!

"Venus isn't human," Candice went on. "Nor is she an Enhanced. She told Poppa that she was a hybrid. What you are. I don't know how it's possible or if I believe her, but I do know one thing: In exchange for spreading Red Fever and Stars, she wanted a private audience with the Allseer. Poppa was willing to give it to her only if he became successful in getting the Allseer's attention. Although . . . I don't know if he really meant it. As manipulative as he was, I know he couldn't have wanted such chaos. That's all Venus brings. He probably would have found a way to wipe her out once he got in the Allseer's good graces."

"I imagine you haven't heard from Venus since?" Sage asked.

Candice shook her head. Sage got back on the couch, sitting and thinking.

"I think things here have been too riled up to make any moves," Sage said. "For Venus, anyway. After Marchello's death, there was the council, and now it's Louis because Agathe is dead, but even he hasn't been here to receive her."

"Do you think she's plotting her next move?" Candice asked. "I mean, should we do anything?"

Sage wasn't sure. But rare was the hybrid that actually wanted positive change. It truly sounded like hybrids had way too much time and power in their hands to hold still, as evidenced by X@me, Big Brother, and now this Venus. X@me had gone around experimenting with reproduction, so it was obvious he had never even met or heard of Venus, but what about Big Brother? He had been carrying something in that bundle . . . but he wasn't the issue now. Could Sage stand by and allow Venus to plot her next move? Louis was back in town, so how much longer would she wait to cash in on Bram's promises?

Sage figured she'd talk to Damian about it. Later.

Today, she planned on enjoying her day with Candice, Olivia, and the twins. They were visiting the Royal Amusement Park, the number-one attraction for any Diamond City resident. It had been featured in *The Royal Court* in seasons one and five. Thinking of it, Sage did feel silly for ever watching that stupid series. She thought long and hard about Louis' actions against Bram and pinning the blame on Damian, but she didn't have the energy or the strength to be mad about it. Besides, Geoffrey was at her door.

"Sage!" Geoffrey chuckled.

He embraced her tightly. Sage hadn't realized how tall he was until now. Her head fit comfortably beneath his chin, right over the scar on his throat. When she pulled back, she realized it was gone.

"Thanks to the cream," Geoffrey said happily. "Sonia and L told me that the doctors in Centerfeld are super efficient. I think the leaders were a bunch of psychopaths who would cut people for fun, so they created Rub-And-Gone."

Impressive. Sage couldn't see any remnants of that nasty gash Shenzi had left behind. She smiled.

"I really hate to ask, but . . ." Sage hesitated. "Do you have some leftover?"

"Actually, I brought some." Geoffrey showed her the tube. "Candice wanted some for that scar she has on her thigh."

Sage narrowed her eyes. "And how the fuck would you know she has a scar on her thigh?"

Geoffrey held up his hands with a laugh. "She told me!"

"Why, Aunt Sage?" Olivia teased. "Do you have any ugly scars you want to cover up?"

"Oh, yeah," Sage sneered. "The one on my ass that says Wyatt."

Geoffrey gasped. The cute old lady that was standing behind him furrowed her brows.

Sage's face fell from embarrassment. She had totally not seen her there.

"Oh, Sage," Geoffrey chortled uncomfortably. "This is my grandmother, Cleo. She really wanted to meet you."

Wyatt's daughter, possibly. Definitely the generation after. She was exactly what Sage had pictured in her head: A small, black senior citizen with gray hair in a bun. Despite the curve of her back and the wrinkles on her face, her eyes were small and intense. She wore a thick pair of glasses that magnified everything a lot more than necessary. Sage felt like someone was looking at her through a microscope.

"Is this the great Optimum?" Cleo asked, fixing her glasses for a better look. "She's nothing but a girl."

"Um." Sage's cheeks were really burning now. Was that a compliment?

"But she's 119 years old!" Olivia announced. "And she'll be turning 120 in the month of Faith!"

"Enhanced certainly are peculiar," Cleo said. "We have old minds in young bodies. Truly a danger to us all. But what am I saying? I am in the presence of the Optimum. And you, my dear, have saved us all. You have constantly put your life on the line for others. While we have heard the stories of the Unification War, Geoffrey told me all about the heroism he experienced firsthand. I never got to thank you for sticking next to my boy when he was pulled aside for Red Fever." She bowed her head. "Thank you. But another thanks is in order, an even bigger one, for you have personally saved my boy's life." Her eyes got bigger. Her thin lips trembled. "You gave him your blood."

"I-I wasn't going to let him die." Sage cleared her throat. She was fighting not to get emotional. This was Wyatt's *daughter*.

"I don't have much to offer you, for we left Winterfeld in quite a hurry, but Wyatt tells me you're in love."

Sage's cheeks were on fire. This was way too much. Candice was smirking and Olivia was hopping up and down.

"He says that you have captured the Warlord's heart," Cleo went on. "And so what better gift to give you than a Soulmate Bracelet? Candice and Olivia tell me you love wearing jewelry on your wrist. And weapons, too." Cleo offered her a box. In it was an empty Soulmate Bracelet. There were ten spaces for charms in between the fine jewels.

"Don't worry, Aunt Sage," Olivia said. "We'll make sure Damian buys the right charms! We all know you love Star Raider, cars, pizza, boiled eggs, swords, boots—because you leave them laying around—hair products, dogs, churros, and hot guys!"

"Wow," Geoffrey said. "That's impressive, Olivia."

Candice showed off her bracelet. "Geoffrey bought me all my charms."

"Thank you." Sage took the bracelet from Cleo. "I would just hate to take this from you if it's your only one."

"Please." Cleo waved at her. "I had a store in Winterfeld. I sold these all the time. You can buy charms pretty much everywhere, but the most expensive part is the band itself. Those are real diamonds in there, you know."

They were glistening like crazy under the light. Definitely at least a carat each. It made sense that these were prohibitively expensive, but what didn't make sense was the "I sold these all the time" bit.

Sage held her breath. "Wait... are you the founder of these bracelets?"

"Yes, my dear," Cleo said.

"So you're the woman in that fairy tale?"

"If by 'fairy tale' you mean my life's story, then yes," Cleo said happily. "There is definitely a story behind these bracelets, and it is mine. They've become a trend in Winterfeld among youth. You're old, but I think you can appreciate the true meaning of love."

"What?!" Sage exclaimed. "You're the woman who founded Winterfeld?"

"I didn't establish Winterfeld, no. I was one of the early settlers, so I can see why people would get confused."

"Did Damian know this was her?" Sage demanded of Candice, who laughed and shrugged.

"Probably not. He probably just heard the story somewhere, but he had no idea that Geoffrey's grandmother was the woman who lost her husband."

"Thank you." Sage bowed her head to Cleo. "Truly."

"I heard you had babies." Cleo clapped her hands together. "May I please see the little darlings?"

As Cleo got acquainted with a happy Castor and Pollux, more

visitors arrived. Sage was surprised to see Gertrude, a reluctant I-have-to-if-I-want-to-impress-her Turtle, Sonia, L, Sword Devil, and Tai standing in the hall.

And Preacher?

"The Forefathers bless us!" he exclaimed, raising his hands. "The Optimum and her offspring have accepted us on this journey!"

"I kind of invited them." Candice beamed.

Sage chuckled. "Sounds good to me."

"Do you know"—Sonia wrapped her arm around Sage's—"how long I've been waiting to see that amusement park?"

"She is obsessed with *The Royal Court*." L rolled her eyes. For someone who was battle hardened, she sure looked casual today: sweatshirt, capris, and boots. Her long black hair was in a messy bun on the right side of her head. Usual attire for the month of Strength, but not for someone who called themselves a Lex Warrior.

Everyone had comfortable wear today. Even Sword Devil, who liked to hide behind her hair or armor, looked like a regular college student. Preacher, however, couldn't be paid enough money to join in on the fashion train. He had the traditional psychedelic mask and white robes, regardless of the fact they'd be walking around in public. He wouldn't want the Squids looking down at him.

Sage thought about Samson. She actually checked the phone she had found at the base near Winterfeld. No messages yet.

"Well?" Sonia sang. She looked so crazy with spiky hair, but today was a day to let go. Damian had given them all permission to go crazy, whether Louis liked it or not, and that's exactly what they were going to do. "Shall we go?"

Sage beamed. "We shall."

W hat didn't they do at the amusement park? It was across the capital from the palace, bordering the Color District in the north, and it was *huge*. Actually, huge was an understatement, because there was no way they'd be able to walk all this in one day. When they got the map, Sonia marked their trail, starting with the west side. If they went clockwise, they'd hit each section in this order: Sun Town; Water The Plants, Kids, and Yourself; the Pyramids of Heart; Mystical Escape; and then the Night Dreamers. According to Sonia, they were supposed to go in the right order because all the sections represented a certain time of the day.

"Everyone knows that," L grumbled. "That's why we should start at Night Dreamers, where there's no one right now."

"That's boring!" Sonia whined. "It's not even nighttime!"

"Children of the Lolligo, do not fret!" cried Preacher. "We shall start wherever destiny takes us!"

"Destiny says we go to Night Dreamers!" L argued.

"No way—Sun Town!" Sonia exclaimed.

"Can you stop fighting?" Turtle spat, covering his ears. Listening to bitches so early in the morning was pure torture. "Why don't we put it up for vote?"

By show of hands, Sun Town won ten to one (Preacher didn't vote, because he didn't interfere in destiny). So Sun Town it was, despite how much L complained about it. Sage supposed it wouldn't have been L if it was any other way. It was pretty entertaining to hear her insult the attendant who asked her for an ID when she went for a beer.

"Are you kidding me?" L rasped. "Do I look like a fucking teenager to you?"

"Just protocol, ma'am."

"But you didn't ask her!" She pointed at Sonia. "And she has a baby face!"

"Can you just show him the damn ID and not complain so much?" Sonia snapped. "Stars!"

"What do you think?" Sage held her babies to her chest, kissing each of them in the nose. They both giggled at her. "Kinda loud, isn't she? Just like Dada, but in a different way."

"They really are gorgeous," Gertrude said, sipping on her cherry slushy. L was the only one consuming alcohol at this time of the day. The Sun Spot was hot and bright, with the lines at the roller coasters over an hour long. Candice, Olivia, and Geoffrey were hitting up each one, and to Sage (and everyone else's) immense amusement, they dragged Preacher along with them for good luck.

"I have been chosen!" he declared as he got in line. "And I am honored to accept!"

Cleo stayed by the gift shop. Sword Devil and Tai were competing with each other on Ring Toss. Sage knew those games were rigged, but those two made every shot and were accumulating quite the number of prizes.

Castor and Pollux couldn't participate much here, but they were sightseeing. Sage promised she'd take them on a few of the water rides in the next section. There were some suitable for babies.

"I appreciate your compliment," Sage said to Gertrude, who puckered her lips at Castor and Pollux and blew them kisses.

"The babies look so cute! I can't get over how much they look like Damian. No offense, Sage."

Sage shook her head. "None taken." She took a seat in one of the benches. It was a nice, shady spot under a tree. She had a portable fan to make sure the babies were cool. "I know they look like him. Not sure if that's a good or bad thing."

"I think anyone would be thankful for his looks," Gertrude said. "True."

Gertrude sighed. She took a seat next to Sage. "I'm sorry for leaving you and them."

"Don't be," Sage said. "You did what you had to. If anything, I should be thanking you for everything you've done. You've followed me into battles, nearly gotten yourself killed, and gone through your share of bullshit."

"Isn't that what we've all been doing? If you're listing my heroisms, then how about we list yours? Starting with the day you took off from Diamond City on your own, battled a bunch of Squids, gave birth to those beautiful darlings, dealt with Damian, faced off against Emerald City, confronted Blackburn, stayed in hiding for three months, and then fought some crazy-ass hybrid impregnating women."

Sage laughed. "Damn. When you put it like that, it sounds like it sucks to be me."

"Nah." Gertrude smiled. Her freckles stuck out more. Her hair was a coppery red, freshly cut, and there certainly was a glow about her. "I don't see it that way at all. I see a woman I aspire to be, someone who has balls even though they are a woman. After my surgery, I was afraid that I'd lose my tenacity. Men are taught to be strong leaders—it's what brings honor to the family. And while I was different physically, I knew this"—and she touched her heart—"hadn't changed. I had even more drive to become an Enhanced and fight against the Allseer. So that's what I did. That's why I've stuck to the Warlord's side no matter what. That's why I believe in him and what he stands for."

"Did he tell you about what happened in Emerald City?"

Gertrude shook her head. "No, not a thing. I don't know. I mean, I wasn't there to see it for myself, because when we ... um ... left you." She sighed, ashamed. "We returned to Centerfeld. Surprisingly, it was still in one piece. That's because Damian had left to negotiate with the Allseer, but we had no idea in what state he was in. Sonia and L told us Takeya and the other two had gone with him. We were terrified that we had lost him for good, but there was nothing we could do. We had to wait for him to return, and eventually, he did. He came back with an army of soldiers that joined us in the fight in Winterfeld. You saw them there, right?"

Sage nodded.

"I'm not sure how he managed it," Gertrude said softly. "Well, Damian can manage anything because he's so damn charming, but all this scares me a bit. When we traveled to Centerfeld for the first time many years ago, he refused to give in to Franco. Franco was dying to get him in his bed, both as a partner and as a part of an orgy." Gertrude bit her lip. "I don't knock it if that what's you like, but there was something dirty about Franco. Manipulative, and Damian is too loyal to betray Ileana just because he wanted hot, explosive sex. My point is: Damian refused then because he had nothing to lose, but what if he wasn't able to refuse in Emerald

City? What if he sold sex because he was desperate to get to you?"

Sage said nothing. Her twins were gurgling for attention.

Gertrude raised her hands. "I didn't mean to upset you. I really don't want to ruin this moment, but I know you know that Damian will do *anything* for you. That man loves you to the moon and back and possibly to the farthest reaches of the galaxy. Did you know our universe is expanding because of all the dark matter—"

"Gertrude," Sage said softly.

"Right." Gertrude finished her slushy. L was probably drunk by now. "Sorry. Can I say one more thing, though? I'm really glad you and him are back together. You guys make an awesome couple. And adorable babies."

Sage kissed her twins' noses. She smiled at them. "Thank you, Gertrude. Speaking of couples, how are you doing? After Little Man and all . . ."

Gertrude took Sage's hand. The sincerity in her eyes was even more blinding than the sun. "I'm sorry I acted like such a fucking bitch. How I made you feel like shit, even if I really didn't mean to. I was mad at the whole goddamned world for taking away the only guy who looked twice my way. God, it wasn't your fault—you're the one who told us to run. We stayed like fools because we wanted to protect you."

"I'm sorry," Sage said quietly.

"*I'm* sorry," Gertrude said again. "And to answer your question, I haven't really been looking. I'm focused on training and just dealing with all the shit here."

Sage glanced at Turtle, who was standing close by, sipping on his own slushy. He was the only one on earth who liked pineapple flavor.

"There's nothing between me and him," Gertrude stated quickly. "Nor will there ever be. He hurt me too deeply."

"Everyone has their asshole moments," Sage said. "Damian once asked me which man was desperate enough to bed me. I guess the answer was him."

Gertrude laughed. "Gosh, I remember that day in the throne room. That was intense. I honestly thought that Commander was going to kill you before we even had the chance to work with you. We had never seen another hybrid fight. Even Damian didn't like to after being exiled from Diamond City. We always knew there was something special about him, but we had no idea it was because he was a hybrid."

"How about Emma and Sally?"

"They're fine," Gertrude said with a smile. "I actually helped them pay off the apartment in the Cut District. Emma's become a seamstress, and she's making toys for a good cause. Cool, huh? I told her to make you a Star Raider plush. Maybe she'll start a new line. I don't think Louis will be against *Defenders Unite!*, do you?"

Sage didn't know. And she also didn't know how to share what Candice had told her about Venus with anyone else, even Damian later that night.

She and the crew got back at one in the morning, after watching the light show in Night Dreamers. Sage had bought Castor and Pollux these cute star pajamas with matching hats. They were warm and fuzzy, so the twins fell asleep right away. Sage had just nestled them into their crib when Damian burst through the door, calling for them.

"Darlings!" he called like an overgrown cockatoo. "Where are you, darlings?"

The babies didn't cry, though. They just started laughing, and it'd probably take forever to put them back to sleep, so Sage let Damian handle them while she went to take a shower.

There, she did the deepest thinking yet. She already knew she'd have to pay the Carat District a visit, talk to and deal with this Venus that Candice had mentioned. Actually, Venus scared Sage greatly. Since Bram's death nearly a year ago, what could she have been planning?

When Sage came out of the shower, her heart melted at the sight she found on the bed. Although Damian hadn't changed his clothes yet, he was sprawled on the pillow, his boys in each of his arms. The three of them were fast asleep.

Sage didn't want to disturb that. Thankfully, the bed was big enough for her to slip into her side undetected. She got to lie there and watch her family for a few minutes until she heard a buzz.

At first, she thought it was Damian. He always had a gazillion phones and gadgets in his pockets. But then she realized it was coming from behind her, so she turned around and saw that the Squid communicator was on.

Samson?

Sage grabbed it. Hands shaking and heart thumping, she read the message in Lolligo.

Are you safe?

Sage's first question was: Was this really Samson? There were ways to prove this, of course.

Yes. What's my favorite food?

The boiled egg.

"Samson!" Sage croaked to the communicator, nearly squealing with joy. She checked Damian and the babies—still sleeping—and escaped to the balcony for some more privacy. She stepped outside, as silently as a mouse, and completely ignored the glorious view of the training field with the Cut District in the background just to stick her face in the screen.

You found Herman and Tyrus, Samson said. *Are they eggs now?*

Yes, Sage typed ferociously. She had so much to say, but she had to prioritize her words if she was going to get the important answers first. Who knew where Samson was now, or if he was in danger himself. *I didn't know Lolligo did that.*

Well, now you do. I didn't know either until I got here.

I love you.

Sage's lip trembled. She didn't know where that had come from, but she sobbed. Suddenly, she was overwhelmed with the desire to have Samson meet her babies, carry them, and spoil them like crazy. She just wanted a big, happy family.

I love you, too, Sage.

Sage held the communicator to her chest. She thanked God for giving her yet another gift. Yes, this was a gift. Samson was well and alive somewhere. That's all that mattered right now.

Please come, she typed. *I want you to meet Castor and Pollux.*

Are they well?

Yes.

I'm not sure how, but why am I not surprised?

Sage furrowed her brows. *What do you mean?*

Your babies would be the ones to survive. Those hundred years we lived together showed me that you are something special, Sage.

Actually, it wasn't me. It was Damian's sperm.

Sage wanted to laugh, because it was true. Had she tried with anyone else, she would have been like one of those corpses in Smallfeld. Her babies wouldn't have survived.

I would love to see you, Samson said, *but I cannot. I have been in the middle of a civil war here at home.*

So much to talk about, so much to talk about—Sage didn't know what to type without writing paragraphs about the who, what, where, when, and why. Samson kept it short.

Some of us want alliances with the humans. Others complete isolation. Similar to what's happening in Diamond City. Except, while it's political for you, it's racial for us. Some Lolligo despise hybrids and don't want them anywhere near here.

Is it true that the Lolligo want to dominate us? The humans?

Yes.

Sage's heart dropped. She waited for Samson to say more, but maybe he was waiting for her reaction. She typed with shaking fingers, *You want unity.*

I want our races to get along. You and I were able to prove that it's possible.

What can I do to help?

Nothing. I think you have enough on your plate.

Lolligo hate humans.

Terrified.

There has to be something we can do.

Right now, there isn't.

Emerald City wants to defeat the Lolligo, Sage said. *Damian says they're the enemies.*

Yes. I suppose, in a sense, we are. Some Lolligo want a complete raid of Abloudor. They want to level all human settlements to the ground.

Is that why you took Wren? To learn how to defeat hybrids?

Yes.

Maybe we can do this the peaceful way?

That's what I'm trying to do. But, Sage, listen: Diamond City and everything around it is dangerous. The Outskirts have been ravaged by unknown forces and it's only going to get worse.

Ravaged by hybrids. Sage told Samson everything she knew and what Candice had told her that morning. It was a while before Samson typed back.

Don't go alone.

That's why Sage would ask Damian first thing in the morning. Right now, she couldn't dream of waking him to tell him there was a crazy bitch in the Carat District sending drugs and diseases everywhere. Carat had always been notoriously shady and cruel, but perhaps Venus was the reason why.

Sage returned to bed, but she couldn't sleep. Not when there was another fight on the horizon and she felt as weak as ever.

CHAPTER 23

Once a Kilstrong, Always a Kilstrong

"My two angels, you're fast asleep
If only you knew how much I weep
because you are so beautiful, my pride and joy
My two angels, my own two boys.
When you open your eyes, my heart leaps to the sky
I can't speak, I can't breathe, I can't even lie.
You'll grow up one day to become grand like a star
But for right now, I'll keep you just as you are.
If I could hold you forever, I would find a way
Nothing will separate me from you, or keep me away
I love you through thick and thin, no matter what you choose to be
My two angels, grow wings and be free."

age was wrong—she had fallen asleep. And she had woken up to Damian's very quiet and soothing lullaby. He was still lying next to her in the same half upright position from last night. The boys continued to sleep in his arms.

"Good morning, darling," Damian said happily. How did he look so good, even after a stiff night on the mattress? He hadn't moved from that spot. The pillow was all wrinkled, yet his hair was perfect. "How did you sleep? I'm afraid I didn't even hear you come out of the shower."

Sage smiled. "I slept all right."

"I heard you had a blast at the amusement park. I'm sorry I couldn't join you—I had a lot to take care of with Kilstrong. The situation in Mousafeld was getting a bit rowdy: The rebels there are jittery from all the delays, and they want security. I thought it was time we bring them back to Diamond City, but Kilstrong convinced me it was better to keep them there until we reconcile with Emerald City. On top of that, there have been rising cases of Red Fever throughout Diamond City. Despite Nova's treatments, there seems to be yet another strain."

Sage sat up a bit.

"I'm sorry," Damian said quickly, sitting up some more, too. Castor and Pollux finally stirred. They gave sleepy yawns and started hiccuping. That meant they were starving. "I didn't mean to wake you up with all the bad news, but we need to talk. And I need to feed my little darlings." Damian kissed their heads. "I love their pajamas. Candice and Olivia told me you got it at the park."

"I should have gotten you one, too," Sage grumbled.

"Both of us, so we'd be matching."

"I'll make sure to ask if they have those in XXXXXXXXX-Large next time."

"You mean the same size as my penis?"

"The same size of the bruise you're going to get when I smack you over the head."

Damian laughed. "I'd rather you smack other places, darling."

Sage rolled her eyes. "Think of something else other than sex. Why don't you go feed the boys?"

"If I had my plastic nipple, I could do just that."

"They don't need a plastic nipple to suck on when they have bottles. They especially don't need one attached to your man boobs, Damian—you'll scar them for life."

Damian arched a brow. "Did you just call my pecs 'man boobs'? You seemed to like them a lot the other night. You sucked my nipples so hard I thought you were trying to milk me."

"Maybe I was," Sage said. "And you're as dry as a well." She shook her head. "Useless, really."

"Forgive me," Damian purred. "But if you try other body parts, I guarantee you'll find plenty of milk."

Sage threw a pillow at his head—Damian jumped before it hit him. Cackling, he gave her the boys so he could shower at last.

Sage thought of Samson as she changed them on the table. She was so happy that she had spoken to him last night. While Lolligo were fighting each other over how to handle the humans, Samson was safe and that was all that mattered for now. Somehow, they'd work out the issues. Once Diamond City and Emerald City were on the same page, they'd deal with the Lolligo and achieve some sense of peace.

Sage convinced herself of it. She kissed her boys on the head, and finished dressing them in an airy onesie that was perfect for a hot muggy day like this one. Temperatures wouldn't plummet until next month. Diamond City would experience its first snowfall of the year, then, too. Whenever it happened, school was cancelled, businesses closed, and people celebrated.

Damian came out of the bathroom without a shirt on, and that's when Sage remembered Geoffrey's medication. As he entered the closet, Sage saw the tangle of scars on his back, which looked ten times worse than she remembered.

"Are the boys wearing white?" Damian asked while rummaging through his clothes. "I think I will, too."

"Damian, wait." Sage grabbed the tube of Rub-And-Gone from her night drawer.

"Darling, the closet's layout doesn't allow us to use the walls, but if you want a quick one, I can get on the floor."

"What the hell are you talking about?"

Damian gave her a sultry smile. He blew her a kiss.

"Oh, shut up and turn around!" Sage stepped up to him, squirting a glob of that cream onto her palm. It was cold and tingly. It was supposed to repair broken tissue in just hours. According to Geoffrey, it stung quite a bit, but it was worth it and so much better than any laser surgery out there. Centerfeld truly was a gold mine of helpful inventions.

"What is that?" Damian asked. He held still, surprisingly, and didn't fight her as she rubbed it all over his skin.

"It's for your scars," Sage said. "Geoffrey's is gone."

"Where did you get that?"

"Sonia and L."

"Of course. But I thought my scars didn't bother you."

"They don't. But why walk around with them when you can get rid of them?" Sage got every visible lash on his back. She turned him around and faced the biggest scar he had on his body. That one, Blackburn had given him many years ago. That one, Damian had carried on his chest for so long.

"Do you want me to?" Sage asked him. She felt inclined to. Perhaps it meant something to him.

"Do it," Damian said. He was grimacing, but that's because he felt the needles and pins from the cream already working on his back.

"Are you sure?"

"You're right, darling. Physical scars don't mean anything, do they?"

"They don't." Sage applied the cream to his chest, too. "But sometimes the ones who give them to us do it out of spite. And so why not have the power to erase it as well?"

Sage avoided his eyes as she said that. She also held back a wave of tears.

His mother hadn't just lashed him. She had skinned him alive.

After Sage was done with his chest, she stepped out of the closet. She put the cream aside, dried her eyes with the backs of her hands, and washed up in the bathroom. It didn't take her long to change out of her pajamas and into something comfortable. She didn't plan on leaving the suite unless Tai wanted a game of fastball, or Sword Devil was ready to "duel to the death." Sage certainly hoped not. She didn't feel any more rejuvenated than she had last night despite the sleep she had gotten.

Sage watched Damian pick up the boys. She engraved the sight of him holding them to each of his shoulders in her mind. She smiled as he walked by and kissed her forehead.

"Let's see if the suite is still in one piece, yes?"

Candice and Olivia were still knocked out because all was quiet in their rooms. The pups were the ones trotting up and down the hall, sniffing for intruders or suspicious activity, but they hadn't destroyed anything. They were simply waiting for their masters and started hopping like rabbits when they saw them.

"How did they do yesterday?" Sage asked Damian on their way to the kitchen. "They were with you through all the meetings."

"They were perfect," Damian said brightly. "They are trained beasts."

"And follow your every command."

"As should the world."

Sage rolled her eyes. She served the pups some raw meat in their bowls, which Candice and Olivia had decorated to reflect their names. With the pups feeding, Sage cracked some eggs into a skillet and cut up an onion. Damian was at the table, feeding the twins with their bottles.

"Where did you learn that lullaby?" Sage asked him. "The one from this morning. Are you a singer, too?"

"I can sing," Damian admitted. "I just don't do it."

Sage arched a brow. "Really?"

"Yes."

"Can you sing something for me?"

"I'd rather not, darling."

"What?" Sage said, gaping at him now. "Are you *shy?*"

Damian cleared his throat. "When it comes to singing? Yes. I don't like singing acapella, either—I prefer accompaniment."

"Now I totally want you to sing for me."

"Not any time soon, darling."

"Please?" Sage couldn't contain her glee. She *finally* had something to annoy Damian with, and she skipped right over to him to rub it in his face. She hugged his head, kissed his temple, and pleaded with him, but the bastard didn't budge.

"Nope," he said.

"Fine, then for my birthday," Sage said.

Damian's eyes widened. He stared at Sage, as if he had never seen anything quite like her. The look freaked her out, and Sage actually jumped, wondering if there was something in the kitchen about to attack them. The omelet was ready, so she went to tend to that, but why did Damian look like a deer caught in headlights?

"Your birthday," he croaked.

"What?"

"I-I never asked you when it was!"

"Damian," Sage said patiently. "I technically don't have a birthday—"

"Everyone has a birthday," Damian said at once. "Even if ours wasn't traditional. Just because you didn't come out of a vagina doesn't mean that you don't have a birthday."

"What is it with you and your fascination of things coming out of vaginas?"

"It's not a fascination—it's a fear."

"Yet you certainly love putting things in there." Sage laughed at her own comment.

Damian frowned. "Your birthday, Sage?"

"Month of Faith, Day 31."

Last day and month of the year. As a teenager, Sage had cherished those nights. They had been the best of her life. Blowing out candles on a cake then watching the fireworks from her window alongside Aurora? She wouldn't have traded that for the world.

"Month of Faith?" Damian said. "And you never said a damn thing last year when we were already a couple?"

"I'm going to be 120 years old," Sage quipped. "Is that really something to celebrate?"

"Of course it is."

"Forget it, Damian."

"Do you not want me to sing for you?"

Sage served their omelets without answering the question. She left the ingredients out for Candice and Olivia to use whenever they got up. She joined him at the table with their glasses of orange juice.

"Fine," she said tightly.

"What do you guys think?" Damian said to Castor and Pollux over his shoulders. "Should Dada sing for Mama?"

Sage just really wanted to see how Damian was going to eat with a pair of babies on his back, but he did. Castor and Pollux looked like two little chihuahuas waiting patiently for their owner to finish breakfast. It was crazy how they didn't cry, scream, or throw tantrums like babies usually did. Sage wondered if it had something to do with instinct, as if they could tell when parents were in the room and could detect when danger was nearby. Because there was none of that, and they were constantly fed and tended to, maybe there was no reason to seek attention.

"I only trust Dr. X."

Sage looked up. "What?"

"Dr. X," Damian said, sipping orange juice while patting Pollux's butt. "I only trust him to see the babes."

"Absolutely not."

Damian arched a brow. Sage scowled.

"No, Damian. No one is seeing our children. No one is *poking* or *prodding* our children for anything. Got it?"

"Darling." Damian leaned forward. He gave her an earnest look that Sage didn't like because that meant he was trying to convince her. "Are you not concerned?"

"Concerned about what?" Sage said.

"They are hybrid babies. Actually, they're babies of two hybrids and we have no idea what their compositions are or if they're in good health."

"*I'm* a hybrid, too," Sage said patiently. "And I grew up just fine without seeing doctors. I will not, for any second, put their lives at risk. I refuse to let any doctor or scientist lay a hand on them. They are not experiments, Damian, especially not for some crazy coot in Mousafeld."

Damian held up a hand. "I never said experiments. I just thought they should have someone monitor their growth, is all."

"No."

"And if they get sick?"

"Then we'll deal with it," Sage said angrily. She had no idea how she was going to finish her breakfast now, but she didn't like where this was going. Why was Damian mentioning Dr. X now? Did he want to clone the babies? Did he want to create an army through them? What kind of ulterior motives lay beneath those words? No, Sage refused—she wouldn't allow it—not her babies—not like Wren and then the shitstorm that had come after—

Castor and Pollux started crying. They wailed loudly, and Damian got up to rock them. But no amount of soothing got them to settle down when Sage was having a breakdown of her own at the table. The worst part was the pups joined in, barking like they never had before. She put both hands on her temples, her eyes burning as if someone had set them on fire. Damn it, what was wrong with her?

Candice and Olivia came out to see what was wrong. Damian already knew how to fix the distress, so he gave them the wailing boys, shushed the pups before they made things worse, and went over to Sage's side right away. He got down on his knees, put his hands on her arm and shoulder, and pleaded her to look at him with a silent nudge.

"Darling," he said softly.

Sage shook her head.

"Darling, please look at me. I, in no way, meant to offend you or make you uncomfortable. I was simply suggesting medical care in case the boys ever needed it, but I will do nothing unless you give me permission. We are a team, and we do nothing without consulting the other." Damian took one of her hands and kissed it. "Please look at me."

Sage didn't want to when her eyes were full of tears. She had to wipe those first with her other hand.

"I understand why you're traumatized."

"Do you?" Sage whispered. She was facing the kitchen doorway. Damian was at the far end of her peripheral right now. "Did you grow up knowing that you were made in a laboratory?"

"Yes," Damian admitted. "I knew my brother and I were not natural by any means. We were a combination of Squid and human, and I was repeatedly lashed at our church until it stuck in my brain."

Sage finally looked at him. Damian was as serious as ever. He had very light makeup on his face this morning.

"We are hybrids," Damian said quietly. "And we were tasked with killing the Overseers and driving away corruption. It was a gift, an honor, to hold Squid blood."

"I knew I was a hybrid, but I didn't know a goddamn scientist put me together like a puzzle piece in a test tube," Sage said. "Any thought that I was conceived because of . . . love . . ." She looked away again. She covered her face with her hand and held in her sob.

"Darling." Damian got up to embrace her. He brought her to his chest and whispered against her temple. "Just because you were conceived in a test tube doesn't mean your parents didn't love you."

"My mother sold Wren!" Sage cried. "Wren was the commodity! It could have been me! It could have been me stuck in a fucking laboratory my whole life! And all the happy memories with Aurora, my nieces and nephews, the pizzeria, and then you wouldn't have ever existed! I got lucky, didn't I?"

"So your mother didn't value you," Damian said, holding her tighter. "But everyone else here does. Your nieces adore you. Our comrades will do anything to ensure your safety. When they ran away from Blackburn, they came to Centerfeld to get help.

"Unfortunately, some parents are trash. Like you, my biological Squid father left me with chosen parents in the Clarity District. I will destroy the world for Cushion, who is the sweetest woman I've ever known, but my foster father was cruel. That's why I had to kill him."

Sage gasped. She looked up at him. "You . . . killed your father?"

"With my pistol," Damian said. "My first lover, Kevin, gave it to me in school when he found out about the abuse. While my brother received similar treatment, I was more rebellious, so I was punished the most. The last straw for my foster father was finding out about my relationship. My brother caught me and Kevin having sex after school one day, and he told my father everything. Of course, he was the perfect child, so my father believed him. Could you imagine the hell that was waiting for me when I got home? It took me by surprise. My father was ready with his whip, and that's when I got the gun. I shot him in the head. Cushion saw me do it. She actually took the blame for it. My brother was there when it happened, so he told the police the truth. The entire district was after me, but I had already run away and taken refuge at the small church down the street."

"I'm sorry," Sage croaked. This time, she couldn't stop or hide the tears.

"It's not your fault, darling." Damian kissed her temple. "It only took me three more years to meet you. If that's what it took for our lives to cross paths, then so be it.

"What I'm trying to say is that who our parents are or aren't can't affect the kind of life we live. It does, in a sense, but we can't let it shape us into who we are. You might not have had the ideal parents, but what difference does that make now? Regardless of how you were born or who birthed you, you would still be here with me, right? Besides . . ." Damian wrinkled his nose. "What human would want to have sex with a Squid?"

"They're asexual." Sage chuckled wryly. "They—um—spit up eggs that hatch into themselves again."

"Right," Damian said slowly. "Fascinating. Sex is more fun."

"Maybe to you, but perhaps spitting up eggs isn't so bad. What would I give to ignore the urge to tear off your pants and ride you like a bull? Maybe I'd make more levelheaded decisions."

"Darling," Damian purred. "Tell me that the next time you're having the climax of your life."

Sage laughed. "I'm only kidding." She leaned her head against his with a smile.

"Sage," Damian said. "Again, I'm sorry that I upset you. I know that your upbringing was no walk in the prairie. I understand the trauma, and I respect your decision to keep the boys away from doctors. But if we ever did need one, Dr. X is it. Definitely not any of these idiots at Heart or anything like that."

Sage nodded. "All right."

Damian pulled up a chair so he could sit next to her. Still rubbing her shoulder, he asked, "What else is bothering you?"

"I feel weak," Sage whispered. And she didn't know why. Everyone could tell there was something wrong with her, but maybe she didn't want to confirm it. She felt like such a hypocrite, claiming she didn't want to see doctors but then complaining about her health. The never-ending tiredness since the pregnancy hadn't ebbed. If anything, it had gotten worse. That last fight against X@me had totally drained her.

"While you might not have been at a hospital pushing twins out of your body, you still went through a pregnancy," Damian said to her. "The boys still used you as a source of nutrition, both when they were inside you and then when we took them out. You fed them your blood three times a day, sometimes more. That's a lot of Cells you lost. Here." Then, with his teeth, he ripped open a gash in his wrist. He offered her his blood.

"I'm not a vampire!" Sage exclaimed, shuffling back. "What is it with you and blood lately?"

"During sex it's pleasurable as hell, but this is for health reasons."

"Don't be gross, Damian!"

"But you need Cells, darling."

"Fine, but not like that." Sage grimaced. Now she felt nauseous. "Isn't my body supposed to automatically make Cells?"

"You've lost too many in a short period of time," Damian said. "Every time you bleed or get struck with Slainium, it slows you down." He took a glass and let his blood drip into it.

Sage watched in disgust as he filled it a quarter of the way and then offered it to her.

"Or would you like to inject it instead?" Damian asked.

"Inject it," she said quietly.

Damian got up to get a syringe. Because Sage had calmed down, the babies had, too. Candice and Olivia were in the hall, wondering if it was safe to come out, and Damian told them they didn't have to hide from anything. There were no secrets here.

Sage appreciated that, although she wished Candice and Olivia didn't have to witness Damian inject her with all that blood. They didn't make faces. They looked a little worried.

"You're not feeling well, Aunt Sage?" Olivia asked quietly.

"She'll be fine," Damian said, kissing the spot where he had pricked her. If only all nurses did that. "She just needs to rest."

And that was the thing: Sage couldn't rest. She hadn't even told him about Samson's messages or Venus. She decided to omit the first and get right to the heart of their problems, which was directly connected to the third wave of Red Fever spreading throughout the city.

"I need your help," Sage said.

Damian took the babies from Candice and Olivia, who went to make their breakfast. Damian turned to her and arched a brow.

"Do you require my services?" he asked silkily. "What position would you like to try tonight? I'm sure Candice and Olivia can babysit while I satiate you. *All* you, darling, whatever you want me to do. If you want my personal advice, I'd say some nice, thick, slow tongue is what you need. A face ride. And now that I mention it, we have yet to try that one—"

"I don't need sex!" Sage spat as the girls laughed. That was such a lie, but this would have been tons more amusing if she wasn't about to confront another crazy-ass hybrid in the Carat District. She told Damian everything she knew, and she saw the shift in his mood instantly.

"Venus," Damian repeated. Perhaps he wanted to know what the name felt like on his tongue. In his mind, he must have been thinking of a plant with teeth and not the Roman goddess of love because he made a face. He thanked the girls when they served him more orange juice. "And she is the source of our problems?"

"Seemingly," Sage said. "I'm not sure if she's made any moves lately, but if people are coming down with Red Fever again, then I think we need to talk to her. I wanted to go, but I don't want to do it by myself."

"Absolutely not. We'll go together. We'll bring a few of our allies, as well—"

"No, Damian. I don't want them to get hurt. If we have to fight, what chance are they going to stand against a hybrid? X@me was so powerful because he was consuming Cells. It sounds like this hybrid does the same if she goes around terrorizing people with her presence alone."

"Very well," Damian said. "We'll go pay this woman a visit. The only question is: where on earth is she? The Carat District is not a very specific location."

It was scary, and Sage wanted to know how the hell Candice and Olivia knew this, but the two girls had a location. It was a building in some gambling sector, a squat warehouse where illegal contraband and drugs were stashed until they were ready to be sold. Nobody on the outside knew that, though, because it was disguised as a storage space for old cars. The manager charged entrance fees and everything.

"We actually went on a few tours while Poppa went to talk to Venus in the back," Olivia said. "Apparently, those are cars from the Old World. From before all the Nuclear Devastation."

"Really?" Sage said.

"Yeah, they actually had wheels. Isn't that cool?"

Sage supposed it was. There was a lot to be desired in the Carat District, but like Clarity, they offered a lot of history and insight into the Old World. Sage wished she had the time to do some thorough research, to truly figure out how Abloudor, their current world, had come to be, but she hardly had a chance to breathe. Perhaps when all this was over. Once her pizzeria was stable again, she'd take a trip to all four districts and continue on her quest of exploration.

Her pizzeria.

Sage grew depressed thinking about it. As she and Damian prepared to head out because there was no time to waste, she truly wondered if her life would ever be normal again. Louis was doing all in his power to stabilize the city by making public appearances and updating everyone on their current situation, but something felt horribly wrong. Dirty. It was hard not to think of Bram and the sort of orders Louis had given to a rebel gang of Enhanced to have him executed. This had all been a ploy to get to her, so why wouldn't Louis be trying to do the same now?

Damian packed some clothes and food into a backpack. They were heading to Sage's house of old, what she liked to call her safe haven. She and Aurora had grown up there—they had shared such fond memories together there—but no one knew that's where the Optimum hailed from. It was also conveniently close to the Carat District border. Sage wished she could take the girls and the twins with her, but they were safer in the palace under the watchful eye of Damian's rebels. But just in case . . .

"I need the both of you to hang on to this." Sage gave them each a syringe filled to the hilt with her blood.

Candice's eyes widened. Olivia gasped.

"Aunt Sage!"

Damian had just replenished her with blood, and here was Sage giving it freely, but this was absolutely necessary.

"If any shit goes down," Sage said to them strictly, "you turn yourselves into Enhanced and you fight for your lives. Got it?"

"What about Louis?" Candice croaked. "What if—"

"Don't worry about him." Damian stepped into the room, backpack over his shoulder. He gazed sternly at the syringes, but said nothing about Sage's decision to equip them with power if they needed it. "Kilstrong will not be a threat to you or anyone we call an ally. First of all, he would not risk becoming Sage's enemy. Secondly, even if he did risk it, he has to eliminate all my rebels and the Lex Warriors to get to you and the boys. Thirdly, he knows he doesn't stand a chance of doing that because he has no military."

The three waited for Damian to continue. He did.

"Kilstrong has no allies left now that Blackburn has managed to turn all his soldiers against him," Damian said. "He allowed Blackburn to create a ton of Enhanced in an effort to find me and Sage in the Outskirts. He thought they were loyal to him, but they aren't. Either way, the Diamond City military is under my command. They surrendered to *me*. So I am all that Kilstrong has left." He raised his chin just a little. A seriousness fell over his face like a curtain, a reflection of Damian Sage had never seen before.

"For now," Damian added softly. "Until I renounce my title."

Sage's heart started a painful thudding in her chest. Her fists clenched involuntarily. Not because she wanted to beat up someone, but because she fought to contain her emotions toward that decision.

Good or bad? Good or bad? Good or bad?

Sage had a horribly hard time making up her mind. Ultimately, she came to a conclusion.

Neither.

"So you're not going to be Emerald City's Allseer anymore?" Candice asked quietly. "Why?"

"Because I have a family to raise, Candice," Damian said. "Your aunt and I were never meant for the political arena. We will stand down and let others do the ruling while we live the rest of our lives in peace. I think we've earned it."

But what if there was no peace? What it the rulers of both Emerald City *and* Diamond City joined forces to seize them? And once Damian renounced his title, what power would he have to say otherwise?

Sage was worried. More: She was terrified. She had so much to say, but she kept quiet because she was still internalizing the whole situation and analyzing the key details. When she pocketed her communicator (no messages from Samson today) and grabbed her phone, she saw Louis' urgent message.

It changed everything.

You're not safe. Damian is a monster. He threatened my guards with those mutts, and actually stabbed one of them in front of me. He cut off all his body parts with his sword—your sword—then set them on fire. He said they weren't even worthy enough to feed his dogs with.

Damian wrapped an arm around Sage. "Once a Kilstrong, always a Kilstrong," he said. "Those bastards can dish out punishments, but they can't take any in return, can they?"

Sage wanted to say that Louis wasn't like the other Kilstrongs, but she quickly realized that wasn't the case at all.

Louis was just like the other Kilstrongs. Sneaky and manipulative to get what he wanted. There was no refuting that, so Sage accepted it.

She had to if her family was going to survive.

CHAPTER 24

A Home to Come Back to

Sage and Damian used a private aircraft to travel to the Cut District. It was small—the size of a standard car—but it was fast, and for Heart residents only. Driving around with the royal crest turned heads in air traffic, but no one could see inside the cabin. The windows were tinted to the max, offering a privacy that Sage appreciated at the moment. She didn't want anyone staring at her or watching her watch them.

Right now, the city was in clear disarray. Electronic billboards flashed with demands from everyday citizens. The most disturbing question was: *What have you done with Allseer Agathe?!* Just like that—no mincing words. Of course, Heart continued to filter and restrict free press in times of unrest. Sage supposed she did pity Louis in that regard, because exposing the truth about Agathe wasn't easy. How the hell was he supposed to tell an entire city that Agathe had been a scheming bitch?

Once in a while, Sage did see fastball announcements. Finals between the Cut Porcupines and the Carat Lions were starting next week. Fastball season was always between the month of Light and month of Strength. Each district had a total of ten chosen teams, and only the top team from each district made it to the finals. The Porcupines always brought it home, though, so Sage always bet her money on them. She could count on the Porcupines to win by two points easily.

Sage smiled. She rested her head against the window, watching the skyscrapers fly by. Like always, it was drizzling. Was this really because of the Squids? Kind of dumb ...

Or maybe it wasn't. August had created a bio-dome, hadn't he? Maybe there was a bio-dome over Diamond City, too. Maybe the Squids had put it there and set it to raining after the humans betrayed them. Maybe they wanted to "purify" the humans, flood them out like God had the people in the bible, and now all the citizens of Diamond City were paying for it. Plantations and food sources were all indoors thanks to the never-ending drizzle. The humans here were coping, but for how much longer would they be able to do so? According to Samson, there were some pretty aggressive Squids waiting to wipe them out ...

"... Darling ... ?"

Damian was calling her. His voice was so soothing.

"Are we really going to run the pizzeria by ourselves?" Sage mumbled. "Damian, get the door."

"Darling?" Damian touched her arm.

Sage looked up. She had been asleep. Her head was heavy enough to prove it, and the look on Damian's face said something was wrong. It wasn't like her to doze off like that, especially after a full night's rest.

"Sorry." Sage rubbed her eyes. "As I mentioned before, I'm fatigued."

"Darling, we're here."

"Here" meant that they were finally at the house. It hit Sage like a bolt of lightning and she sprang right up, gazing at the little house deep in the outskirts of the Cut District that she used to call her home. City-life had become a dominant force after the Unification War, and, unfortunately, these suburban neighborhoods didn't see a whole lot of traffic. Association companies were aloof and knew there wasn't a lot of money to invest, so the houses were old and decrepit. Unlike the steel city high-risers were made of, these were all concrete and drywall.

Sage stared. For a long time, actually. She felt like she was in a time warp, seeing the house as an eighteen-year-old adolescent, not a 120-year-old woman. As the minutes ticked by, her vision got blurrier. God, why was she so emotional lately? She wasn't pregnant anymore, so it couldn't have been her hormones unless something else was going on ...

"Darling," Damian said softly, when it was time to snap her out of it. Or else they might have been sitting there the whole night. The lights weren't on, so it was awfully dark.

"Damian, I can't do this!" Sage declared, whipping her head away as if someone had slapped her. She started shaking in her seat, knees quaking like a little school girl's. "I can't!"

"Darling, look at me—"

"No, this is a bad idea—let's just stay at a hotel—"

"Sage," Damian stated seriously. He grabbed her chin, forcing her to look at him. His eyes were intense in the dark car, outlined in black like usual, but they seemed darker still. Their gaze bore into Sage, calming her a little, but not enough to stop her from crying.

Again.

"I miss her," Sage croaked. "I-I miss her, Damian ... I-I wanted to give her my Cells—turn her into an Enhanced—but she said no. She refused. She told me she wanted to die a human, but was it because she didn't want to become a monster? Like me?"

"We're not monsters," Damian said. "So get that our of your head. People have a choice to do with their lives as they please, how to live it and how to die. We have to respect those choices no matter how much the result hurts. Do you understand?"

Sage lowered her head in defeat. She took deep breaths, hands clutching the edges of her seat. She stayed like that until Damian went to fetch her on the other side. He had to pull all her body weight because Sage's legs weren't strong enough to sustain her.

Sage clung to him like a child. He smelled so incredibly good, his hair so soft on her face. She didn't want to let him go and look at the house over his shoulder. She wanted to stay like that for a great while longer. Damian carried her like a baby, scooping her up against his chest and taking her down the beaten pathway to the front door.

"I used to knock," Sage whispered, eyes full of tears. "A-and Mom would answer . . . She'd let me in, and I'd put my backpack down and plop on the living room floor to watch Defender's Unite! with Aurora."

Damian nuzzled her head. He unlocked the door as if he had done it a thousand times before and pushed it back.

Sage smelled vanilla. Spray. Someone had sprayed here the last time before vacating. She had a feeling it was Bram, maybe to cover up his tracks or the scent of all the sex he'd had with Venus. Sage's thoughts were at war with each other because of it, throwing her into a semi daze as Damian set her down and waited for her to take him through the house. While Sage gathered her wits, Damian took a look around himself. She saw him in her peripheral, his eyes completing a full sweep of the space that smelled like old beneath the fresher scent of vanilla.

There was nothing special about the house. Perhaps the new furniture, TV, and tables were from a good brand, and maybe those photographs on the walls told stories of the past, but no one would be able to tell this was the Optimum's house. Unless they recognized Sage as a child. Damian barely did.

"Darling?" he rasped, looking at a picture of a six-year-old Sage. "Is that you?"

Chubby cheeks, freckles, and pin-straight hair in a bowl cut. Yes, before hormones and the never-ending humidity of this city had set in.

Damian laughed. He took a closer look, completely enraptured by how different Sage looked. He studied her baby features with an attention only he had, the one Sage loved so much, then turned to her with a tenderness in his eyes that made her forget her troubles.

"Beautiful," he said. "You were a gorgeous child."

"I'm glad you think so."

"But you're even more gorgeous now."

Sage sighed. "Stop being a sap."

"I'm not—it's true."

"I think you were gorgeous from the moment you were a fetus."

Damian laughed. "Let's take it back a bit further than that—how about when I was still a sperm and an egg?"

Sage rolled her eyes, but she laughed, too. "Sure. It was a match made in heaven, with the chances of creating the most beautiful embryo in the world at a near perfect 99.9%."

"More like 100%."

As Damian continued looking at the photographs on the wall, Sage wandered into her room of old. The house was big enough to accommodate a family of three, so she had always had the privilege of privacy. That didn't mean she had kept to herself every night, though. Often, Aurora would come visit and they'd stay up till morning just talking. About anything. Mostly boys, *Defenders Unite!* episodes, and their mother, who, a lot of the time, wouldn't come home. It'd be up to them to pick up on all the chores.

Candice and Olivia must have stayed in this room. Everything was tidy and recently dusted. Although many Aurora descendants had used this house, there were still items that belonged to Sage. The desk that she used to do homework on was still standing strong a hundred years later. Her old novels were stacked neatly on the shelves. And Candice and Olivia must have found her bulletin board of hot guys from high school because it was on the wall. Of course, August had never made the cut, and Sage had learned an important lesson: Boys with a doll face didn't necessarily have brains.

Even the one she was with now.

Sage grinned to herself as Damian came to investigate who had caught her eye as a teenager. He tsked.

"Was that really the best you could do?" he said. He made a face at the boys, as if they were pictures of skunks instead.

"That's what there was. And what's wrong with Wyatt?"

Wyatt was a freaking hottie. Sage had forgotten how much until she was looking at him now, his sharp features with a nose he had inherited from his white mother and a perfect darkness to his skin that had come from his father. One time, he had told her his mother was of Canadian descent and his father was from South Africa. Regardless of where they were from, their genetics had come together nicely. It showed in Wyatt's entire family, all the way down to Geoffrey, who—Candice could agree—was hot. It made competitive machos like Damian super jealous.

"I didn't say there was anything wrong," Damian clarified. "I just think the lot was average."

"They were all still in puberty, Damian."

"So?"

"It makes a difference," Sage said. "They weren't fully developed."

"That doesn't matter, darling—you can tell what those features will become. When the base is mediocre, the rest of the building will be, too."

"Are you really that picky?"

Damian chuckled. "Of course. Do you think I'm attracted to just anyone? It's never just about looks—it's about appeal, too."

"You mean people who are raring to have sex with you?" Sage said.

"That's definitely a part of it."

"Well, that can't be because I didn't think about sex when I first saw you."

Damian arched a brow. His devious smile curled into a grin. "Really?"

"No," Sage said with a straight face. Her answer was a lie, of course, because *beautiful* was the first word that had popped into her head when she first laid eyes on him. Sexual fantasies had soon followed.

"Don't lie, darling."

"I'm not." Sage took a seat on the bed. She felt tired. "You were sitting in a damn palanquin. Do you think I was impressed by that? Hell no. I had my eye on Turtle the whole time."

"According to the scriptures, lying is a sin, darling. And those words you just spewed out are a clear and blatant lie. *Turtle*? Please.

You know that Gertrude is my number-one informant, and her report was very clear: All you could talk about was me."

Sage was blushing a stupid red. Damn Gertrude. Damian laughed.

"Well." He ran a hand through his hair. "Whether you masturbated to Turtle at night or not, it doesn't take away from *my* beauty, does it? Clearly, if we're a couple now. Just admit it, so we can put this behind us: You were attracted to me from the moment you laid eyes on me. Am I wrong?"

No, Damian wasn't wrong, but Sage wasn't about to admit it for the life of her. Nothing he did was going to get her to talk, either—not his kisses, his nuzzles, or his laying on top of her when they embraced.

"Why are you so hot?" Damian pulled back immediately. He touched her forehead and neck.

"Maybe because you make me hot," Sage said with a smile. "You're the best kisser I've ever met."

But this was a different kind of hot. Damian knew it, and that's why he didn't laugh. His eyebrows drew down in concern as he got off her. Sage's eyes were already closed and she was dozing off.

She wasn't sure what happened next. Damian must have changed her into some comfortable clothing and tucked her into bed, because she woke up like that. As she rubbed her eyes, he was entering the room with a bowl of soup. Oh, God, Sage hoped he hadn't overdone it on the salt again. Then she remembered Damian had become an incredible cook. His food was safe now.

"I made you soup," Damian offered. He set it on her lap as he sat down on the bed next to her. "And extracted more of my blood for you."

He had a syringe in his hand. Sage let him inject her before she started eating, just because she didn't want to be staring at that blood as she spooned broth into her mouth. Plus, she needed the strength. When Damian finished, he sat there and watched her.

"This isn't bad," Sage complimented. "At least you're learning something."

Damian didn't smile. The worry he had inside was eating away at him, making him fidget with the rings on his fingers. He had them all on today, except for the Diamond City one. Sage wondered what he had done with it since that horrible night on the *Mistress*. Sage had had every right to reject him then, but she felt bad about it now. She certainly wanted to make amends, even if wedding plans were far from Damian's mind.

"Sage," Damian said when she finished her soup. "Darling . . . we need to talk about this. About your condition."

Damian was treading cautiously, because Sage already knew what he was going to suggest. He didn't beat around the bush, either.

"If you don't improve by the end of the week, I'm taking you to Mousafeld to see Dr. X."

Damian tensed. He waited for her to yell and start crying. Sage didn't. Not because she didn't have the strength, but because she was going to acknowledge that there was something seriously wrong with her. *Really* wrong with her. The pregnancy was long over, so why did she still feel like she was dying? Why was she getting weaker every day?

"We're going to take care of this situation with Venus," Damian went on, "and then we're going straight to Mousafeld."

Sage settled back in the covers. They smelled clean, the polyester soft. She absolutely hated satin. Damian loved it because he was a silk god.

"Fine," she concurred quietly.

Pleased with her answer, Damian didn't have to fight her anymore. He took her empty bowl and went to clean up in the kitchen. He also showered. Sage didn't fall back asleep right away. She had the communicator in her hand, and decided to tell Samson about her sickness.

I'm sick, she typed. *I've never been sick. Is it normal?*

It always took him a while to answer when he didn't have the communicator in reach. God only knew what he was going through in his city. Sage wasn't in any rush because she had Candice and Olivia to talk to. She also got to see Castor and Pollux, both of who were ready to sleep. They gurgled when they recognized her on the screen.

"They're so beautiful," Sage complimented as Damian finally joined her in bed.

"Look at who they have as a father, darling," he purred. "Of course they're beautiful."

Sage let him take over the cooing. As soon as she curled into his side, eyes on her precious boys as they laughed with every stupid thing Damian did, she fell asleep again.

The next morning, Damian got up early to make breakfast and get ready for the day. When Sage woke up, she was alone in bed with the communicator's screen lit up on the nightstand. Sage nearly sprang to her feet to grab it—she reached over, and with shaking hands, she read what the message said.

That's not normal, Sage. We don't catch bacteria and viruses.

Sage's heart started pounding. Her breathing got very tight. She sat up some more as another message came in.

It could be because of the pregnancy, but you said it was getting worse.

Yes. Sage gulped. Then she wrote, *Do Lolligo ever get fatigued like this?*

No. The only time Lolligo show signs of fatigue is when they're about ready to reproduce. That's because their bodies are dying and ready to give way to new life.

Sage's head was spinning. That was its attempt at making sense of what Samson was saying and relating it to her own condition. Clearly, Sage didn't reproduce like Squids did, but did having babies have something to do with her deteriorating state? She hadn't forgotten Fido's fate, how the mother had lain aside and allowed her own pups to eat her.

Is that because Fido had known she was going to die?

Sage's eyes filled with tears. Fear, true fear like she had never felt in this room—in her life—struck her like lightning. She had spent so many nights here talking to August, watching chaos descend upon the district as Overseer Callus ordered the military to quell rebellions, and formulating escape plans with her sister, but none of that compared to now, when she contemplated her own death and what it'd mean.

Not just for the city. But for her family. Damian, her babies, and Candice and Olivia.

Don't worry, though, Samson said. *You've given birth and used a lot of your blood to feed the babes. Keeping drinking the Warlord's.*

But why couldn't Sage calm down? Why did she nearly fall when she got out of bed and have the sudden urge to cry because something felt so horribly wrong?

"Darling, are you awake?" Damian called from the kitchen.

Sage went to the bathroom to compose herself. She washed her face, brushed her teeth, changed her clothes, and convinced herself that she actually felt a bit better today. She didn't feel as fatigued as last night, and she tried with all her might to look at the positive side of all this. Perhaps Samson was right and this was just a phase. She didn't reproduce like Squids, so why would her body die? Wasn't she indestructible?

Sage's train of vicious thoughts got cut short when she entered the kitchen. She got quite the shock when she saw the full-fledged breakfast ready for her consumption: eggs, hash browns, toast, sausages, and juice. Damian must have had food delivered that morning, because there was no way these perishables had lasted that long in the refrigerator. There were ways to preserve items for years, but this looked too fresh to have come from a sealed container. It wasn't just the food, either—Damian had another dose of blood ready for her. With the way he moved and from the set determination in his eyes, he looked like a mother taking care of her children.

"Damian?" Sage pressed. She hadn't sat down yet. "What bug bit you?"

"We're going to get this over with," Damian said, taking her arm and finding a vein. He did it with such gentleness and precision that Sage never felt the needle. Perhaps he could be a nurse, too. "This thing with Venus."

Just as Sage pictured Damian in scrubs, she thought of a vicious woman with the facade of a tiger. She also remembered with painful vivacity how Candice had described seeing her on top of Bram in this very kitchen. Sage's stomach twisted itself into a knot, but Damian's words kept her attention.

"We're going to Mousafeld after this, darling," Damian said, eyes boring into hers, hypnotizing her to comply. "I can't stand to see you like this, and I don't know if this is normal."

Sage said nothing. Despite the number of rebuttals at her disposal—*What the hell would Dr. X know? Samson said I'll be fine. And didn't you say we were waiting until the end of the week?*—she couldn't argue. She sat down at the table and looked at her food. Then she turned her head and looked at Damian.

"How are you feeling today?" he asked.

"A little better," Sage admitted. "But…maybe you're right. Maybe it'd be a good idea to get checked out."

Damian held her hand. That meant Sage only had her left to start on those hash browns. They were her favorite breakfast item. "I know you don't like doctors," he said sincerely. "But I swear to you Dr. X would never do anything to hurt you or use you in a manner that you don't consent to. He would never take your blood to create more Enhanced or sell it on some online market."

"I know," Sage said quietly. "He really respects you. He told me once that he looked up to you during the Unification War. Is he from the Clarity District?"

"He is," Damian said. "We met in school, where we talked about ideas of resistance. We became a couple not long after that. It was a bold move, especially in Clarity, but we were daring—"

Sage nearly jumped out of her chair. She stumbled away from him, but quickly caught her balance. She stared at him, shocked, because for the first time since she had met Damian, she finally learned who Dr. X was.

"Kevin?" she whispered. "And you never thought to tell me that was your first lover from Clarity?"

"Would it have made a difference?" Damian said. "We were

experimenting at that age. We weren't even really in love with each other. We just wanted sex and dreamed of running away to a better world, one that didn't exist. So if we wanted it, we had to make it a reality. Me, especially, since I killed my father and became a wanted man. Kevin went on to finish school while I stayed hiding at a church for three years. I was too devastated and demoralized to think about fighting, so I thought of fashion instead. And when I couldn't even get that, well, you know that I had to do something, so I joined the resistance—"

"Are you *fucking* kidding me, Damian? WHY DIDN'T YOU TELL ME?!"

"Again," Damian said patiently, "what difference would it have made, darling? Kevin and I acknowledged that we weren't truly in love with each other. He went on to have a wife and kid of his own, but he never stopped respecting me and my goals. He swore to always stick by my side, and he has. He has never betrayed me, nor I him, and we have remained allies to this day. After we were exiled from Diamond City, so many of the rebels let go of their past lives. It was the only way to survive the new one that awaited us in Mousafeld. We don't think of the past, because it's too painful."

"I'm your wife!" Sage yelled. "And you're always prying into my 'past', so why can't you come clean and tell me everything about yours? You didn't tell me about Cushion, Dr. X, or your plans with Agathe, but more than that: You didn't tell me you were a hybrid! What else are you hiding from me, Damian?"

"Is that what you call it?" Damian asked calmly. " 'Hiding'? I don't 'hide' anything. I've never lied to you. All these new tidbits you're learning about me is natural. We've each lived a hundred years. I don't know about you, but that's a lot of stories to tell. Now you know about Kevin, but let's not forget about Wyatt—how many times did you have sex with him?"

Sage threw a knife at him.

Damian caught it. "You see? There're things you haven't told me, too. Do you expect me to believe he was just a friend when you wear his class ring everywhere?"

"*Wyatt,*" Sage panted aggressively, "wasn't a lover of mine. And this ring was a gift from Geoffrey that holds a lot of meaning—it is a memento from the times of the Unification War, so it has nothing to do with how badly I want to have sex with him. I told you about August—"

"Sorry, darling, but no, you didn't. I figured it out and asked you about it later. You knew damn well we were going to Wolfeld, and you never said a damn thing about being past lovers. Why? *Because it didn't matter.* It was in the past and no longer applied to the present. And if you want to continue playing this little game, how about the goddamn fact you never told me you loved pizza or owned a restaurant?"

Sage clenched her fists to stop herself from pummeling him, but she came to the painful conclusion that he was right. Maybe. But that didn't mean she had to stand here and take it, so she was about to beeline for her room to get ready, but Damian caught her like a fastball, holding her still.

"Admit that I'm right," he said.

Sage's lip trembled.

When Damian kissed her, Sage tried to bite him. He let her clamp on to his lips, because he didn't mind a wild, bloody make-out session before breakfast. Sage had to pull back because she was still angry with him and didn't want to entertain his desires.

"Your mother," Sage said. "Your real one. You knew she was the Emerald City Allseer, but you never told me anything."

"First of all, I never met her," Damian said. "Secondly, I had no interest in Emerald City. My concerns were you, the babes, and our situation *here*, in Diamond City. Understand?"

"Fine, what about Ileana and Phoebe? Did you know that Phoebe wasn't your blood daughter?"

Maybe Sage was crossing a humongous line with that question, and it sounded so dirty when asked in that tone, but she wanted the answer. Damian didn't hesitate to give it.

"I did," he admitted. "I knew she wasn't mine. I knew that, as hybrids, we couldn't reproduce unless it was with each other. At least, that's what my brother and I speculated. After the Unification War, he slept with a lot of women and realized he couldn't conceive. Although we weren't friends nor talking to each other much, he brought it up in one of our arguments. This was before my rebellion, when I realized he wanted the Optimum solely to reproduce. He thought that's what I wanted, too, so he was trying to get me to do his dirty work and find her on his behalf."

"So reproduction was just a speculation?"

"Yes," Damian said. "As it has been for a lot of hybrids."

Smallfeld. Right. But that horror show didn't deter Sage's train of thought.

"Did you want me because I was the Optimum?" she asked him. "Because I was a hybrid?"

"Darling." Damian held her cheeks. He gazed lovingly into her eyes. "I fell in love with you long before I realized what you were. Did you honestly think I thought you were the Optimum. Some girl with horrible hair in a tattered jacket—?"

Sage hit him and Damian laughed.

"Is it not true, darling?"

"Asshole!" she hissed at him.

"But your hair is much better now," Damian said brightly. "And you haven't worn that tattered jacket since. Thank God."

Sage turned from him and crossed her arms with a huff.

"But I didn't know you were the Optimum, darling," Damian continued, swinging to her front again. "I thought the Optimum had already moved on with her life. I certainly didn't think she'd be happening across my camp a hundred years later. So the answer is: I loved you way before I found out what you were. And I still do. I'm not sure I will ever stop loving you."

Sage glared at him.

Damian chuckled nervously. "Why are you looking at me like that?"

She wasn't. If only he could see what she truly felt like inside. How Samson's words about her potential fate swirled around inside her like vomit in a toilet. It took everything she had to keep it to herself. There was no point in speculating about it. They were going to see Dr. X regardless, so what did what-ifs and maybes matter now?

That's what got her through breakfast. Sage ate everything Damian had served her. His cooking had definitely improved.

"I love you, too." Sage said to Damian, although she was looking at the hash browns. She smiled. She supposed she really did love them as well. There was something about the crunchy exterior with the soft, salty potato interior that sent her taste buds soaring.

"I know you do, darling." Damian beamed. "I know this sounds trivial, but you have cured all my scars. I looked at my back last night, and there is not a single blemish anywhere. I can be a nude model now."

Sage glared at him. Damian laughed.

"Wouldn't you want to see me on magazine covers?"

"I see you in real life and that's enough."

"True." He gazed dreamily at her. "That's all that matters, isn't it? And I will make all of your wonderful dreams come true. Whatever you want. Whatever you desire. Whatever you need to raise our children into handsome men. After so much fighting, you deserve it."

Sage looked up at the wall. There was a painting of a castle there. She wasn't sure if it was Heart, because Heart hadn't existed a hundred years ago. Perhaps seeing those spires every school morning had inspired her to want more than just ... this. So she had fought for it, just like Damian had.

"I'm sorry." Sage choked on her laughter. Orange juice dribbled from her lips.

Damian arched a brow. He was sipping coffee. "Something amusing you, darling?"

"Dr. X? Are you for real?"

"What?"

"*He* was your lover from high school?" Sage choked again. It had just finally hit her. "That guy is creepy! Wyatt beats him by a landslide."

"I don't think he's creepy. Don't be so quick to judge."

"He's creepy, Damian. He has huge eyes that look like a pair of x-rays or something and he's just . . . ugh."

"Yes," Damian agreed. "But you haven't seen his penis."

Sage laughed her head off. She shoved at Damian, who laughed, too.

"Next time I see Cleo, I'll make sure to ask for a picture of her father's penis so I can see what it looks like." Sage shook her head. "Don't they all look the same anyway?"

"No," Damian said honestly.

Sage sighed pleasantly. If only all her mornings were just like this moment. That's why she clung to it with all her might.

CHAPTER 25

The Carat District

Maybe because they were about to head to the Carat District. Sage had only been there a handful of times as a tourist and sightseer. She wasn't one for casinos, dog races, and gambling (unless it was for fastball), so her visits revolved around the extraordinary hotels, parks, and museums.

She had stayed at the Golden Rail, a unique hotel featuring architecture from the Old World. The century was apparently mid 2000s, just a few hundred years before radiation had wiped out most of humanity. The hotel still stood as it had many years ago, with its cathedral-like structure and round pointed roofs. Because there had been a lot of French settlers in this area, which was known as Quebec back in the day, its original name was "Fairmont Le Château Frontenac". It overlooked a river that used to be called the St. Lawrence River, and was walking distance from a cathedral of old. The area was beautiful and historical.

The same went for the parks, a lot of which had been turned into zoos to preserve the only bit of wildlife Diamond City fostered, and the museums, like the kind Candice and Olivia had visited when seeing Venus. So much to learn. It had been some time since Sage was interested in the past.

People from the Carat District dressed differently, too. Men were in suits and jackets while women wore more traditional dresses and boots.

Unlike the Color District, no one liked to stick out here. No matter the area, notorious gangs were always surveying the streets and secret dealings went on in alleyways. Now that Sage and Damian had crossed the border and were cruising around on ground level, she could smell where there was the highest probability of trouble.

On their way to Venus' warehouse, they passed by a hospital. There was a long line of ambulances racing around the back, transporting people on stretchers. While some looked like the victims of gun violence, too many of them were on ventilators.

As Damian kept driving, Sage noticed a few people sitting on the sidewalks, resting against the sides of buildings or trash cans. Their coats were too shabby and dirty to have been cleaned recently, and the dark splotches on their skin said that they had seen better days. Beneath the light drizzle, they wobbled around like zombies. One guy was throwing up into an open bin.

When they passed by the liquor store, Sage noticed a gang standing off in the corner, in the dark spot between the dumpster and emergency staircase. She counted five. A pair of women walked by, having just picked up some booze, and were stopped by one of the grinning gangster men.

Damian was about to go now that the light was green, but Sage stopped him immediately. She had her sword, but Damian wasn't going to let her get her hands dirty.

"Stay, darling," he said.

Sage didn't, of course. She got out to watch Damian approach the gang getting ready to have the rape-fest of their lives. There weren't enough officers in the district to patrol low-key crimes like this, taking place in near darkness and away from public view. So the white battle armor that was so prominent in the Cut District was nonexistent here. People treaded cautiously, but some never made it out with their lives. Faces peered out from those dark windows from as high as the thirtieth floor on some complexes, but who was going to call for help?

Damian had his pistol, and he finished the gang quickly with a gunshot to the head. He didn't even bother hiding it. Like an executioner, he just blew their brains out and allowed the women to escape, unscathed.

The both of them were in awe that a hero had come out of nowhere to rescue them. A night of picking up some rum for their party later could have ended in death. They embraced Damian, fearing for his safety, because the Feather Boys' friends would soon be looking for revenge.

"Are you ladies all right?" Sage asked the women as they rushed by her.

"Yes." They both made haste before they were seen. "Thank you!"

"Hey!" shouted someone from down the street.

Sage looked over and saw more roaches scurrying out of their nooks. It looked like the Feather Boys had lookouts, and these three gangsters were twice as big with bulging muscles. It showed through their button-ups and jackets.

Like a domino effect, everyone on the street scrambled away from them. In fact, the entire block cleared out. Sage soon saw why: The guy in the middle was holding a bazooka. Sage hadn't seen one of those since episode 23 of *Defenders Unite!*, and she couldn't begin to wonder where this gang had gotten one.

Could this be Venus' doing? Distributing weapons and funding chaos?

"Eat this, asshole!" bazooka-guy fired. A missile came flying out of that long tube.

"Damian!" Sage cried. She made for him, but stopped when she realized that Damian had this under control.

Damian took cover behind a mailbox as the missile smashed into the sidewalk. The boom was deafening and the explosion rattled Sage's bones. Fire and smoke erupted before her eyes, debris raining down on the entire street like rain. Damian had just barely dodged that. Sage couldn't see him past the crater that had nearly taken out their car, but at least there were no casualties. Everyone had done right in running as soon as these gangsters had shown their faces.

Sage rushed them. For her, it was easy taking out a trio of humans. She did it quickly, then gazed down at their bodies, at the rocket launcher on the sidewalk.

Primitive, Samson would say. After Nuclear Devastation, humanity had sought other means of fighting in wars without the use of such destructive weapons. At the end of the day, these weapons caused more damage to innocent civilians and buildings than to opponents themselves. Squids were powerful beings, and so were hybrids . . . so were Enhanced.

They were perfect for war.

"W-whoa!" someone croaked.

Sage looked up and found two tiny faces behind a dumpster. Trained to survive, these kids had taken cover just as quickly as everyone else. The sight of a bazooka was enough to make anyone cower.

"Are you like some super woman or something?" the little girl breathed wondrously.

"And is that super man?" the little boy peered at Damian, who ran over to Sage at last.

He still looked perfect, even after evading a missile. There wasn't a single hair out place or a speck of debris on his clothes. He looked ready to strut down a runway. He really didn't belong in the Carat District, which was why he was such a sensation among the population. People peered out of windows and from behind doors to see who their heroes were.

"Darling, are you all right?" Damian checked her, but Sage shook her head.

"I'm fine, Damian." Sage got closer to the children. Damian put away his pistol. "Where are your parents?" she asked the boy and girl.

"We don't have any," the little girl squeaked. "We're from the Carat Orphanage over there."

"What are you doing out here by yourselves?"

"We, um . . ." The little boy swayed on his feet. "We wanted candy, so we snuck out. The caretakers don't know that one of the windows is busted and the pane can be removed."

"You know it's dangerous to be out at night, right?" Sage said.

"We know," the little girl said sincerely. "But we really wanted some candy. One of our friends is being adopted, and we wanted to make her feel special."

"Here." Sage gave them Louis' credit card. She couldn't believe she still had it after all this time, but it was serving her beautifully now. "Go to the discount store and buy as much food and candy as you can. Then go back to the orphanage and tell the caretakers that Allseer Louis will let you buy anything you guys need."

The little girl gasped. "Even the new Star Raider toys that are coming out? I heard they're starting the series again!"

"Nah, the Shadow King is the coolest!" the little boy exclaimed.

"They should totally be together."

"Ew—gross!"

"It's not gross!" the little girl argued.

"Come on." The little boy grabbed the little girl's hand. "Let's go back before we're caught. The police is coming."

"Thank you for the card, ma'am!" the little girl called to Sage. "And, sir!" she said to Damian. "You're really good-looking!"

The two disappeared into the alley.

Damian chuckled. "Spirited, aren't they? I just hope they didn't see the bodies." He turned to the three corpses on the street. The Feather Boys' reinforcements, all decapitated.

"Is this really the norm here?" Sage asked quietly. She still had the sword in her hand. "Then things have gotten worse, not better. Look at how long it's taking the police to respond to a fucking missile going off. I'll have to talk to Louis . . ."

Damian wrapped an arm around her. "I will do that. Trust me.

As soon as we get back to Heart, I'll make sure he fixes up all these districts."

Sage looked up at Damian. Little fires were still burning from where the missiles hit, but they'd go out eventually. What lit up even more were Sage's eyes.

Damian furrowed his brows. He had never seen a look like that in her before, clearly, because Sage had never given him one like this.

"Please be the Emerald City Allseer," Sage said softly. "Please."

"Darling, we've already talked about this—"

"I don't give a fuck what we've already talked about. I'm telling you again: I want you to be the Allseer. I want you to have the power, because things are not going to get better, Damian. You know better than anyone that all those council members are thugs who thrive on all this bullshit. That's what Venus does: She creates chaos because the government pays her. *Bram*, head of the Private Guard, paid that bitch to cause trouble. She had her sights set on the Allseer, and God knows what would have happened if she had ever wormed her way into Marchello's ranks. She could still worm her way into Louis'."

"And that's why we're going to stop her." Damian held her face. "Right—?"

Sage smacked his hands away. "You don't get it, do you? How many Venuses are out there, Damian? How many in Emerald City, too? If your mother was a nightmare, then it's ten times worse over there than it is here and people need a righteous leader, and I know you are, Damian. Despite what a monster you were in Mousafeld or what other people say about you, I know you'll do the right thing. I know you'll also keep Louis in line, in case he gets any batshit crazy ideas."

"Sage—"

"Do it for me," Sage said. "Please. And I'm not asking you to abandon our children—you can take them with you. *I'll* go with you."

"But what about Candice and Olivia?" Damian said angrily. "What about your pizzeria?"

"Candice and Olivia are old enough to choose where they want to go. If they want to stay in Diamond City, then they stay. If they want to come with us, then they can do that, too. As for my pizzeria, I can always start another one in a new city." Sage smiled. "I think Emerald City is in need of good pizza. Desperately. And not that shitty stuff that Dough sells in Mousafeld, either—*my* pizza. Number-one in Diamond City. Five fucking stars."

The wheels seemed to be turning in Damian's head. A slow smile spread across his lips. He opened his mouth to speak, but Sage cut him off again.

"Marry me," Sage said.

Damian blinked at her. He looked a bit dumb with his mouth half open like that. The sirens approaching them from afar were getting louder.

"I'm not getting on my knees for you, but I want you to marry me."

Damian's eyes softened at last. "Darling . . . we don't have to. I've learned that marriage is just a show. What matters is our dedication to each other, whether a paper says that we're together or not. Plus, you already referred to yourself as my wife this morning."

"I want it official," Sage said.

"Why?" Damian asked her gently.

"Because I want to be with you forever, Damian. Fuck, isn't it obvious?"

Damian was still staring at her like she was an alien. Maybe this next part would snap him out of it.

Sage didn't have a ring, but she did have the Soulmate Bracelet that Cleo had given her. Sage hadn't worn a bracelet since using her Slainium ones on the Squids in the Outskirts, and she wasn't going to resume now. This bracelet was too girly for her. The charms she had bought for Damian were pretty badass, though.

"All right," Sage said, sheathing her sword and taking out the bracelet. She stepped over to him. There were bodies on the floor and a crater just a block away, but everything else in that moment ceased to exist. Especially for Damian.

"I got you ten charms," Sage went on. "You've got one for fashion, makeup, cigars, milkshakes, swords, *The Rainbow in Me*—they actually had a charm for that show—the Diamond City flag, dogs, twin babies, and a heart." She smiled at him. "Because even when you didn't have one, you still did."

Damian was shaking. Sage clipped the bracelet on his wrist. It was a perfect fit. She was super happy with her accomplishment. Damian was so overwhelmed that he fell to his knees. Actually, he prostrated himself at her feet like the drama queen he was.

But this was no act. This was pure, unbridled emotion. When the police finally arrived, they ran over to them immediately. One hunched over Damian and asked, "Sir, are you all right?!"

"I don't think my husband is well, no," Sage said to them. "You might have to take him to a hospital."

Damian was sobbing so loudly he might have lost a limb. He clutched his head, still curled into that tiny ball of his, and rocked back and forth on his feet.

"Sir?" said one of the officers. He was in that white battle armor, but he wasn't safe around Damian. "Come with us—"

Damian swatted the officers away—hard. Then he looked up at Sage. Eyes all red and runny, and with his lip trembling viciously, he gritted his teeth. He wanted to speak, but he couldn't.

"Ma'am, do you know what happened here?" asked another officer as more arrived to investigate the scene.

Sage had to explain, because Damian was still picking himself up from the ground. He took deep breaths and wiped his eyes. His hands were still shaking. Actually, he was still sobbing.

"The Emerald City Allseer?" the officer gasped, when Sage told him exactly who Damian was. If his helmet were transparent, Sage would see his wide eyes. If she could read minds, she'd hear, *This crying dolt is an Allseer?* "S-seriously?"

"Yes," Sage said. "He's just undercover, inspecting the streets of Diamond City. So far, we both agree Allseer Louis has quite a bit of work to do."

Sage was in conversation with the officers for a long time. She didn't have to reveal who she was because Damian's status was enough to get the officers to back off. Or else, they probably would have spent a long night at the station answering more questions about why they were taking the law into their own hands. Sage found that ridiculous when the police here sucked. Nevertheless, it was clear that average people didn't stand a chance against these gangs.

Sage had to help Damian back into the car. He wasn't capable of driving at the moment, so Sage took control. Every time she glanced at him, she saw him looking at his bracelet. He used his fingers to touch each of the charms.

"Pretty accurate, isn't it?" Sage said happily.

Damian looked up at her. His eyes were full of new tears. He had cried more today than Castor and Pollux had in their lifetimes. "Yes," he whispered.

"It was easy. Picking out the charms, I mean. There was a store full of them at the Royal Amusement park."

"Yes," Damian said.

Sage patted his leg. "You see? I pay attention, too. Like when you fix your eyes, you always do the left one first even though you're right-handed—"

"Yes, Sage."

Sage looked at him.

Damian looked like he was about to blow up with emotion. He did, actually—he broke down and sobbed like he never had before. Sage had seen him cry plenty of times, but never like this. His face turned red and he started wheezing. It sounded like someone was torturing him.

So dramatic, Sage chuckled to herself. She had to fight her own tears.

But Damian's tantrum went beyond drama. This was a display of true, unbridled happiness after a lifetime of hell and suffering. After so many instances where, perhaps, living had not been worth the pain. At long last, Damian had reached his light at the end of the tunnel.

Damian held his face and shook his head. Sage had to rub his shoulder to calm him down. Eventually, Damian composed himself enough to wipe his eyes and say, "I'll marry you. I'll marry you, Sage, my darling, my life, my love, and my heart itself."

They actually applied for a marriage license on the way to the warehouse. It was quick, because there was no one in the clerk's office at the time, and all they had to do was show ID and sign a few papers. The license would take some time to be processed and become official, but that was fine. Damian still wanted the wedding ceremony of a lifetime, and he said he'd get on it as soon as they were done with all the Diamond City drama. The biggest one was coming up now.

It made sense that the closer they got to the warehouse, the more isolated the district felt. The Gambling Den was supposed to be famous, but there weren't a whole lot of people out on the streets. The rain never stopped, destroying wayward papers and vomit bags in the corners. Even the casinos were dim, signs blinking lazily. Guards stood by, but all the guests were already inside and out of sight. Sage could hear the bells and whistles from within, as well as collective groans from players who had lost a shit-ton of money. It was easy to pull up on the sidewalk, but this sector wasn't like the one they had come from.

Sage and Damian were drawing tons of attention here. Not only were they dressed differently, but it was super quiet and desolate. Maybe Sage could blend in a bit better with her drabby look, but Damian was in a glossy leather jacket with silver pants and boots. He looked like a black gemstone in a bucket full of weathered rocks. He had red eye shadow, too, which he had fixed on the way here. He didn't look like a drunken fool, so everyone knew he was here for some kind of business. The guard in front of Venus' warehouse couldn't stop staring.

"Come on, darling." Damian handed her the sword again.

Sage shook her head. "I can't take it. That sword is yours."

"And if you have to fight, you intend on doing so with a dagger?"

And a gun. Sage didn't feel right taking away Damian's main weapon. She was so foolish for having lost hers.

"I will make sure to gift you another." Damian kissed her head. "But for right now, I would feel better if you used yours instead. Mine," he amended.

Right. So Sage took the sword and strapped it to her back. For Damian, it was easy to hide his weapons. Regardless, they wouldn't be getting inside the warehouse without a check-in, but Damian didn't plan on being very discreet.

He entered with a bang, shooting the security guard in the ankle then pushing his body aside. The cashier dropped to the floor and hid behind the front desk while customers scurried behind the cars on display in the middle of the room.

Candice and Olivia were right: the cars had wheels. Sage had only seen them in pictures before. She managed to read "Toyota Corolla", a model from the year 2001 that had come from a country called Japan. She wondered what it was like to drive one of those.

It wasn't like Sage to remain idle amidst a struggle, but she really didn't need to do much. Damian took care of anyone who might be a threat.

More security came out to see what was going on, but they weren't expecting an Enhanced—much less a hybrid—to barrel his way inside.

"Sir, please," said one of the sensible security guards, hands up. He was probably stalling for time, ready for Venus' Enhanced to come down from their highs or card games to take a look at who was paying them a visit.

"Venus," Damian said. "I want to see her."

Her lackeys were already filing into the room, weapons raised and pointed. All were Enhanced. Privileged and with plenty of power to boot, their confidence seeped into the room. That was until they assessed their opponents and realized they weren't up against a couple of drunks who had wandered in here by accident.

"Well, well," drawled the guy at the head of the group. He had long hair like Damian, blond a pretty boy who liked to get down and dirty with whoever was willing. He didn't have a shirt and his zipper was untied, but he didn't care about formalities when he was

Venus' lapdog. He had black lines coming out of his eyes, a signature feature from whatever gang he affiliated with.

"What is this handsome hunk of a man doing here?" Lapdog purred, looking Damian up and down. "Didn't care for the cars of old and decided for a bit more excitement? The afterparty doesn't start until midnight, darling."

"I want to see Venus," Damian said again. "Or I cut the penises of your partners over there and you won't ever be having fun with them again."

Lapdog stared hard at Damian. But no matter how hard he tried, he just wouldn't be seducing him. Unfortunately for him, there wasn't much flesh to ogle at, either. He'd have to use his imagination when it came to Damian's body and what might lie underneath his clothes. Sage didn't care for the inspection, but she didn't intervene if Damian was building momentum.

"Would you truly be so cruel, darling?" Lapdog said, more serious now.

"Don't call me that," Damian spat. "The only one who's allowed to is my wife." He waved Sage over. "Come here, darling. I don't think these buffoons have ever seen the Optimum in person."

If anyone had been ready to insult Sage's average looks, they quickly shut their mouths when they contemplated the possibility of this being the girl who had united their districts. Thanks to her, they received plenty of funds and goods from the Allseer, who made sure to provide some care for even the lowest and filthiest of districts. The gangs here would have died out quickly otherwise. Without funds, there'd be no shit to buy and sell. No one liked police in white armor, but everyone liked money and handouts. Add the tourism, and that was the only reason this district still functioned.

"Optimum," Lapdog said. His eyes cut her up like a pair of knives. He licked his lips, as if he'd like nothing more than to taste what Sage had in between her legs.

If Sage thought that Damian was possessive and promiscuous, then he was nothing compared to this guy. So many red flags popped up in Sage's head that she got dizzy. Whereas Damian was caring despite all his sexual innuendos, this guy couldn't think of anything else. That's what he lived and breathed for. That's what his guys behind him all yearned for every second of the day.

"I'll prove it to you," Sage said. "Look at me like that again, dipshit, and you'll lose your goddamned eyeballs. I'm a woman, not a piece of meat for you to stick your dick into, and you'll treat me as such. Or did mommy never teach you to be a true gentlemen?"

"Holy *shit*." Lapdog laughed. "The mouth on this one!" He looked at Damian. "And *she's* your wife? No wonder you don't need anyone else—"

Sage didn't need a sword when she had a dagger. The dagger always came in handy in moments like these, when all she had to do was fling it and watch it hit Lapdog's eye with a satisfying *shleck*. When his guy friends all realized their god had just lost an eye, they moved for their weapons, but Sage already had the sword drawn.

"Don't move," she said to them. "Or I'll cut you all down so fast you won't even know what hit you. Your friend over there already has Slainium moving fast through his body, so one of you should tend to him if you want him to live. As for the rest, I need you to take me to Venus."

"FUCK THIS BITCH!" Lapdog howled. "KILL HER!"

Funnily enough, no one moved. Only two of them edged toward Sage, as if gravitating toward the newest and biggest bully in the playground. Lapdog knew how to work his dick, but he wasn't very moving as a leader. Especially one who had lost his eye.

"Didn't you hear me?!" he continued howling. "Kill her!"

No matter how Sage cut it, this guy was a clear menace to society. She knew that the other men huddling beside her weren't much better, but at least they weren't following through with his orders. They knew when they were outmatched, and so they stood by and did absolutely nothing as Damian finished Lapdog with a gunshot to the head.

Besides, this was a raid. Sage already knew that nothing good came out of those rooms in the hallway, ones she peered into as Damian led them through one of the most dangerous hideouts in the city. It was true—orgies and prostitutes were the least of it—Sage saw the stacks and stacks of reddish powder, the Stars drug that had nearly killed Damian in Mousafeld. She saw the makeshift laboratory in another room, probably where other drugs and diseases were tested before distribution. A set of double doors at the end of the hallway said there was a secret parking lot in the back. What sort of people came by on a daily basis, picking up orders and readying for mayhem? Hadn't one of those people been the Private Guard at one point?

"S-sir," stammered one of the men behind Sage. He was trying to get Damian's attention. "Please, wait. Let us explain."

"There's nothing to explain." Damian barged into every room. Anyone who tried to attack got a bullet in the face. There were plenty of Enhanced at work here.

"S-she's not here—Venus—there's something wrong!"

Sage didn't have a clue what they were babbling about until Damian stopped dead in his tracks. He stood at the doorway to the last room in the hall before the exit. Although it was dark, Sage could tell that the walls were painted a dull jade, perhaps Venus' favorite color. Fitting for a backdrop of killer plants that robbed life, not sustained it. This must have been Venus' private quarters, but why wasn't she coming out? And why was there light sobbing coming from within?

Sage walked up behind Damian to see what he was looking at. At first, Sage didn't quite understand it.

A . . . cocoon?

CHAPTER 26

An Unexpected Fate

Sage didn't understand what on earth she was looking at. She knew it was a cocoon, the life-sized version of the one butterflies emerged from, but she had no idea what was inside it. It hung in the center of the room, stringy flesh attached to the ceiling, walls, and floor. The cocoon hovered right above the bed and all the disturbing regalia that was far from royal. Sage swore that silver contraption in the corner was a tooth filer and that the shiny blades on the tray next to it were for experiments. Either on Venus herself or willing participants. Bags full of white powder on the table were most definitely for a good time and the human bones in the translucent jars on a top shelf were mementos of victims . . . or lovers.

Next to the cocoon was Big Brother. Sage recognized him instantly, and her hand went right to her sword again, but she didn't point it. Big Brother, so tall and tough when she had been battling his brother in the Outskirts, was crying. He was holding his face and sobbing like a schoolgirl who had been rejected by her lover. This was nothing like Damian when Sage had proposed.

This was out of grief. Pure, torturous grief.

"My God!" Big Brother wailed loudly. "My God . . ."

"What is this?" Damian asked. He didn't care about introductions or anything else if it wasn't the answer to his question.

When it was obvious that Big Brother wasn't going to respond, one of Lapdog's pretty boys stepped forward instead. At this point, what was the use in keeping any secrets from the enemy? Damian looked ready to start shooting again. This was only going to end in death if they didn't explain themselves.

"Miss Optimum," said the pretty boy politely. He had wavy brown hair, a nice long nose, and full lips that were still swollen from kisses and whatever else he had been using his mouth for the past few hours. Like his friends, he, too, didn't have a shirt on. At least his trousers were zipped up, though. And at least he spoke to Sage like a human being. "Please … listen. Venus isn't … well …" He cleared his throat. "Not quite herself."

"Where is she?" Damian demanded. "What the fuck is going on here?"

"That's just the thing, sir—w-we don't know. I mean, we don't know what's going on—but Venus is in that cocoon."

Sage's eyes widened. She looked from Polite Guy to his friends, to the people crowded in the hallway wondering why the intruders hadn't been dealt with yet. She tried to find validity in that statement, and it was hard to tell if it was truth when all she had was her opponents' anger and aggression to contend with. No one really cared about Venus when there was an intruder in their hideouts.

"What do you mean she's in that cocoon?" Damian hissed. He grabbed Polite Guy by the neck and slammed him into the wall. He slapped him and yelled, "Speak so that I understand you, boy!"

Polite Guy's eyes welled with tears. Sage stepped up to Damian and kept him under control. She used softness in her tone to address Polite Guy.

"How is she in that cocoon?" Sage asked.

Polite Guy shook his head. "I-I don't know. We don't know. It happened just a few days ago. One morning she was up and about, and the next … well … she was in there."

"And the cocoon just came out of nowhere?"

"Yes," Polite Guy said. "Jared went to check on her, and that's what we found."

Jared must have been Big Brother. Sage continued asking questions.

"Has she ever done that before?"

"No, never."

"Did she complain about anything or act unusually before it happened?"

Someone laughed, making Sage jump. The laughing was low and wry, like someone accepting defeat in the face of so much irony. Sage just didn't know what the ironic part was yet. She didn't understand why Jared was crying and why he looked so miserable.

"My sweet Optimum." He smiled crookedly. It was so horrible that Sage started a fierce trembling. "I saw you fight my brother the other day . . . and it was magnificent. He deserved it, didn't he, for all the women he raped?"

Sage drew her sword and pointed it at him. "For all the women he and *you* raped," she snarled.

Jared laughed again. His hair was so oily that he probably hadn't washed it in days. His flannel was unbuttoned at the top and his pants were stained with what looked like piss. As if he hadn't even had the strength to go to the bathroom.

"Why would I rape women," Jared whispered, "when I found the love of my life? Venus is the epitome of what it means to be a woman. Fierce . . . loyal . . . strong . . . and oh-so good in bed . . ."

"With a knack for violence and spreading diseases," Sage said. "Fantastic."

"You don't understand." Jared shook his head. For someone who was a hybrid, he looked weaker than an old man of eighty. There were enough lines on his face to prove it. "You live in your fairy tale of Defenders' Unite!. I understand, because I, too, saw the show when I was a child. But I have long since grown up, Optimum, and realized that we, as hybrids, have humans to put in order. We did it with the Overseers, and now we have to do it with the rest of the population. We have to hand-choose those who are worthy enough to become Enhanced, share our blood with them, and create a new civilization of people. The old times are over and done with. Humans destroyed each other with nuclear war, and now it's time for a new race to thrive.

"The only problem was that Enhanced weren't enough," Jared went on dismally. "They are still so very ... human. Destructive. Selfish. Weak. It was my blood, but it wasn't my genetics. I wanted a baby. And my sweet Venus ... well ..." He smiled weakly. "She gave me two. And they are the sweetest angels. You should know, Sage— don't you have two of your own? I saw them when you battled my brother. Gosh, they are adorable."

"Stop talking about my children!" Damian spat.

Jared nodded. "I saw you, too, my precious Warlord—how you came to her rescue and swept your children into your arms. You love her, don't you? So much that your heart hurts when you think of her and your soul starts singing when you make love to her, yes?"

Damian drew Sage to his side, as if Jared were about to kidnap her. But it didn't look like he'd be moving out of that chair any time soon.

Jared laughed. He laughed so loudly that it sounded like someone had uttered a joke in his ear. He covered his face and kicked his tired feet. He just couldn't stop because of the—oh—*irony* of it all. Falling in love and finally having children was a dream come true for a hybrid. After so many long quests and so many attempts at reproduction, he had finally done it ... but at a cost.

"The question is ..." Jared came down from his chuckles. "Are you prepared to lose her?"

For the first time since stepping into the room, Sage could smell the rot. A room that probably housed its share of scents from steamy misty perfumes and provocative bath salts now stank like a crypt. As if something was decomposing, dying. And the fear in Sage was so great, that her knees actually buckled.

"Lose her?" Damian sneered, holding her tightly. "And what makes you think that I'm going to lose her, love? Just because you lost yours?" He nodded at the cocoon. "Because she took some freaky drug and killed herself?"

Was that it? Could that be it? So maybe this wouldn't happen to Sage, after all . . .

"Tell me, my sweet Sage," Jared said. He looked at her again, eyes droopy, red with exhaustion, and lined with old dried tears. "Are you feeling fatigued? A bit under the weather? Hormonal, not because of the birth of your children, but because everything just makes you sad? You don't think that your body is trying to tell you something?"

"I'm no doctor, but even I know those are symptoms every woman experiences after childbirth," Damian spat. "Postpartum depression is common and completely treatable. How dare you talk shit about my wife as if you're her doctor, as if you know what's going to happen to her.

"I want to feel sorry for you, but I don't. All you've caused is misery in the Outskirts alongside your brother and your reproductive experiments, and all your beloved in that ugly cocoon has caused is even more misery among the streets of Diamond City. Unforgivable. So you know what? I hope the both of you rot."

Damian kissed Sage's head. "I love you," he said to her for everyone to hear. "Don't listen to them, darling. Let's go home."

There really was nothing else for them here. As Damian went for the door, Jared spoke up.

"And what about you, my precious Warlord? Are you not guilty like I am? Slaughtering and torturing people for the hell of it? Starting a rebellion against the Allseer because you wanted power over this city? Then you're exiled and you bully others into making alliances with you to attain the same damn thing you've always wanted: power." Jared met Sage's eyes. "I'm surprised, Optimum. For someone as righteous as you, you have not seen through this man's shenanigans?"

"No one is perfect," Sage said. "Not him . . . nor me. And I have accepted Damian and his past for what it is. All I know and all that matters is that he cares about me and our city."

Jared laughed. "Oh, is that what he's led you to believe?"

Damian pulled Sage out of the room. Sage was glad, because she had heard enough. If she had to listen to one more person talk shit about Damian, she was going to explode. Already, she couldn't walk, and she wasn't so sure it was because of the anxiety. That's what Damian chalked it up to. He picked her up and carried her the rest of the way to the car, putting on a spectacle in front of customers and thugs alike. A war-torn man carrying around the Optimum? Strange . . .

"Come, darling." He kissed her before putting her in the car. "Let's go home."

Sage's mind was still in a whirl from the fact that they hadn't met Venus—that they had witnessed her in a cocoon instead. They had just up and left without further investigation, abandoning a very dangerous hybrid with his Enhanced lackeys. Despite all that, Damian still looked determined to leave: He turned on the car and sped down the street. Had seeing the cocoon bothered him much more than he was letting on?

"Who knows what that bitch was up to," Damian reassured her. "Are you seriously going to let that bastard's words get to you?"

"Why did we just leave him behind?" Sage said, panting a little. "Damian, he's dangerous!"

Damian's hands tightened around the controls. Sage sat up a bit more.

"Damian!" she said again.

"Didn't you see him?" he whispered to her.

"See what?"

"He was heartbroken."

Sage wasn't sure what that had to do with anything.

"He's dead," Damian whispered, even softer still. If Sage didn't have above average hearing, then she wouldn't have heard him.

"He's not dead," Sage said. "He's very much alive."

"I'm not sure you're understanding me. He's *dead*. He's so devastated that it would be a miracle if he ever left that room. I've . . ." Damian hesitated. Thank God for autonomous vehicles, or Damian would have crashed into the side of a building. He was the definition of a distracted driver, someone who was clearly lost in the past.

Sage didn't know why the hell she was so slow at piecing all this together, but Damian had to spell it out for her.

"I went through it," he said finally. "The time that you asked me to leave you alone on the *Mistress*. The day that I had to pack my things and reside in Centerfeld while you took some time for yourself. Of course, I respect anything that you wish of me, so it wasn't about me leaving—it was about how my leaving affected *you*."

Sage waited for more. Damian's eyes were glossy.

"I couldn't stand to see you like that," Damian croaked. "Curled up on a bed, wasting away in front of our children. You were a woman who had lost everything, and when we first met...you were a woman who had fought for everything. You had lost your will, and that broke me." He swiped at his eyes. "Because *I* had done that to you. I had destroyed you. And I hated myself so much in that moment that I wanted to kill myself. I didn't have any weapons, so I started clawing at my arms. Rockstar had to restrain me and Preacher took me aside to calm me down. He recited some scriptures that helped me relax. He told me to give you time...and I did. I prayed every damn day that you would forgive me. I don't pray to Squids—I prayed to whatever higher power there is out there. I truly believe there has to be something good up above or there wouldn't be anything good down here. So I asked and I asked and I asked...until you came to me, darling." Damian reached out to hold her hand.

Sage took it. She was staring out the windshield. She fully understood what Damian was saying now.

"We spent a glorious night with our allies," Damian went on with a trembling smile. "We ate, danced, kissed, and accepted each other fully and whole-heartedly. But that doesn't take away from the fact that I experienced the heartbreak of a lifetime. More than when I was rejected by a damn school in the Color District. But, you see, there was hope for me. I had faith. I love you and I know you love me, and love conquers all, even in the ugliest of times, so I knew we had a fighting chance.

"But Jared?" Damian chuckled wryly. "He doesn't stand a damn chance. His beloved is in a cocoon. Who the hell is going to fix that?"

"Worms go into cocoons," Sage said softly. "And then they become butterflies."

"Do they all become butterflies, darling?"

"Most of the time, yes."

"But are there any guarantees that that's what they're going to become?" Damian said. "What if they die? Do we truly know what Venus did to earn such a long period of darkness?"

"She had babies," Sage said quietly.

Damian slammed on the brake, making Sage lurch forward. She threw out her hands, or her face would have hit the dashboard.

"Damian—!"

"Don't say that!" Damian exclaimed. His face was red and veins were popping out of his temples. "Don't say that, damn it! Who the fuck has ever heard of going into a cocoon after giving birth? You gave birth months ago! Almost a goddamn year now! What does that have to do with anything?"

The only time Lolligo show signs of fatigue is when they're about ready to reproduce. That's because their bodies are dying and ready to give way to new life.

"It's what happens to Squids," Sage admitted. "And I'm part Squid. So—"

Damian slammed his hands on the controls. He looked like a big baby throwing a tantrum.

"You don't spit out eggs!" he yelled. "You gave a lot of essence to those cocoons when we took them out of you, but in no way did we slit your wrists and drain you of blood. You're a little fatigued from the whole process, but that doesn't mean a *thing*. You know what?" He took a deep breath to compose himself. People were honking at him and swerving around them, but he took his time fixing himself in the rearview mirror. He actually darkened his eyeliner and brushed his hair. It would have been funny had Sage's heart not still been pounding.

"Kevin will have the answers," Damian finished. He sounded like he was talking to himself more than to Sage. "Dr. X will know what's truly going on with you. That's who we're going to see right away. We're going home, darling, so make your calls to the girls, and then we're heading out to Mousafeld. Got it?"

Did Sage really have a choice? In this state, if she said anything contradictory, she'd be fighting an uphill battle. Chances were she wouldn't win. Damian was deadset in his decision to take her to Dr. X, and while Sage absolutely dreaded it, she was more terrified of her fate. She couldn't stay idle when her life was at stake, when they just didn't know what would happen. She had to do something.

Sage fell asleep on the way back home. Damian didn't try to keep her awake, because he was throwing all his hope on Dr. X. He was so determined that he got out of the car by himself. He headed toward the house to pick up their stuff, when something stopped him.

Sage heard voices. It was impossible to discern who they belonged to when she was in a car and they were far off. She had to open her eyes and release a heavy sigh, because the brain fog was insane. Her vision was blurry and her surroundings were spinning like a carousel. It took her a while to stabilize herself. When she was fully awake, she gasped at what she saw.

Candice and Olivia? Here with the boys? And not just them— Louis and his advisor, Darius, were here, too. They were both white in the face, stricken and horrified, as if they had seen a ghost. Sage wanted to know what the hell they were doing here—because no one other than her family was supposed to know about this place— but it was obvious there was a grand emergency. The six of them looked like they had just run from something.

Sage's heart dropped like a ball. It hit the ground with a splat, and she nearly followed had urgency not driven her to walk then run to her distressed family. She wondered where Gertrude and the others were in all this mess. If they weren't here, then they had stayed at Heart for some reason, and that reason could only be one that Sage dreaded with every fiber of her being.

An invasion. An attack.

"SAGE!" Louis called like a banshee as soon as he saw her. Amazingly, he had the Squid eggs in a bin by his feet. He lugged them around as if his life depended on it. Maybe he was hoping they'd hatch into his bodyguards if he took care of them, or maybe it was his extreme loyalty to Samson, but now Sage questioned everything when she knew Louis had pulled his own form of sneaky behind her back at Mousafeld. "SAGE!"

Damian drew his sword and moved in front of Louis so quickly that no one had a chance to react. He pointed the blade right at him.

"One more step, Kilstrong," he said steadily. "And I decapitate you."

"Fuck you!" Louis exclaimed. "Fuck you, asshole! You don't own her!"

"No, I protect her. She is in no mood for your bullshit right now—she needs to see a doctor, and I'm going to take her."

All eyes flicked to Sage. Even Castor and Pollux, one in Candice's arms and the other in Olivia's, looked at her. Their eyes were big and awake. There were dried tears on their cheeks from crying, fear, and anxiety. But whatever was happening at Heart could wait when their mother was clearly sick.

"What's going on?" Sage said angrily. She stomped over to them, trying hard not to trip. She was so damn dizzy and her heart rate was out of control—this wasn't normal—but by God she couldn't collapse here. Not now. Not in this mess. "Why are the girls here?" she choked out.

"Aunt Sage, we had to run!" Candice said, running over to her with Olivia in tow. They went around Louis and Damian to reach her. "W-we had to—there was an invasion! The Lolligo have invaded us!"

"What?" Sage rasped.

"It's true, Optimum," Darius said, looking a bit weak in the knees himself. "We received word of unidentified visitors and knew without a doubt that the Lolligo were here to take control."

" 'Received word'? From who?"

"Security at the northernmost border of Diamond City as well as in the capital, my lady. The Lolligo have touched down in airships all over the Clarity District and are marching their way to the capital. No Claritian would dream to attack the beings they worship, so for the Lolligo, it becomes quite simple. They are demanding an audience with the Allseer. We all know why, of course."

"Why?" Sage sputtered. This wasn't making sense to her at all—how could they be here to take Diamond City by force if Samson was their Prime? Wasn't he fighting to make sure the Squids didn't do anything rash? "How do you know what they intend? Did they march into the capital and make themselves at home, demanding power?"

The look on Candice and Olivia's faces said they didn't know—they had been pushed out of the palace by Gertrude and the others before they could ask any questions. At some point, Louis and Darius had jumped in on that escape.

"DON'T YOU GET IT?!" Louis roared. "SAMSON IS DEAD! HE LOST THE WAR!"

Damian lowered the sword and pulled out his phone. He communicated with Josiah and Jarka, who had become his second-in-command since the fiasco with his mother in Emerald City. Sage's brain was too jumbled to make out the conversation exactly, but Louis proved an effective translator.

"Oh, great!" he sneered. "Let's call in Emerald City, too, while we're at it! I bet this is what you were waiting for, wasn't it, Damaris? The Lolligo come marching in, and it's Emerald City to the rescue! How fucking convenient."

Sage stared at Louis. Candice and Olivia did, too. Darius had a tight look on his face as if he was holding back a sneeze.

"This is what he's wanted all along!" Louis went on, glaring down Damian like a beast. Hatred spewed out of his eyes, making them the darkest blue Sage had ever seen. "Power, so he could take over Diamond City. He admitted everything in our last meeting—what he did when he got to Emerald City, how he slaughtered his mother, crowned himself Allseer, then recruited the military to defeat his brother at Winterfeld!"

"You *fool*," Damian spat. "Does your pea-sized brain not understand a damn thing I've told you? You make it sound like I'm a killer, but I only did what I had to for the good of the people. Now it looks like I'll be exercising that power to clean up this mess because you weren't able to hold down a military. You put all your trust in Blackburn instead of me and Sage, and now you have no one and you're cowering like the sniveling rat you are. Stars, the whole fucking Kilstrong family is the same: They lean toward the person with the most power and search for ways to stab them in the back so they can take it for themselves."

"I'm not my father!" Louis yelled. "And how dare you presume otherwise, as if you know a damn thing about me! I didn't have a choice but to trust in Blackburn—"

"Who proceeded to use little girls as hostages," Damian sneered. "Brilliant."

Louis had to control himself, or no one would believe a damn thing he was saying. He tightened his fists and took a breath before continuing in his defense. "I had no choice. In hindsight, I was wrong, but let's talk about the now—"

"The Squids are invading, and that's all you can think about? Your title?"

"Of course it is," Louis breathed. "Because I still can't decide what's worse—you or the aggressive Lolligo!"

"What you think is irrelevant," Damian sneered. "I won't let you take advantage of this city. Both Emerald City *and* this city need help, and I plan on guiding both to prosperity."

Louis guffawed. He looked for Sage across the lawn. "Sage! Are you listening to this maniac? Are you seriously going to take his side? Are you that blind?"

"Damian," Sage said, despite the roaring in her ears. "A-are the Squids really here?"

"Yes," Damian replied. "Our forces have already sighted them."

"N-no," she croaked. "S-Samson can't be dead . . ."

"We don't know that for sure, darling. Don't listen to this fool spew misinformation—we will get to the bottom of this. The Lex Warriors are holding their ground at the capital while Emerald City moves in from the east. I don't know what's happening from here, but rest assured that no shots have been fired yet."

"You can't let him do this, Sage!" Louis exclaimed. "You see where this is going, don't you? He was exiled from this city for that exact reason—because of his power-hungry quest to rule—and now it's finally coming true! He swore in Mousafeld that he'd let me and my sister rule, and now look at how he's turned the tables on us! First, he plotted behind our backs with my sister to use you, and when that didn't work out, he ran off to Emerald City to get rid of his mother and recruit a bunch of soldiers—which we don't even know how the hell he did that—and then he kills Blackburn—conveniently— and controls me by threatening me every step of the way!"

"What other way is there to get you to do the right thing?" Damian sneered. "Aside from using Candice and Olivia as scapegoats, you pin the blame for Bram's death on *me* behind my back? After we all thought it was a suicide, you spread false rumors about me so you could manipulate Sage. How do you explain yourself there, Louis?"

Louis drew his sword. It shocked everyone, even Damian, who didn't let it show for long. This was his chance to finally kill Louis and end the Kilstrong line. Louis didn't care that he was up against a hybrid—he looked determined as hell to cut Damian into pieces.

"Stop!" Sage cried.

The two weren't going to listen. The fire was burning too greatly, and extinguishing it would require more than just words. Sage didn't have a sword, but she did have a dagger, so she jumped in front of Damian's lunge before he could strike Louis.

Everyone already knew who the victor in that scuffle would have been. Damian would have cut Louis to the ground in two vicious slashes—as easy as serving a piece of pie. It didn't matter that Louis had worked on his fighting skills—he was no match for someone like Damian, who had beaten Sage in battle already. Twice.

Perhaps a Sage in her prime would have bested Damian, but she was far from it now. The most she could do was deflect his blade with her dagger, and even that didn't turn out quite right. He nicked her in the wrist, a small cut, but that's all Slainium needed to enter the bloodstream. Sage didn't let the burning or the pulsing show on her face. She kept a stern gaze on Damian, who was gawking at her, horrified that he had just struck her.

"No fighting," Sage said steadily. "Please, Damian. Please ... no fighting. We've had enough. This city's had enough. Cutting him down isn't going to fix anything. Louis will work with you because he respects me. But please don't turn into a bloodthirsty tyrant. I know you're better than that."

"SAGE!" Damian yelled. He dropped his sword and took off. He got to Sage, grabbed her wrist, and clamped his mouth over her wound. He started sucking her blood right away, to take the Slainium out. Maybe it worked. Either way, Sage sagged against him.

"What's wrong with her?" Louis croaked. Even he knew Sage had never crumbled like this. Her face had never turned pale like sour milk and her arms and legs had never looked so ... skinny.

"Kevin!" Damian exclaimed. "We need to get her to Mousafeld! Right away!"

"Damian." Sage caressed his cheek. She still had the word *Allseer* pounding away in her brain. She still had so much to say, even if she had already said it all. She had already told Damian everything. She loved him and their children with all her heart; Candice, Olivia, and Geoffrey were depending on him now; and the futures of Diamond and Emerald City rested on his shoulders. "I ... want to sleep. Please."

"Darling," Damian croaked. "We have to take you to see Kevin. How else are we going to help you?"

"What's wrong with her?!" Louis demanded.

"Can't I just rest for a little bit?" Sage said softly. Damian was so beautiful. Who had a long perfect nose like that? "I want to be with my girls ... and our boys ..."

"I understand, but your health is more important right now."

"I . . . just . . ." Sage's eyes welled with tears. When she blinked, they came running down her cheeks. She saw airships in the sky, dark and sleek. She saw curvy, Lolligo print on the sides. "I-I don't think I have enough time . . ."

"What do you mean?" Damian choked. He held her tighter. "Enough time for what, darling?"

"Damian." Candice stepped over. "I think we should do what she says. Can't you call Dr. X to come?"

"But wait—why doesn't she have enough time?"

Sage curled into Damian's chest. She started shaking. Damian buried his face in her head and sobbed as if someone was tearing out his heart all over again.

These cries, Sage noted, were completely different from the ones earlier, when she had proposed. While those had been heart-wrenching, they had been filled with hope and love. These were painful, tearing out of his very soul. These were the ones Sage had hoped never to hear again.

"Please don't leave me, darling," Damian croaked, caressing her hair. "No, no . . . Don't do this to me . . ."

"WHAT'S HAPPENING TO HER?!" Louis roared, brave enough to finally come closer, because Damian wasn't paying attention to him anymore. Candice and Olivia didn't really know the answer, so they stood by, watching with tears in their own eyes. The twins were silently crying, too.

"Please," Sage whispered to Damian. "Take me inside."

She couldn't stand much less walk. Seemingly, neither could Damian, who slumped evermore into the ground, as if he had lost the will to go on. Candice and Olivia were the ones who had to place their hands on his shoulders, get him to do as Sage requested, and fill him with hope that she could be saved. From what, no one but Sage and Damian knew.

t some point, Damian got up. Because the next time Sage opened her eyes, she was in bed.

Candice and Olivia were in a shirt and house shorts, curled up beside her with the babies in their arms. Louis was sitting in a chair next to her, watching her intently, with Darius standing right behind him. Geoffrey was by the window, looking out at the moon when he got too emotional at the sight of Sage. Mega Woman was at the foot of the bed, drying her eyes with some tissues. Preacher was in the corner, calming everyone down by reciting some old Squid scriptures. They must have put the six pups to sleep, because Green, Red, Orange, Blue, Violet, and Yellow were curled up on the rug. Gertrude and Turtle were standing by the doorway, speaking very amicably with each other. Rockstar and Eye Candy were in the hall, peering into the room every once in a while. Sailor, Butcher, and Clara were in the living room, voices soft like everyone else's, as if they were at a funeral. Sonia and L must have been somewhere close by. Sage wouldn't have minded hearing them bicker one last time. They usually didn't when in the presence of Tai and Sword Devil.

But wait . . . if everyone was here . . . then what had become of the Squids?

"Aunt Sage?" Candice leaned over her. She caressed Sage's face, pushing hair out of her eyes. "You're awake. How are you feeling?"

"Really weak," Sage said softly. She felt like shit, but that was the least of her worries when the last memory she had was of airships flying over the Cut District. "What happened? The Squids?"

"We're going to be fine," Gertrude offered. "We're in the middle of a nasty power play, but things are looking good for us. We have more than enough numbers to hold them off if they think starting a war is the answer."

"Oh my God," Sage choked. "T-they want to take over?"

"Yes," Gertrude replied honestly. She was getting glares from everyone in the room for making Sage worry, but that's what Sage loved about her: honesty, even seconds away from what felt like death. "We are trying to keep the peace, so we have council members from both cities doing the negotiating. But we also rushed over here when we learned about your condition. We are here to keep you safe no matter the cost."

"Where's Damian?"

"He went to get Dr. X," Mega Woman said. Her eyes were puffy and her nose was red. Holy shit, was she crying over Sage? "He didn't trust anyone else to fetch him, so he hopped on a ship and took off."

Sage shook her head. "Does he think the ship would crash if someone else drove it?"

" 'No chances,' he said." Darius crossed his arms. "He punched my nose to get to my aircraft."

"Trust me," L sneered at him, stepping into the room with Sonia in tow. "I would have done the same to any snot-nosed politician."

Sage took another good look at everyone's faces. She saw a mix of sadness and devastation, with desperate attempts to smile and make her feel better. Some couldn't manage it, though—they broke out in tears. Even the pups were whining. Blue and Violet had their front paws on the bed, amber eyes swimming in grief.

"Can I have a sheet of paper and a pen?" Sage asked quietly. "Two papers, actually."

Sonia went to get it. She was back in seconds. No one questioned why Sage wanted to write at a time like this, although this could be a sign she was feeling better.

Sage sat up just a little. She didn't recognize her own arms. They looked like they were withering away before her very eyes. Those long skinny fingers weren't the ones that had gripped a sword a hundred years ago. Nevertheless, she still had a grip, and she could write. So she wrote her first note.

Darling,

I love you with all my heart and soul. Perhaps that is my biggest flaw, but you have made my dreams come true. I can rest as the happiest woman on earth. You have shown me true love and passion. You've given me two beautiful boys. Raise them well. Show them what it means to be a fair and just ruler. Show everyone what you can do as an Allseer. You've fought hard to attain it.

Yours forever,

Sage

Sage put it on the nightstand. Then she took the second paper and wrote her final note.

To my beautiful Castor and Pollux,

You're too young to remember your mother, but I love you both so immensely that it actually hurts. You carry my legacy of defending the helpless against the cancer of corruption. I know the two of you will fight and ensure no one is ever taken advantage of. As hybrids, we fight for justice. We make peace and use our powers responsibly. Your mother . . .

"Aunt Sage?" Candice shook her.

But Sage was fast asleep again. And this time, she didn't wake up. Not even when Damian screamed outside her door.

Epilogue

"You're my end and my beginning
Even when I lose I'm winning
So tell me when you hear my voice, can you feel all my love for you?
It grows greater by the day, like a balloon in my chest
All the things that we've done, all the things we've yet to do
I will wait for you, darling, because I know you'll make it through
Darling dear, I'll hold you for an eternity
I'll make you feel my love through the pain and adversity
When the evening shadows and the stars appear
I'll drive away all your fears
When the run rises and the light shines
I'll kiss your lips, our bodies intertwined
From the first time I saw you, I knew that you'd be mine
From the first moment we spent together, you filled my heart with joy
You gave me the confidence to finally see
That if I worked hard enough, together we could be
One day, I'd ask you to marry me and you'd say yes
We'll be together always, to the world I profess
Darling dear, I'll hold you for an eternity
I'll make you feel my love through the pain and adversity
When the evening shadows and the stars appear
I'll drive away all your fears

When the run rises and the light shines
I'll kiss your lips, our bodies intertwined
I could sing a thousand songs about you but what good would that do?
They'd all say the same thing: I can't do this life without you
There's something in your smile that gives me strength to carry on
And there's something in the way you used to look at me that lingers even
when you're gone"

Sage heard the words just barely. It sounded like she was underwater, listening to someone speak from up above. It was warm wherever she was, encased in a darkness that didn't scare her but soothed her. Either way, she appreciated the singing voice.

She was fairly certain she had heard it before.

Acknowledgements

The hardest part of writing the book, actually. Acknowledgements don't get easier—they get harder. Don't let anyone tell you otherwise.

I started my publishing journey in May of 2023. This could not have happened without Kira and James and their beautiful cover design. Julie and Ryan Scheife, as well as Matt and Molly from Mayfly Design, thank you for formatting this manuscript and helping me get it out into the world! To my incredible artist, Kiwi Byrd: thank you for the beautiful depictions of my book and for bringing my characters to life!

Although I've always had incredible artists and designers who put my book together, I had zero followers across all my social media platforms when I started. I couldn't name a single person on Bookstagram. Since *Diamond City* took off, I can say I have met a group of incredible readers who are more than just readers—they are friends and my support in this sometimes very bumpy journey

For anyone who's published, you know the writing is the least of it. It's the exposure, the posts, the reels, the shares, and the hype. That, I cannot do on my own. That, I had titans standing behind me

Kariany, your incredible support knows no bounds. You drove across a state to come see me at my first book signing and I tear up every time I think about it. Not only that, but you've read *Diamond*

City twice, beta-read *Emerald City* twice, read a historical fantasy romance (I know that's not your genre), and are well on your way to finishing Ruby. Wow. Ready for Sapphire? *MAYBE*

Kayla Miller, what can I say? Your posts (and hair) are beautiful and I am honored to have been featured on your page. Your positive energy is infectious and I love when you come up on my feed.

Aja, where would *Emerald City* be without your glorious charts? Thank you for your brutal honesty, because *Emerald City* in its beta-phase (Kariany and Marissa, you know this is true!) was … heh-heh … pretty bad. I think your chart with all the spots that needed tweaking got me off my butt pretty quickly.

Marissa Eckel, I'll never forget you were one of my first *Diamond City* reviewers and you said you wanted to sleep with a copy of *Diamond City* on your bedside. Thank you for your kind words!

Valery Archaga, you know your reviews and reactions are priceless. I am so grateful that you signed up for my ARC and that we have become fast friends! Good luck on your own publishing journey—you are incredible.

Mikaela Harris, you are a beast at reading and there is nothing more rewarding to an author than a reader who finishes their book in less than twenty-four hours and in between working shifts on the farm!

Hannah and Thaela, your posts are beautiful and I am honored you featured *Diamond City* on your page! Thank you for your support and for helping me spread the word in the Bookstagram community!

Shandy and Tiffany! My gals! Thank you for beautifying my images and posts! I don't know what kind of magic you do on those reels, but they mean the world to me!

Danielle Johnson, if it wasn't for you, I wouldn't even know how Instagram works. I was totally lost on how to reach more readers, and honestly, because of you, I met Katie! (Who's pretty freaking awesome). Thanks for your reviews and support! I knew you enjoyed Emerald!

Nora Ellen, you also know how to work magic on my posts and

I am forever grateful. I think you hold the record for fastest person to ever read *Emerald City* in literally five hours with a glass of wine in between. Wow.

Ashley Gonzalez, you were one of the first to buy a signed hardback of *Diamond City* back in July when I still didn't have a functioning shop on my website. Do you know how much that meant to me?

So these are just *some* of the Bookstagram people. Now it's on to the people who have to see me on a day-to-day basis and have become the foundation for me staying sane as I navigate the publishing world.

Aris, my thanks goes to you once again. Although we're no longer working together at school, do you realize the impact you've had on my life? You and I brainstormed all the manuscripts I have on my computer. I am so thankful to have met you.

Cassandra, you continue to influence my life because I can't stop thinking about all the times we've spent together and all the conversations we've had. I love you and miss you!

Armando . . . need I say more?

Claudia, Brooklyn, and Bronx: you always put a smile on my face. Thank you for your support of *Diamond City* and my crazy publishing journey!

Simone and Kyle: you always greet me at the gym with a smile and show me it's possible to get through life's toughest moments while keeping a positive attitude. Wow.

Micah and London: I don't think the two of you realize how you've influenced my life yet. You stick to what you like to do and become the very best at it regardless of setbacks. I am forever impressed.

Andrew, I will continue to say that you inspire me to be the best. Or else you're going to glare me down and shake your head and I wouldn't want that.

Ronald, the superman from Steelhouse. You were the first to preorder the kindle version of *Diamond City* and wave it around at the gym. You continue to believe that I can do anything. That might be true, but that's only because I look up to you!

Soolmaz, I have great respect for you and your entrepreneurship. I see what you do and how you do it and it inspires me to be the same way with my book business. Thank you for always believing I can hit PRs both in and out of the gym.

Danny? Did you really break into the presidential archives to get that copy of *Diamond City*?

And now onto the three people who have been with me through thick and thin.

Mom, it means the world to me when you support me and my writing. You know how to keep me focused on what matters and how to bypass obstacles. Thank you for coming with me to my book signings and for guiding me on this journey called life.

Richard, when you play your sax, you remind me to do what I love no matter what. And that, for me, is what I need to keep writing and pushing to do better.

Robin, you have changed my world. I know you know it.

I know there are so many more people who supported me in this journey, but *Emerald City* is already pretty long, and I'm going to wrap this up. I just wanted to say, once more, thank you to everyone who's supported me out there!

Thank you, readers, because without you, I wouldn't bother publishing. I hope you've been able to find enjoyment in my work and that *Emerald City* has kept you entertained with its never-ending drama. I hope I didn't rattle you too much! I promise *Ruby City* will be coming soon!

And, last but not least, I'd like to thank my Heavenly Father, Lord Jesus Christ, and Mother Mary for giving me the inspiration, dedication, and persistence that it takes to write and publish a novel from beginning to end. I have a feeling that doesn't come from nowhere.

Thank you!

About the Author

Astrid Cole has a master's in English Literature from Florida International University. Although she enjoys all subjects, she started writing fiction in high school and hasn't stopped since. When she's not plotting her next novel, she's teaching students history and hitting the gym. A former bodybuilder, running and exercise are a part of her daily routine . . . and so are playing video games and watching horror movies. *Diamond City* is her first published novel.

Coming Soon

Look out for the next installment in the *Diamond City* series, *Ruby City*, coming in fall of 2024! Join Ruby Kilstrong as she fights to defend her family and friends against new and old foes alike. Unfortunately, monsters and Lolligo are the least of her worries when betrayal, romance, budding friendships, past tensions, and deadly secrets are at every corner.

Check out my website www.astridcolebooks.com for the latest news, special editions, and future books!

www.ingramcontent.com/pod-product-compliance
Lightning Source LLC
Chambersburg PA
CBHW021329310726
48971CB00001B/42